GODS ON CAMPUS

KAYLA CLAIRE

KICKOFF

KICKOFF

ONE

ZOEY

Today is the day. I'm going to tell him. I'm going to grab Z by the shoulders, sit his ass down, look him in the eyes, and say, "I want a relationship. Make me your girlfriend."

I pull into the parking lot outside my dorm. The anticipation crashing through my body has nothing to do with the fact that it's the first day of my last year in college. Nope. The mini avalanche in my stomach and the smile on my face are all because of Z. After a summer apart, I'm *finally* going to see him again—and more than that, I'm womaning up and telling him how I feel.

We've been dancing around this thing for a year now, a will-they, won't-they, on-again, off-again, friends-with-benefits relationship that could inspire several seasons of good TV. And that will all end today.

I step out of my car into the 102-degree Southern California heat and stretch my arms above my head, welcoming the warm sun on my skin after the two-hour drive back to Olympia University. I shoot off a text to Z, letting him know

I'm back on campus, and then I get to work hauling my carful of boxes up to my new apartment.

Tour Guide Fun Fact #1: Our founders based Olympia University on Greek mythology. That means all of our campus accommodations are named after Greek gods and goddesses.

I'm on the fifth floor of the Athena and Aphrodite Campus Apartments—my home for the next year. Signs that Tessa moved in already are all over the place, and my heart swells. It was a long summer without my best friend by my side. The small kitchen sink is already chock-full of dirty dishes, and tie-dye throw pillows dress the lime green couch that matches the lime green walls. Tessa's remaining decorations are strewn about the floor, waiting to be hung.

Tessa isn't here now, so I'm alone, making three trips to my car and back, dumping the suitcases and boxes in my room. Normally, I'd be more careful with my stuff. Today it doesn't matter. The faster I unload, the faster I can get to Z.

I check my phone again, just in case I missed anything. Nothing. No response.

I shrug it off. It's the first day of classes, after all. He's probably busy.

The smaller voice in my head, though, says *maybe there's someone else.*

Twice now Z has taken a break from me to date another girl. But he always comes back to me. Besides, the way he's been texting me lately? I *know* we're good.

I glance around my room. I have a few hours before class. I

guess I could start unpacking while I wait. Honestly, I had kind of planned on just dropping my stuff off and jumping his bones and *then* having that all-important defining-the-relationship conversation. Because I'm a responsible adult like that. I'm already dressed in a cute halter top and tiny shorts, makeup done—the whole shebang. I figured I might as well look my hottest self if I'm going to get laid today, and I really *do* look my hottest self. I'd spent the whole summer hiking. *Hellooo* toned thighs. Z might come in his pants when he sees me.

When my phone buzzes in my pocket, my whole body smiles. I drop the pile of shirts I'm folding into an open drawer and then rub my palms on my thighs. My heart pounds out a giddy rhythm.

I open his text.

Z: I'm not sure I can meet up today…

And just like that, all the good vibes go whooshing out of my body. He can't meet up? Doesn't he realize he's about to have several hours' worth of toe-curling, mind-numbing sex? And then again after my class?

Me: Oh no! Are you sure? Why not?

Z: I went to this frat party with my friends a couple of nights ago.

Me: Okay?

Because that explains nothing.

Z: It was a lingerie party, which was fun, but I felt kind of guilty being there because of my gf.

My heart makes a croaking sound, and then it stops pounding. Did he say gf?

What the fuck. What the actual fuck.

My heart takes off again—faster than before, trying to

get to the top of a mountain. It's like a slap to the face. I stare at those two tiny letters.

I Urban Dictionary *gf*, just in case I'm missing something, but nothing else seems to fit. It's not a George Foreman grill, he wasn't in a good fight, and I don't think he feels guilty because of his goldfish.

Z has a girlfriend. And it's not me.

I take a deep breath. I need to be logical. This was never a for-sure thing. Just because he sexted me most of the summer didn't mean he would be waiting for me when I came back. And yet, I want to yell at him. I want to unleash hell.

But I can't. I have no right.

Me: Yeah… that's a weird line to balance.

Z: And that's kind of why we can't hang out today. Like she was chill with the frat party, but I don't think she would be comfortable with me hanging out with someone I've had sex with.

I sit on the floor, strangling the phone in my hand. Now I'm just someone he's had sex with? Aren't we at least friends? We were friends for months before we even started hooking up.

Besides, that's all he ever told his friends we were. Friends. Just friends. He kept our fuck dates hidden from them. So it wouldn't be that hard to continue being my friend. It's not like he'd have to face any judgment from them.

I keep blinking at my phone, wishing I could blur away this whole thing.

Me: So, what does this mean?

Z: Huh?

Me: If you can't hang out with me, is our friendship over?

Z: No, woman, ofc not. I just think we need to tone it down until my relationship with her settles down. Maybe you and I can text like once a week?

I'm reduced to a scheduled thing. A once-a-week text.

The happy, giddy feeling I had when I first arrived is gone. Not gone—murdered. By Z. That fucker. He's decided we're over just when I thought we were starting.

Z: Is that okay?

Is that okay? What the hell is wrong with him? Of course it isn't okay! My hopes and dreams are crashing down, falling beside me, shattering like a glass of perfectly good cold brew hitting the floor. But there's no reason to tell him that. There's no reason to tell him I'm hurting. There's no reason to tell him anything at all.

Me: Yeah

Because what the fuck else am I supposed to say to all that?

TWO

ALEX

I do not have time for this right now. I'm already so ridiculously late. I glare at my phone, tempted to ignore it, but my mom will just keep on calling. Sighing, I swipe to answer the call.

"Alex!" My mom speaks before I even get the chance to say hello. "Are you on your way to class?"

"Yeah," I lie. "Almost there." I was supposed to head to campus right after dropping my younger sister Lucy off at middle school, but I rushed back home when I realized I forgot my lesson plan—and my coffee. I found my coffee right away, because priorities, amiright, but now I can't find my goddamn lesson plan. I press the phone up to my ear, using my shoulder to keep it in place, and search my desk. I fling papers across the surface and open notebook after notebook, looking for anything that resembles the set of notes I drew up last night.

"Oh my gosh, I can't believe it! My baby is all grown up

and teaching his first class!" she cries with far more enthusiasm than I have right now.

"I'm just the TA for the class," I remind her. I don't want her getting any wrong ideas in her head. She would love nothing more than for me to become a professor like her and Dad. They both love the academic life. That's where they are right now, on sabbatical in Spain together, teaching classes. As much as my mom wants this teaching assistant position to call my name, I'm just here to see if it's the right path for me.

My lesson plan isn't here. Shit.

Shit, I think again. I'm not supposed to be cussing anymore. I slipped up once when I moved back home and received the silent treatment for days after that. They left me with strict no swearing rules before they moved across the world, leaving me in charge of my little sister.

"I know, I know, but that's step one, right?" she says. I can imagine the flippant wave of her hand, brushing away my protests. "I'm so proud of you."

"Thanks, Mom," I say, crouching down to glance under my desk, still looking for my damn lesson plan. "Listen, I gotta go. I just parked."

And thank the gods of finding things, because there's my lesson plan, a single sheet of now slightly crumpled lined paper, chilling under my desk. I reach to grab it, and when I stand back up, I bump my head into the side of the desk. Fuck—fudge. Fudge. I bite my cheek to keep from hissing and pray my mom didn't hear the bang, or that she thinks it's the car door.

"Of course, sweetie. Call me later and let me know how your class goes," she says. This was one of the nicer phone calls we've had lately, so I tell her I will before I hang up. I stuff my lesson plan into my backpack and then glance at myself in the mirror.

Should I dress more professionally? I want to be the chill TA, the one everyone likes. A lot of my teaching assistants in college would just wear T-shirts and jeans. But I still want my students to respect me. I know what my dad would say—"dress your best to do your best." But then again, my dad can be a kind of weird guy.

Right now, I'm wearing my lucky shirt. It reads "Hero of Canton." It's a reference to my favorite show, *Firefly*. I figured I could use a little luck on my first day, but so far that luck hasn't kicked in.

I button a collared shirt over it. At least this way, my tattoos are covered. I wasn't planning on wearing a collared shirt, but it's good to start your first day looking professional, right?

I want this to go well. Even if I'm not sure if I want to pursue the academic life, there are lots of reasons being a teaching assistant just made sense: connections with my professors, desperately needed experience for my resume, a chance to prove to my parents that I can be responsible. After my fuckup of an undergrad, I owe them. If everything goes according to plan, after this semester, my mom won't feel the need to call me and make sure I'm making it to my first class on time.

I rush to my car, and I'm halfway to Olympia University when I realize I forgot my coffee on the kitchen counter. Again. I sigh in defeat, gripping the steering wheel in annoyance. Today is just not my day.

A crazy thing happens though when I reach campus. I find a parking spot right away. Someone pulls out right as I get there. That almost never happens.

I'm early.

I rap my knuckles on my steering wheel, trying to decide whether I have time to stop at the Caffeine Cart on campus on my way to the engineering building. In theory, I should have plenty of time to grab a coffee and still make it to my class. Besides, I'll teach better if I'm caffeinated.

Fuck—fudge it. I'm gonna do it. If there's anyone who can make this happen, it'll be me.

ZOEY

I have no memory of pulling myself off the floor or wiping the black mascara streaks from under my eyes. But when Tessa finally comes home, I'm lying on top of the blue, stained dorm mattress. I haven't unpacked my bedding yet—honestly, I had assumed I'd spend the night in Z's bed. Stupid of me, really. This was the third time he had a girlfriend since we started our fling. Third. Fucking. Time.

I wrap my arms around my stomach, curled up in the fetal position, glaring at the wall in front of me. It's yellow, dirty, and stained. Little marks are all over the wall where the previous occupant had hung pictures.

"Babe, we need to get going!" Tessa's voice calls through the apartment. She sticks her head in my room. Her dark brown curls are tucked into a messy bun on the top of her head, and she's full of smiles. Tessa's one of the brightest people I know. It's like she carries a sun inside of her everywhere she goes. Just seeing her makes my heart feel a little better. Just a bit, though. "Nice room." Open cardboard boxes are everywhere, and my purple duffel bag is vomiting clothes onto the floor. It's a hot mess. I only got back to campus a couple hours ago, and already my whole life is a steaming pile of garbage

"Do you think you can get an STI from lying on this thing?" I ask her.

She grimaces. "I prefer not to think of all the nasty things that were done to the mattress before I got here," she says with a shiver. "But to answer your question, yes. You now have herpes, I'm almost a hundred percent positive."

I try to think how I would normally respond and force out a laugh. "You should either be a doctor or a statistician. I see either of those being a great career move for you." I don't want to tell Tessa about Z yet. If I do, I'll have to retell the whole embarrassing story. Tessa knows how much I was looking forward to today, and I know she'll instantly try to comfort me, smothering me with her love and support. I'm not ready for that attention.

"Or an epidemiologist." She waggles her eyebrows. "Combine them both." She nudges a box to the side with her foot, taking a couple steps into my room. I pull myself off the mattress. "What kind of person moves in on the day classes start?"

"The kind whose internship doesn't end until three days before school starts."

"Oh yes, I forgot about your fancy-schmancy science-y internship." Tessa uses a fake haughty voice, waving a wrist full of jangly, colorful bracelets through the air. "See, I was smart and stayed at home watching Netflix all summer. For the sole purpose of getting here early enough to unpack *before* classes started."

I wonder how different things would be if I had stayed at home all summer. I wonder if Z and I would be together now.

"Bullshit. You haven't unpacked a single thing yet," I

say. I know Tessa. I'll call her bluff. I weave through my room, spotting my backpack in the corner and then slinging it over my shoulder.

I rush toward her, and she reaches out her arms for a hug. I duck under them, racing out the door.

"Hey—where are you—don't you dare!" she yells after me. I yank her door open.

"Ha!" I yell in triumph. There are half-opened boxes, suitcases, and bags piled everywhere. Her room is even more of a mess than mine.

"Yeah, yeah." She waves a hand at me. "It's only 'cause I went out the first night I was back and was too hungover to do anything for the rest of the weekend."

"How did you even get all this stuff here?" I ask. "How many trips did it take you?" Tessa lives close enough to do multiple trips, but that still seems like such a hassle.

"Nah, bitch, I rented a moving van," she says. At this, I do laugh. Of course she would. "How did *you* even fit all that stuff in your tiny-ass car?"

"Mad packing skills. UPS should hire me."

We head to the door together, but I pause in front of the bathroom mirror we share. I swipe my fingers under my eyes, cleaning up the smears of makeup. I look so good, it hurts my soul a little bit.

"Hun, you're gorgeous, but we're gonna be late," Tessa calls, holding our apartment door open.

"Since when do you care about being late?" I ask, slipping on the pair of sandals I left by the door. We walk out into the open-air hallway of the A&A apartments.

"It's the first day, I've got to make a good impression."

"It's syllabus day, it doesn't count." I link my arm through hers as we walk together. It's been a long summer without her. Heck, it's already been a long day without her.

"If I get herpes from your nasty dorm mattress body, I will hurt you."

Tessa and I are only two minutes late when we slip into the back of the large lecture hall. This is a lower division mythology course we've both been pushing off until our senior year, so we'd have something fun to take together. Tessa's a psych major and I'm geology, so except for elective classes we have almost no overlap.

The professor is just starting his introduction, so we pull out our notebooks, slouching low in our seats. Everyone else around us looks slightly panicked, furiously taking notes as he writes the office hours and email on the board. Freshmen.

"So, first Olympia game is this Friday. You in?" Tessa asks. I smirk at her. If she's going to start a conversation, she doesn't care nearly as much about syllabus day as she claims to.

"Of course." I don't need to ask her what game is this Friday. Tessa is obsessed with all things soccer. She's dragged me to all of Olympia's games, men's and women's, since we met our freshman year. Her obsession with the men's soccer team is borderline crazy, but I'll give her this. Every single player on that team is ridiculously hot, and their record is insane. Last year, we finally beat out Heyward University for the University Champions Cup and are currently ranked number one in the country.

But the fact is, those guys *know* they're good. I haven't met a single person on that team who isn't too cocky for their own good. They may be beautiful to look at, but I would never want to date a soccer player.

Tessa, though, has a different opinion. "Let me tell you, I wouldn't ever date a freshman, but their new blood is hot."

She pulls up the app on her phone, showing me the team roster for this year. There're obvious ones: Like Eddie Fuentes, our starting goalie and Tessa's hero, and Jonah West, our top forward and Tessa's number one crush-from-afar for the past four years, but I see what she means about new blood. Some of the freshmen are kind of cute. Tessa shoves a picture of Kacen Karlson in my face to prove her point.

Normally, I'd be excited to talk about the upcoming soccer season and objectify the players, but right now I couldn't care less who is good-looking and who's injured. In fact, the more Tessa talks about guys, the more my brain drifts to Z.

Z's full name is Zeus, but he always goes by Z. He literally chose this campus because of all the Greek mythology references. He wanted to feel like a god when walking around this campus, not that he ever was one. Unfortunately, when the mythology professor in front of us mentions Zeus, Z's face is all I can picture. He's cute. Not Olympia soccer team hot, but good-looking. He has this boyish charm and could freak out with me over every single nerdy movie. He knows everything about me. All of my secrets.

I can't believe it's just over.

Maybe I should go talk to him in person. Just to make sure someone hadn't stolen his phone to play some shitty practical joke. Or maybe to yell at him for the abuse he's putting on my heart.

By the end of class, I've made up my mind. I'm going to talk to him. I know his schedule. He has a class in the engineering building right after mine ends. I could walk by casually. If I go the long way, the building is on the way back to my apartment.

I ditch Tessa and make it all the way to the engineering building before I wonder if this is a bad idea. What if he's there with his girlfriend? What if she walked him to class? I don't want to see that. I'm not at all emotionally prepared to see him with another girl. To watch him kiss her, laugh with her, hold her hand.

I'm a couple steps down the hallway when I start to slow. The space is clearing out as everyone escapes into their classrooms. I'm a sitting duck out here. If Z glances out one of these windows, he'll notice me right away.

Oh god, this was a mistake.

I stop walking and spin around, trying to sprint out of this building as fast as possible—only to crash into someone. Hot liquid pours down my stomach, burning my skin.

"Oh fuck," I say, trying to pull my too-tight shirt away from my body. "Who the shit drinks hot coffee in September? It's still summer!"

The guy in front of me looks wide-eyed and panicked. He shoves a hand through his short, dark hair.

"I'm so sorry," he says. "I didn't know you were turning and I—fuck—fudge." He glances at a door down the hallway, and then back to me, where I'm lifting the small crop top away from my body as liquid drips down from it, splashing onto the concrete floor. I think I might be flashing him my breasts, but I kind of don't care right now. I'm in pain, dammit.

But the coffee isn't boiling. It could be worse.

"You need to get that shirt off before you get burned," he says, but he mutters it, almost to himself. He's just working out ways to solve this problem.

"I'm not stripping right here."

He shoots me a quick smirk. "I know, I'm just late. I don't know what else... " The smirk falls from his face. He's unbuttoning his shirt now. I don't understand why, since there are only a couple small splashes of coffee on it. He takes off the button-down, revealing that he is *built*, his biceps straining the material of his T-shirt. His arms are pure muscle, and tattoos cover almost every inch of his brown skin. He slips out of his T-shirt now too and—holy fuck. He's gorgeous. I don't think I've ever seen a man this well-proportioned.

Before I can even ogle him properly, he's tossing me his T-shirt. "Put this on instead," he says gruffly. I grab it with my free hand. He's already buttoning back up his collared shirt. He makes his way into a classroom, and I'm almost *positive* that it's the same classroom Z is in. The door swings shut behind him, and I'm left standing there, in a puddle of coffee, my body on fire, and his T-shirt in my hand. What the hell just happened?

THREE

ALEX

It's official. The caffeine gods are against me today.

I can't believe I just dumped my coffee on that poor girl. I had been speedwalking to class—totally set to make it on time, too—when she spun around and ruined my dreams of caffeine. I hope she's okay. Coffee can burn like a motherfudger. She seemed more angry than hurt, though.

She was gorgeous. There were a thousand and one reasons not to be checking her out, but I couldn't help but notice she had been cute as hell. Long, toned legs, wavy blonde hair, an outfit that could kill. I don't even know if she realized she flashed me during that encounter. I looked away as soon as I noticed, but that image is burned into my brain.

I walk into my classroom, shaking my head. If I don't get the image of her pink nipples out of my mind, "tits" is going to be the first word out of my mouth, and that's not how I want to start my teaching career.

The classroom is packed. There're no seats left and two guys stand in the back, leaning against the grey wall.

Hell. I have no clue how to work the waitlist. I run a hand through my hair. I don't know how to do any of this.

It's a sick joke, me being a TA for a semester, molding minds.

"Hey everyone," I say. Damn. My voice is shaky. I don't get a shaky voice. Ever. I'd been the team captain of my soccer team for the past two years. I'm pretty sure my pregame speeches were the freaking reason we had so many victories. "Thanks for showing up. I know it's week one, and it makes zero sense to have a discussion meeting before you've even had a lecture, but Professor Harrison wanted us to meet anyway." I roll my eyes, and it earns me a few chuckles. I grin. Maybe I *can* pull this whole cool TA thing off.

"So I'm Alex Adams. I got my bachelor's in mechanical engineering at Heyward University and am now at Olympia University working toward my master's. Discussion is mandatory, and we will have quizzes almost every week." I glance around the room, and so far the class seems like they're with me. It's unnerving to have this many people stare at you. Sure, there're thousands of people in the stands at a soccer game, but they all blend together. You just zone them out.

"Other random facts about me," I say, trying to think of something cool I've done in my life that doesn't revolve around soccer. I don't want anyone here to figure out who I am. "I've been skydiving twice." I listen to the noises of approval. "I love rock music and superhero movies."

The class is quiet, nodding along. I glance down at my lesson plan. *Fun Facts. Class Intros.*

"Okay then." I glance back up at the class, resisting the

urge to run my hand through my hair again. Instead I curl my hands into fists and then release them. "Why doesn't everyone introduce themselves. Tell me their name, year and a random fact about themselves."

I motion for the girl in the front to start introductions and I don't miss the way she smiles at me, fluttering her eyelashes. I just give her a nod. Even I'm not stupid enough to flirt with someone in my class.

"I'm Abigail," she says. "I'm a third year and I practice yoga. Religiously." She winks at me.

Fudging hell. I gesture for the next person to go. Quick. They do, and we continue down the line, and it gives me a moment to take a couple deep breaths and collect myself.

I recognize one guy from the Olympia soccer team—Daniel. Truthfully, I was hoping to never run into anyone from the team. Olympia has been Heyward's biggest rivals these past couple years at nationwide tournaments. Most of the soccer guys will probably recognize me—and then ask questions I'm not ready to answer. Like what the hell I'm doing here.

Daniel seems too busy eyeing Abigail to piece together that we've battled on the field before.

A nervous-looking guy named Zeus is the last to go. "I'm Zeus, but I go by Z." His laugh is kind of nervous too, so I smile encouragingly at him. My mom would be so proud. "I'm a third year. And a fun fact about me is tomorrow is my one-month anniversary with my girlfriend."

I resist the urge to roll my eyes. "Congrats." I don't understand people who feel the need to celebrate their relationship every month, but I guess that's part of my role as TA. To be more understanding.

"Awesome. So, since you haven't had class yet, I thought

I'd just review a few topics you'll need for this week's homework. And then let you all go a little early."

I turn to the whiteboard. This is the part I was most scared for—but my pregame jitters are gone. I'm in the middle of the match now, so it's all about following the plan and getting down to business.

The rest of my lesson runs smoothly. At the end of class, I get a couple questions about a discussion syllabus, which I assure them will be posted by the end of the night. Which it will be. Right after I write it. A couple kids hang back after class to ask me questions about joining this discussion section, and I write down their names so I can figure out how the hell to do that when I get home.

All in all, it wasn't that bad. My mom might be right. This could be my future.

I leave the classroom last, trying to get rid of that depressing thought. The mostly dried puddle of coffee lingers on the floor of the hallway, reminding me I still haven't had my daily dose of caffeine. Maybe third try is the charm?

Hopefully Cute Blonde Girl isn't hurt. Those breasts were too perfect to be marred by coffee burns.

Freaking sucks I lost my lucky shirt, though. At least I can go to sleep at night knowing I didn't leave some poor girl stranded in coffee-soaked clothes.

I push open the doors of the engineering building and the heat hits me like I'm face to face with a car engine. You would think after being home for the whole summer I'd be used to the weather, but no. Still not acclimated to being back.

Blonde hair peeks out from behind a large oak tree. I

smirk as the girl I spilled coffee on spots me and makes a beeline straight toward me.

"Were you hiding back there?" I ask. Is it just me, or does she look even hotter in my shirt? It hangs down to the edge of her shorts, so it looks like she's wearing that and nothing else.

"No. Well, not from you at least." She offers me a huge smile, even if it seems slightly forced, and then sticks her hand out. It's full of a large coffee. "I figured I owed you a new one," she says with a shrug. Thank you, caffeine gods. I greedily reach for sustenance.

"You're my new favorite person," I say, taking a grateful sip.

"I'm everyone's favorite person." She winks, flipping her hair over her shoulder. I chuckle. Gotta love a girl with confidence.

"How'd you know what I ordered?"

"It was written on the cup you left behind. Not that I understood what was in the boxes, but when I took it to the barista, she did." She holds up the cold brew in her hand. "And I got myself something that is acceptable to drink in the summer. Just to show you what it would look like."

I want to laugh again, but I feel bad. I literally dumped hot coffee on her. That should be a punishable crime. She *seems* okay. I mean, she bought me a freaking coffee when I should be the one apologizing. "I'm so sorry. I wasn't paying attention—"

"Greater men than you have been distracted by my legs."

"No, I—"

"Honestly, It's no big deal."

"Are you okay? Did you get burned?"

She waves me off. "I'm fine. Wasn't the worst thing to happen to me this morning."

If getting hot coffee dumped on her isn't the worst thing to happen, I kind of want to ask what is. But she purses her lips together, like she regrets what she said, so I don't press her.

"My name's Alex," I say, sticking out my hand.

"I know, it was written on your coffee cup." She smirks. "I'm Zoey."

"Nice to meet you. Part two."

"Part one was you dumping your coffee on me?"

"Part one was you crashing into me for no good reason."

"Yeah, part one isn't quite as nice as part two." She holds up her coffee cup. "This time we both have coffee. And it's *inside* the cup. Way nicer."

"Are you kidding me? I gave you my lucky shirt. That's the nicest I'll ever get."

She looks down and picks at the shirt she's wearing. "This is your lucky shirt?" She turns to look back up at me, and those damn blue eyes are shining with mischief. Hell—she's real cute. "I don't even know what it means."

"Blasphemy," I say, even though I'm not surprised.

"'Hero of Canton,'" she reads out. "What the heck is that?"

I chuckle. "*Firefly.*"

"*Firefly?*" she asks. I nod. "*Firefly?*" she repeats, waving her hand in a circle, expecting me to explain.

"Aaand that's it. Our friendship is officially over," I say. I walk away from her, but she follows me across campus, laughing.

"You're leaving without your lucky shirt?" she teases, spinning a little and pulling at the hem to show it off.

"True, I'll take that now." I reach toward the hem of her shirt, and she laughs, slapping my hand off.

"You've literally asked me to strip in public twice today. I should report you to Olympia University PD."

"Olympia University PD isn't a thing."

"Okay. I'll report you to the bullshit security guards that pretend to walk around campus sometimes."

"I'm terrified. Seriously. There's no way I could outrun those dudes." I bend my arm and flex my bicep, smirking at her. She smirks right back at me.

"I hate to break it to you," she says, laughter dancing in her eyes. "But you need leg muscles to run. Not arms." Normally, when I flex for a girl, you can see the hint of desire in their eyes. I've spent the last four years practically being mauled, lines wrapping around parties with girls who wanted to get their hands on me. With Zoey, there is nothing. Zip. Nada. No desire whatsoever.

Maybe I'm losing my touch.

It doesn't matter, I remind myself. *You're Responsible Alex now. No girls.*

"I hate to break it to *you*," I say, "but I've been playing college soccer for years." I drop my voice and step into her space. What can I say? Old habits die hard. I want to see if I can put that little spark of lust in her eyes. "I think I've got the leg muscles to outrun them."

She throws her head back and laughs—at me. Then she continues walking across campus, and I'm following her this time. "You're a liar," she sings. What the—

"Am not." I jog a step or two to catch up.

"You are though," she says. "My friend is obsessed with the men's soccer team. She's dragged me to all the games. And *you*,"—she jabs a finger at my chest—"are not on the team."

I snort. "Of course not. I wouldn't play for those losers."

Now she's the one confused. She scrunches up her face. "First off, Tessa would kill you if she ever heard you call them losers. Didn't they win the University Champions Cup last year?"

My muscles stiffen. Yes. They did. And it's not something I want to relive.

"And second, who the fuck else would you play for if you go to college here?"

"Didn't your parents ever warn you about making assumptions?" I tease.

We're in the middle of campus on the busy center walkway, and Zoey flips around, transitioning into walking backward so she can face me. She tilts her head up in defiance and shrugs. "Okay then, prove me wrong."

"I'm a grad student—"

"You're not a grad student."

"Uh, yes I am."

"This morning you walked into a third-year class."

"I'm the TA."

"Oh," she says, biting her lip. "Oh shit."

"How did you know what classroom I walked into?" I eye her. Then mock gasp. "Was the crash this morning just a setup so you could finally meet me?"

She laughs. "You're so full of yourself."

"I mean, you've already seen all this," I say, gesturing to my abs. "I have good reason to be full of myself." I'm laying it on a little thick, but I kind of want to get a reaction out of her.

She just rolls her eyes at me. "Where'd you play soccer then?"

"Heyward University."

"Damn," she whispers. "Were you any good?"

"You actually follow college soccer enough to know that school?" I hadn't thought she would. Heyward's on the east coast, so the only time we would ever play Olympia was if either team made it to the University Champions Cup. Sure, because we are the top two teams in the nation, the rivalry is intense. But if she only went to Olympia's home games, she never would have heard of Heyward. All the flack I was giving her about making assumptions? Yup. Backfires to bite me right in the ass.

"Like I said, Tessa's obsessed."

"Who's Tessa?"

"My best friend, roommate, and soulmate," she says with a sigh in her voice. I smirk at her, and she sticks her tongue out at me. I'm actually impressed at how well she's walking backward right now. She weaves through students during their passing period like she has eyes in the back of her head. "I just know the team name 'cause you were in the finals. I never saw any games or anything."

That's good news. The tension in my shoulders dissipates. She doesn't know who I am, or that I wasn't there for the final game. I'm still bitter about it. Obviously. We would have won the stupid game if I had been there, because, to answer Zoey's question, yes, I was damn good.

"Does Tessa know you've been following me?" I ask, steering the conversation away from soccer.

"If that was even remotely close to true, wouldn't I have had better intel and known you were a grad student?"

"You were creeping down the hallway and hiding behind trees," I counter.

Her bravado falters. With a slight smile, she spins back around to walk beside me, taking a sip from her coffee.

"You never explained this properly," she says, pinching

at my shirt again. It seems like we both have things we're avoiding talking about. I can roll with that.

"My poor shirt doesn't belong with someone who doesn't appreciate it," I lament.

"I appreciate it just fine. It's clean and not dripping with coffee. It's my new favorite shirt."

"It can't be your favorite shirt if it's my favorite shirt."

"Who says it can't be both of our favorites?"

"Because I'm the only one of us who actually knows what it means!"

Zoey laughs again. She laughs a lot, and it's doing great things for my ego. "So explain," she says.

I'm not sure where we're going. It doesn't seem like she has a class or anything she's trying to get to. We're just walking around campus. I know I had promised I'd use this time for studying, but my first actual class isn't until tomorrow. In theory, I *should* have time to read the chapters tonight. And write my class syllabus. And figure out the waitlist. And, you know, take care of a tween in between all that.

So I point out a spot on the lawn, under the shade of the tree, and Zoey nods, sitting down beside me. That's one pro of being back. It might be as hot as playing soccer in the desert, but at least there're trees everywhere.

I explain my lucky shirt, and the awesomeness that is my favorite show. She says she'll take my word for it.

There's something about Zoey that makes her easy to talk to. She's flirty and sweet and calls me on my shit every chance she gets. And not once does she try to hit on me. I've never hung out with a girl *not* trying to hit on me. It's... nice. It means we can talk about stupid things, like the proper temperature of coffee, or how the movement of a hummingbird's wings contributes to science, or if riding dragons would actually be practical.

This thing between Zoey and me, it feels natural. Like we've been ragging on each other since we were born.

Hours have gone by. Coffees have been finished. I've propped up both our backpacks and am lying back against them. Zoey's on her elbows and stomach, head propped in her hands. And I'm doing an excellent job of keeping my eyes off the curve of her hamstrings extending from my shirt, thank you very much.

"So as my new friend—" I start. She tucks a strand of hair behind her ear and winces. "What?" I ask, warily.

"Are we friends?" she says, that wince still in her voice.

"Yes."

She makes an *if you say so* face and then shrugs, hesitant. "I *guess* I could consider being your friend."

"Are you kidding me? We're already best friends."

"*Tessa* is my best friend," she tells me, reaching over to pat me on the arm. "How many times do I have to tell you this?"

I groan. "Fine, attack me like that. I only wanted a friend." I press my hand to my chest in mock pain. She doesn't fall for it.

"I guess you could fill out an application. There's a huge waiting list, though, just so you know."

"Application?"

"A friendship application," she says. She has a completely straight face, like a friendship application is a totally normal thing to have. I can't tell if she's messing with me or not. I've found out that with Zoey, you never know.

"And what's on this friendship application?"

"The normal getting-to-know-you stuff. You know—

your major, where you're from, assorted favorites. That way we can skip all the small talk."

"Is small talk that terrible?" I ask, curious.

"It's the worst. Absolute worst."

"Didn't you figure all of this out when you were doing your recon?"

"I take it back. Small talk isn't the worst. You're the worst."

I laugh. "You wouldn't have set up the crash this morning if you thought that."

She shifts, and the shirt rises to reveal one side of her jean shorts. They're short. Really short. And the position she's lying in makes them look even shorter.

I drag my gaze back to her eyes. I think the gods of celibacy might be messing with me for shits and giggles. I've pledged to be Responsible Alex this semester, and that means no hooking up whatsoever, and then boom—they give me Zoey.

"Jeesh, mark the box for big-ass ego in your friendship application."

"You have a box that says big-ass ego?"

"It's a scale. The top of which is big-ass ego."

"And I have a big-ass ego?"

"Obviously." She reaches up, dragging her fingers through her sun-streaked hair so it tumbles down over her shoulders. I suppress a groan. It's been three months since I've taken my vow of celibacy and I need to friend-zone Zoey. Fast. For my sanity.

Although, for the record, she doesn't seem all that interested in me in the first place.

"Fine. Send over the friendship application. I'm not afraid to compete against Tessa."

"That's only because you haven't met Tessa. Besides..."

She winks at me. "I'm only fucking with you. There's no friendship application."

"So, we're automatically BFFs then?" I tease, just to piss her off. She flicks me on the forehead. Apparently we're already at that stage of our relationship.

"No, Mr. Big-Ass Ego. Give me your phone."

"Why?"

"So I can give you my number and you can get your lucky shirt back. I have to go to my next class."

I unlock my phone and pass it to her. She types in her number then tosses my phone back to me. I catch it easily. We both stand, brushing grass off ourselves, and I return her backpack.

"I'll be expecting a friendship application," I call as she walks across the grass.

"And I'm expecting to start shooting rainbow laser beams from my eyes any day now," Zoey says over her shoulder. "See you around."

I turn toward the library so I'm not tempted to watch her walk away.

FOUR

ZOEY

I can't sleep. You would think being so drained would knock me right out, but no. I'm lying in bed, staring at the ceiling, wondering how it's possible to get so emotionally and physically attacked on my first day back.

During dinner, I finally confessed to Tessa about Z. Monday nights were always our bonding nights. She cooks, I clean, we watch whatever show we're working our way through. After the sixth time my alfredo pasta made a circle around my plate, she demanded to know what happened. And she was *pissed*. Not once did the words "I told you so" come out of her mouth, and I loved her a little more for it.

I close my eyes and all I see is Z's stupid-ass smile.

Tessa and I have this theory about the universe. You're in charge of your own decisions, but the universe gives you a little shove sometimes, makes sure you meet the people you are supposed to meet, when you are supposed to meet them. Z and I never should have crossed paths. We were in different years. He was an engineering major. I was geo.

But, at the start of my third year, he was in three out of four of my classes. He was sweet, had a nice smile, exuded good guy charm.

Then I started to run into him everywhere. At the restaurant where Tessa and I had our date night, in line at the coffee shop, the rock climbing wall at the gym. So I listened to the universe. I introduced myself.

A month in, we were best friends. Inseparable. I actually hung out with him more than I hung out with Tessa. *And Tessa and I live together.* We both knew it was more than friends though. His eyes would follow me from the moment I stepped foot in the classroom, to the moment I sat down next to him. I would laugh at his jokes that weren't that funny, just to see his face light up each time I did. Two months into our friendship I kissed him.

Then? We were fucking on every surface imaginable.

I sigh, popping my eyes open again. At least there's only six more days until his "weekly text." We'll still be friends. It's terrible, but I'll take him in any form I can get him.

I wish I could push him out of my head. The only time today I *wasn't* thinking about Z was when I was talking to Alex. There was something about talking to someone new. You get to introduce yourself as who you want to be, the very best version of yourself. A version of me who wasn't tied to Z. Alex wouldn't think to ask me about Z. I could just be myself for a few moments.

It's weird though. I think he's Z's TA. They'll see each other every week.

An exasperated sound escapes from my lips. Apparently, it's true. All roads lead to Zeus. That prick.

I curl my hands into fists. I need to get my mind off him.

I sit up in bed and grab my laptop.

I smile while drafting the document, fingers flying

across the keyboard. I can just imagine Alex's face when he reads it.

An hour later, I look up Alex's email in the school directory and press send.

ALEX

My little sister wakes me up by whacking me on the top of my head. "We're late."

I panic stumble out of bed, snatching my phone to check the time. We should have left ten minutes ago. Fuck —fudge.

I race into the kitchen, calling out to her over my shoulder. "Did you get breakfast?"

Lucy trails after me, dragging her shoes across the floor, arms crossed. "No."

"Fudge." I rip open the pantry door, crouching down to see what we have. Empty shelf after empty shelf greets me. I frown. Apparently, I really need to go shopping. Like yesterday. "Want applesauce?"

"No."

"Here, take this, eat it in the car." I shove a box of cereal at her face.

She pushes it back to me. "Without milk?" There's attitude dripping from her pores. I don't blame her. It'll be my fault if she's late.

"Did you get lunch?"

"No."

I groan. I reach into my pocket, only to realize it's my pajamas and my wallet is not there. I sprint back to my room, grabbing my wallet out of my jeans from yesterday.

"Get in the car," I yell to Lucy. I can tell without turning around that she's rolling her eyes.

I run back through the house, reaching the car at the same time she does. I yank the car door open, throwing myself into the seat and turning the car on. She inches the door open and thunks down into the seat, arms crossed, apparently on a mission to punish me.

It was completely my own fault I slept through my alarm this morning. I had stayed up late writing my syllabus and preparing for my first classes today. I guess I hadn't realized how badly I needed sleep after that.

I back my car into the street and then toss Lucy my wallet before I speed down toward her school. "Grab what you need for lunch."

"School lunch is gross." She props her feet on the dash, her face still scrunched up in anger. She fingers open my wallet, as if touching it might give her some unspeakable disease, and draws money out. She drops my wallet on the floor and glares out the window.

"I'll make it up to you after school. We'll get ice cream or something." Anything to make her hate me a little less.

"A double scoop." She doesn't even glance in my direction.

"A double scoop," I confirm.

"I'm going to be late if you don't speed up, you know." She doesn't seem all that upset about being late. It's just a way to torture me.

"Haven't you heard Dad's speech on why you shouldn't weave around cars?" I ask. I know I've heard it enough times throughout childhood that it's ingrained in my head.

"Yeah, but Dad also believes we're haunted by a family of ghosts." I don't remember other seventh graders being full of this much sass, but when the moody teenage years hit

Lucy, they hit her hard. Without our parents here, her attitude has only gotten worse.

"There have been quite a few hauntings around the house," I say, flicking on my blinker. My casual driving does not reflect the stress I feel inside. At all. If I don't get her to school on time, the school will send out a tardy email. That will go straight to my parents' inbox. My family already all think I'm a fuck-up who can't take care of Lucy for the semester. Hell, they left me a *written* list of rules to follow while they're gone. That's how much they don't believe in me.

And that's why I have to be Responsible Alex this semester. I have to prove them wrong.

And so far? I'm failing. I haven't broken any of the rules but... I side-eye Lucy, who has her arms crossed and has turned her back on me as much as she can in a car. Yeah. She's not about to give me any glowing reviews.

"You know you're not wearing a shirt, right?" She grumbles.

"I was in a rush."

"It's weird. Can't you drop me off like around the block?"

"There is nothing embarrassing about me being shirtless." Because really, there isn't. Until last year, I'd played soccer all my life and it's paid off. Loads of people would kill to see me shirtless. Hell, maybe I should go and flirt with Lucy's teachers and see if I could get them not to send out that tardy email. "Besides, weren't you the one who mentioned how late we are?"

Lucy scowls at me. "As if that's my fault?" She jabs her finger at my chest. "*You* messed up. Just like you're messing up everything else."

We slow to a stop at the light. The car ticks between us.

For the first time, Lucy is looking at me, and the anger I see from her slitted eyes is enough to make any man want to run away. But I don't. My past is something I have to face.

I know why she hates me. When I left for college I disappeared from her life. Didn't call, didn't visit. And then when I finally did come back, it was bad. I hate myself just as much as she hates me for the way I distanced myself and continued to throw my life down the fucking drain.

But I'm better now. I want to fix it.

We pull into her school in silence. I know I should apologize. For today, for last year, for everything. I've said sorry too many times to count at this point, but she deserves to hear it again.

Lucy hops out of the car and slams the door shut before I can even get a word out. She walks up to the school like she doesn't have a care in the world, not even rushing to make it to class on time.

In fact, I think she's slowing down.

Hell, she's not even going to make it through the doors before the bell rings.

I hang my head. It bounces against the top of the steering wheel.

My parents are going to kill me.

FIVE

ZOEY

Tour Guide Fun Fact #2: Olympia University is home to 25,000 students and hopes to grow to 27,000 students in the next two years.

And yet? It feels tiny. I'm walking past the huge glass research labs and the white, columned buildings, under the large oak trees and across the barely surviving Southern California lawns and I realize: Z could be anywhere. He could be walking to the library, or getting food in Zeus's Square, or watching me from behind the window of one of these buildings. My skin crawls, like I'm under a magnifying glass and he's watching my every move.

My heart rate only calms when I'm sitting in the lecture hall for geo. I'm actually excited for this class. We're going to be spending a lot of time in the field on weekends—gathering measurements and mapping—so that means hikes and camping trips, which I always prefer to being stuck in a classroom.

Beyond that, Professor Heath teaches this class. He's already setting up at the front of the lecture hall, wearing hiking boots, jeans, and a nebula T-shirt. He's kind of hot, for a professor, and is a constant source of discussion among the geology students that swing that way. He's kooky, but then again, most geologists love rocks a little more than they should.

When he starts class, I take some of the most diligent notes I've taken my whole college career. My pencil fills every inch of the page. Even if he's just talking about the syllabus, which I memorized religiously before I even arrived on campus, I want to remember every word that comes from his mouth.

Professor Heath's research lab is my dream position. He leads the volcanology department and runs one of the most prestigious research labs on campus. He normally takes one or two undergraduates—seniors only—to be his lab assistant and support the grad students in his lab. The thing is, even though he's young, he's already a big name in geology. Every senior who has worked for him has gone on to immediate job placement, even securing jobs within the United States Geological Services. USGS is literally my dream. I've been waiting two years to try and become a research assistant, boosting my resume by working for other labs, completing an international summer internship. All for this moment.

My hand itches to check my phone. I put it on silent for the first time since Z ended things. But...what if he texts me? Tells me everything he said was a mistake? What if he decides we only needed to wait a day between texting instead of a week?

I take a deep breath and refocus on Professor Heath.

I'm not about to throw away the most important class of my college career over a boy. Even a cute one.

My hand still twitches.

After class, I dash down to the front of the room to speak with Professor Heath. I am not above befriending my professors for a leg up in life, and I've already taken two of his classes just for that purpose.

I practically glow when he greets me by name. We set a date to meet in his office hours and go over some of the research I participated in over the summer.

I exit the air-conditioned classroom, feeling a tiny bit better for the first time since the end of my nonexistent relationship. The sun washes over my skin, and my good vibes last for all of two seconds before I dive for my phone.

My adrenaline skyrockets. My heart jumps to my throat.

Five unread texts.

Unknown Number: It's not fair I have two pages to fill out and you don't.

Unknown Number: You should fill out the application too. So I know how to woo you.

Unknown Number: Woo you into being my best friend. Not like wooing dating.

Unknown Number: Just to be clear.

Unknown Number: I'm only trying to steal you from Tessa. Nothing else.

It's Alex. I deflate. Yeah, I had a good time with Alex yesterday. He's funny, good-looking, and way too confident for his own good. And yeah, okay, if I had met him at any other time, I might have tried to be something more with him. His muscles are insane.

But I'm just not interested in him. I can't be. I'm not at

all mentally ready for that. My heartbreak has decided to display itself in the form of nausea and chest aches and I can't even stomach food, much less stomach the thought of a new guy.

Besides... I think I just got friend-zoned.

Me: The whole point of a friendship application is for me to decide if I even want to be your friend.

Alex: Please. We're already best friends.

Me: No. Tessa is my best friend.

Alex: For now.

I snort. But I find a seat near Zeus's Square and fill out the friendship application. Then send it over to Alex.

I get his shortly after.

We're surprisingly similar. While he's a summer baby and I'm a winter baby, we have the same favorite band, and we both love superhero movies and geeky TV shows. He did check "big-ass ego," so I'm proud of him for coming to terms with his condition.

For his essay section, all he wrote was: you've seen me shirtless.

He's ridiculous. Absolutely ridiculous.

Alex: Good taste in music.

Me: Ditto. How is seeing you shirtless a reason for me to be your friend?

Alex: Because who wouldn't want to be best friends with this sex god?

Me: Why are you like this?

Alex: A lot of hours in the gym.

Me: Not what I meant.

Alex: I know. When can I pick up my lucky shirt?

Me: Meet me at Hades's Fountain.

I left Alex's shirt in my room. I wasn't expecting to see him today. Normally, I wouldn't invite a man I've just met back to my dorm, but there's something about Alex that puts me at ease.

Still, I shoot off a text to Tessa and tell her to investigate Alex Adams in the engineering department if I go missing.

Then, I make my way to Alex.

ALEX

I'm the only one sitting on the edge of Hades's Fountain. It's a nice day out, so plenty of people sit on the benches and tables that surround the walkway, but I'm by myself enjoying the mist from the fountain.

I grew up on this campus. Both of my parents have been professors here my whole life, so when I was little I used to go to lectures with them or terrorize the students by riding my skateboard through the hordes of people. It's exactly why I didn't want to do my undergrad here. I already knew everything about this campus.

Like its stupid, classical Greek mythology theme. There are three fountains across the center of campus, Poseidon, Zeus, and Hades. Loads of people sit at the other two fountains, but there's a weird stigma where people tend to avoid Hades's Fountain. Some people say you get a semester of F's if you sit on the fountain, some people just say it's a semester of bad luck in general. It's bull. I've been swimming in this fountain since I was six and never had any issue with my luck. Besides, athletes are supposed to be the most superstitious out of everyone, so if I can get over it, so can the rest of the student population.

"You really shouldn't be sitting there," Zoey says as she walks up to me with a teasing smile. I can't help checking her out. Those shorts that she's wearing just highlight the fact that she's got legs for days, and my pulse accelerates like I'm running agility drills. Just because I've banned girls doesn't mean I don't notice them. Particularly if those girls look like Zoey. "It'll be a whole semester's worth of bad luck."

"If I don't get my lucky shirt, it'll be a whole semester's worth of bad luck," I grumble. I don't know why I'm so in my head about this girl, but I don't like it.

"You do you," she says, shrugging at me. "But when you start failing all your classes, you can't say I didn't warn you."

"I'm too smart to fail my classes."

"Fine, when you can't get any pussy, blame it on the fountain," Zoey says with another shrug. I burst out laughing. Well, then. I appreciate her bluntness.

I push up off the fountain and gesture to myself. She tilts her head, unimpressed. "Do I look like someone who can't get some?" I question, teasing her. What's the harm in flirting anyway? She doesn't back up when I step into her space. She doesn't blush either. Just holds her ground.

I like that.

"I mean," she says, completely unfazed while eyeing me up and down. "You're eh," she says with a hand movement. "Like you *were* really hot, but now there's like this bubble of bad Hades's juju floating around you and it kinda cancels out the hotness."

I laugh. "Take me to my lucky shirt then so I can cancel out the bad Hades juju."

She grimaces. "It's gonna take more than a lucky shirt, but we can try."

Zoey's room is a disaster. She warned me about it before I stepped foot in her space, but I wasn't expecting it to look like the whole men's soccer team had been living in just this one room. For a week. And they didn't own a trash can or dishwasher.

"I told you," Zoey says, weaving her way through the mess and hopping over the strap of a duffle bag.

"Did you get attacked or something? Was there a zombie invasion I didn't know about?"

"How do you *not* know about the zombie invasion? Tessa and I were killing zombies with kitchen knives left and right."

She holds out my lucky shirt and I snatch it from her, not about to let it out of my sight again.

"I haven't had time to wash it." She rubs the inside of her arm, eyes trailing around the mess. Her cheeks are a little pink now, and I feel bad for teasing her. "Zombie invasion and all."

"That's fine," I say, hugging my shirt to my face, over-dramatic as hell. But her laugh makes it worth it. "I'm just glad it's back where it belongs."

It smells like her. And coffee. But there's that sweet scent that's all Zoey—maybe vanilla? It's nice. Probably the closest I'll get to a girl this whole semester. Being Responsible Alex kind of sucks.

Zoey shoves me from her room and closes the door behind her. We end up on the couch and fall into the same banter we did yesterday. It's easy. No stress. A break from everything else crazy in my life.

And every time she laughs, or flicks me, or flips me off, I regret pledging to be celibate this semester. But I know myself. I'm an all or nothing kind of guy. If I don't commit fully to being Responsible Alex, then I won't do it at all, and that's not fair to Lucy.

My eyes trace Zoey's face, her smile, the dimple she has on her left side, the freckle right above her collar bone. The sad look that crosses her face every time she glances down at her phone.

Hell, just because I've sworn off women doesn't mean I can't be friends with one. I mean, I'm allowed to have friends. My parents can't ban me from that.

"It's official," I announce. "I'm showing you *Firefly*. What are you doing Friday night?"

"Pretending to study," Zoey says. I smirk. "What?"

"How about you pretend to study at my place instead, and we can have a movie night?"

Lucy and I have a weekly movie night every Friday. We switch off who gets to choose the movie, and this week it's my turn. I don't think Lucy will mind that I'm inviting a friend over. Lucy acts like she wants nothing to do with me anyway.

"Yeah," Zoey says with a shrug, glancing down at her phone again. She's been holding it in a death grip the whole time we've been on the couch, checking it every few minutes, scrunching up her nose each time she shuts down the screen again. I would think she's sending the super-secret signal that it's time for me to leave, but when I offered earlier, she practically begged me to stay. This time when she checks for notifications, she blows air in her cheeks, then releases it saying, "Yeah. Why not?"

· · ·

It isn't until I leave her apartment an hour later that I realize I never told Zoey about Lucy. And I should have. Hell, what if Zoey thinks this is a date?

Goddammit. Can't even ask a girl to a movie night right.

SIX

ALEX

"Will you pass me a napkin?" I ask. Lucy sits at the dining room table in front of me. The table feels huge without my parents there. When it's just Lucy and me it's too quiet. Lucy passes me a napkin.

I've ordered pizza. Again. I've never been a great cook, but I should probably figure out some other way to feed us. We can't live off takeout for a whole semester.

"So how was school?" I try. Lucy rolls her eyes at me. I swear that's the only facial expression she ever does anymore.

"Fine," she says. She stuffs a huge bite of pizza in her mouth, presumably so she doesn't have to answer any more questions. My mom always used to do this thing when she picked us up from school. She'd say, "Tell me three things that happened today that I don't know about already." She would honestly hold me hostage in the car until I told her about my day, and I assume she did the same with Lucy. I wonder if I should try this—holding Lucy hostage until she agrees to talk to me. I sigh. Probably not the best way to get her to forgive me. I try for a less parental tack.

"I sat on Hades's Fountain today and got my lucky shirt back—so Hades's Fountain can't be that unlucky, right?" I ask her.

"Maybe your lucky shirt is now an unlucky shirt." I see her lips tilt up in a smile at the thought of my misery. It's about as close as I'll get to a real smile, so I'll take it.

"Nah, I think I'm just so awesome, I turned Hades's Fountain lucky when I touched it." Lucy rolls her eyes and goes back to eating pizza. "Do you have any homework?" I ask. "I can always help, you know. I'm quite good at math. College degree and all that." Talking to Lucy has me talking like I'm in middle school and the girl I have a crush on is right next to me. I have no clue what to say and all my goofy spews out.

Lucy and my dad used to gather almost every night at the dining room table, with art supplies or papers spread out to work on. She's been back in school three weeks already but hasn't asked me once.

"I'll just video chat Dad later."

"Oh." I get why she hates me. From her perspective, I moved out when she was nine years old and barely reached out to her beyond that. Sure, I'd come home for the summers, but those were spent at the gym and cut short for training camp. I'd come home for the holidays if I didn't have games or practices. But honestly, for the past four years, we weren't anything more than acquaintances, and now I'm here demanding to be both her brother and her parent.

But I've been home for three months now. You think she would cool it with the attitude.

Lucy sets her plate down and steps away from the table.

She's barely eaten a slice. Can she really not stand me that much?

"You should eat more," I say.

"You're not my mom."

"But I am in charge. That's not nearly enough food for you."

"Maybe I'm just full because you took me for ice cream earlier today."

"I thought that's what you wanted—"

"—or maybe," she says, kicking her chair into the table. "I'm sick of never-ending pizza."

"And maybe I'm sick of never-ending eye rolls," I fire back. She flinches. Dammit. I shouldn't be getting into an argument with her. I take a deep breath. "I'm sorry, I'll order something different tomorrow."

"Mom used to cook for us," Lucy says, crossing her arms. "It's not like you can't."

"Luce, I set off the fire alarm the first night—"

"Mom and Dad taught me to never give up, so I'm sure they tried to teach you that too. It just didn't stick," she yells.

"Well then why didn't you go live with them?" I yell at her. "I thought you wanted to stay here with me?"

"I wanted to stay here," she says. "Just not with you." She turns on her heel and marches out of the room.

"Where are you going?"

"To call Mom and Dad."

"You know they can't cook you dinner through a screen, right?"

She turns around to face me, points at her eyes, and gives me the most dramatic eye roll of the whole night. "Just watching them eat good food would be better than another slice of pizza." She storms out of the room, and I hear the door to her bedroom slam shut.

God. Fucking. Dammit.

My papers cover the dining room table. It's the first week of school and I already have more work than I can imagine. Lucy hasn't come out of her room since our fight earlier. I've reread the same paragraph three times before I finally give up, leaning back in my chair.

I don't know what to do about Lucy. The only reason I'm even bothering with this whole Responsible Alex bullshit is to try to win her back. I hate that I was such a failure that even my sister hates me.

I have the strange urge to text Zoey. I don't even know her that well, but hearing her laugh right now would be nice. I could use a smile.

I pull out my phone to text her, but before I can even type a message my mom's picture flashes across the screen with an incoming call.

Lucy totally ratted me out.

"Hey," I say, picking up the video call. "Didn't realize I could still get in trouble when you were halfway across the world."

"Was it something I did, Alex? Is that why you're like this?" my mom says. I guess we're launching right into this then. I rest my elbows on my table, propping my head in my hand. I get the sense I'm going to be here for a while. My mom and dad are sitting at a dining room table somewhere. I assume it's at one of my mom's cousin's houses, because there are about five other people in the background, rushing around the kitchen. I wish I wasn't interrupting her family time with this, but then again, she's the one who chose to call me.

"What did Lucy say?"

"That you aren't feeding her properly! You told us you can do this, Alex—"

"I *can* do this," I argue. My mom is the one reaming me out, while my dad sits by her side, looking awkward and uncomfortable. His gaze keeps getting pulled away from the screen, like he can't be bothered with this conversation. But I know better. He gets distracted by everything, all the time. The curiosity is what makes him a good professor, but sometimes it sucks when you're talking to him, and he hasn't heard a word you said because his gaze got snagged on the spine of a book.

"Apparently not—"

"Mom. I can do this. Lucy is overreacting. I'll only feed her salad from here on out. It will be okay."

"I got an email saying she was late to school the other day."

I groan, wanting to hit my head against the table. Instead, I straighten my shoulders, glaring at my mom head-on. Because I *know* I can do this. She just has to give me a chance.

"I slept in after my first day of school because I stayed up late writing my syllabus that night. Lucy was only five minutes late."

"Your syllabus should have already been written," my dad says, mild and unconcerned but choosing that moment to chime in.

"Thanks, Dad."

He shrugs with a smile, and then his gaze gets stuck on something in the corner of the room, and he's tuned out again.

Sure, that first day I might have been a little unprepared, but I've got this now. I've figured out what I need to be doing. I have proofs scattered all over the table right now because I'm studying.

"You know you can always call us if you have any questions," my mom says, sounding softer now. "I had to call my mom every other day when I was first raising you."

"I know." I nod, but I have no intention of calling them. I can do this, dammit.

"Honey," my mom says, looking tired, letting go of a bit of the fight. "I'm just worried that this is too much for you."

"It's not." I shake my head. "I know I messed up last year, but I'm doing better now."

"You're not still sleeping around, are you?"

When my mom says that, Zoey's long legs are the first thing to pop into my mind. And then the image of me gripping her hair while she's laughing, sliding down onto her knees in front of me. I run my hand over my face. I really shouldn't be thinking of Zoey like that. When I'm around Zoey, I don't have to be Responsible Alex or the idiotic guy I was before. She doesn't know me like that. I'm just Alex. It's like a breath of fresh air, taking a brief break from the mountain of responsibilities.

I'm not going to mess that up by thinking with my dick instead of my brain.

Besides, I promised my mom and Lucy *and* myself that I'd be celibate for the semester. "You don't have to worry, Mom," I tell her. "I'm not sleeping around. Wouldn't do that around Luce."

"Good." My dad nods as if he's been there the whole time. I suppress the urge to laugh.

"Remember the rules," my mom warns.

"I've got it, I've got it. Stay sober, stay celibate, don't cuss in front of Lucy, ace my classes—"

"And take care of Lucy," my mom yells. "That's number

one. If I get one more notification that she's late or one more call that you're not feeding her properly—"

"Ma, I swear. Only vegetables from here on out." I raise my hands in the air in surrender and try to give her my best innocent boy smile. She narrows her eyes at me. One of her cousins calls to her, though, so my mom slides out of her chair, pointing her finger at me.

"I love you. Now don't mess this up. I'll call you again tomorrow."

"Love you too." I chuckle.

That just leaves my dad and me there. He looks at the phone and clears his throat a couple times.

"How are classes going?" he asks.

"Good."

"Good, good. That's good." My dad and I have never been close. My mom and I will have full-on yelling matches, sure, but she's also who I've always felt closest to. I know what she's thinking. She doesn't mince her words. My dad and I sit there a couple seconds longer in awkward silence.

"How's Spain?" I finally ask. His face lights up, and he tells me about his current research project. I try my best not to zone out and pay attention, but it's not the most exciting stuff.

The academic life has never appealed to me like it did my parents. But it's kind of all I've known growing up, so it's worth a shot as my plan B.

When our conversation falls silent again, it's my dad's turn to speak first.

"So do you think this is something you can see yourself doing?"

That's the big question, isn't it? If I can do this for the rest of my freaking life?

Instead of playing soccer.

I know what my dad wants to hear. So I crinkle up my eyes and smile at him. "Maybe."

We hang up after that.

Zoey's contact information is still pulled up on my phone. I let out a deep breath, running my hands through my hair again. I shoot Zoey a text.

Me: Two days till Friday.

She responds instantly. Is the woman glued to her phone?

Zoey: No shit? Why doesn't my calendar tell me these things?

I text her back, smiling.

Two days till Friday. Hopefully that will be enough of a break that I can manage the rest of my responsibilities.

SEVEN

ZOEY

After a summer apart, my friends and I are meeting up in the same place we always do: Boba Land. It's a boba place about five minutes from school, and it's been our favorite place since freshman year, particularly because of the section we've fondly named Nerd Corner. Nerd Corner is in the back of the shop with big comfy lounge chairs, and swinging chairs, loads of board games, stacks of comic books, and a huge collection of movie and book-themed pillows and stuffed animals. And if Nerd Corner wasn't enough of a draw, they have the best coconut boba in a ten-mile radius. Tessa and I have tested it.

There are five of us here: Me, Tessa, Eileen, Derek, and Naomi. We were tight freshman year, but we've kind of started to drift apart. I don't know what this year is going to be like, but I'm already feeling uncomfortable. It feels like I'm hiding something by not telling them what happened with Z.

"So how was Professor Heath?" Naomi giggles. She's

never actually had a class of his, but she's fully aware of how hot he is.

"Oh shit," Eileen says. She has her long black hair shoved into a messy bun on the top of her head, and she's curled up in her chair—wearing plaid pajama pants—as if she's about to fall asleep there. I'd bet five bucks that she's been in her pajamas all day. If she didn't work as a tour guide with me most days, she'd probably never wear actual jeans. "Was that today?"

"Yup."

"Damn. Slept through that." Eileen sighs. Her missing a geology class and me giving her my notes is a pretty regular occurrence. She's still damn smart though, and she always shares her study guides, so it's a pretty good trade-off. "At least I made it to my Disney class though. It's gonna be great." All of us adopted the same philosophy when it came to classes: get the hard stuff out of the way as early as possible so we could take the fun stuff senior year.

"I hate my dance class," Naomi complains. "I thought I was going to learn something cool, but I got stuck in improv. How is improv even a dance?"

"What the hell? When I took Dance 1, I got stuck in ballet with Professor Wren. I died. Literally died," Derek says. He and Naomi are sitting in one of the oversized egg chairs. They swear they aren't a couple, but they've always acted as close as one. As if to prove my point, Naomi reaches over and grabs Derek's boba to take a sip. Then she makes a face and hands it back.

"Why does your drink taste like death?"

"You taste like death," he responds.

"That doesn't even make sense," Eileen cuts in.

"And when did you taste her?" Tessa waggles her eyebrows at the two of them.

"Ohmygod, can we please not go there?" Naomi squeals. Then she does a dramatic shiver. "So gross."

"Speaking of two people who need to get together already," Eileen says, turning to me. I sink further back in my chair—hugging one of the pillows to my stomach, as if that would save me from what's to come. "How are you and Z doing?" Eileen finishes.

I open my mouth to respond. Then close it. What do I even say? That he broke up with me? We weren't even officially together.

Naomi looks at me in horror. "Girl. You and Z aren't still friends with benefits, right?" Before I can even respond, she lowers her voice. "'Cause I saw him, like the other day. With someone else."

I shut my eyes against the pain that sentence brings me.

"No way. Who?" Derek demands.

"I don't know her! They were over by the engineering building. I saw them making out."

"What?" Eileen and Derek shriek in unison. The whole situation is freaking embarrassing, and I really wish my friends weren't currently recapping it for me. Tessa glances over at me. Her nostrils widen with anger, and she's about one step away from her pissed-off warrior princess face.

"Wait," she says. "He was kissing someone else, and you thought Zoey and Z were still together, and you didn't think to tell her?

"Well I didn't know if they were together or not," Naomi says. Then she turns to me. "I'm sorry, girl, I just didn't want to overstep my bounds, you know?"

"Overstep your bounds?" Tessa demands. "You're *her* friend. Not Z's."

"It's fine." I shrug. "Zeus and I aren't a thing. He has a girlfriend now."

They sing a song filled with pity notes. I bite my cheek. This is why I didn't want to say anything.

"It's fine, I'm fine, don't worry," I lie.

"I never liked him," Eileen says. "I think I told you that. He was never a good fit for you."

"I told you," Naomi says. "Friends with benefits never ends well. People always catch feelings."

"Honestly, you should have listened to us," Derek says. Then he turns to Naomi. "Is his new girl cute?"

"I mean, she's not Zoey hot. But she's cute," Naomi says.

"I honestly can't believe he thought he could do better than you," Eileen says. "Where does he get off? He is such a jerk."

"Yeah, he's a boy and you need a man," Derek says with a laugh, flexing his non-existent bicep to show me.

"I mean, he just did this to you so many times." Eileen shakes her head. "He seemed like such a good guy in the beginning too."

"I never understood why you even bothered with him anyway," Naomi says. "After all the shit he put you through?"

Yup. That about sums that up. I'm an idiot for catching feelings, and if I had just listened to my friends in the first place, I wouldn't be sitting here, strangling the poor pillow, feeling miserable.

But some small part of me thought that maybe, after each time he chose a different girl, that we were meant to be. That's why we kept coming back to each other.

But they were right, and I was wrong.

"I did a stupid," I agree. Can't really argue with them for being right.

Tessa makes a disgusted noise in her chair beside me. I look to her, startled. But her gaze isn't directed at me. She's glaring at Naomi, Derek, and Eileen. She's in full warrior princess mode now.

"Zo?" she asks me, and I can hear in her voice that she is barely keeping it together. "Can you still give me a ride to my thing tonight?"

I don't know what thing she's talking about, but I nod, grateful for the escape.

"We should go then," Tessa says, standing. I nod and follow her.

"Wait," Derek says, frowning. "I wanna know more about Z's new girl."

"Girl, you didn't give us any deets about what happened!" Naomi says. Tessa links her arm through mine and pulls me out of the boba place. The anger is radiating off her, and once we get outside the glass doors she lets loose.

"Oh my god, we need new friends," she announces. "Honestly, Zoey, the only reason I didn't attack them is because I knew you wouldn't want a scene."

"They were right." I stumble over the asphalt. My body is dead tired, my legs barely even lifting off the ground.

"No. They absolutely were not right. They have no right whatsoever to invalidate your feelings like that. They were treating you like shit."

She yanks on the passenger side door to my car, but it's still locked. So she yanks on it five more times angrily before I finally find my keys. Then she throws herself down into the seat.

"Did you notice how not one of them asked how you were feeling? They just launched into 'I told you so.' Motherfuckers!" She jerks angrily against the seat belt. I reach over to her and put my hand on her shoulder, trying to calm her down. She throws her hands in the air. "Even if they thought Z was an ass, they shouldn't attack *you* like that. It's your life, your decision. Not theirs."

"Tessa, I'm fine. It's okay." She looks at me, her brown eyes searching my face, trying to confirm that I'm telling the truth. I try my hardest to keep my shame and embarrassment hidden. Instead, I smile slightly. "Thank you for getting us out of there."

"Anytime, babe," she says. "Anytime. Now let's go home so I can binge all of *How to Get Away with Murder* tonight and hope I pick up some things."

I laugh. "Your method is to automatically spring for murder? You'd be a terrible murderer."

"Not if I learn how to get away with it."

I shake my head. The drive is only five minutes back to our apartment, and when we get inside, Tessa does load the TV before flopping on the couch. I decline her invitation to join her though.

I go to my room, making sure to lock and close the door behind me. I put in my headphones and then I curl up on my covers and finally let out all the tears, the ugly, quiet, heartbroken sobs that I had been holding in for days.

"Okay, so I've been looking up clubs all morning," Tessa says, joining me at the table.

"What the heck do you mean 'all morning'?" I say, glancing at my phone. It's nine-thirty. "The morning doesn't start for like another thirty minutes. This is still nighttime."

Tessa rolls her eyes at me and continues. "And I think there's this creative writing one that sounds kind of cool. And this other crafty one where you just do crafts all the time. And I considered sports clubs, but then I was like, nah. Not our thing."

I blink at her. And then I blink again. "Did I miss something?" I ask. "Why are we joining clubs?"

"Operation Make New Friends," Tessa says, as if it's obvious. I raise my eyebrows at her and take another reluctant bite of my instant oatmeal. I scrunch up my nose, and Tessa smirks at my meal. I flip her off. It's not like I have the energy to cook anything else in the morning. "I stayed up all night—"

"You haven't been to bed?" How the hell did she look so good after pulling an all-nighter? I got a solid six hours last night, and my eyes are way puffier than hers.

She waves me off. "Anyway, I've decided I don't have what it takes to be a murderer."

I snort. "No shit, Sherlock."

She narrows her eyes at me but continues. "So instead of murdering them, we are just going to pretend that they don't exist and build ourselves a new friend group. I've already deleted them all on social media."

"But the effort," I groan.

"They were shits to you last night. Honestly, we should have dropped them a year ago," Tessa says.

"I guess," I say. Tessa is being overdramatic, like she always is, but it's one of the many things I love about her. Besides, I would be fine not hanging out with Derek, Naomi, and Eileen for a while. She's right. Last night did suck. And it's not like I'll totally cut them out of my life. I'll still see Eileen in class and at work.

But maybe Tessa's right. We could do with some new friends.

Like Alex.

EIGHT

ALEX

"You invited a girl over for movie night?" Lucy asks. Then she starts making kissing noises.

"It's not like that." I groan. I look around the living room, which is kind of a disaster right now, and try to figure out what I have time to clean before Zoey gets here for movie night. Lucy stands a few feet away from me, hands on her hips, her judgy expression showing exactly what she thinks about me inviting a girl over.

But what if Lucy's right? What if Zoey does think this is like a date or something?

If I just leave everything there—the empty chip wrappers, dishes, and random notebooks lying around—it shows I didn't put effort into this. Besides, Zoey's room had been even worse.

"If you pay me, I won't tell the parents," Lucy says, holding her hand out for money. I narrow my eyes at her.

"There's nothing to tell."

"You *promised* them you wouldn't bring over random

girls anymore," she says, her eyes twinkling. She's enjoying extorting me, the little shit—ship. The little ship? This whole not swearing thing is a fudging pain.

"She's not a random girl."

"Then why don't I know her?"

"Because you haven't met her yet."

"Then she's random," she says with a nod as if it's settled and I owe her money.

"Luce, it's not like that. She's just a friend." I'm trying to argue against seventh-grade logic. Lucy sticks her hands back out. I run my hands through my hair. "What the hell are you even going to tell them? That I had a friend over to watch *Firefly*?" Because, officially, the rule is not to hook up with any random girls. As far as I know, there's not a clause prohibiting movie nights.

"We're watching *Firefly*?" Lucy shrieks, eyes and mouth wide in horror.

"Aren't you excited?" I ask her, false sweetness in my voice. I know Lucy hates *Firefly*. I also know she's wrong and that it's a masterpiece.

"No," Lucy says, shaking her head. "Movie night is our thing. Don't ruin it."

I didn't even think Lucy liked movie night. It's something I kinda forced on her so she'd hang out with me, so I feel a little guilty making her watch it again. But then again, she might just be saying all this to extort me for more money.

"I'm not ruining it. I'm bringing it to a whole new level. Besides," I say, resisting the urge to stick my tongue out in victory, "it's my turn to choose."

I grab the bags of takeout Thai food from the kitchen. I spread out the food on the coffee table in preparation.

"Oh thank god," Lucy sighs, approaching the food. "It's not another salad."

True to my word, I got takeout salads for Lucy and me the past few days. And I figured curry had more vegetables than pizza, so we have Thai food today. Don't know how long I can afford this, the stipend for being a TA is next to nothing, but at least Lucy's getting vegetables. No more phone attacks from my parents.

"Oh, so you like takeout now?" I tease.

"Nope." Lucy rolls her eyes and reaches for a paper bowl. "Just sick of salad."

When Zoey rings the doorbell, I start to get up to answer it—but then I think of an even better way to set the tone for the evening. Just to absolutely make sure Zoey knows this isn't a date.

"Lucy," I whisper-yell.

"What?" she asks, annoyed.

"Go answer the door."

"I'm eating."

"Please?"

"It's your 'friend,'" she says. I don't miss the way she air quotes "friend."

"I bought you ice cream." Didn't think I was going to have to break out the big guns this early, but here we are.

Lucy rolls her eyes and mumbles something about her being the real adult here, but she stands up and walks toward the door.

"I heard that," I call after her.

Good. Zoey will know right away that I'm here with my sister, and, therefore, this isn't a date. I don't want it to be a date. I mean sure, if it was a different semester, I would be figuring out how to get into Zoey's pants, because Zoey is

freaking hot as hell. But there's no version of me that would
have wanted a date. Right?

ZOEY

Alex's house is like a legit suburban house, with a
landscaped front yard and a huge wooden door. I knock on
that door, and glance around. It doesn't seem like somewhere a college student would live. *He's a grad student*, I
remind myself. Maybe a year from now, I'll be mature
enough to live in a house like this too.

The door flies open. I'm expecting to see Alex in front
of me, but I have to lower my gaze to the small girl glaring at
me. She's cute, but I'm kinda concerned about the fact that
she looks pissed to see me. Oh God, what if I'm at the wrong
house? I want to glance down at my phone and confirm the
address, but this girl is just staring at me.

"Hi, I'm Zoey." I give her a small wave.

She narrows her eyes at me. "So you're the reason we're
watching this again," she accuses. The wind blows, sending
the girl's black curls flying all over her face, making her look
even angrier than she seemed in the beginning.

I burst out laughing. I'm at the right house, alright. How
many times has Alex made this poor girl watch *Firefly*?

Alex comes around the bend and is suddenly standing
in the doorway. My heart does a strange dance in my chest
because *damn*. My head might be fucked with thoughts of
Z, but there's no denying Alex is good-looking. He looks
even better in casual clothes and bare feet than he does in
his normal school clothes. Right now, he's in gray sweat-

pants and a worn, navy T-shirt that looks good against his darker skin.

"This is my little sister, Lucy," he says, putting his hand on her shoulder.

I just nod in response. I wasn't expecting Alex to be one of those people who still lives at home. He has this air of confidence that I thought came from being independent and sure of himself.

It's actually kind of sweet, though, that he does live at home.

Alex welcomes me inside. I follow him down a hallway to the living room. There are books everywhere; shelves are double stuffed, stacks cover the top of the dusty piano, precarious piles are pushed up against the wall. The place is also a bit of a mess. There's spilled popcorn, a leftover pizza box topping one of the books stacks, papers on the floor, and dishes left on other surfaces. I have the urge to clean, but I doubt Alex wants me fingering all of his stuff.

Alex already has Thai food laid out on the coffee table and *Firefly* cued up on the TV. He plops down on the couch, a couple feet away from me, an arm thrown across the back.

And then he blatantly checks me out while I'm standing in front of him. His eyes start at my ankles, slowly snaking their way up my legs, until, halfway up my body, he flicks his eyes away from me and to the wall. His hand squeezes in a tight fist, and his eyes close.

Oookay. I don't know whether to be offended or relieved that his eyes couldn't make it all the way up my body.

I plop down on the couch next to him, a few feet away. I'm not entirely sure why Alex asked me here tonight, or what his intentions are. But sharing a couch together feels more...intimate than I expected it to.

"Do you want curry?" Alex asks, gesturing to the cartons and paper bowls in front of him. "I got a vegetarian one for you."

"See, friendship applications are helpful," I tease, trying to recover my spirit.

Alex shakes his head at me, letting me know how crazy he thinks I am for having a friendship application. I reach for a bowl, even though my stomach is rolling a little bit.

"And now, drum roll please," Alex says, banging two fingers against the coffee table. Lucy rolls her eyes, and I roll mine back at her. "It is time for the world-renowned, number one nerd show of all time, the one, the only, *Firefly*."

Alex glances over at me and winks. I get the sense he's being extra goofy for Lucy's sake. He presses play.

Halfway through the episode, I grudgingly admit that Alex was right. It's pretty good. Right up my alley.

Lucy, obviously, does not agree with me. She collapses backward in the armchair she's sitting in, draping herself over the side, a dramatic hand crossed over her forehead. I grin. That's totally something Tessa would do. Alex glances over at her but doesn't say anything.

Lucy lets out a sigh. Then a groan when that still doesn't get her the attention she wants. I laugh.

Alex pauses the show. "Yes, my queen?" he asks, turning toward her.

"Queen?" she asks him, skeptically.

"As in drama."

"You're such a jerk." She crosses her arms. "You know I hate this show, and the first episode is sooooo long!"

"It's an hour and a half of pure awesomeness," Alex reassures me, before turning back to Lucy. "And I promised you ice cream."

"And yet, where is it?" Lucy asks, motioning to the coffee table covered with the now mostly empty takeout cartons.

Alex grumbles but pulls himself off the couch and walks toward their kitchen.

"We can change it to something else," I offer Lucy.

"No, we absolutely cannot!" Alex yells over his shoulder. I smirk at him.

"It's okay," Lucy whispers to me. "I'm going to make him watch something terrible next week."

"You two need to stop whatever plotting is going on here," Alex says, walking back toward us, a carton of mint chocolate chip in one hand, cookies and cream in the other. He holds up three bowls and spoons in between them, and a bag of M&M's. As he weaves around the coffee table and back to the couch, I really can't help but notice the way his biceps are bulging out from beneath his shirt. His hips are slim and his legs seem strong and powerful. I have to wonder how much time he spends in the gym. If I wasn't so heartbroken right now, my poor hormones would be struggling to process the fact that I have over six feet of a god bod stalking toward me.

When he sits down, it's closer than before. So close I can feel the heat radiating off his body, the weird magnetism between our thighs. I reach for the cookies and cream. I ate a whole bowl of curry earlier. Being around Alex and Lucy is the perfect distraction, so I might as well eat some ice cream while I still have my appetite.

"What do you think so far?" Alex asks, glancing at me out of the side of his eye while he loads up his ice cream.

"It's honestly so good."

"Boooo!" Lucy calls from her chair.

"I'm going to be binge-watching it instead of doing homework all the time now."

Alex lets out a sad sigh and then pats my leg. His hand feels warm against my thigh, and my body flushes. "And you've discovered the tragedy of *Firefly*, my friend."

"That you spend all your time binge-watching?"

"It's only one season," Lucy says with a gleeful smile, pouring M&M's into her mint ice cream. "Alex literally cries himself to sleep about it."

"I do not." He reaches for an M&M, just to ping it off her forehead.

"Oh why oh why couldn't there be a second season?" Lucy cries, deepening her voice, pretending to sound like Alex.

"You're such a brat," Alex says.

"What, it's not like you're trying to impress her," Lucy says in a singsong voice. "She's not a random girl, right? If she's your friend she should accept you for who you are."

I have no clue what they're talking about, but the fact that Alex isn't trying to impress me is probably a good sign. In fact, he hasn't tried to make a move on me all night. Besides sitting close to me, the whole situation has been extremely friendly. Lucy and Alex are battling something out with their eyes.

"Fine. You can have another bowl of ice cream," Alex says.

"I'm gonna get weak with you in charge," Lucy says with a glare at Alex.

"How on earth are you going to get weak?" he argues, throwing another M&M at her.

"Because every time you mess up you bribe me with ice cream. And if I don't get my proper nutrients, my muscles won't form." Lucy turns to me. "And he messes up a lot."

I can't help the giggle that comes out of my mouth. Their relationship is honestly really cute, and it makes me wish I was closer with my siblings.

"Well, what am I supposed to bribe you with? Salad? I'd never get you to do anything that I need you to do."

"Cold hard cash, dude."

"You're like, seven. Are you saving up for the pencils that smell like fruits or something?"

"Just think what Mom and Dad will say when they come home and I'm not able to walk on my own."

"Or maybe you're trying to get that new Tamagotchi. That was my goal when I was your age."

"They'll have to lift me out of the bed."

"Do you want me to stop getting you ice cream? Fudge popsicles child."

"Fudge popsicles are your solution?" I ask with a grin. "No wonder you're messing up so much."

"See what I have to deal with?" Lucy whines. I snort.

"I try not to cuss in front of Lucy," Alex says. "So I've been saying things like fudge popsicles instead."

"So you were just cussing me out right there?" Lucy demands.

"Can I unpause now?" Alex sighs.

"Fine. Only because I'm leaving to go soak my wounds in peace. You owe me five bucks for that," Lucy says, loading up a couple of extra spoonfuls of ice cream into her bowl before getting up. "What the hell is a Tamagotchi anyway?"

"You'll get ice cream," Alex says, gesturing to her bowl. Lucy narrows her eyes at him, about to fight him, but Alex hits play and she scurries out of the room as fast as she can, taking her ice cream with her.

"So... one more?" I say at the end of the second episode.

"I told you space cowboys were amazing."

"I still don't understand your lucky shirt."

"You will," Alex says. The sun has gone down outside, so the blue light of the TV is the only thing illuminating the room. We're alone, on the couch together, in the dark.

He's leaning back against the couch, eyeing me through half-lidded eyes.

I need to tell him I'm not available.

"Where are your parents?" I ask instead. I figure any mention of family will shut down any sexual notions he has.

"They're in Spain teaching for the semester."

"No shit?"

Alex snorts, grinning at me. "Yeah. Both my parents are professors at Olympia. They decided to take a sabbatical together and take off for the semester."

"Why'd your parents choose Spain?"

"My mom has some family there." Alex stretches out, propping his feet on the coffee table and leaning back on the couch, resting one hand behind his head. He seems like the type of guy that knows that's just showing off his arm muscles.

So I smirk at him. He smirks back, still peering at me through those smoldering eyes.

"So it's just you and Lucy here?" I ask.

Alex nods. "I'm taking care of her while they're gone."

"So you're like a full-on parent now?" He's basically my

age. His face is partially obscured by shadow, but I can make out the purple bags under his eyes, the lines of worry etched into his forehead. I couldn't imagine raising a kid on top of college work, even if it's just for a few months. It's admirable though, that Alex is raising his sister.

Alex leans toward me. "Obviously I don't have a clue what I'm doing." He drops his voice to a whisper. "She's going to have no muscle by the time my parents come home."

I can't help the laughter that escapes my mouth. "Why don't you cook her something healthy then?"

"When do you think I learned how to cook?"

"In college?"

"Uh, no. I was burning like a thousand calories a day. I lived off the dining hall and takeout."

"Sounds like the life."

"Yeah, it kind of was," Alex muses. He looks away from me and up toward the ceiling. "I honestly can't decide if I miss soccer or sex more."

I don't know if he's propositioning me or not with that comment. I rub my palms off on my jeans and play it like it's a joke. "You're hot, I'm sure you can find someone around here to have sex with you." *Just not me.* Alex chuckles, tilting his head so he's looking at me again.

"Oh I know I could," he says. His gaze lingers on my face before dipping lower for a moment. My chest warms. Alex is too gorgeous for his own good. Even when I'm heart-broken over another boy, his sex appeal is enough to mess with my hormones. Then, once again, his gaze flicks away. He leans back, so his neck rests on the back of the couch and his face is pointed toward the ceiling. He sighs. "But I've sworn off women for the semester. Parenting and all that."

"No shit?" I ask again. Because Alex seems more player than parent, I would have assumed he was getting laid on the regular.

"I don't want to be bringing home random girls around Lucy, you know? Besides, it's just a semester." He sounds sad as he says it though, like a child whose favorite toy was taken away.

"You poor soul," I say with fake sadness, reaching over to pat his arm. Even though it probably sucks for him, I feel a hundred times more comfortable around him now that I know sex is off the table. This whole being my friend act isn't just some move. He genuinely wants to be my friend. "I would never *ever* in a million years agree to giving up sex for four months." Even as I say it out loud, it doesn't quite ring true to my ears. Over the summer I didn't have sex once. I kept waiting to come home to Z. So it's already been what— three months for me?

"I never thought I'd be counting down the days until my parents come home."

"What if you were in a relationship? Then it wouldn't be a random girl you're bringing around Lucy."

"Oh god," Alex groans. "Can you imagine the added stress and effort of a relationship? I'm already parenting, teaching, and trying to get a master's. A girlfriend is a no-go."

"Would it ever be a go?" I ask, because Alex doesn't give off the relationship vibe.

"Probably not," he admits. "But this is what you're for, my new BFF—"

"Tessa's my BFF."

"—you can fill me in on all of your sexual exploits and I'll live vicariously through you."

I wish I was having sexual exploits. With Z. I can't imagine anyone else.

I wonder if Z is fucking his new girl. She's probably doing everything with him that I want to do.

"In your dreams, perv," I say, reaching over to grab the remote off the coffee table. I press play. Alex leans back, legs still on the coffee table, adjusting so he faces toward the TV. I bring my legs up, crossing them underneath me, and leaning back beside him, finally getting comfortable in his house.

NINE

ZOEY

A week came and went and I still had no text from Z. There were plenty of texts from Alex over the weekend, way too many from my mom, and hundreds from Tessa despite the fact that she lived in the same freaking apartment. None from Zeus though. And what was the reason for even having a phone when the person you wanted to text you wouldn't text you?

I bite my lip, turning my phone over in my hand.

Should I text him?

Around me, students swarm, dashing to swoop tables as soon as someone leaves them. The courtyard around Zeus's (as in the Greek god, not my sort-of ex) Fountain is surrounded by most of the food joints on campus. It has loads of outdoor tables and study spots but they are impossible to get because the square is always packed with students. I scored Tessa and me a table outside The Bolt—the best coffee shop on campus—the minute I got out of class, and she is currently inside buying both of our lunches while I hold down the fort.

Z was the one who suggested weekly texts. He said that would be enough time for him. But I had expected him to reach out first. I didn't want to seem needy or clingy. And what if he was just saying that, and didn't want me to text him at all?

I bite so hard my teeth slice through my lip. I soothe over the spot with my tongue, tasting the slight tang of blood in my mouth. Fuck it. I set my phone down. I'm a bigger woman than this, I don't need to text him.

"Hey babe," Tessa says, slipping onto the bench seat in front of me and passing over the cold brew and half a veggie sub.

"Thank god," I say, greedily reaching for the coffee.

"I did not even wake you up that early," Tessa says. I narrow my eyes at her. She totally woke me up that early, singing Broadway tunes while she cooked us avocado toast and eggs. I think Tessa noticed I wasn't eating as much because she started cooking the both of us meals way more often. She bursts out laughing at my narrowed eyes. "It was nine a.m., Zoey."

"My alarm was set for eleven."

"Your alarm was wrong."

"How can my alarm be wrong? It's *my* alarm."

Tessa's face changes from good-natured to panicked. I turn my head, following her gaze, even as she reaches for my hand to—what? Provide comfort? Turn me around so I don't see?

Walking across Zeus's Square is—speak of the devil—Zeus. He looks so good, the sun reflecting on his blond hair, a friendly, real smile across his face. He is hand in hand with a girl. She's adorable, and the complete opposite of me, with the most magnificent eyeliner I've ever seen. If I tried for hours my eyeliner would never look like that.

Z whispers something in her ear. She laughs. He laughs too. He looks at her with such adoration that he can barely take his gaze off her to watch where he's walking.

He never looked at me like that.

They're a few feet away and he still hasn't noticed me.

I don't know whether to go say hi to him or if I should launch myself under the table and hope he doesn't spot me. Oh god. What if he just walks right by and doesn't even notice me? Or, worse, what if he does notice me and then doesn't even acknowledge me?

I push myself up from the table. We're supposed to still be friends, right? It would be normal to say hi to him after not seeing him for a few months. I glance back at Tessa, and she smiles at me encouragingly. I'm glad she's here.

I step toward him, and Z glances up. He notices me, and I see the panic on his face for only a second before he rearranges it into one of his classic, charming smiles.

Fuck me, he's got a nice smile.

"Hey," I say, my smile too bright and my wave too energetic. I've stepped into tour guide mode.

"Hi Zoey," he says. "It's good to see you."

"You too," I offer. It's like we're strangers.

"This is my girlfriend, Clara," he says. Clara gives me the cutest wave. It kind of hurts that she's not more intimidated by me.

"I'm going to grab us a table, babe," she chirps. She kisses him on the cheek before disappearing into the mess that is Zeus's Square. She doesn't even try to stake her claim on him or anything.

Z looks awkward. He stuffs his hands in his pockets and glances at the ground before making eye contact with me.

God. It's like he doesn't even want to be here, talking to me. That can't be right, though. We used to talk about everything.

He smiles at me, and it's like the whole world gets a little bit brighter.

"I can't believe you traveled the world," he says. "How was Italy?"

"I loved it," I say. It's true, I loved every minute of it. But... *was it worth losing Z over?* the lousy voice in my head asks. There's no version of myself that would ever give up on my dreams for a guy, but I can't help but wonder what would have happened to Z and me if I had stayed.

My heart is fucking breaking.

"That's good. I can't wait to hear all of your stories." Good. That means he's not ghosting me. It's just a mistake that he hasn't texted yet.

"And I can't wait to tell them to you," I say with a giggle and a hair toss. Fuck. That was too flirty. I don't know how to act around him anymore.

"Give me your top moment. Go."

"Every hike we did in the Apennines Mountains. It was incredible. I've never seen anything like it."

"That sounds like a Zoey thing for sure." He nods. He looks around at the square, and I don't think he even spots his girlfriend before he says, "I have to go, Zoey, but it was good running into you."

"Yeah," I say, still all bright fake smiles. "I'll talk to you soon."

He walks away without even responding, effectively ending the awkwardest conversation ever.

It didn't used to be like that between us.

I sit back down at the table. Tessa and I are both silent. It's like when you finish a good show, and there's the empty hollowness in your soul as you wonder what you're going to do with your life next.

There was something about Z that made the endorphins in my brain trip over themselves.

"I want him back," I say. My voice sounds deflated, even to my own ears.

Tessa's cheeks hollow. It's her thinking face. She's silent for several moments, just watching me, chin propped in her hand. Finally, she sighs. "Let's get him back, then."

And then she hatches a plan. The main ingredient: a fake boyfriend.

TEN

ALEX

When I step out of class on Monday, I'm kind of hoping Zoey will be waiting for me again. I don't know why she would be there, but we have been texting pretty consistently. Not gonna lie, ever since movie night I've been trying to find a reason to hang out with her again.

Who I see, though, isn't Zoey.

"Hey man, I'm Eddie—"

"Eddie Fuentes. Yeah, I know who you are," I say, returning his handshake. He's been the goalie for Olympia University for the past two years and he's damn good. Almost no goalie sees play time their rookie season, but Eddie did. He became their starting goalie first game of his freshman year. The kid is insane.

"Daniel told me you were teaching this discussion," he says, nodding over to Daniel, who's leaning against the wall outside of the classroom, a hand in Abigail's hair. "I hope you don't mind. I wanted to talk to you."

"Sure, shoot." I run a hand through my hair. I actually

have no clue where this conversation could go, and I'm a little nervous.

"How would you feel about coming out of retirement?" he asks.

"Is Olympia that desperate?" I joke. We both know full well that as a grad student there's no way in hell I could play for their D1 team. I've already used up my four years of eligibility.

"Our club team is," Eddie says. "West and I coach it, and let me just say, West would come in his pants if he knew we could get you on the team." West as in Jonah West. He's a fast-as-lightning forward for Olympia, and whenever our teams played each other it was always my job to shut him down and never let him get the ball. And I was damn good at it too. But it meant he and I were constantly fighting on the field. I don't have particularly fond memories of his tactics. I was always covered in bruises after those games, and one time I ended up with a black eye from his elbow that lasted for weeks.

"I doubt that." After three years of battling, there's no world where Jonah West would be thrilled to see me.

"He's not as much of a dick off the field as he is on it. I promise."

"Still, I wouldn't have the time."

"It's not a huge commitment. Practice two days a week, and on some weekends we have games."

I want to think about it. I can already feel the anticipation in my toes just imagining being back on the field. There's nothing in the world like having a ball at your feet.

But Lucy still hates me. I haven't finished my homework for class tomorrow. My students just turned in thirty quizzes for me to grade.

I promised my parents I would try this, and I'm already falling behind. I don't need another commitment.

"I can't."

Eddie's shoulders hunch in. "It was worth a shot. Our team would have been seriously overpowered with you on it anyway."

I flash him a classic Alex Adams smirk, the one I perfected over the years of compliments. "Good luck with your season." I'm not a complete jerk. Contrary to popular belief, I do possess some manners.

Eddie nods. "If you ever change your mind, we practice Mondays and Wednesdays from seven-thirty to nine-thirty. Come by anytime. Seriously."

The following week, I do manage to find Zoey. "Zoey," I call, sliding into a chair beside her. "Just the woman I wanted to see." The energy of Zeus's Square buzzes around me. Zoey and another girl are sitting at a metal table, soaking up the sun in the middle of the crowded square.

"I'm the only woman you know on this campus," she jokes. She rests her head in her hand, leaning on her arm as she looks at me. "Strike that—I'm the only *person* you know on this campus."

"Not true," I say.

"Name one other woman you know—and they can't be your student."

"This is Tessa," I say, gesturing at the girl across from Zoey who is watching the two of us with an amused smile. She chokes on her bite of food when I say her name.

Zoey glares at me. Then she relents, sighing. "How'd you guess?"

"Every other word out of your mouth is Tessa. I kinda figured you don't have any other friends."

Tessa laughs. "Well, he's not wrong," she says. Zoey gapes at her.

"Well, he *was* wrong until about a week ago when you decided to unfriend everyone we ever met."

"They were being dicks," Tessa says, matter-of-factly. "But it seems that you made new friends without telling me."

It's been over a week since I saw Zoey for movie night. I wonder if I should be offended she hasn't told Tessa about me.

"I'm Alex. Zoey and I are BFFs," I tell Tessa, trying my hardest to keep a straight face.

"Uh, no you're not," Tessa says. I can't see her eyes through these badass aviator glasses she's wearing, so I can't tell how upset she is. She points to herself. "I hold that role."

Zoey shrugs at me. "I told you."

"So where has Zoey been hiding your hot body?" Tessa asks, pointing at me.

I give her my best panty-dropping smirk. Tessa doesn't even blush. Zoey gives me a Lucy-worthy eye roll. Are all the women at Olympia indifferent to my charm? Or is it just the women who hang out with Zoey? I spent my college career perfecting that smirk, I know it works. "In a box under her bed. She only pulls me out when she needs a boy toy."

"Zoey, you're not doing this right." Tessa turns to her, gesturing at me. "You need to have this man on display all the fucking time. Look at those arms."

"Should I strip for her too?" I offer.

"You've stripped for her?" Tessa demands, slamming her hands on the table. She doesn't even care when people seated nearby glance at her. Zoey tries to cut in, but Tessa cuts her off, throwing her hands in the air, and a collection of bracelets on her wrist jingle as she does. "Why was I not informed of this?"

"Why are you here, Alex? Don't you have class?" Zoey asks.

"I got out early. And I knew you'd be here." I don't miss the look Tessa gives Zoey, a little half smile and eyebrow raise. Zoey ignores her and narrows her eyes at me.

"Tessa, did I ever tell you how Alex and I met?"

"Nope." Tessa pops the "P."

I groan. I know exactly where this story is going.

"I was walking along, minding my own business, and then boom, there he was, throwing his coffee at me."

"That's not at all how it happened." I swear, if Zoey's best friend believes that, it would suck. Zoey's my only friend so far.

"I think it was an act of love," Zoey continues. "He just didn't know how else to express himself."

"How the hell did you make that jump?" I mutter. Zoey winks at me.

"I mean you're impossible not to love. Your body, your hair, your brains, your personality. If only he had as much to offer," Tessa says, gesturing at my body. I make a face at her. Don't know what she's talking about. My body is great.

"I have lots to offer." I'm torn between amusement and annoyance. Are they always like this?

"I'm sure you do, sweetie," Zoey says, leaning over and patting my hand. She grins at me, the brightest smile I've seen since I've known her, and I know she's joking. I burst up out of my chair anyway in fake exasperation.

"That's it. I'm out of here. You two are ridiculous."

"We know," they say in unison. Zoey sticks her tongue

out at me, and I'm kind of thrown by how cute she looks doing something childish like that.

"I'm gonna go get a burrito, and when I come back this whole attacking the new guy thing better be over."

Zoey laughs, a full-body, head-thrown-back laugh, and then waves me away before turning back to Tessa.

About ten minutes later I return to the table, foil-wrapped burrito in hand, and I'm able to catch the tail end of their conversation.

"He would be perfect," Tessa is saying, practically bursting with excitement as she tugs on Zoey's arm.

"I barely know him." Zoey's shoulders are hunched in, like she doesn't want to be discussing whatever they're talking about.

"You know enough. Besides, he's hot as fuck. And we've been searching for someone for over a week."

"Tessa, no. That's awkward. I'm not going to do that."

"Then don't." Tessa shrugs. "But if you want to go through with the plan? *This* is how it works."

Zoey taps her coffee cup against the table, and I take her silence as a moment to break into the conversation.

"You're not going to do what?" I ask, slipping into the chair next to her. She starts and turns to me, a blush spreading across her face. Once I'm there though, she sets her shoulders straight and tosses that hair over her shoulder, all attitude and smiles.

"Flash the men's soccer team with Tessa," Zoey says.

Tessa snorts. "You would if you knew we could get away with it," she says. "But no, that's not what we were talking about," she tells me.

"Tessa—" Zoey warns. Her voice is panicked. There's something she doesn't want me to know.

Even though that makes me even more curious than

before, I'm not going to press her. I'm not a complete jerk. Kinda sucks that Zoey doesn't want to tell me, but I've learned from living with Lucy that people have their secrets, and they can get really angry if you step too close to them. But maybe that's just Lucy.

"This better not be about *Firefly*," I say, trying to change the subject for Zoey's sake. "If you watched without me..."

"I didn't, I swear. I've been waiting."

"Are you where her sudden *Firefly* obsession came from?" Tessa asks, pointing an accusatory finger at me.

"Guilty."

"Ugh." Tessa groans, shaking her head at me. "But *no*, this is about Zoey's need for a—"

Zoey dives across the table, slapping a hand over her best friend's mouth.

And holy hell.

I have a view right down Zoey's shirt. Does she just not wear a bra?

The first time I saw her breasts was because I had dumped hot coffee on her. I had other things to freaking worry about. But right now *all* I have to think about are how perfect Zoey's breasts are, the pink outline of her nipple that I'd love to put my lips on.

For the past three months, I've been dating my right hand exclusively. It's the longest freaking relationship I've ever had. The swells of Zoey's breasts swaying inches from my face is by far the most action I've had in months.

"See, he'd be perfect. He already can't keep his eyes off your tits." Tessa has somehow managed to wrestle Zoey's hand away from her mouth.

"Shi—shoot. Sorry, Zo," I say, dragging my panicked gaze to her face. I'm such an idiot. If I lose my only friend because I can't keep my eyes where they're supposed to be I might not ever forgive myself.

Zoey smacks me lightly on the forehead as she sits back down. "It's only 'cause he's in a drought. And my breasts are awesome." She shimmies slightly, and I curse under my breath, rolling my eyes toward the sky, trying to ignore her teasing me.

Thank god she's not mad. "True story," I mumble, feeling guilty.

"I still think it's a good idea," Tessa says.

Zoey bites her lip.

"I have to go to class," Tessa continues, getting up out of her chair. She kisses Zoey on the cheek before whispering, "Ask him." And then she leaves.

Zoey does not want to ask me. That much is obvious. She props her chin in her hands and glares at the table. Her blonde hair comes down to frame her face, and even with that angry scowl, she is still way too good-looking for my sanity. Why couldn't I have met her at *any* other time period in my life?

"Are you finally going to explain what I'd be perfect for?" I ask her, mimicking her position, propping my head in my hands and smirking at her. She turns her glare in my direction.

"Ask him, she says." Zoey shakes her head, leaning back in her chair. "Like that's not fucking awkward."

"It doesn't have to be. I don't bite, I swear." I wink at her. She rolls her eyes. Then she takes a sip of her iced coffee.

"Fine, if you want me to start guessing, I can," I say. I lean back in my chair, crossing my feet under the table.

"You need a nude model for an art class and you finally figured out that I'm an example of male perfection."

Zoey snorts.

"I mean, first time I stripped, you only saw me without a shirt. I get that you're trying to think of ways to get my pants off too."

"You're such a perv," she says, shaking her head at me. But she's laughing.

"In all honesty, Zoey, I have no shame. You can ask me anything." Because I don't want her to feel uncomfortable with me. If I can help her, I want to help her.

Zoey bites her lip again and glances away from me, observing the rest of Zeus's Square. "Fucking Tessa," she says with another head shake. At first I don't think she's going to say anything else. Then finally she looks back at me, facing her problems head-on.

"The last relationship I had kind of sucked," she says, putting air quotes around the word "relationship." I don't know anything about relationships. And I have no clue how this can possibly lead to her asking a question, but there's a sad look in Zoey's eyes and I get the sense that I should take this as seriously as she is.

"Sucked as in it was bad or sucked as in it ended?"

"Both?" She rubs condensation off the side of her coffee cup, staring at that instead of me. "When it was good, it was really good. But we were really just friends with benefits, so there were other girls too. I was the stupid one for getting feelings." She sighs, flicking at her cup and shaking her head, like she can't believe she ever did anything like that. "He didn't tell any of his friends about me. Not one. Like fucking me was some dark secret. And now he has a girlfriend. It all just kind of sucks." She swirls the cup in the air now and then glances to me, shrugging.

I blow out a breath of air. I'm really out of my league here. Don't know how to handle any of this. But I do know one thing. He's an idiot for not bragging about being balls deep in Zoey. "When did it end?" I ask.

"Start of the school year," she says. So like, two weeks ago? No wonder she looks so sad right now. She smirks at me, trying to hide the pain in her eyes. "That's actually how I met you."

"We met because you knocked my coffee over."

"You, like, literally threw your coffee at me, I swear," she says, laughing. "We met because I was following my ex." She puts "ex" in quotation marks again. "He's in your class."

"No way," I say, racking my brain, trying to figure out who it could be. "One of my students did that to you? Who?" Most of the guys are pretty nerdy and definitely couldn't handle Zoey, let alone Zoey and another girl.

But then again, they didn't really handle Zoey, did they?

"Do you know Z?" She lets out a resigned sigh. I stare at her, trying to see if she's messing with me.

"Z as in Zeus?" I ask. She nods. She can't be serious. Zeus is... fine. He's fine. I don't know him that well, it's only two weeks into the quarter. But he was totally cheating off his friend during our quiz today. Cheating on the first freaking quiz. I let it slide because it's not like I didn't do the same thing every once in a while when I was doing my undergrad. But cheating on the first quiz definitely isn't a good sign for the year.

Zoey's still not looking at me. It's the first time I've really seen her without her shield of confidence and laughter. She looks like she just lost the biggest game of her career, and it kind of makes me want to punch Zeus in the face. How against the rules is punching one of your students? "You dated him?" I finally ask.

"Not dated really," she says. "I mean it felt like it to me, but I guess not to him." Zoey's braced like I'm about to throw all the judgment in the world at her. I *do* think Z's a weird choice to get all hung up on. Zoey's way out of his league. But if she's hurt by this, she's hurt. I'm not going to question it.

"So what do you need me for?"

"Well." She scratches at her arm. "Tessa has this master plan to make him jealous so he'll want—yeah. Just to make him jealous. She thinks I need a fake boyfriend."

She looks at me. I look at her.

I sigh. Of all the things to ask of me.

"I'm not sure I have time for that, Zo." Because I really, *really* don't have time for that. I have way too much going on, when the hell would I have time to fit in a whole fake relationship? Some of my old teammates were in relationships and that was the most time-consuming shit I've ever seen.

And why does she even need to make him jealous? This better not be some scheme to get him back. Zoey deserves way better than that.

"I know, I know. But he's in your class, so it wouldn't be that time-consuming. We'd just flirt before or after class or something. When he was around." Zoey starts talking faster as she gains confidence in her plan. "You wouldn't have to take me out on an actual date. Obviously."

"Obviously," I echo. Hell, she's being serious right now. I hate to tell her no, but, "I don't have time."

"I could babysit for you," she offers. "Whenever you want. And I don't really want to be someone who plays games—"

"Then don't."

"But it's not really hurting anyone, is it? I mean, you and I will be fully aware what this is." She gestures between us. "And if he really has moved on, he won't be hurt by the fact that I'm with you. I'm just... testing it."

I'm holding in a sigh. I can see it all over her face that this will hurt someone—her.

My first instinct is to tell her no again. Lucy hates me. I should be spending as much time with her as I can if I want her to like me by the time my parents come back. And I know they don't want me leaving Lucy with a stranger. Not that Zoey's a stranger. We haven't known each other long, but it feels like we've known each other for years. Actually, if I was going to have anyone babysit Lucy, it would probably be Zoey.

I run a hand through my hair. I *know* I shouldn't ask this next question. It's too tempting. But now that the idea has been planted in my mind, I have to ask.

"What are you doing Monday and Wednesday nights?"

"Pretending to study," she jokes. "I could babysit."

I crinkle the leftover foil from my burrito into a ball, tossing it from hand to hand.

This could actually work. *Hell*—this could actually work.

"Can you cook?" I ask.

Zoey grins at me. "Not like Tessa, but I know how to add broccoli to a pot of pasta."

"That's more than me." I run my hand through my hair again.

If I don't have time for a fake relationship, I definitely don't have time to be going to soccer practices twice a week. And I know my parents would be perfectly happy if I never touched a soccer ball again for the rest of my life.

But this is the most excited I've been since I've moved back home.

"Okay," I say.

"Okay?" she asks in shock.

"Let's make this thing official." I refold the foil into a huge ring that's more bracelet than ring. I reach for her hand and slide it on her finger. "I vow to continue checking out your breasts and to make outrageously sexual comments anytime Z is in earshot."

She grins at me, tucking her hair behind her ears. "And I vow to feed Lucy properly to counteract everything you're doing."

"By the power vested in me by the idiots who hired me at Olympia, I now pronounce us fake boyfriend and girlfriend."

"You may fist bump the fake girlfriend." Zoey holds out her fist.

I fist bump her, but then I grab her hand, pulling her closer so I can growl in her ear. "If we're going to be fake dating, you better be expecting a hell of a lot more than a fist bump."

"I'm counting on it." She winks.

That's when the reality of the situation hits me. I'm allowed to have my hands all over Zoey. I'm allowed to touch her however I want. Feel her body against mine. Hell, maybe even her lips against mine.

And still. Not. Have. Sex.

What the hell did I just get myself into?

ELEVEN

ALEX

Unsurprisingly, Lucy did not mind that I was leaving her for a few hours. She looked way too happy about the fact that this was going to be a regular thing actually. She didn't even threaten to tell Mom and Dad about me leaving her with Zoey.

I haven't told my parents about the babysitting arrangement yet. I already know they wouldn't approve—either of soccer or leaving Lucy with a babysitter they haven't met.

But it's not like I'm *actually* playing soccer again. It's just a club team.

That doesn't stop the spark of adrenaline I get when the smell of freshly cut grass hits me—bringing back twenty years' worth of good memories. Thank the sports gods that Olympia is a soccer school. It's filled with tons of real grass fields—no turf in sight—maintained to perfection. I'm itching to get out there.

My future teammates sit at the edge of the field, lacing

up their cleats and putting on their shin guards. Eddie Fuentes and Jonah West are sitting on the team bench, relaxing before practice starts. It looks like they already have cones set up on the field for passing drills.

It's weird. I've spent the past four years of my life playing against Olympia, and now I'm going to be playing for them. West might not even let me on the team. We might have tripped each other on the field a few times, accidentally on purpose.

West turns his head when he catches sight of me. His eyes widen. His mouth falls open. Fudge me. He's gonna send me right back home, and I'll only get to smell the field, not actually play on it.

"Oh sweet baby Jesus," West says. "That can't be— No. Oh my god." He's standing on the bench now, watching me as I walk up. I keep waiting for the part where he tells me to leave.

"Believe it." Eddie smirks up at him, his back arm still resting casually across the bench, barely nodding at me, as if he knew I was going to show up this whole time.

"Alex fucking Adams," West says, shaking his head in disbelief. "On my team? This is the best motherfucking day of my life!" West yells at the sky.

The guys who are already sitting on the grass and lacing up their cleats are staring at me and obviously have no clue why West is freaking out right now. I freeze. I didn't expect this response from him either.

"Careful, man, your hard-on is showing," Eddie says mildly. West hops off the bench and rushes to me, practically jumping into my arms when he throws his arms around me. I half hug him back, patting his shoulder blades a couple of times. I don't know what to do here. Maybe

Eddie was right and West is only a jerk when he's on the field.

"This is the strangest welcome to a soccer team I've ever gotten," I say, still encased in West's arms.

"You mean your new coach doesn't normally jump into your arms the minute you get there?" Eddie asks, walking over and trying to pull West off me. West grips tighter though, rocking back and forth, saying things like "You are my hero, our savior."

"Surprisingly, no," I say. "Although, I might put in a request that all my future coaches do this. It's more fun."

Eddie finally wrestles West off me. "That's why you're here, right? You're going to play for the team?" West whispers.

"Planning on it," I say. He gets this big goofy grin across his face. I guess he's not gonna kick me out.

"Sweet baby Jesus," West repeats, looking like he's in a daze. "Alex fucking Adams."

"Didn't think you'd be this happy to see me," I drawl.

"Are you shitting me? We are going to kick ass this year."

I chuckle. I guess that's true. West was always competitive. You have to be to compete at the level we did. If he truly thinks I can help this team then I guess that explains his eagerness to forgive.

"I told you, man," Eddie says. "West doesn't hold a grudge. It's not his style."

"Nah, his style is dancing like he's possessed every time he scores," some guy with red hair calls from the field. He's leaned back on his elbows, gear already on.

"I will make you run suicides, Matty, don't think I won't," West says, pointing a finger at him. But then he turns to me. "And what happens on the field stays on the field." He claps me on my back again. "Holy fuck am I glad you're on my team now instead of playing against me."

Jonah West wants me here. He doesn't hate me at all. Weirder things have happened in my life, I guess. I can roll with this.

But I can't deny that part of me was hoping he would turn me away.

I love this sport more than anything in the world. Playing it again—at this level—just makes me realize everything I lost out on. Dreams of going pro crashed and burned within a week. My whole future totaled.

Feeling the snap of the ball at your feet, sprinting down the field, getting lost in the adrenaline rush of the game, making that perfect pass. It's great. It's fantastic.

But it's not the same.

I get why Eddie and West are so stoked I'm on this team. A lot of these guys are good, some of them might even have semi-pro potential, but it really isn't up to the standard of a D1 team. The fitness isn't there, the passes aren't as crisp, crosses are a hit and a miss. The speed of play feels like it's in slow-mo.

Doesn't mean I'm not grinning like an idiot when I'm sweat-soaked and done with practice.

"You want to come out with us?" Eddie asks. "A bunch of us normally go to Crosslands after practices. My brother and his freshman friends from the D1 team normally try to crash."

I shake my head. I haven't been to the bar right off campus since I needed a fake ID to get in. And as much fun as it would be to go out with the guys, I really can't. "Nah. I'm taking care of my sister and have a babysitter to relieve."

Beyond that, I'm a little worried. I haven't been anywhere that tests the limits of my sobriety yet.

Eddie just nods. I get the sense that not much rattles this guy. Probably why he's such a good goalie. "Maybe a different time then. I'm glad you came out. It's gonna be a good season."

TWELVE

ZOEY

I still can't believe I asked Alex to be my fake boyfriend.

At the time, it made sense. Tessa and I had sat down the night after I ran into Z and hatched a plan. The theory: if Z sees me happy with someone else, he'll get jealous and realize what he's missing. And then maybe—just maybe—he'll want me again.

When you say it like that, it seems plausible. But right now I'm pretty sure I'd fucked up asking Alex to help me out with this.

And today is supposed to be our first outing as a fake couple. I'm supposed to walk Alex to class. Flirt with him outside his classroom. Touch him and giggle and whatever else I can think of and hope Z notices me. All this for a guy.

I hate that.

But desperate times call for desperate measures, and I am sure as hell desperate to get this sadness out of my system.

After mythology, I stand at the edge of Poseidon's Fountain. I spot Alex weaving through the crowd of students toward me. His strut is confident, and his cocky smile is huge when he spots me. He obviously isn't stressed about this fake dating. I, on the other hand, am brushing off my clothes, even though I know there's nothing on them.

Normally, I'm not this self-conscious. But nothing about what I'm about to do is normal for me.

"Hi, girlfriend," Alex says with a grin. Then he frowns. "That didn't sound right. How do people in relationships greet each other?"

"Normally a 'hey' works fine," I tell him.

He shrugs and gestures across campus. "You ready to do this thing?"

I nod. I can't bring myself to speak. The nerves tumble through me like an avalanche. We walk in step toward the engineering building. Alex is talking to me, but I can't seem to concentrate on anything he's saying. He's trying to take my mind off my nerves, I can tell, but he keeps asking me questions about babysitting Lucy that we already went over when he first got home Wednesday night. He literally asked me every question he could, making sure everything had gone well. It's cute how overprotective he is of her.

We reach the building and I stop walking. How are we already here? This is a stupid idea. What if Z sees right through this and realizes what a clingy bitch I am?

"You know you don't have to do this, right?" Alex asks softly. I look at him and he shrugs and grins. "You can do the healthy thing instead. Which is *not* fake an entire relationship to make him jealous. Just in case you didn't know."

"Fuck off." I shove him lightly.

He puts both hands in the air. "Don't shoot the messenger."

"Because *you're* the designated messenger for all things healthy relationships?"

"I've never actually been in a relationship," Alex says cheerfully. "So yeah, someone messed up when they chose me for messenger."

"Fuck me. We're doomed." I groan and turn around, but Alex grips my inner arm, keeping me close to him, and then slides his hand down into mine.

"But I've hooked up with more than my fair share of girls," he says. "Trust me, I know how to create chemistry."

I want to slap that proud smirk off his face. Instead I take a deep breath and nod. I've come this far already. I have to at least try, right?

Alex opens the door to the air-conditioned building, guiding me in with a hand on the small of my back. I have the urge to press my fingertip to the heart rate monitor on my phone, just to see how crazy off the charts it is right now. Alex curls his arms around my waist, pulling me against him. His fingers dig into my skin between where my crop top ends and my shorts start. I tense under his touch. Alex, for his part, seems perfectly relaxed.

He gives my skin a squeeze, like he can't stop himself from touching me. Then he releases me and threads his fingers through mine.

I'm busy panic-scanning the hallways. My Z radar is going off and—boom. Sure enough, there he is. Waiting outside the classroom and talking with his friends. He hasn't noticed me yet. His Zoey radar isn't up to standard. I can't stop myself from checking him out. Why does his smile have to be so adorable?

"Zoey," Alex says, a little rough, a little exasperated, a little entertained. He turns me so I'm standing with the wall at my back and he's blocking out the rest of the hallway.

"You're with me? Remember? Don't be looking at other guys like that."

"I can check out other guys if I want to," I say. Because even if I was in a relationship with him, my man can't tell me what to do. Alex rolls his eyes. He actually looks a lot like Lucy in this moment, dark curly hair, eyes pointed toward the heavens

"I just mean that if you want this to work, you have to seem into me." He drops his voice and leans toward me, resting an arm on the wall beside me. "You can't give me that scared look you're giving me now."

"I'm just nervous." Which is not me. At all. I can count on my hands the number of times I've been this nervous. I glance over Alex's shoulder. *Shit.* Z is looking directly at me. I tear my gaze back to Alex's, whose eyes are crinkled up as he smirks at me.

"Is he looking?"

I nod.

"Good," Alex says, that self-assured smirk still covering his face. He starts to lean toward me, and—oh fuck. Is he going to kiss me? I don't think I'm ready for that.

He passes my mouth to whisper in my ear. "Woman, you have zero chill." He places a hand on my hip again. "Look at me," he says, and I do. His eyes shine with mischief. He likes playing this game. "Now touch me." I take a deep breath. This was my idea. I can do this.

I reach a hand out, gripping his bicep.

Okay. I get why he has a big-ass ego. His biceps are insane. They're on a whole other level. I can't even begin to wonder about the rest of his body. Soccer isn't even an arm sport.

"Now hug me," Alex instructs. "That's all. You're hugging me goodbye before class."

Without any more prompting, I reach my hands around his neck. His out-of-this-universe arms circle tight against my waist, holding me to him for several long seconds.

"There's the confident Zoey I know and love," Alex jokes. I can feel his voice pressed against my chest.

When we separate, Z and his friends are gone. They've already gone into the classroom. I hope he noticed me. I hope Alex and I were convincing enough. I hope he still likes me enough for this to even affect him. Please *please,* universe, let this be successful.

Alex walks toward the door of his classroom. Just before he disappears inside, he turns, grabbing me by my belt loop and pulling me toward him. He grins down. Damn, he really is tall.

"You may be good for me, Zoey Hawthorne." He flashes me a grin and then shows me his phone. "I'm a whole minute early today."

THIRTEEN

ZOEY

Eileen sits next to me in our geo class. I haven't informed her of Tessa's Operation New Friends endeavor, and I don't plan to. Eileen and I have been friends for years. We work together, we have class together, we study together. We've never been super close, but I think Tessa, as much as I love her, might have been a little overdramatic with the whole "we need to ditch our friends" move.

"Why is he so dreamy?" Eileen whispers, leaning into me, resting her shoulder on mine.

"Professor Heath?" I ask, smirking.

"Yeah." She sighs. It's a well-established fact that Eileen has had a crush on him since our freshmen year. I think it's weird. While I can admire from a distance that he's good-looking, the fact that he's a professor would just make it too creepy for me to ever have a crush on him.

Kind of like Alex. Not that he's creepy or anything. But he's the sort of guy where I *know* he's attractive, but I'm not attracted to him. Which works well for fake dating.

Once I got over my nerves, yesterday wasn't bad. I haven't heard from Z—still. But I definitely think he noticed Alex and me. Which is okay. Yesterday I was just laying the groundwork. Next week I'll be a better fake date. Alex won't have to give me so much instruction.

I almost roll my eyes, sitting in class. It's not like I actually *need* dating instruction. I probably have more experience with it than Alex does. Yesterday my nerves just got to me. I froze.

"Honestly," Eileen whispers to me, as Professor Heath continues to lecture. "That man is beautiful."

At this, I do roll my eyes. I'm glad I'm not Eileen attracted to him, because it would majorly fuck with my plans of working in his research lab. The deadline to apply is next Friday. I've been perfecting my application all week. And now, my hand moves at rapid-fire speed, trying to make sure I don't miss a single thing he's talking about. What if he asks me something during the interview to make sure I was paying attention in lecture? Not that I have an interview yet, but still. I have to be prepared.

"I might apply to be his lab assistant," Eileen says.

My pencil stills against the paper. What the actual fuck?

Eileen has known since day one that this lab position is my dream. She's never once mentioned being interested before.

"Really?" I ask, trying to keep my voice calm. I can't have a monopoly on a job.

But this job is my baby. Not only is Professor Heath's work fascinating, but I've been working toward this since my freshman year, making sure I have above and beyond the required experience to apply.

Professor Heath's connections could literally change my

life after college. And I *need* a good job after college. I can't move back home.

"I mean, I know you're applying too. You've been talking about it forever," Eileen says. "But I looked into it, and it's a really good position. And he's a really good teacher." She finishes on a sigh.

I want to scream. I mean *obviously* it's a good job! That's what I've been telling her since day one. But she never cared back then. She thought it was stupid I dedicated so much time to something I wouldn't even have a chance to apply for until my senior year.

Logically, it doesn't make any sense to get upset. Applications are open to all geo students, Eileen included. Just because Eileen only goes to half her classes and always copies my notes and is only interested in the position the week the application is due does not make her any less deserving.

I calm the laser beams shooting out of my eyes. "I think you should do it." See, look at that. I even managed a smile.

"Really?" She grins at me, her messy bun flopping around as she gives me a side hug. "That means the world to me."

I hug her back. And then I try to go back to taking notes. But my mind and my heart are racing each other and can't seem to stop.

I need this position.

Both of my brothers have already graduated college and have moved back home. One of my brothers plays video games all day and doesn't even have a job. He just keeps "writing," saying he's putting his creative writing degree to good use. Ask me if he's finished anything in the four years he's been back. My other brother tries. He really does. But even with a college degree he can't get hired. He's working at a coffee shop.

I know from the years of watching them, a college degree isn't enough to get you even an entry-level job anymore. You can have the best GPA, an awesome cover letter, tons of college-level work experience. It still isn't enough.

And my parents really can't afford for me to come home too. As much as my mom says she wants all her kids under one roof, she's working two jobs trying to feed all the extra mouths at home.

I need a good job when I graduate, not just a coffee shop job. I need Professor Heath's letter of recommendation like I need my coffee every morning. It's the ticket to my future.

I glance sideways at Eileen. She's actually taking notes for once, while I'm sitting here, not being able to concentrate. I take a deep breath, centering myself like I'm preparing for battle, and then get to work.

Fake dating attempt #2 takes place the following week.

We were supposed to meet up before his class again, but Alex called to say he was running late and would have to reschedule. So much for me keeping him on time.

Z still hasn't texted me. It's been three weeks now.

My friends (besides Tessa, who is a queen, always) haven't reached out to me at all, and they don't *know* that Tessa wanted me to drop them. They just heard about my breakup and never reached out again.

Tessa and I have yet to find a new group of friends, despite her insistence on dragging me to club meetings.

An eighth grader ate too much before my tour and ended up puking at my feet.

All in all, though, even though my life is kind of a hot mess right now, I'm smiling waiting for Alex. The sun is out, I'm double fisting coffee, and am about to see the man who thinks he's my best friend. All good things.

Besides, I really think this fake relationship has a fighting chance. I have no nerves this time. I'm wearing my shortest shorts, my tightest top, and am ready to flirt my ass off. That'd get to anyone, right?

When class lets out, Z and his friends are the first group of people out of the door. He stops when he sees me.

"Hi Zoey," he says.

"Hi." I wave to him as well as I can with a drink in my hand. He stares at me expectantly. I stare at him, keeping my eyes on his face. I will *not* check him out. He looks confused and finally opens his mouth when I don't say anything else.

"Are you—are you waiting for me?"

"Oh. No." I try to sound like the idea is preposterous. Wait for him? Of course not! Well not *technically*, in this situation. Am I waiting for him to eventually realize how awesome I am and come back to me? Yes. Yes, I am. "I'm waiting for Alex."

"Alex as in..." He trails off and points back to the door of the classroom. I nod. I peek through the window and can see Alex talking with a student who stayed behind because he had a few extra questions. That's alright. I can hold my own against Z. I just have to stall him until I can get Alex out here.

Z's friends shift their weight back and forth, waiting politely to the side for this conversation to be over. I don't know what they think is happening here, but I know for a fact that Z never told them we were hooking up. They're engineers though. It's not that hard to add two and two together.

"What's going on with you two?" Z asks.

Is it just me, or do I detect a hint of jealousy? I fight to keep my smile down.

"It's still new." I shrug, leaving it at that. He knows I'm way too sensible. I'd never immediately jump into a relationship with another guy right after him.

Alex finally comes out of the room, and he makes a beeline straight toward me. "Hey babe," he says, kissing me on the cheek. He wraps an arm around me, pulling me to him, and I can't deny I fit pretty freaking nicely against his body. I'm tall, so it's hard to find someone tall enough that I fit tucked against him like this. God knows Z wasn't tall enough.

Z narrows his eyes, and I grin up at Alex. I like that his arm around me doesn't feel possessive. He's not staking his claim. It just feels comfortable, like he can't help but touch me. Alex is right. He is good at this.

Alex winks at me, his eyes twinkling with the secret we're keeping.

"This is for you," I tell him, passing him a cold brew. He smirks at me and raises an eyebrow. I know what he's thinking, *an iced coffee? You're ridiculous.*

I give him a smirk full of attitude right back. *So you know what a proper summer drink tastes like.*

His lips quirk up at the edges.

"Thank you," he says, taking a sip. "You're the freaking best. I was desperately in need of caffeine."

"Aren't you always?" Because between raising a middle schooler, teaching classes, taking his own classes, playing soccer, and being my fake boyfriend/self-proclaimed BFF, the only extra thing Alex has time for is coffee. He just laughs.

"Are we still on for tonight?" he asks, his eyes glued to mine. He asks it with enough heat and tension in his voice to make it seem like we're doing way more tonight than babysitting and soccer practice.

"Of course," I murmur, placing a hand on his chest. On his really well-developed chest. God bless the universe when it shoved Alex directly into my path. He really is the perfect fake boyfriend. With over six feet of soccer-playing muscle, it would be hard for anyone to deny that Alex Adams is hot as fuck.

I cast my gaze back to Z's, and his mouth is pressed into a supportive smile. Is he being supportive because he thinks he has to, or because he actually is happy I found someone else?

"Hey Z," Alex says. "I didn't know you two knew each other."

I pinch his side where Z can't see it.

"Yeah, we're—" he starts. We're what? Ex-fuck buddies? Ex-best friends? Exes? Acquaintances? I don't know what we are now and I doubt Z knows either. "Friends."

I fight to keep my snort in. If we were friends, he would have texted me when he promised he would. If we were friends, would I know what he sounds like when he comes?

Alex does snort though. "You mean you're actually friends with someone besides Tessa?"

Z laughs at that, like he's part of some inside joke, but Alex doesn't even glance at him. His eyes are glued to mine. His stare is hot and heavy, like he's trying to communicate some secret with me, but I'm not getting it. It's too much.

"Are you ready to go get lunch?" I ask.

"Lead the way," he says. And we walk away, hand in hand, without even a backward glance at Z.

ALEX

"Admit it," Zoey says, poking me in the chest.

I shake my head.

"Come on," Zoey complains. "Say 'Zoey, you are the queen of all things coffee.'"

So yeah. The cold brew is good. I would totally drink it on a regular basis. But I dug my grave on hot coffee the minute I dumped it on her when we first met.

"Just imagine," she sighs. "If you had dumped that on me instead of burning coffee."

"Then we wouldn't have been friends," I say. "Because I never would have had to give you my lucky shirt, which is the whole reason we discussed *Firefly*, which is the whole reason you came to my house. So burning coffee for the win."

"I guess I did get a really good fake boyfriend out of it." Zoey and I are still walking hand in hand across campus. Z and his friends exited the building right after us, so we're sipping our cold brews and holding hands while he can still see us. It's weird. I don't think I've actually ever held a girl's hand before. It's not bad. Zoey's hand feels nice inside mine, all small and stuff.

But it's also another wicked hot day in SoCal. Not exactly the best hand holding temperature. Not sure I would do this again. I'll rate sweaty hand holding maybe a two out of ten.

A girl squeals beside us and we watch as she rushes into

Z's arms. He picks her up, spinning her around like they've been apart for days, not hours. Zoey slumps beside me.

"That his girlfriend?" I ask. We watch as the group crowds around a picnic table, the girl settling into Z's lap. Zoey can't seem to tear her gaze away.

"Yeah." There's so much disappointment in that word. I don't understand why Zoey's hung up on him. At all. But she is.

"Here, come with me," I say, pulling her toward the grass right off Zeus's Square.

"Aren't you supposed to go study?"

"I can do that later. Come here." I sit underneath a tree and pull Zoey down toward me. "Let's rub our fake chemistry in their faces." I settle Zoey between my legs, so she leans back against my chest, and I stack our backpacks behind us so I can lean against those. I catch a whiff of her shampoo as she pulls her hair over one shoulder. It's vanilla and sweet and I kind of want to bury my nose in her hair.

And then I realize I can.

"What're you doing?" she asks, laughing.

"Giving them something to look at," I mumble, nose still in her hair.

It's dangerous, having permission to give in to my temptation. I want to touch every inch of Zoey. But I'm also just going to be teasing myself the more I continue. I can't actually *act* on any of it. The minute Z's gone, Zoey will be out of my lap and I'll be living like a monk again.

But for now, I let my fingers slide across Zoey's bare thighs. Her legs feel like heaven. Smooth and silky and toned.

"God, I love SoCal," I groan. My fingers glide up, dipping under the edge of her shorts, before traveling back down toward her knees.

"'Cause it's October and I'm still wearing shorts?" Zoey asks. She's absolutely unaffected by my hands on her.

"Bless the California sun gods," I respond.

She glances over her shoulder to smirk at me. "Well, if we're going to be here a while, I guess I could get to know you too." One of her hands comes down to the outside of my thigh, and she squeezes. I flex for her and she laughs.

She always laughs so easily.

"What position do you play?" she asks.

"Attacking mid, usually. But I can play anything in the center."

"How's an attacking mid different than a center mid?" she asks.

"Depends on the formation."

"Explain." She waves a hand in the air.

"Well if you're playing a 4-4-2..." I start. And I draw out the shape of the formation on her thigh while I talk. Four little, tiny X's for defenders. Four X's for midfielders. Two forwards. Line after line, I know we're both watching the smooth glide of my tanned finger against her pale skin. "That's me," I say, pointing to the higher mid, supporting the forwards. "It's my job to feed them perfect passes and take shots on goal."

Zoey nods. Is it possible to get high off her shampoo? "What other formations do you play?"

I don't know if she's asking because she wants me to draw on her thigh some more, or if she actually wants to know. Either way, I'm happy. If I can't be playing soccer, the next best thing is to have a hot girl in my arms and the next next best thing is talking about soccer.

We spend a half hour going over different formations. I don't miss how often she glances over at Zeus throughout the conversation, but, in her defense, he keeps glancing over here just as often.

"Tessa is going to be so proud of me," she says, grinning. "I'm going to wow her with my soccer knowledge next time we go to a game."

Is it just me, or is it really kind of a turn-on that Zoey's a soccer fan?

She glances again at Zeus, and I sigh, shifting her so she's resting in my lap.

"So what is it about him?" I ask. There's got to be *some* reason a girl like Zoey is all messed up over a guy like Z. Maybe he's way better in bed than I thought.

"What is it about soccer?" she counters.

I pinch her thigh. "You're saying you love Z as much as I love soccer?" I challenge. "'Cause all future guys in your world are screwed if that's the case."

Zoey pinches her lips together. "See, okay. I've dated a few guys, and I've slept with a few more. And I really feel like it's hard to tell sometimes if you actually have legitimate feelings for someone, or if you've just spent so much time with them it's grown into a relationship. With Z, it was easy. I knew immediately that I liked him."

"How is it difficult to tell?" If you're in a relationship with someone, wouldn't you know that you like them? I wouldn't even attempt a relationship in the first place if I wasn't one hundred percent sure.

Zoey shrugs against me. "It just is. I'm shit with emotions. If someone flirts with me, I'll flirt back."

I laugh. "I get that. Feelings suck." Probably why I haven't had a single relationship in my life.

"But that's the thing. You know when people get married or fall in love and you ask them how they knew they found the one? And their response is always 'you just know.'" She's staring straight at Z when she says, "With Z, I just knew."

I don't want to argue with her, but it seems to me, based on the fact that he was an idiot who broke up with her, that it was not, in fact, meant to be.

Zoey turns in my arms and waggles her eyebrows at me. "You'll appreciate this, Mr. engineering major." She pats my chest. "Because I'm shit with emotions, through extensive trial and error I've actually developed a foolproof test to differentiate between guys I have actual feelings for and guys I don't."

"Oh yeah?" I raise my eyebrows at her. "What's that?"

"Are you sure you can handle hearing it? It's pretty spicy stuff for your celibate ears."

"Bring it."

"It's called the Blow Job Test."

I burst out laughing. Of course it is. Zoey isn't one to sugarcoat anything. "Please elaborate."

She grins at me. "Perv. I knew you'd want to hear it."

"Of course I do. It involves you and blow jobs. Listening to this story is going to be the most action I've gotten in months."

"It's not a story. It's a test," she clarifies. "I give the boy in question a blow job, and if it felt like a chore and I'm not enjoying it, I don't actually like them. But if I'm excited to be slobbering all over their dick, that means the feelings are actual real feelings."

Goddammit. Zoey isn't allowed to say stuff like that while sitting in my lap. It's sending my thoughts—and blood—to all the wrong places.

"How do you know it's feelings and not sexual chemistry?"

"Because even if you have sexual chemistry, there is

absolutely nothing hot about giving a blow job. It hurts your jaw, it's stressful, and the girl gets nothing out of it. I used to think I hated blow jobs."

"But you don't?" I can't stop myself from asking.

Just like I can't stop myself from imagining gathering Zoey's perfect-smelling hair into my hands, feeling the soft strands slide through my fingertips as she sucks me.

I'm not attracted to Zoey. Well I mean, I *am*, but it's nothing I would ever act on. She's my friend, and I want to keep it that way. I'm just getting all confused because she's in my lap talking about blow jobs, for Christ's sake.

"No," she says. She has an evil glint in her eyes when she leans in to whisper in my ear, nibbling a bit on my earlobe before she speaks. "When it's a guy I have actual feelings for? I fucking love sucking him off. There's nothing hotter in the world than watching his reaction to my lips around his cock, hearing his moans, and feeling him get harder against my tongue. I could do that shit for hours."

Hell.

It's all I can picture now. Zoey looking up at me as she bobs up and down my shaft, loving every second of it.

I shift underneath her, trying to pull her body off mine. She smirks at me, laughter in her eyes.

"I can feel your boner, dude." She cackles. "I told you your celibate ass couldn't handle it."

"Why couldn't I have a freaking normal BFF?" I ask the sky. "One that doesn't sit in my lap discussing her love for blow jobs."

"*Hate*," she corrects. "It's a hate. There's only been one person in my life where I actually enjoyed giving them."

If I didn't want to murder Z already, I do now.

And to make matters worse, Zoey shifts away from me, looking back over to Z and his girlfriend, cozied up at the lunch table. She frowns, all the joy she found in teasing me floating away. "I wonder if she gives him blow jobs as good as mine."

My first instinct is to say something sexual. Flirty. I'm like her. I stay away from feelings and all that crap and live in the sarcastic world. It's why Zoey and I get along so well.

But I can tell that's not what she needs right now.

I slide my hand into her hair, turning her gently toward me. "Don't think about that. This fake dating thing is supposed to make him jealous, right? So he wants you again? It'll work. He's checked us out this whole lunch." Her gaze bores into mine, eating up everything I'm telling her. It's a lot of pressure. "You're amazing, Zo. And he's an idiot for not seeing that."

She bites her lip, and it makes me want to groan. She's so gorgeous, and drawing attention to her lips like that isn't helping my sudden raging attraction to her.

"What if the fake dating thing doesn't work?" She whispers.

"Then you do the healthy thing and move on, like I previously told you to do," I tease. "And I got to spend a few weeks with a hot girl in my arms talking to me about blow jobs."

"And what will happen to us after this is over?"

I smirk at her. "Come on. You do know the second F in BFF stands for forever, right?"

FOURTEEN

ZOEY

I'm lying in Alex's bed, staring at the ceiling, while he gets changed for soccer. Alex wouldn't care if I watched. He has no shame. And I'm really, really tempted to pick my head up and just take a quick peek. I mean, his body has to be close to perfect, right? Every muscle of his that I've touched so far *feels* defined. I haven't seen them. But actively checking out your friend, even if they're godly hot, feels like it's a no-no.

I listen instead to the rustle of his clothes as his jeans hit the floor.

Keep your eyes on the fucking ceiling, Zoey.

"How's it going with Lucy?" I ask. Anything to distract myself.

I hear him sigh. He sounds utterly exhausted. "I'm on a first-name basis with everyone at the ice cream parlor near Lucy's school."

I laugh. "You know, if you ever need me to babysit Lucy anytime besides practice, I totally can," I tell his ceiling. It's been something I've been meaning to offer for a while. Lucy's such a sweetheart, and Alex is constantly doing so much. I'd do it even if he wasn't fake dating me.

Alex snorts. And I think I can hear him sliding a shirt over his head. No clue if it's coming off or on. "I don't do anything else."

"Didn't you grow up here? Don't you have friends?"

"No."

I prop myself up on my elbows to look at him, and I can't deny that I'm a little disappointed he's already dressed in a T-shirt and his soccer shorts. He bends over, though, as he reaches into his soccer bag, giving me the perfect view of his ass in those shorts, and I fall backward on the bed, staring back up at the ceiling again.

"Why not?" I ask.

Alex grumbles but doesn't actually say anything.

"It's your winning conversation skills that drove them away," I joke. The bed dips as he sits down next to me.

"I don't know, Zo. I have people when I have people. I don't like actively try to make friends." He leans back on his elbows so he can smirk at me, because he knows that's what Tessa and I are doing right now.

I roll my eyes at him. "Well, you should. It's fun."

"I have you." He grins at me. "And I really only have room for one ridiculous person in my life." I shove at him and he laughs. "The soccer guys go to Crosslands after practices, but that's the closest I've come to being invited out."

"You should go," I tell him. Because I'm a good friend like that. He shakes his head. But he has so much responsibility on his shoulders all the time. He needs a break. "I'm serious. All I need to do is study tonight, and I can do that just as easily here as I can at home."

He runs a hand through his hair, considering it. The tattoos on his bicep pop. I try my best not to notice.

Don't get me wrong. My feelings for Z are still there and one hundred percent in place. But can't a girl appreciate an attractive male when she sees one?

I poke his tattooed, built, turn-on-worthy bicep. "Go out, Alex. You need a break. I've got this."

"Have you always been this bossy?"

"You only drink cold brew now, right?" I ask. He smiles. Even though he refuses to admit it, I know it's his new favorite way to drink coffee.

"You'll text me though, right? Anytime you want me to come back? Or if you want to go home or anything?"

"No."

"Zoey," he warns.

"Fine, fine, I will," I relent. Because I know he won't go out unless I do.

He pushes up off the bed and then offers a hand to pull me up too. I follow him out of his bedroom and into the kitchen while he fills up his water bottles.

This has become my standard Monday/Wednesday. I come over early before his practice, and we watch *Firefly* or work on homework. Then he gets ready and I babysit Lucy until he comes back. The Adams house is starting to feel like my second home.

"So you'll go?" I ask as he zips up his soccer bag and slings it over his shoulder.

"Are you sure you're okay with this?" he asks, his eyes searching my face.

"Absofuckinglutely."

He narrows his eyes at me, and I make an oops face. Yeah. Probably shouldn't be cussing when Lucy's only a hallway away. But then the corner of his lips lift in a smile.

"I'll go then."

He walks toward the front door. I check my phone and then yell at him from the counter. "You're early again." I laugh. Because Alex isn't ever early to anything unless...

"It's soccer," he says, matter-of-factly. As if it's okay to be late to everything else in your life, except for soccer. I mean, that probably *is* what he thinks. It's a little concerning, but I let it slide.

"Kick ass," I call.

"Always do," he responds, before letting the front door swing shut behind him.

"Lucy, we've ditched the fun police," I yell from where I'm still sitting on the counter. "Come hang out."

Lucy pokes her head into the kitchen, a mass of curls peeking around the doorway. She glances around, confirming Alex is gone before bringing her whole body into the room.

I know Alex likes to face everything with humor, but I can tell it bums him out that she's avoiding him so much.

"Hi Zoey," she says, all smiles now that it's just the two of us.

"Hey yourself." I grin. "You got any homework left tonight?"

Lucy shakes her head. "I did it all before you came."

"Atta girl," I say, jumping off the counter and grabbing my backpack from the living room. Each time I come over we've been doing something fun together after she's done with homework. The first night we played board games, and Lucy kicked my ass at Monopoly. Seriously. She won twice in the span of two hours. I didn't even know that was possible.

The second time, I brought canvases and we painted. The third time I raided Tessa's recipe cards and we made a fancy dinner for ourselves.

Lucy is practically bouncing on her toes in the kitchen now, waiting for me to return.

"So what are we doing?" she asks.

"I am going to introduce you to something special, something I hold near and dear to my heart."

"Which is?" She rolls her eyes.

"Slutty brownies." I whip the ingredients out of my backpack, doing the whole dramatic reveal thing. Alex would probably kill me if he knew I was teaching Lucy the proper name for them, but she's in middle school. I'm sure she's heard worse. I set the brownie mix, cookie dough, and Oreos on the counter.

"That looks like way more than brownies," Lucy says.

"Exactly. That's why they're slutty." I waggle my eyebrows at her. "Because there's so much that goes in them." I've never been a fan of the word "slut." If a woman wants to have safe, consensual sex with someone (or *some-ones* if you're Naomi at any concert ever), I say she should go for it. Whenever and with whomever she wants, and she shouldn't be labeled as anything besides a normal fucking human.

Doesn't mean the slutty brownies joke doesn't make me cackle every time I hear it.

Lucy snorts and rolls her eyes. I spin toward the fridge and start gathering the other ingredients.

"Don't tell Alex I said that," I call over my shoulder.

"Wouldn't dream of it."

I kind of wish she would. It would make Alex feel better that Lucy is at least talking to him about *something*. Even if it's me saying the word "slut" too many times in his kitchen.

Maybe I should do something so outrageous that Lucy just *has* to talk to him about it.

"So how was school today?" I ask as we get started whisking brownie batter.

"School was school." She shrugs. "Mrs. Berry absolutely lost it though when Andrew refused to spit out his gum. She said the F-word twice in front of everyone."

I snort. "Andrew should have spit out his freaking gum then." I take a leaf out of Alex's book and *don't* drop the F-bomb in front of Lucy.

Lucy laughs. "Did you know my parents literally made Alex a list of rules to follow while I'm gone? And no cussing is at the top of them?"

"Really?" I ask. I get why he shouldn't do it in front of Lucy, but Alex has basically cut it out of all aspects of his life. Which is intense. If that's how he wants to live his life, it's fine, but I wish he knew it was okay to be human.

"It's a stupid rule." Lucy rolls her eyes. "I've already heard it all."

I kind of doubt she's heard it *all*. But yeah. It is kind of a stupid rule. And the fact that it's at the top of the list?

Lucy jerks a thumb toward the wall behind the dining room table. I never noticed it before because books are stacked on the table practically as tall as the note.

I walk over to it. Whoever penned it has nearly perfect handwriting, so I know it couldn't be Alex.

1. No swearing around Lucy.

2. No random girls

3. Stay sober

4. Pass your classes

5. Don't leave Lucy home alone

6. Water the indoor plants every Monday

The list goes on. There are seventeen different things

his parents want Alex to be in charge of. But it's the first five that really get me. It explains a lot. His personality right now, why he's always stressed about everything. Why I'm babysitting every time he leaves and the fact that he doesn't stay out or go out with his friends. *Why he's celibate.* I mean it's right there. *No random girls.* That's his parents' Lucy-appropriate way of telling him not to get his dick wet.

Alex is trying so hard to follow all of these rules. He's trying so hard to be a good brother.

But Lucy doesn't see that. And I'm not gonna ruin her night by trying to convince her otherwise. She gives a brutal silent treatment.

"No random girls, huh? This was Alex's semester to be gay," I say mildly, smirking at the list.

Lucy giggles. "I almost told on him when he brought you over the first time."

I fake gasp. "How could you?" I say, pointing the brownie spoon at her.

She raises her hands in the air. "I didn't know you back then!"

I shake my head, pretending like I'm giving her a hard time. We continue baking brownies, shooting the shit, and end up grabbing a deck of cards to pass the time while the room fills up with the smell of chocolatey goodness. I also make us salads that we pick at. I promised Alex I'd feed her veggies, but I don't want her to get so full she can't enjoy the brownies.

I close my eyes as the smell of brownies brings back another memory. Z and me, stumbling and sneaking through my apartment at two a.m., trying not to wake any of my roommates up as we made brownies. Batter splashed up onto my cheek as I stirred, and he licked it off. Then he just continued to drag his lips across my cheek. One kiss turned into seven, and then I was sitting on the table and his head was between my thighs.

The Z memories are floating through my brain less often now, but when they hit, they hit hard. I rub at my chest, opening my eyes and glancing around the room to find something to distract myself with.

"Lucy," I sing, making my voice as upbeat as possible, as she gets up to find ice cream to go on top of her brownies. I'm lounging in a dining room chair, my feet propped on their table.

"Yes?"

"Your makeup looks beautiful."

"Oh." She shrugs. Then she rolls her eyes and shakes her head. "I messed up on the eyeshadow."

"Stop, stop, stop," I say, covering my ears. I know I'm being overly dramatic, but I feel like I'm about to teach my first lesson as a babysitter.

"What?" Lucy asks, horrified. "Did I do it that badly?"

I shake my head. "Of course not. When I say it looks beautiful, I one hundred percent meant that it looks beautiful. But if there's one lesson I have to leave you with, Lucy, it's to own your compliments."

She looks at me, confused. She walks back to the table and sets the ice cream down, passing me a spoon.

"You put effort into looking pretty today. It should be acknowledged and appreciated and the world should worship you." Yeah. I earn a big eye roll for that one. "But sadly, you'll probably only get a couple compliments throughout the day. So don't write off the ones that you *do* get. I feel like it's a woman's first instinct to explain why that compliment doesn't actually count. But it *does* count and you *do* deserve it."

"But that seems so... rude," Lucy whispers.

"Nah, babe, that's some BS society pushes on you." Lucy is looking at the table now. I don't want to scare her, but this is something I truly believe in. My confidence didn't come from nowhere. "If someone compliments you, say 'Thank you, I know.'"

"Yeah... I'm not gonna do that," Lucy says.

"No, come on." I reach out and grab her hands. "You've got to be your own pump-up squad. No one else is going to do it for you. The way you talk about yourself affects the way you see yourself." I squeeze her hands and wait until she makes eye contact with me to say the next part. "You should never put yourself down for the sake of politeness."

Lucy still looks disbelieving though. So I lighten up and take a bite of my slutty brownie, which are definitely God's gift to the universe.

"If you're not comfortable with that though, you can start by just saying 'thank you,' that's always classy," I tell her. "Now how freaking good are these brownies?"

Lucy laughs, relieved we've finally moved on from the subject of owning your compliments.

It's not exactly true that no one else is going to be your pump-up squad. I'll definitely be part of her squad, just like I'm part of Tessa's and Alex's. Just like they are both members of mine. Tessa is the best pump-up squad there is.

But I had to live the first seventeen years of my life without Tessa. And I was so much younger than my brothers that my mom was always busy driving them around. I was just stuck in the car. I didn't get one-on-one girl time like this. I didn't have someone explain the concept of fake it till you make it. I had to teach myself and crawl and scratch for every inch of my self-confidence.

I tap my fingernails on the table a couple times, staring at the wood grain beneath my plate.

Have I lost a bit of my confidence through this whole Z experience? Here I am, telling Lucy to define her own self-worth, and I've been basing part of my self-worth on what a guy thinks of me.

That... sucks. I never thought I'd be that girl. I frown at the brownies in front of me, but I can't bring myself to swallow another bite. I'm not hungry anymore.

FIFTEEN

ALEX

When I get home, Zoey is sitting cross-legged on my couch, laptop resting on her thighs, sweatshirt hood pulled up over her head, hard at work. It's nearly midnight.

Going out with Eddie and West was fun. They introduced me to Eddie's younger brother Carlos and a couple other freshmen that come out with them. They're something else. I forgot how much energy freshmen have, and the stupid decisions they make. They spent most of the time trying to force Brandon, who seems quiet as hell, to go talk to random tables, and, despite the fact that we were all sitting around the same table, they yelled the whole night. My ears hurt. Were nights out always that loud? But Zoey was right. It was a good break from all the work I have to do.

It was the first time I'd been out to a bar since the start of my sobriety. I kept thinking someone was going to judge me for my club soda. That's what would have happened on my old team. But no one here cared, or even said anything, and I'm suddenly more at peace with being Responsible Alex than I have been in days. Zoey made that possible.

"Hey," she says, rubbing the sleep out of her eyes. She pushes the hood down.

"Hey yourself." I set my soccer bag on the tiled floor by the door. "Is Lucy asleep?"

Zoey nods. "Yeah, I checked on her about an hour ago, and she was out."

I walk by Zoey anyway, and down the hallways, pressing my head against Lucy's door. If I listen closely I can hear the sounds of her deep breathing.

I make my way back to Zoey. "How'd everything go? Did I stay out too late?"

"Everything was great! We made slutty brownies, so you have some leftovers in your fridge."

"Some?"

"Yeah, we probably ate more than we should." She flashes a smile at me, all bright white teeth and perfect pink lips, and it brightens up the room. I turn on the lamp next to her. "Thanks. And no, you didn't stay out too late. I told you I'd be up working."

I settle into the couch beside her. I know she should be going, and I should be getting some sleep, but I don't want her to go. "What're you working on?"

Zoey lets out a sigh. "A research lab application. I've read over it so many times, it's killing me."

"Let me look over it," I say, reaching for the computer. She passes it to me gratefully. And then she curls into a ball on her side of the couch, waiting for me to provide feedback.

I scan her resume, her cover letter, and the brief essay she wrote. It's impressive. Really impressive. Besides the lack of grammatical errors, as far as I can tell, Zoey has done a lot. She's already had two internships, studied abroad, part-time jobs. Way more than I had accomplished at her age.

"You're a campus tour guide?" I smirk, looking up at her. I can see it. She's got the preppy look for it.

"You couldn't tell by my walking backward skills?" she teases.

"Actually, it does explain a lot." I read back through everything again. "How do you have time for all of this?" I ask.

She shrugs. "How'd you have time to play D1 soccer and graduate?"

"Professors make time for that. They understand when you're skipping classes for sports. Professors don't make time for the students working two jobs and doing whatever the heck" —I squint my eyes at her resume again— "GIS mapping is."

Zoey laughs. "I guess I just want it, so I make time for it."

"It looks really good, Zo," I say softly. She reaches out her arms from where she's curled up. I pass her laptop back to her.

"Thanks."

"There's no way you won't get it."

She shrugs. "We'll see."

"Are you really worried?" I ask.

She hesitates, biting her lip before nodding. "It's just that... I've been working toward this research assistant position for years, and it's really prestigious so I have no idea if I've done enough. There are probably people who have done more. I should have joined clubs, like the hiking club or something."

"It says here you did a ridiculous amount of backpacking in Italy." I point at her resume and the internship she did over this past summer.

She stretches out on the couch like she's trying to push the negative emotions from her body. Her jean-clad calves land on my thighs. I rest my hands on her legs, and she doesn't even notice.

I notice though. Heat spreads over my thighs from everywhere we're touching, and my heart races just a tiny bit faster. Because her legs are in my lap. Am I in freaking middle school again?

"If you don't get it, there will be other positions, right?" I ask.

She shakes her head. "Not like this. This is a huge deal. It's got a huge amount of funding, and everyone who's had this position in the past has gone on to get jobs with USGS or NASA, and I need that opening." She lifts her arms over her head, bending over the side of the couch. Her shirt rises up, showing me her toned stomach, and I can definitely admire how all those hours of hiking have paid off on her body. "Getting hired is about who you know, right? This is how I get known. This is my shot."

"Let me look it over again," I say, reaching for her laptop. I know how it feels to mess up your one shot. I don't want that to happen to Zoey.

I have to move her legs off me so I have room for her computer, and my thighs feel cold without them. She sits up beside me, rereading her application as I do. Her love for geology is apparent, oozing off the screen. The way Zoey feels about hiking and the environment is the same way I feel about soccer.

"It's good. It's really good."

Zoey shakes her arms out and then rolls her shoulders back. "Okay. Fuck it. Let's do this."

She takes the laptop from me, puts everything into place, and then presses submit. That's something I admire about Zoey. Once she decides to do it, she doesn't second-guess herself.

"I should play a victory song," she says, smiling, already scrolling through the music on her phone.

"You should." I nod. "Quietly."

She laughs softly, then starts playing "In The End" by Linkin Park. The opening makes me smile.

"This is your victory song?" I demand.

She crosses her arms. "You got a problem with that?"

"There's so many better Linkin Park victory songs."

She shushes me. A sudden thought of horror goes through me. "When you say Linkin Park is your favorite band, you do know more than just one song, right?"

Zoey glares at me. I haven't seen the full force of Zoey's glare before, and it's honestly kind of scary. "One. Even if I only did know one song, they can still be my favorite band. And two. I'm offended. Offended as fuck. I know every song."

"*Every* song?"

"Every song. Try me."

We spend the next thirty minutes singing pieces of different songs, quizzing each other on different albums.

And yeah. She goes toe to toe with me.

She might be as big a fan as me.

"*Might* be?" she demands. "I'm totally a bigger fan."

I shake my head. "Aren't you forgetting something?" She looks at me, confused. I gesture to my arm, but she just looks at me like I'm crazy. "How have you not seen my tattoo yet? I've literally stripped for you."

"I'm sorry I was more worried about the boiling coffee dripping down my tits," she says. I don't know if it's because

I'm tired or sex-deprived, or the fact that Zoey is rocking like the greatest pair ever, but I can't stop my gaze from traveling down when she says the word "tits." She's in a sweatshirt, and I can't see anything, but my stupid brain can't seem to understand that this is exactly what I should *not* be doing right now. "Hey, eyes up here, perv."

"Sorry," I say, flicking my gaze back up to her face. She's smirking at me. "Here, quid pro quo," I offer, reaching for the hem of my sweaty practice shirt and ripping it over my body.

"What's your logic?" Zoey demands, not checking me out at all. "It's suddenly okay to be checking me out if you strip for me? This is the problem with the world."

I chuckle. "Just showing you my tattoo, Zo," I say, twisting my arm so it shows my inner upper bicep.

"Which tattoo?" she asks. "You have like twenty—oh." She reaches out and then stalls for a second, her gaze dragging back up to my eyes. "Can I?" I nod.

Her fingers are light across my skin, barely there, as she traces the Linkin Park logo etched across my skin.

"I got it a few years ago," I say. Her eyes are glued to my skin, where she keeps tracing and retracing the logo. God, why do her fingers feel so good on my skin? "It was right after Chester died—"

"It's the hex logo," she finishes. She rubs her thumb over the design again. I'm not sure if I'm imagining it or not, but her voice sounds all breathy, like I'm actually affecting her for once.

Zoey's touched my body before, been in the same room with me while I'm changing, seen me shirtless, sat in my lap, been held in my arms, and not freaking once has she ever seemed affected by it. My ego was strong enough to take it, but still. Some part of me kinda wished that it wasn't so easy for her.

But right now? Zoey's cheeks are flushing, and I can see her pulse racing in her neck we're so close.

And the stupid part of it is I can't even appreciate it because my breaths are coming faster too, the longer she keeps her hands on me.

I just keep inhaling the scent of vanilla and getting dizzy.

I've had lots of girls' hands on me before. You'd think I'd be used to this. It must be the fact that I haven't been touched in months. It could be anyone touching me and I'd be reacting like this.

But honestly—how the hell am I getting this wound up from her just touching my arm?

Her gaze finally drags away from the tattoo, but she just stares at my chest and my arms, her gaze dipping lower to my abs. I smirk at the way her eyes get stuck on my skin.

"How many tattoos do you have?" she asks, taking her time drawing each and every one with her eyes. Some of them actually mean something to me. Some of them I just got because they looked badass. But Zoey honors each and every one of them.

"Seventeen. One of the guys on my team did them." There's an electricity humming between us, and I feel the strange need to ground us so we don't get shocked.

"Which one is your favorite?" she asks in that same stupid-sexy voice.

I twist around to show her the tattoo on my shoulder blade. It's a couple lines, geometric shapes mashed together. It actually looks pretty cool. "Lucy drew this on a napkin one time when she came up to visit me."

Zoey's fingers trace that tattoo too. "Does she know you have it?"

I shrug, feeling her hand on my shoulder blade while I do. "I'm not even sure she remembers drawing it."

Zoey is quiet. But I can still feel her hand on me. "You're a good brother, Alex," she whispers.

I choose not to comment on that. It's nice that Zoey sees this side of me, but she didn't know me before. Instead, I flip around to face her again, and her hand never leaves my skin, so when I'm finally looking down into her eyes, and she's looking up into mine, her hand is resting on my chest. There's tension. She can't seem to remove her hand from my body, and I don't want her to. We're staring into each other's eyes, as if daring the other person to take a step forward, to make the first move.

Zoey snatches her hand away.

"We still on for the library tomorrow?" she asks. She stuffs her laptop and various study supplies back into her backpack. Her hair falls in front of her face, and she doesn't look at me while she packs up.

"Of course." I don't have pockets in my soccer shorts, and right now I kind of wish I did. I don't know where to put my hands.

I don't bother putting my shirt back on.

"Tell Lucy I had fun." She's standing up, already halfway to the door. She glances at me and smirks. Back to unaffected Zoey.

"Thanks for babysitting."

"Thanks for fake dating me." I don't miss the way she stresses "fake."

I stand up, watching her walk out the door, making sure she gets to her car okay. Then I close the door and lock it behind me.

What the hell was that?

I know Zoey is attractive. She's sexy as hell. But then again, lots of women are attractive. It doesn't mean anything.

There's just something about Zoey that's getting under my skin. And I'm not sure I like it.

ZOEY

I'm shaking the whole drive home. It's just because it's late, I tell myself. It's because I'm nervous about finally submitting my application.

It has nothing to do with having my hands all over Alex's body. That goddamn perfect body. It's all hard muscles and taut skin and never-ending tattoos. He's gorgeous in a way that shouldn't be possible.

When I'm lying in bed that night, all I can think about is that skin, those eyes. The intensity of his gaze when he was staring down at me.

I have to physically remind myself that I'm fake dating Alex to get Z. I want Z, not Alex.

That doesn't stop my mind from running all sorts of places with Alex that it shouldn't.

SIXTEEN

ZOEY

I hate the way that names can get stuck in your head. *Zeus.*
When it's someone you really like, every time you think
their name, it brings a smile to your face. I used to wake up,
and the very first thought on my brain would be Zeus. Just
his name. And after his name, images would flash through
my brain—us laughing together, in bed together, running
around campus at midnight together—and then I'd text him
first thing in the morning.

I programmed my brain to think his name probably fifty
times a day, and now it's stuck. I don't know how to delete
the program. It's like the worst fucking song stuck in my
head. On repeat. His name is the first thing in my head
when I wake up, it flashes through my brain at random
times during the day. At night, his name rests on the tip of
my tongue, wanting to be formed.

I would do anything to never think his name again.
Burn the word "Zeus" from my vocabulary.

But when you're taking a Greek mythology class, that's

impossible. Professor Coleman spent the last hour reviewing topics we should know for our midterm—and I swear, he's said the name Zeus fifty-seven times. Fifty-seven. I counted.

"I need to drop this class," I mutter to Tessa as we exit the lecture hall and step into the sunlight. She flips her sunglasses down over her eyes, and my miserable—but gorgeous—face is reflected in her lenses

"Don't do that. You let him win if you do that," she says.

"I know, I know," I say. "I would never. It just sucks." We walk through campus toward Poseidon's Fountain, where I agreed I'd meet Alex before we go to the library.

Things with Alex got weird last night. I should probably apologize for all the feeling up I did of his body. But sitting through this class really reminded me what I'm doing this for. I like Z. It's as simple as that.

"Okay, who the fuck names their kid Zeus anyway? Do they know how much Zeus cheated on Hera? It's like they wanted their son to be a cheater," Tessa bursts out. I think she's trying to make me laugh, but it makes me a little sad.

"He didn't cheat on me. We weren't actually together."

"Bullshit, babe," Tessa says. I don't know if it's the badass sunglasses or the way Tessa always walks with her shoulders back and her head high, an air of haughty confidence, but the absolute certainty in her voice grabs my attention. "You two were a couple, he was just too chicken-shit to admit that."

"But—"

Tessa stops walking and holds up her hand to silence me. She pushes her sunglasses up on her head, so she can stare me dead in the eyes, placing a soft hand on either one of my cheeks. "You're fucking Hera, babe. You're a queen. You're a motherfucking goddess. And he's going around fucking all these tree nymphs and mortal girls instead of being loyal to you. That's not okay. And you know what you're going to do? You're gonna kick his little lightning god ass."

I burst out laughing. It does make me feel better, a slight surge of power inside of me. It honestly is his loss that he's not with me. I loop my arm through Tessa's, and she drops her sunglasses back down her face as we walk down the brick walkway again. "You're going to ace this midterm."

"Honestly, myth is my favorite class right now. These gods have more drama than *Grey's*."

We sit on the wide concrete rim of Poseidon's Fountain, the cool water misting over us as we wait. The weather is still warm, and the sun feels wonderful on my skin. I close my eyes and take a deep breath, inhaling sunshine and mist. Tessa's right. It's really not worth it to miss out on a day like today because I'm thinking about a guy.

"Are you daydreaming about me?" the guy I'm *not* thinking about asks. I pop my eyes open to see Alex smirking at me. He passes me a cold brew and keeps the hot coffee in his hands. I think he continues to get hot coffee just to piss me off.

"Hello to you, too, Mr. Big-Ass Ego," I say, tossing my hair behind my shoulders. "Thank you for the coffee."

"Where's my coffee?" Tessa asks.

"Didn't know you were going to be here." Alex shrugs.

"Well that's just poor planning," I say. "You should know by now that Tessa and I are a package deal."

Alex grins, raising his eyebrows. "So when I'm fake dating Zoey, I'm really fake dating both of you?"

"Exactly," Tessa says, patting him on the shoulder, while I hiss.

"Don't say 'fake' so loudly."

Alex and Tessa ignore me. "Are you a cold brew girl like Zoey?"

"Tea, actually," Tessa says, "You don't want to see me with any more caffeine than that."

"Noted," Alex says. "You two ready?"

I nod, hopping up from the fountain, before reaching out a hand to pull Tessa up. We walk toward the science library.

Tour Guide Fun Fact #3: We have three libraries on our campus, and our science and engineering one is by far our best. It has huge windows, loads of study spaces, and each floor has a different level of volume, ranging from practically yelling to completely silent.

Tessa and I normally study on a whisper-level floor. We make our way to the staircase, and I turn to smile at Alex over my shoulder.

"How was practice last night?" With all of his help on my application, our Linkin Park competition, and the shirt-less-moment-that-shall-not-be-mentioned, I never asked.

"I'm still rusty, but it's coming back." Alex never talks much about soccer. Sure, he's taught me about formations and positions, but he normally doesn't talk about his personal experience on the field.

"Practice?" Tessa questions, her footsteps slowing as she glances over at Alex. Her eyes bug out wide. Then she blinks several times. "You play soccer?"

"Yeah." Alex shrugs.

We walk out into the stacks of books and collections of desks. I'm about to explain to Tessa that he plays for the

club team, not the D1 team, but when I glance back, Tessa
has come to a complete stop, staring at Alex.

"Holy shit. You're Alex Adams," Tessa whisper-yells.
Everyone around us shushes her, but she just waves them
off. Alex runs a hand through his hair, looking uncomfortable while he glances away. "How the fuck did I not put
that together?"

"You know who he is?" I whisper. Because even if I
don't mind all the attention we're getting from Tessa's
yelling, I'm still respecting the whisper law.

"You don't?" Tessa asks, shaking her head. "God, I have
failed you. This man right here," she says, stepping forward
toward Alex, then patting his arm. "This man is college
soccer royalty."

Alex's face has drained of color. His cocky, Mr. Big-Ass
Ego smirk is still in place, as if saying *yeah, I am damn good,
I know I'm damn good*, but beneath that I can see the panic
in his eyes. I know I've only known him for a little bit, but I
can read him well enough to know that he does not like this
conversation—at all.

Tessa's still fangirling though, staring up at Alex with
awe in her eyes. She keeps glancing back to me as she
explains. "He's been voted the top college soccer player two
years in a row now."

"Why didn't you tell me?" I ask Alex.

He runs a hand through his hair. Again. "I told you I
played soccer."

"What the hell are you doing here? Why aren't you
playing professional soccer out there somewhere? Didn't
you get signed?"

Alex shakes his head, looking at the ground now, but
doesn't explain anything.

"Holy fuck. I'm friends with Alex Adams." Tessa shakes her head.

"Who said we were friends?" he teases, trying to derail the soccer conversation. But his voice is tight, and his shoulders are clenched.

"We're a package deal, remember?" Tessa says, gesturing to me. "If you're friends with Zoey, you're friends with me."

Alex needs out of this conversation. Now. He's spiraling. And Tessa has just met one of her idols. She's not about to let this go. I shoot a sharp glance toward Tessa, but she doesn't even notice.

I wrap my arm around hers, dragging her with me. "Come on, package deal," I say. "Let's go find somewhere to study where you can't annoy so many people."

Alex shoots me a grateful glance. I lead our trio to the back corner of the library, where we find a cluster of empty tables together. I can tell Tessa still wants to ask Alex questions, but I convince her to study.

I keep glancing up in Alex's direction, and he just keeps staring at the papers in front of him. I know he can feel my eyes on him, but he refuses to look my direction. His knee bounces. His cheek twitches. His heavy head rests in his hand.

Alex used to be the best player in the nation, according to Tessa, and there's no one I trust more than Tessa on this subject. He hasn't mentioned that to me once. And he brags about himself *all the time*. Why avoid a subject where he has serious bragging rights?

Tessa leaves to go to the bathroom. Alex sits up from his hunched position, leaning over to me. Our faces are only an inch apart. Our breath mingles. His forehead is almost resting on mine.

"Stop staring at me."

"I'm not staring."

He reaches for my hand, which is starting to sweat now that we're so close. He rubs his thumb over my fingers, and my nerves dance up my arm, pulling at my heartstrings. "I'll explain later. I promise," he breathes.

I nod. I can barely manage any words beyond that.

"It's just—I can't—" He breaks off, shaking his head. His eyes still have that panicked look in them.

"It's okay. I can handle Tessa," I whisper, squeezing his hand.

He smiles at me gratefully, and that pulls at my heartstrings too.

SEVENTEEN

ZOEY

"Holy shitballs," Tessa says, walking into my room without knocking. I spin around in my desk chair to face her. "It's clean."

It's true. I've finally unpacked everything. Boxes have been recycled, laundry has been washed, surfaces wiped down. In perfectly placed, color-coded buckets I've arranged my pens, pencils, and highlighters.

It's spotless. Just the way I like it.

"I could have been naked in here," I say.

"Nah, you weren't." She waves a dismissive hand at me.

"How would you know? You just barged in."

"I hate to break it to you, Zo, but even during solo sessions you're loud." I flip her off, and she laughs, flopping onto my bed. "Thank god it's finally clean. My room was beginning to be a disaster."

This is how it always works with Tessa and me. Whenever the mess in her room gets too overpowering for her she just comes and hangs out in my room instead of actually cleaning.

Tessa's fully laid out on my bed now, talking toward the ceiling. "I don't understand how, as college students, they expect us to have time to clean our rooms and feed ourselves in between all of the studying."

"And yet, there's always time for Netflix."

"Obviously," Tessa says. "So, are you excited for Haunted Nights?" she asks in a spooky voice, referring to our local Halloween-themed amusement park. I give her a look. She knows I hate scary things. I love her enough to watch horror movies with her, but she knows I don't like it. Tessa bursts out laughing. "Why are you going then?"

"Because this is a really good opportunity for Alex and Lucy, and he asked me to be there," I tell her, making my tone final. Tessa gives me a knowing smile, and I just know she's going to overanalyze a situation that does not need overanalyzing. "Fine. Go. Get it over with." I groan, closing my laptop and awaiting my lecture.

Tessa points at me. "See, even you think there's something fishy about this."

"There's nothing fishy about it."

"You are going on a very real date with a guy you're supposed to be fake dating."

"It's not a date. Alex and I are just friends." I dust imaginary crumbs from my desk.

"I'm just saying, your room is clean."

"So? My room is always clean."

"Not when you're heartbroken, apparently." I narrow my eyes at her. She holds up her hands in mock surrender. I screw up my nose at her. Pretty sure that my emotional well-being and clean room status aren't connected. Pretty sure.

Although, lately, I have been thinking less about Z. His name doesn't make my heart twinge anymore.

"Get out of here with your psychology witchcraft," I say, making shooing motions at her.

"But your bed is so comfy," she groans, snuggling further into my blankets and pillows. "Mine is covered in unfolded laundry."

"Well, whose fault is that?" My phone pings on my desk. Alex is waiting for me downstairs. I grab a couple sweatshirts and my phone. "I have to go, babe, enjoy your nap."

"Will do," she says with a lazy thumbs up. I leave my room, Tessa still in my bed. She calls out to me without lifting her head from the pillows. "He doesn't have to be a fake date, Zo. I still have those earplugs!"

"He's celibate," I call back. Because, apparently, that's the best response I can come up with. As if Alex hadn't banned sex, we'd be fucking right now.

Which is absolutely not the case.

Luckily, Tessa doesn't overanalyze that statement.

Alex is sitting in the front seat of his mom's SUV, grinning at me as I make my way over to him.

"Hey," he says as I open the door.

"Hi." I wave at him and try not to blush. "Hey Lucy," I say, waving at her too. She grins at me before turning back to her friends and giggling.

Alex introduces me to the car, and they barely say hello before debating which musical to sing next. Lucy is all laughs, which means Alex is all smiles. The whole drive to the amusement park, he seems absolutely unfazed by the middle schoolers belting out show tunes. He's dressed in a light gray, long-sleeve shirt that showcases his biceps perfectly, both hands in position on the steering wheel. At one point, when Lucy bursts out with a deep, happy laugh, he looks over at me and winks.

Tessa's words have put these weird butterflies in my stomach. I knew, objectively, that Alex was hot. It's part of what made him a great fake boyfriend. But for the first time I'm really tracking how his muscles look under his shirt, flexing and moving so gracefully as he tilts the steering wheel. How cute his eyes look crinkled up and shining when he smiles. The line of his tattoo that escapes from his collar, swirling its way toward his neck.

Is it possible to be into two boys at once? Because I might have a tiny crush on Alex Adams.

"You're just going to let them roam by themselves?"

"I'm a cool chaperone," Alex says.

"Always so humble," I mutter.

"It's what Lucy wanted. I'm trying to win her over here," he says, leaning into me. We're talking in hushed tones so our voices don't travel to the group of tweens, gripping their tickets in hand and bouncing on the balls of their feet, in line behind us.

"I'm surprised she wanted to do this. I would not have the guts at her age," I say, trying not to shiver. I don't like jump scares, and I don't like that people are actively trying to scare you. I mean, you don't know who's hiding behind those costumes. What if someone broke in, dressed up as a clown, holding a very real chainsaw? I'd be trying to act all brave, not flinching while they rushed at me, and then— boom. I'd be dead. It's terrifying.

"You're not into scary things?" Alex gives me the side-eye.

"Is anyone?" I counter.

"I am," he says with a shrug. "It's why Halloween is my favorite holiday."

"Halloween isn't anyone's favorite holiday."

"I literally just said it was mine."

"You're the exception to a well-established rule." We finally hand over our tickets and are ushered into the park.

I *do* love the Halloween aesthetic. Orange and purple lights glow from all the lanterns, pumpkins line the walkways, spiderwebs cover every inch of the storefronts. But scare zones are a no-go.

"So if you don't like scary things," Alex says, keeping his eyes on Lucy as he speaks. "Why'd you come?"

I bite the inside of my lip. I honestly don't know why I came. I just knew I wanted to be here, spending time with him.

"You're not as cool of a chaperone as you think you are," I stage-whisper. "Someone needed to up the cool factor around here."

The side of his face betrays nothing. I look for a flicker of disappointment, relief, anything. He only turns to me once the last of Lucy's friends have made it into the park, a smirk on his face. "Is that so?"

"Obviously."

"We'll see who's the cool one when we go through the mazes," he warns me. Then he turns to the group of middle schoolers who have gathered around him. He becomes an all-business chaperone, telling them what time to meet back here, to use the buddy system, and to program his number into their phones. Then, he sets them free. They take off, map and battle plan ready, moving at a mix between a speed walk and a jog. Alex turns back to me, running his fingers through his hair, and I'm standing here, staring. Responsible Alex is actually a fucking hot version of Alex. "Ready?" he asks me, a teasing grin on his face.

I show him one of my new Halloween nails. The middle one.

I nearly shit myself the first time someone jumps in my face. We're walking through a scare zone to get to the mazes. Smoke wafts from the ground, bright lights fill the air, rock music that I know Alex and I both love pierces the night. And I would love all that if it wasn't for the fake-weapon-holding-creatures slicing through the fog with one purpose: scaring perfectly innocent people. Like me. A man on stilts with a bearded silicone mask walks toward me, his gait long and confident. I freaking know it's coming and still shriek when he dives, bending over, sticking his creepy mask right in front of my face.

Alex chuckles as I huddle closer to him, pressing our sides completely together. Our upper arms are squished together, and Alex doesn't seem to mind that I'm stealing comfort from him. He probably doesn't know that I'm not above using him as a human shield.

"Isn't this great?" Alex asks. He turns around so he's facing me while he walks backward, and I instantly miss the warmth of his arm against me.

"No," I say, shaking my head. "It will be once you fall on your ass though." I nod toward the people he barely avoids. Alex glances behind him quickly to make sure he's not about to trip and then glances back to me.

"What, you don't believe in my tour guide skills?" he boasts. A man in a cloak and mask holding this huge sword starts approaching behind Alex.

"I absolutely do not. Takes years of training to be as

good as me," I joke. Is it terrible that I want Alex to get scared?

The cloaked man jumps out from behind Alex, swinging his sword at him. Alex doesn't even flinch. Nope. Not one freaking muscle in his face twitches. And then the motherfucker smirks. I hate him.

When Alex proves impossible to faze, the cloaked man pivots, and suddenly there is a sword three inches from my face, and a masked face tilted sideways, peering at me. "Oh fuck no!" I yell, diving around the man and reaching for Alex. I bury myself in his chest, hiding my face so I can't see any of the creepy people around me. It's definitely not the smartest move in a true horror situation, but I'm banking on the fact that these are just actors.

Alex wraps his arms around me, keeping me tucked under his chin. He walks backward, pulling me with him, and we shuffle over painted cobblestones together. His sweatshirt is soft against my face, and I take a deep breath of his detergent and body wash, and a scent that is so masculine and *him* it puts me at peace. Surrounded by masks and weapons, I feel safe in Alex's arms.

"Damn, Hawthorne, I thought you were supposed to be a badass." His voice is right by my ear, all deep and gravelly and definitely filled with laughter—at me.

"I am a badass. I'm a badass who doesn't like the idea of getting murdered, and therefore avoids creepy things. You never think the people who go into the dark basement of a murder house are badasses. No, you think they're idiots, because they are idiots for walking right into a creepy death trap. Therefore, I'm a badass, not an idiot, because I don't like creepy death traps."

"We might need to work on your proofs, babe," Alex says when I finish my rant. I tilt my head up to glare at him, right as a masked creature makes a weird purring noise in my ear. I jump, and Alex's arms tighten around me as I bury my face in his jacket again.

"Get me out of here," I moan. Alex flips around, tucking me under his arm and I burrow into the side of him. He guides me forward and I squint my eyes, as if seeing everything around me through little slits will make people less likely to jump out and scare me.

"I agree though," Alex says lightly. "Avoiding creepy death traps does make you an intelligent badass."

"I know."

"Intelligent, badass, gorgeous, and humble." Alex chuckles. "If only slightly irrational."

"Keep the compliments coming, they're distracting me."

"You took *all* of those as compliments?"

"Mmhm."

"And you say I have a big-ass ego?" Alex mutters under his breath. I grin. We step out of the fog and out of the scare zone. The amusement park is back to normal Halloween vibes, less murdery and more decorative. I take a deep breath of relief. Or I call it that. Really, I think I'm just trying to get one last whiff of Alex before I have to let go of him. He smells good. Really good. It's intoxicating, makes me almost dizzy on my feet while it fills my lungs.

And his arm around me...

I've always been someone who chooses to fend for herself. I've never been in a relationship before where I would place my entire trust in a guy to protect me. I've always kept some little part of myself locked away, even with Z.

I've never felt as safe in a guy's arms as I did with Alex right then. And with my eyes closed, letting him lead me, that was a few seconds of me, trusting him with my entire self, completely.

We untangle ourselves from each other and continue into the park.

ALEX

Usually, the Halloween mazes aren't that exciting. It's obvious where all the jump scares are. It's easy to catch the tiny traces of movement before they even happen.

Stumbling through a maze with Zoey, though? That has my heart pumping like I'm in the second half, down a goal, and there's only ten minutes left in the game. In part, it's because it's fun anticipating her reactions. The woman is terrified of literally everything here. I've seen her speed through a yellow (but basically red) light for Christ's sake, and *this* is what scares her.

Zoey screams as air shoots out of a wall at us. She hugs me even tighter, if that's possible. Her two arms are wound around my bicep, clinging on so her chest is pressed firmly against my arm. And even though I don't want to admit it—I know that's the other reason my heart is beating so damn fast. Zoey has been all over me tonight, and it doesn't feel fake, or like she's using this as an excuse to cop a feel.

She *trusts* me.

She might be the only person in the world right now who does.

And it doesn't hurt that even through her two sweat-shirts, I can feel the softness of her breasts as they squish against me. I like having Zoey all over me.

We shuffle along through the maze, following the

people ahead of us. "Why won't they move faster?" Zoey complains. The maze smells like mist. We weave through cutouts, and every once in a while an actor, standing in wait to scare some poor, unsuspecting soul. As someone screams ahead of us, she jumps and then winds one hand down, interlocking her fingers with mine. Her palm is sweaty, and she's squeezing me so hard I swear I can feel her pulse racing. Her other hand is tucked around my bicep, plastering her whole side against my body.

Please, Halloween gods and goddesses, let me have the strength to make it through this night without making a move on Zoey.

"It's actually better for you this way," I say. "You know where all the scares are because it happens to them first."

"Nuh-uh, I don't need you mansplaining a horror house to me," Zoey says. I step forward into the next room, and wet strings hit my face. Zoey curses when they hit her, tucks her head down, and follows me blindly.

"I'm just trying to make you more comfortable."

"You're doing a shitty job of it. Go back to the compliments thing."

I laugh. This freaking girl. "Okay, Zo, whatever you want," I say, trying to keep my voice as calm as possible. We step into the next room of the haunted house, and Zoey shrieks. It's filled with strobe lights and an actor is brandishing a knife right in our faces. She grips me harder, and I lead her around the actor and out of the room. "Do you know how ridiculously funny you are?"

"I do," she mumbles, nodding into my shoulder. She glances around for scares.

I continue pulling us forward. "You're also super smart, have freaking fantastic taste, and you're as dedicated as an athlete."

"I'm great, aren't I?"

I chuckle, continuing to talk to her in soothing tones as I lead her around the next scare. "You're so good with Lucy, and so selfless and willing to help your friends, and—" I kind of didn't realize how much I had noticed all these things about Zoey until I had to list them. Oddly, complimenting her does seem to be helping. She isn't squeezing on to me quite as hard, and she's watching me speak instead of actively trying to figure out what will scare her next. "I love your laugh." My voice is quieter now. I wonder if I'm being too honest. "It's so cute, and I love that you laugh at freaking everything. It's like you're filled with sunshine or some shit."

Fuck—fudge. I shouldn't be cussing. But I feel out of my element here. This kind of stuff is like something a boyfriend would say to a girlfriend, not what a guy would say to his best friend. And the way Zoey is looking at me, with her eyes all wide, says she knows exactly that. God, I need to lighten the mood.

"What else?" she asks. It's practically a whisper.

"You have a totally bangable body."

Zoey laughs—that stupid, cute laugh, right as we round the last corner of the haunted maze. An actor jumps at us, and we both yell. I didn't even notice it coming.

"Ha." Zoey grins, pointing at me. "You screamed. You— oh shit no!" Another character jumps out at her, and she curses, grabbing my hand and pulling me under the exit sign and out of the maze. She takes a deep breath of relief, and I gulp in the outside air too. I need fresh air, fresh thoughts.

I gently untangle my arms from hers.

"Thank you for noticing my totally bangable body," she says, smirking at me, all her confidence back now that we're safe. She shimmies for me, and I have to avert my eyes toward the sky because yup, Zoey's trait of never wearing a bra is apparent, even under all those layers.

"You're too confident," I tell her.

"Not a real thing."

"It is a real thing, you have it." We walk away from the maze, several feet away from each other. Because I kind of need that space right now.

"Having too much confidence isn't a thing. You can never go wrong with confidence," Zoey explains, her voice loud and bright. She's acting like normal, like she didn't have her hands all over me, or that I didn't get too deep back there. But then again, maybe it was normal for her. I bet if she was with Tessa in that maze she would have been all over Tessa and begging for compliments too. "You can be too arrogant, but never too confident."

I shake off the weirdness I was feeling before. "Yeah, I guess that's true."

"Damn right it's true, Mr. Big-Ass Ego. What maze next?" she asks, coming to a stop in the middle of the sidewalk. People race around us to get in lines.

"Want to go find some rides instead?" I ask.

Zoey gives me the most beautiful smile, and damn if it doesn't make my heart beat just as fast as having her hands all over me did. "Oh thank fuck."

The next couple hours are a blur of rides, texting Lucy, and lines. Even though the lines are long, they're not that bad. Zoey and I talk the whole time, like we've done since day one, every conversation flowing smoothly into the next. We've discussed everything from what inventions we would design if we had endless funding, to what my next tattoo should be, to how nervous Zoey is for her research lab application, to how she and Tessa have already decided to have a joint wedding, and we still haven't run out of topics. Our current topic is Zoey making fun of me and the time my mom helped me fix up my car.

"I was sixteen and had just gotten my license."

"You seem like one of those kids who would get their license right away."

"What's that supposed to mean?"

"Like you were one of those jock high school douchebags, showing off your brand new license."

We're standing in line for a roller coaster. Or more exactly, I'm standing and Zoey is sitting on the metal bars, grinning up at me. "Wow. Them be fighting words." I cross my arms, stepping into her space.

"Am I wrong?" She tilts her head up toward me, expression cocky.

I relent, smirking. "No."

Zoey bursts out laughing and then tucks her hair behind her ear. "I'm only on your case because I failed my driver's test three times when I turned sixteen."

"That tracks."

"The fourth time I had to flirt with the guy so he would pass me."

I chuckle. "Honestly, Zo, your driving is atrocious."

"'Cause women are worse drivers than men, right?"

"No. It's 'cause you didn't learn that a stop sign means stop."

"I haven't even run that many stop signs."

"The fact that you've run any is the concerning part."

"Rules are made to keep people safe. If it's one in the morning and no one else is around, do you really need to stop?"

"Rules are rules for a reason, Zo."

"Exactly. To keep people safe. As long as you're being safe, they can be broken." I shake my head at her. "C'mon, are you telling me you've never done a U-turn at an intersection where it said no U-turns?"

I frown. Her smile gets bigger because she knows she's got me.

"Doesn't change the fact that I'm scared to be in your car," I grumble.

"Hey, we can't all be skilled in all areas. Some of us have different talents."

"Driving isn't a talent. It's a fundamental life skill. Like washing yourself." We scoot farther down the line. Well Zoey scoots, I walk. Once we've claimed our space, we turn to each other again.

"Or cooking?" she asks, raising her eyebrows at me, an innocent smile on her face.

I narrow my eyes. "I'm getting better."

"Lucy did tell me you put broccoli in with the pasta the other day." She nods wisely. "I'm very proud."

"Fudge off," I grumble.

"So you were sixteen and had just gotten your license," Zoey prompts, returning to the original story. She has so much energy compared to other people in line. The orange glow of the fluorescent lights and the never-ending waiting has zapped everyone else's energy, to the point where she looks alive and adorable snuggled up in about five sweatshirts and everyone else in line looks like grayed out zombies.

"I really wanted a car, and I knew my parents wouldn't buy me one. So I asked them if I could fix up an old car and make it run again. They're always supportive of a learning opportunity." I shake my head, smiling at the memory. "I remember my dad had wanted to help me. I guess he thought it was a dad thing to do? But he stood there for a good thirty minutes with his hands on his hips, just staring at the car in the driveway. He didn't even say anything, just turned right back around and walked into the house. And then my mom was coming out."

"And she knew what to do?" Zoey asks.

"Yeah. Between her and the internet, we were able to figure it out."

"And next thing you knew, you were a mechanical engineer."

"Exactly." I smile. "It's the only thing that comes close to soccer, honestly."

"But you still like soccer more?" she asks. We scoot farther down the line.

"I mean." I scratch at the back of my neck. Fudge. Is now the right time for this conversation? I glance to the front of the line. We probably have twenty more minutes of waiting. And I trust Zoey. I'd probably end up telling her anyway. Might as well get it over with. "Yeah. I do."

"Why aren't you playing then?" she asks. I don't point out that I am playing. I know what she means. Playing professionally. Getting paid to do what I love. Why the hell am I in grad school?

"Athlete Alex was a bit of a frick-up."

"A fuck-up?" Zoey supplies.

"Exactly."

"So Athlete Alex was before Responsible Alex?"

"Yeah, back when I was enjoying the benefits of being a student athlete."

"So really you were Fuckboy Alex?" She grins.

I scowl. "No. Athlete Alex."

"Asshole Alex?" she guesses again, her face screwed up with fake innocence.

"I wasn't an asshole, Zo." I sigh. I run a hand through my hair, and her eyes track my movements. I smirk. I know that look. The one time she's checking me out is the one time my mind actually isn't in the gutter. "Being a student athlete is hard. Not that that's an excuse. I could have handled everything better than I did. But even during my freshman year, I was trying to party as much as I was studying, and everyone recognized me from the field so I was sleeping with more girls than I could keep track of." It makes my stomach churn just remembering it. I've been too scared to look at Zoey during my confession, but I glance into her eyes now.

There's no judgment there. No hatred or disgust or distrust. I take a deep breath and maintain eye contact with her for the next part. I want to see the moment that understanding in her eyes disappears. "It started off slow, you know, only getting drunk or high at parties. But it's kind of hard to study when you're that wasted. And I needed to keep my grades up for soccer." I feel nauseous now. The line shuffles forward, and I'm grateful for the small break in my story. I mean, any logical person at that point would just stop with the parties altogether. Soccer was always supposed to come first.

When the line settles again, Zoey's staring at me, her eyes shining. The rest of the story falls out of me in a rush. "I started messing around with uppers, and right before the University Champions Cup my senior year, I failed a surprise drug test."

Zoey gasps, her hand flying over her mouth.

I shrug. "It's honestly a surprise it didn't happen sooner. And that shit doesn't fly. That was it for my college career."

"Oh, Alex." She hops off the bars and steps forward, wrapping her arms around me. She's soft and warm and being in her arms starts to melt the hard pit that's formed in my stomach.

"I didn't hold it together very well after that," I whisper in her hair. That sweet vanilla smell comforts me. "I started fucking around even more than before, kind of blew off my whole last semester honestly, burned a lot of bridges I shouldn't have. The real kick in the nuts was when I didn't get drafted."

Zoey still hasn't released me. She hugs me tighter if anything. I need to see her eyes. I want to know if I just lost my best friend. I lean back and slowly tilt her chin up, fully expecting her eyes to be filled with disgust.

But they aren't. They're filled with warmth and sympathy, her lips downturned at my loss. I'm surprised. Doesn't she hate me? She should hate me after hearing all that. Everyone else in my family does.

Zoey's hand finds my cheek, rubbing the stubble there softly. "You know that's not who you are, right?" she asks. "That guy, that's not you, Alex."

And there it is. That's why she doesn't hate me. She doesn't believe I actually used to be like that. "And Responsible Alex is?" I counter. "I can't live the celibate life forever."

"Maybe not the celibate life." She steps back and stares me straight in the eyes, hand resting on my chest. "But who you are is under all this Athlete Alex, Responsible Alex bullshit. You're the guy who worked his ass off to become the best college soccer player in the country. You're the guy who's completely sobered up to be a good brother to Lucy. You're loyal and considerate and—"

I close my eyes. "My parents didn't want to leave Lucy with me." I can't hear any more of this praise. "They didn't even trust me to take care of my own sister. How messed up is that?"

"But you're doing such a good job with her," Zoey says, rubbing her hands up and down my arms. "That sucks they didn't trust you, but you've changed."

I'm about to argue with her on that, but she tilts her head up and presses a soft kiss to my jawline.

I stiffen in her arms. I just told her how important it is for me to be celibate and she's kissing me? This isn't a fake date and it isn't a real date, and we shouldn't have been all over each other tonight.

Someone clears their throat loudly behind us. And then they do it again when neither Zoey nor I react. I glance toward them, and the couple who's been behind us in line the whole time is glaring at us. Zoey and I have been standing here talking, and the end of the line is now several feet in front of us. We walk forward, catching up. The couple continues to grumble behind us.

"People change," Zoey whispers. We're standing side by side now, not looking at each other. "And you've changed for the better. You're a good guy, Alex."

I don't respond.

"Do you want to go through a maze after this?" she asks. I glance down toward her. She's not looking at me, and her blonde hair blows into her face from the gentle night breeze. I sigh.

She's sweet. And probably too trusting. I mean, that's why she's willing to forgive Z after everything he pulled, right? But I don't think I've had anyone care about me enough to want to go through a horror maze when they're deathly afraid of them, just to cheer me up.

I bump her shoulder, in a best-friends, just-one-of-the-guys kind of way. "Let's just go get some snacks instead. I think Lucy and her crew will burn out soon anyway."

ZOEY

The drive back is filled with less excitement than the drive there was. Lucy and her friends are practically dead in the back seats. Most of them are sleeping. Alex and I don't dare talk and wake them, and the silence grows between us.

It gives me time to reflect on everything he told me. I guess I didn't realize how different Alex used to be. I mean, I never knew him then, but I can't imagine him being as terrible as he says he was. And even if he was, the fact that he was able to rise from the bottom and clean up his act completely says a lot about his willpower and personality. It's impressive.

It makes my heart hurt that his parents don't trust him. I'd trust Alex with anything. Even after knowing each other for only a few months, I know it's true. I'd trust Alex with anything.

He deserves a second chance. With Lucy, his parents, soccer, all of it.

The silence stretches on. I wish I could talk to him. When it's just me, alone with my thoughts, surrounded by the smell of him, close enough to feel the heat of his body, my late night brain is starting to roam places it shouldn't.

I remember how it felt to have his arms around me all night, the easy strength, the feel of his palm sliding into mine. I want to place my hand on his thigh, feel that warm muscle encased in his jeans. I want to kiss his neck while he drives, feel his smooth skin beneath my lips.

I'm not sure when the air becomes so thick around Alex and me, but suddenly the only thing I can think of is *him*.

Alex pulls up in front of my dorm building. He looks toward me and flashes me an almost nervous smile. I think he keeps thinking I'm going to hate him for what he did in the past. But I don't.

The past is the past. The Alex I know is the one here. I want to reassure him, but I don't know what else to say.

"Text me when you get to your room, okay?" he whispers.

"Yes, Dad," I groan, quietly.

"I'd walk you up if it wasn't for—"

"The five middle schoolers in your car?"

"Yeah. That." He flashes me his classic Alex grin. One side of his lips is pulled higher than the other. It's a little smug, a little happy, and it's real fucking cute. Like panty-melting hot. How have I not noticed that before?

I give him a little wave and slip out of the car. He watches me walk into the building, and I don't think he has any intention of pulling out of the parking lot until he knows I'm safely in my room. Which is comforting at three a.m.

Tessa is asleep—in her own room—which is probably a good thing, because I wouldn't be able to answer any of her questions right now. I don't even know how I'm feeling.

I text Alex that I got back safely, and he sends me a thumbs up.

My mind is racing as I run through my bedtime routine, removing my mascara, brushing my teeth, changing into pajamas. I just keep thinking about Alex, and everything he's gone through, and how sexy that stupid smirk of his is. And his legs. And his biceps. And, well, his abs that he always claims are *so* great. They are. They really are. Every part of him is stupid-sexy.

My body is humming as I slide between my sheets. My breasts feel swollen and heavy, nipples tight. I keep remembering Alex's body pressed up against mine all night, his hands on my hips, my back, my waist.

Even though there are a million reasons why I shouldn't do this, when my hand slides down into my panties, it's Alex's name burned into my brain tonight.

EIGHTEEN

ALEX

Zoey walked me to class today. She held my hand on the way there while we joked and drank our coffee. She was all positive vibes and sunshine and laughter, not once mentioning what I confided in her. She squeezed my shoulders tight after our hug goodbye, her fingers digging into my shirt. She winked at me when she noticed Zeus looking at us.

Stupid. Freaking. Zeus.

Sometimes it's easy to forget that she's doing all this for him. Zoey is so good at creating fake chemistry I can almost fool myself into thinking she's doing this because she likes flirting with me.

I stomp into the classroom, setting my half-empty hot coffee on the desk. I pull out my lesson plan and then turn to face the classroom.

Abigail sits on the opposite side of the classroom from Daniel now. I don't know what he did to piss her off, but she's been shooting glares at him for several sessions now.

And Z sits in his chair, leaning back, arms crossed, glaring straight at me.

What the hell is he giving *me* attitude for? Doesn't he know he can still have Zoey if he wants her? He's the one dating another girl over here.

When I start my lecture, he uncrosses his arms and leans toward his friends. And then proceeds to whisper to them, blatantly ignoring my lesson.

I'm older though. I can be the bigger man and not get upset. I turn to the whiteboard and start writing out the problem we'll be reviewing this session.

Z's laugh rings out behind me.

My shoulders pinch together. My hand grips the whiteboard marker so tightly, I have to roll out my wrist before I continue writing.

He's not even whispering anymore. He's straight-up talking to his friends.

I wish we had a quiz today so I could catch his cheating ass and kick him out of my classroom. But it's a midterm review day. We're just going over practice problems.

When he speaks again, I snap. "Z," I demand, and he looks absolutely startled in his chair that I'm calling him out. He opens his mouth, eyes wide with panic, glancing at his friends. "You know how to find one of Euler's Equations of Motion from here?"

He narrows his eyes at the board, and his Adam's apple bobs as he swallows. But he puts a smug grin on his face. "Yes."

"Here ya go, then." I toss him the whiteboard marker. He reaches out with both hands to catch it but fumbles it instead and it clatters to the floor. "Why don't you show us?"

He flushes a deep red when he stands up out of his

chair and picks up the marker from the floor. His legs look shaky as he approaches the board.

He glances to me again, hesitating before he uncaps the pen. I cross my arms and wait.

With shaky handwriting, he gets the first step right, but it's obvious he doesn't know where to go from there. He stands there, shifting his weight from side to side, looking absolutely terrified.

I sigh.

He's suffered enough. Well, actually, he hasn't, based on the amount of suffering Zoey has gone through. But I can't do this. This is my classroom and I'm the TA, and no matter how rude he's being I shouldn't be calling him out like this in front of everyone. I walk toward him. "Fantastic job, Z," I say, putting as much sincerity in my voice as I can. "Great first step. Let's popcorn this thing. Who wants to go next?" I take the whiteboard marker from his hand, and he slumps forward in relief before speedwalking back to his chair. "Anyone know the next step?" I ask, holding the marker up for grabs.

Abigail slides out of her chair and toward the board, taking the marker from me. We complete the rest of the problem like this, a new student coming up to the board for each step. Then I take the time to explain it to them.

I run my hand through my hair, grateful when class is finally over. I shouldn't have snapped like that. I'm well aware of where I stand with Zoey. Just because I like her flirting with me doesn't mean she's over Z. I need to back the hell off.

The good news? Z was silent for the rest of class.

. . .

I go out with the guys again after practice tonight. I feel guilty about staying out so late, but after my jealous standoff with Zeus in the classroom earlier today, I kind of needed a break. And Zoey was more than happy to shove me out the door and demand I stay out as late as possible.

I keep waiting for the other shoe to drop. After everything I told her about my past, I keep thinking *this will be it. The last time she comes over. The last time she lets me touch her to make That Prick jealous.*

But she keeps coming back.

When I walk back into my house, I stare in shock. She's cleaned. Everything looks tidy, neat. Dishes have been done, trash thrown away, the endless stacks of books my parents have are all dust-free. I can't believe this girl. I had already been planning to thank her profusely when I got home, but now I might have to upgrade to worshipping her.

She's not studying on the couch. Or the dining room table. I was expecting her to still be up, but the house is silent. I creep down the tiled hallway, turn the knob to Luce's room carefully, trying to be as quiet as possible. I peek my head in. Lucy is fast asleep in her bed. Good. I ease the door closed behind me and continue through the house. Where the hell is Zoey?

My heart starts beating a little crazy as I walk toward my room. If she left Lucy home alone, I'm going to—

Zoey is asleep in my bed. I can make out the slight rising and falling form of her under my covers. I smile a little. It's barely midnight, not even that late. I *could* wake her up, tell her goodnight, and send her back to her dorm. But I don't want to. I stumble in the dark as I realize how freaking much I want to curl up next to her and pull her body against mine.

And technically, this wouldn't break any rule. I'm just going to sleep with her, not, you know, *sleep* with her.

I peel off my sweaty exercise shirt and shorts. I catch a whiff of myself and grimace. I should probably take a shower. But what if she disappeared? Her eyes are still closed now, her breathing still even. I slip into a fresh pair of boxers. It's going to have to do.

What if she isn't okay with me sleeping next to her, though? I'd hope, because she fell asleep in my bed, that she would be expecting me to come home at some point.

"Zoey," I whisper. She mumbles something. "You're in my bed."

She rolls over, giving me even more space.

I'm going to take that as an invitation to sleep in my own bed.

I crawl into bed beside her, and she turns slightly, blonde hair and vanilla spreading all over my pillow. I grin. A sleeping Zoey is adorable.

I don't reach out to her or even touch her. Just lie beside her, listening to her even breaths, breathing in her scent. Lying there beside Zoey, it doesn't take long for me to pass out.

ZOEY

It's dark when I wake up. I don't know where I am, but it's hot. Too hot. It takes me a moment to register that someone else is in the bed beside me, and a whole other moment to calm my racing heart when I realize that person is Alex.

Dammit. I wasn't planning on falling asleep here. I just

meant to lie down for a second. But his bed had been so comfy—and smelled so good. Like him.

I glance back over at Alex. He's gorgeous when he's sleeping. His curls flop over his forehead, his cheek squished up against the pillow. His bare arm escapes the blankets, and my heart trips over itself as it kicks back into gear. Is he shirtless?

It's been almost a month since I saw Alex shirtless, but that image is still burned into my brain. His tattoos, his muscles. I know it's bad, but I've been dying to see him shirtless again.

My hand reaches forward, almost as if it's doing exactly what my brain is telling it not to. I just need to know.

My fingertips feel the heat of his body before they even make contact with his skin.

Oh. Fuck.

My body is shaking as I let my finger barely skim across his chest. I drag it, ever so lightly, over his pecs, down to his abs. Holy damn. Even in his sleep, you can feel the muscles resting there. I don't know what I'm doing. I don't want him to wake up and find me groping him, but Alex has the hottest body I've ever touched, and now that my fingers are here, it's like they're glued to his skin. I can't pull them away. I can't stop my exploration. I touch every single part of his chest, feel the smooth skin, taut over his pecs, biceps, his neck. I let my fingers dance in his happy trail.

Wait. If he's shirtless... what if he's not wearing anything else?

My fingers follow that thought process, dragging down the side of his body, lower, lower, lower until...

They meet the waistband of his underwear. My heart is beating so fast, I'm not sure if I'm disappointed or relieved.

My hand skims over the top of his thigh until I find skin again. He's just in his boxers.

I finally drag my hand away and roll onto my back, staring at the ceiling. My ragged breaths echo around the room and I almost groan. I have a very *very* hot, almost naked Alex lying in bed beside me. How the fuck am I supposed to sleep now?

"Are you done feeling me up?" Alex rasps, his voice sounding all growly and deep from sleep. My body jumps, and it's a sound that goes straight to my clit. "'Cause I was kind of enjoying that."

I glance sideways sheepishly and meet Alex's now wide-open eyes, a sleepy version of his trademark smirk, with the left side higher than the rest, on his face. "Just wanted to make sure you were wearing clothes. Would have been really awkward if you weren't."

"Really awkward, huh?" he says, and I can't stop staring at how bright his eyes are shining in the dark. He's one step away from laughing, I can tell. "'Cause it *seemed* like you were into that."

"Nope. Just your casual, everyday clothes check." I sound more confident than I am. I'm sure Alex can see right through me.

"Of course," Alex says, and his smirk gets bigger, I fucking swear. "It's important to check. These blankets are so big it's impossible to tell what anyone is wearing."

My brain is still slow from sleep, and, let's be honest, Alex's hotness. I don't realize what's happening until his fingers are at my shoulder, feeling the shirt I one hundred percent stole from his drawer. Holy—

"Shoot," Alex drawls, drawing lazy circles with his fingers in the shirt. "Was kinda hoping you weren't wearing that."

My laugh comes out choked. "I'm sure you were, you perv." My laughter dies down, though, as he continues to drag his hand down. His fingers slide directly in between my breasts, and I can't stop the shiver that works its way through my body. I'm sure he notices, but he doesn't say anything. His fingers continue down my stomach, until they reach bare skin, right above my panties, where my shirt rose up while I was sleeping. His fingers linger on my skin there, and my stomach flips and swirls and dips lower with each tiny movement he makes.

My panties are soaked. He finally, *finally* glides his hand down further, only to cross over the thin strip of my panties, down to my inner thigh. I watch his eyes darken when he figures out I'm not wearing anything else besides the shirt and underwear. His thumb rubs my inner thigh, so fucking close to where I need him most. The rest of his hand rests heavy and warm on my thigh. I let out a whimper.

He drags his hand away so slowly, it feels like it takes forever for the contact between skin to skin to break. "Just a casual, everyday clothes check," he whispers.

The moment between us grows heavy. I want to kiss him. I want to press my body against his and grope him like my life depends on it. His eyes keep traveling, flicking between my eyes and my lips.

His tongue wets his top lip. He's debating. And I want it, I want it so bad but... Alex is my friend. He has a rule about not hooking up with girls. I can't force him. Besides, the last friends with benefits situation I got myself into ended in a nightmare, and I don't think I'm ready for that again.

That thought sobers me. I glance away from him, staring at a point on the wall behind his head. Alex gets the message. He rolls on his back, putting both hands behind his head as a pillow, looking up. I steal another glance at his arms, which are absolutely bulging in this position. In the dark, I can barely make out the ink etched into his skin. Why does he have to be built so perfectly?

"Hey, wait a second," he says.

"Yes?"

"You weren't wearing a T-shirt when you got here," he says. Oh. Shit.

"I wasn't?" I ask as innocently as possible.

"No. You were in that sweater thing."

"Oh. Well, it's hard to sleep in a sweater. It's too hot."

"Zoey?"

"Yes?"

"Where'd you get the shirt?"

"From your drawer?" I say, letting it hang like a question.

Alex snorts. "Oh my god, you stole my shirt and my bed. What the hell am I fake dating you for?"

"Bitch, this is best friend privileges," I tell him. "You keep going around *claiming* I'm your best friend and yet you get all bent out of shape when I wear your shirt."

"You are my best friend," he says, his voice serious. It's silent for a moment. I'm hoping this has been settled. "You stole the Captain America one, didn't you?"

"What Captain America one?" I bite my lip and glance over at him. "I didn't even know you had a Captain America shirt."

Alex's body shakes with laughter. "You're not leaving in it. Just so you know. I love that shirt."

"It's just so soft," I whine. "And it's Captain America. I need the shield to protect me from pervs like you."

"Then buy yourself a freaking shield."

"That would be weird. I'm much better off wearing this."

"You should take it off now, in case you forget to later," Alex says.

"You just want to see my tits."

"Obviously."

"Not gonna happen."

"But best friend privileges," he whines.

I burst out laughing. "What the fuck kind of best friends did you have before me?"

"The kind that stripped for me."

"This is why they're no longer your best friends." I turn on my side, facing toward him. I pat his chest. It's warm, and his muscles tense beneath me. Instead of patting him, like I meant to, my hand just kind of stays there. "But don't worry. I value our friendship too much to do that." I mean for it to come out as a joke, but it feels way too serious as it leaves my mouth. It's too true.

"The friends with benefits thing never works, does it?" Alex says ruefully.

"Nope." I pop the word. "That shit fucks you up."

There's too much emotion in my voice. Even I can hear it. Alex doesn't say anything in response. But he reaches for me. Tugs me to him, puts an arm around me, guides my head to his bare chest. I melt into him. He's warm, all soft skin and hard muscles. I snuggle into him, my head finding that perfect spot right around his collarbone. He grips me tighter, hands digging into my back.

I fall asleep in Alex's arms.

I sneak out before Alex wakes up. It took all of my willpower to pull myself away from his warm frame and out into the cold morning air. But I didn't want to acknowledge the fact that since Halloween, I've hardly thought of Z. Alex fucking Adams. That's the name branded into my brain.

And that opens a whole cavern of problems I don't want to get into.

NINETEEN

ZOEY

Tour Guide Fun Fact #4: The geology building was architecturally designed to mirror the mountains that surround this campus. It has arched points and an indoor/outdoor setup that makes it feel like you are walking in and out of caves. Not only that, but the hallways are filled with one of the largest publicly accessible rock collections in the world.

It's like a second home to me. And I'm about to be spending a lot more time there.

I got the interview.

I got the motherfucking interview.

Tessa and I celebrated with donuts before mythology, where, also good news, we've moved on from discussing gods and goddesses to hero stories, like Hercules. Bye, Zeus, you cheating shit. Tessa spends the whole time whispering in my ear about how the Disney movie compares, and I know that soundtrack will be the only thing playing in our apartment for the next week.

I'm practically giddy by the time I head to the engineering building to greet Alex after class. We've hung out almost every day since I spent the night last week, just as friends, and neither of us has mentioned what happened. I'm okay with that. I'll need all the time I can get to focus on preparing for this interview, anyway.

I stand in the engineering hallway, just across from the door of Alex's classroom, waiting for his class to be over. I'm rereading the interview information email from Professor Heath when Alex circles his arms around me from behind. My stomach drops out—in a good way. A real fucking good way. I didn't even know his class had gotten out, and now I'm surrounded by his warmth, his scent, his muscles. It's like every nerve ending in my body is suddenly aware of Alex's touch.

"Hey babe," he says, nudging the hair out of his way so he can kiss my neck beneath my ear. I have to stop myself from tilting my neck to give him more access. He's doing this because we're fake dating—not because he actually wants to. He's putting on a show because I asked him to.

"Hey dude," I say. His arms are circled around my midsection. I wrap my arms over his, rubbing my thumb over his forearm. The drastic difference between my white skin and his tanned forearms all tangled together is hot. Everything about this is hot. Even the possessive way he's gripping me, making me feel like I'm *his*.

"He's not even looking," Alex complains. "And this is like A-plus material over here."

It takes me a second to even realize he's talking about Z. I glance up to where Z is standing with his friends, not even looking at us.

And the horror of realization rushes over me.

I don't care. I'm only here for Alex.

"I mean," Alex says, his voice still in my ear. He places a small kiss on my neck. Then another on my shoulder. "Look at you, Zo. How can anyone keep their eyes off you?"

My shirt is tight and my neckline is low. I know from where Alex is standing above me he has a direct view of the swells of my breasts. Did I wear this shirt today because I knew I'd be seeing him?

No comment.

"It's their loss," I murmur, arching my back slightly, making sure I'm fully on display for him.

"Damn right it is," Alex says. He flips me around, so his arms are now circled around my lower back and my hands come to rest on his chest. His eyes. His eyes betray *everything*. They're smoldering, and my insides feel like magma as I get sucked into his gaze. In this moment, he wants me just as bad as I want him.

"Is he looking?" I whisper. I figure we both know I don't actually care. Alex doesn't even glance in Z's direction. His gaze stays on me. He shakes his head.

"I think..." His gaze flicks from my eyes to my lips. "I think we may need to up the ante."

The world is rushing around me, these little bolts of light and color streaming past, and I'm glued to the ground, stuck here, in this moment, watching Alex lick his lips. Everything around me is too loud and muted, all at once.

Alex leans forward, stopping millimeters away to glance back at my eyes, asking if this is okay. I grip both my hands in his shirt and pull him forward the rest of the way, crashing my mouth against his.

He kisses me back just as vigorously, his hands coming

to the back of my neck to support the force of his kiss. I drown my hands in his hair.

All is fair under the guise of fake dating, right?

It might be his years of being Athlete Alex, but he *knows* what he's doing. His lips feel soft and plump against mine, and when his tongue slips into my mouth it takes all of my willpower to suppress a moan that absolutely should not be released in public.

Kissing shouldn't be this good. It's never been this good before, even with Z. Is it because I've been in a five-month sex drought? Or is it because it's Alex?

My legs are shaky. My emotions are all over the place, and I can't handle it. I'm not sure I'm ready to fall so hard for someone after I just went through this with Z. Especially someone so unavailable. I slowly pull my lips off Alex's. He's staring down at me, eyes warm, full of wonder, still trying to catch his breath.

"Did it work?" I find myself hoping Alex will look disappointed when I ask the question. He doesn't. He's as collected as he always is on our fake dating stints. He casts his gaze over my shoulder and then frowns slightly.

"Yeah," he says. "It did."

TWENTY

ALEX

There's something so satisfying about hearing the proper snap of your foot against the ball. If you hit the ball too low, it makes this flat sound, lifting off the ground; hit the ball too high and you get an empty tap and it thunks to the ground. But if you kick it right in the sweet spot it's a perfect, hollow, snap. Perfect pass every time.

And I've been hearing that snap all goddamn night. West is practically drooling on the sidelines.

I've missed this. The stadium lights, the smell of the grass, the scrapes on my knees, my voice hoarse from yelling while sprinting.

Still can't believe I messed it all up.

"I love you, man," West says after practice, wrapping his arm around my neck, not giving a shit that I'm soaked in sweat. "I truly do. Let me buy you a drink tonight."

"I love not being on an official team." I grin. "All these bribes are great."

We end up at the local bar after practice again.

Within minutes of us arriving, Eddie's little brother, Carlos, who is a freshman on the Olympia team right now, and Carlos's friends Kacen, Brandon, and Maia all show up.

"How do they always know?" Eddie sighs, dropping his head on the table.

The four freshmen crashed our night out last time too. Apparently they follow Eddie everywhere he goes.

"Damn. I needed more time for my ego to recover," West whines.

"What?" I ask.

West drops his voice. "We were playing flying changes today at practice. Brandon beat us all. As a fucking freshman. And he plays defense." West shakes his head at himself.

Eddie shrugs in agreement. "The kid isn't half bad."

West snorts.

"You don't think he's good?" I ask.

"He's the shit," West corrects. "Like a bitty baby Alex Adams."

I laugh. I glance over at Brandon. He has an easy-going smile across his face and carries himself with the confidence of someone who knows what he's doing but isn't flaunting it.

He's not a young version of me. When I was a freshman, I walked around cocky as hell and luckily had the talent to back it up.

"Seriously though," West says, dropping his voice and they start walking toward us. "That kid is going places. In the first month and he already put in more extra hours than the rest of the team combined."

"He showed up to training camp in better shape than the returners," Eddie says, chuckling. "If he doesn't go pro, I'll eat my shoe."

I just nod. I don't say anything. West shoots a glance at me and then gives Eddie a look to make him shut up.

I know what he's thinking. It's what everyone is thinking.

I would have bet a million dollars that Alex Adams was going pro.

And yet, here I am. Playing on a club team. Being coached by players I used to beat on the field. Making friends with freshmen.

So far Eddie and West have been great about not asking me what happened on my old team. They know that I didn't play in the final last year—hell, that's why they won the game last year. If I had been there that score would have been different.

But they were there. I wasn't. And it's my own goddamn fault.

The four freshmen scoot their way into the table. Eddie gets up automatically to separate Maia and Carlos, who are always at each other's throats. It looks like it's second nature to him at this point.

"This is supposed to be socializing for the club team," he complains.

"They are socializing. Look at them all tucked into their tables like sleeping babies," Kacen says.

"They're laughing and very much awake. Why are you like this?"

"You mean how did I just get you to admit that they *are* socializing? Skills. Mad skills."

Eddie groans. "They're supposed to be socializing with *us*. You're not supposed to be here."

"But where's the fun in that?" Kacen shoots Eddie a grin. "C'mon, you know you love us."

"We look like shits, though, hanging out with only D1

players. I don't want them to think we're too good for them," Eddie says.

"You have me," I point out. "Card-carrying club team player."

West snorts. "Yeah, we're hanging out with the guy who could have gone pro. Not elitist at all."

"Oh yeah, you're supposed to be some big shot, right? West can't shut up about getting you on the team," Kacen says, grinning at me.

Brandon eyes me curiously but doesn't say anything.

I shrug and choose to take a sip of my drink instead of responding.

"Hey, your peasant ass shouldn't be bothering such greatness," West says. Then he turns to me. "Ignore him, he has no filter."

"No worries."

"I'm just curious," Kacen says with a shrug. "West has made it sound like he's about to propose."

"I'm not about to propose," West mutters.

"Do you jack off to thoughts of Alex scoring your winning goal weekly or nightly?" Kacen asks.

"Nightly, if you must know," West says. Then he sweeps his hand in my direction. "But fucking look at this man. He's half god, half human."

I shake my head, chuckling. My phone vibrates and dings loudly from where I have it laid on the table in front of me and I thank the texting gods for the save. I really don't know how to respond to any of this without giving too much away. I check my phone to make sure it's not Zoey about Lucy.

It *is* Zoey. But it's not about Lucy.

Zoey: Have you ever noticed your heater makes a creepy noise?

I chuckle before I type out a reply, because yeah. I have noticed that. Every single freaking winter.

Me: Dad says it's ghosts.

Zoey: Yeah…I don't love that.

Me: Want me to come home?

Zoey: No stay out

Zoey: But, just checking, does your dad think the ghosts are dangerous?

Me: He does not. They're a sweet family.

Zoey: Good good. Well Lucy's in bed for the night, I've finished my homework, so I'm just gonna chill with the ghost family apparently.

Me: Wait one second, I'll come home.

Zoey: No need, I'm building a blanket fort for protection.

Me: Just use my bed

Zoey: I can't. Your bed is comfy

Me: So?

Zoey: I'll fall asleep. And then I'll never want to leave.

My palms are sweaty when I go to write this next part, so I wipe them on my shorts.

Me: Then just stay the night

I'm probably pushing too many boundaries. For her, and for me. I'm just tempting myself with what I can't have. I mean, she's into Z. And she's a relationship kind of chick, I can tell. I mean, look how messed up she was over her friends with benefits situation before. I'm obviously not ready for that, and I don't have time for that and—I don't even know why I'm having this conversation with myself, I can't sleep with her.

But kissing Zoey this morning seriously messed with my head. It's my sex-deprived brain grasping at nothing, but I thought if I had just one taste of her I'd be able to make it through the rest of my celibacy in peace.

Nope.

Kissing Zoey was stupid-good. Maybe the best. Ever. And now I want to do it again, even though the whole time Zoey was shoving her tongue down my throat she was putting on a show for Z.

Christ, I don't think I've ever been this into a girl before. How the hell did she get so into my head?

She doesn't respond to my text right away. And I'm too anxious to have her in my bed again, so my sweaty palm is practically strangling my phone waiting for the response. When two more minutes pass, and she still hasn't responded, I drag my gaze up. Cheap beer, sticky floors, tired tables. The smell of it doesn't make my stomach roll anymore, like it did early into my sobriety. It's almost comforting. At least I know where I stand here.

"Really? You just wink at them and then boom—spontaneous orgasm?" Kacen asks. "Can you teach me how?"

I blink. I blink again. What the hell did I miss?

West shows Kacen a smooth wink. Kacen winks back at him. His body turns and his whole cheek gets into it. I burst out laughing.

"Yeah, that's not gonna be how you get a girl to orgasm," I tell him. Kacen doesn't look deterred.

"I just need practice."

He turns to Carlos.

Carlos curses. "Ni te atreves, pendejo." Kacen gives Carlos the world's most dramatic wink. Carlos stands up so he can smack Kacen in the back of the head. "Fucking dumbass."

It sends Kacen's hair flying, and a bubblegum pink stripe of hair that I hadn't noticed before flies with it.

"Uh, Kacen—" I start.

Maia cackles. "You're gonna ask about the pink hair, right?"

I nod mildly.

"I was trying it out. I think I'm rocking it," Kacen says, doing a hair toss for all of us to see.

"Not on purpose," Brandon chokes out between laughs.

Kacen sighs. "Don't judge. It's a family thing."

"He's tried to explain it three different times, but I still don't understand it," Brandon says.

"Does Kacen ever make sense?" I ask. 'Cause, it's kind of true.

"Sometimes I wonder if he failed elementary school so many times his teachers just passed him to get rid of him," Carlos says. Kacen laughs, waving us off.

Brandon is practically doubled over as he tries to explain. "There was something about Halloween and pranking and races and prizes. Really not sure. All I know is when I got back to my dorm in the morning the whole side of his room was pink. Like pink blanket, and posters, and"— he gestures at Kacen's head—"pink hair streak."

"Fucking Kenneth," Kacen mutters, shaking his head.

"Wait, what?" Eddie asks, still looking as confused as I feel.

"My family does a prank war type thing on Halloween," Kacen says. "My brother Kenneth did this to me." He yanks at the streak of hair.

"And you just let him?" Maia asks.

"I slept through it."

The whole table laughs. "How?" I groan. Because

there's no way I wouldn't wake up if someone was dying my hair in the middle of the night.

Brandon laughs again. "Bro, he can sleep through anything. The girl I had over the other night was loud as fuck and this shithead didn't have a clue."

"I do now," Kacen moans. "Don't have sex when I'm only three feet away from you. That's nasty."

"Says the guy who got a blow job in front of everyone at last week's basketball party."

I let them bicker it out, glancing at my phone again. I don't particularly like the way my heart stalls in my chest when I read Zoey's text.

Zoey: Okay

TWENTY-ONE

ZOEY

I'm still awake when Alex creeps into the room, closing the door softly behind him. I listen as he sets down his soccer bag, kicks his slides off, and makes his way toward his dresser. Then there's the rustle of clothes coming off. I keep my eyes closed as he lifts the blankets, letting cool air wash against my skin, and then slides into bed beside me, heating everything up.

I've lain here for the past hour debating whether to leave or not, honestly kind of mad at myself. The fake dating thing is starting to feel kind of... icky. It's impossible to tell if Alex is actually into me or not.

Well, maybe not impossible. He scoots toward the center of the bed, grips my hips, and pulls me toward him until my back fits perfectly against his front, his bare arm resting on my stomach as we spoon.

"You're still awake," Alex accuses. His bare legs press against mine and it feels like my body's on fire.

"Couldn't sleep."

He chuckles, and I can feel the movement throughout my whole spine. "Is being scared of ghosts something I should know about you?"

"You should know everything about me," I tease. "I'm very interesting."

"That you are," he whispers, his voice in my ear. His fingers grip my shirt, drawing it up slightly, giving him access to the smooth skin of my stomach. "Which shirt did you steal?" His thumb makes small movements across my stomach, and my skin is flushing red hot everywhere he touches.

"It felt like a Rage Against the Machine kind of night."

"Mmm." He doesn't say much more than that. Just continues to bury his nose in my neck. I think we both want something more than we can have. I want to shift my hips, press back against him.

But I don't.

We lie there in silence for a few moments, wide awake in the dark.

"When's your interview?" he finally asks. It comes out a reluctant growl.

"In three weeks."

"You feel ready?"

I turn, flopping over so I'm on my back. Alex's arm is still cast over my stomach, and I don't miss the heat in his eyes when I face him. "As I'll ever be."

"Which I'm sure is over-the-top prepared in ways no student has ever been before." His voice is teasing, but I can see it in his face that he's proud of me, impressed with the amount of effort I've put in. I just hope I've put enough in. Eileen got an interview too, and she's yet to miss another class so far this semester.

"It's a lot of pressure," I whisper. I don't normally

confide in anyone except Tessa about this part of my life, the unrelenting ball of stress in my stomach. I figure, if you always have a smile on your face, things will eventually be okay.

"Want me to ask you practice questions?" I like how his first reaction is always to look for solutions to a problem. To take action.

"About to show me your secret stash of geo knowledge?"

"*I* don't need to know geo. *You* need to know it. And then teach me." He smiles a little smugly, and I shift toward him so my body is fully facing him. There's barely any space between our bodies.

I stare at his chest while I speak. "I love it, you know," I say softly, "and I couldn't imagine doing anything else, but it's not exactly a guaranteed job straight out of college."

"Nothing is."

"Says the engineering major."

He flicks me in the side, and I feel a little bad for poking fun because I know this isn't his first choice. But it hit me today. I'm six months away from graduating. I need to be applying to jobs *yesterday*. And if I don't get this research lab position, I'm screwed.

"It looks good on you, you know," he says lightly. "The hiker chick look."

"Damn right it does." Alex and Lucy picked me up last weekend after I got back from one of my backpacking trips with Professor Heath's class. I was stinky and covered in dirt and in about the least sexy hiking clothes you can imagine. Alex smiled at me just the same.

"What are you scared of?" Alex asks, cutting right to the chase. And it's like it all comes spewing out of me, everything I've been trying to keep bottled up for the semester.

"What if I don't get a job? A college degree doesn't

matter anymore. Look at my brothers. They both have degrees and for years I've watched them apply and not get hired. They don't even get interviews most of the time. *You're* in grad school to get more experience because undergrad wasn't enough." I take a shaky breath and I look up at Alex. His eyes are wide and patient and tell me to keep talking. "Your grades were good enough for you to be a teaching assistant but not good enough to get hired?" Alex pinches up his face a little, doing a half shrug of disagreement. I get that's not the full story but *still*. "I don't have a fallback system. My mom can't afford for me to come home. One of my brothers has already moved into my room, and unless I get a good enough salary that I can pay her a shit-ton in rent, she can't afford to feed me and pay for all the extra energy too. It's just not going to happen. And I knew it was risky when I went for geo, that I'd have to work harder. I just—I wanted..." I groan helplessly at Alex. My hands rest on his shoulders, and I squeeze, not knowing what else to do.

"You wanted to chase your dreams," Alex says simply. He runs his fingers through a strand of my hair, "I get it." I know he does get it, and he understands what happens when you don't succeed. He knows how much is at stake. "I know that it's scary, but it's good to go after your dreams, Zo." His thumb comes to my cheek, rubbing slightly. I lean into his touch. "You'll make it. You work so hard, and you want it so much I *know* you'll make it."

Sometimes it just takes the right words from the right person to make everything better. I want to hear them again. "You think so?" I ask.

The room is just bright enough for me to see his eyes, flicking back and forth between mine. Our foreheads are touching. "I know so." He smiles at me without a smidgen of doubt on his face. "You're gonna be this badass, environment-saving, hiker babe, world renowned for her scientific discovery. And when you get famous, I get to tell everyone I'm your best friend."

I smile sweetly. "Tessa's my best friend."

He rolls his eyes. "C'mere." There isn't much farther to go. But he drags me so I'm pressed flat up against his chest, one of his arms cradles my head, tucking it against his neck, and the other has dipped under my shirt, pressing against the small of my back. I throw one leg over his hips, and it feels deliciously good to be pressed this close together.

Alex presses a kiss to my forehead. It's such a cute gesture I almost laugh at the image—this hulking, heavily tattooed, soccer-playing god, holding me so sweetly.

I absolutely want to tilt my head up and shove my tongue down his throat. But I don't. And he doesn't make a move. We just hold each other tighter, pressing against each other in all the ways we know we shouldn't. I let his arms ease the ball of stress in my chest until we fall asleep.

My leg is asleep. That's the first thought to cross my mind in the morning. It takes me a second to blink my eyes against the blinding sun and realize it's asleep because it's pinned under Alex's body. Our limbs are everywhere, and the sheet is so tangled around us I'm surprised it isn't choking one of us.

I slowly pull my leg out from underneath him, trying not to wake him up. It gets caught on the blanket. Shit. Alex rustles in his sleep, his arm around my ribs tightening, pulling me closer against him.

I yank my leg hard, jostling Alex's body in the process, and my leg thunks down on the bed, feeling rushing through it again.

"Stop with the morningness," Alex groans. His eyes are still closed, his face pressed against the dark blue pillow. He looks all soft and sexy and gorgeous. I take this opportunity to let my eyes roam the expanse of his back, all the muscles and tattoos and exposed skin. And his ass. Praise the fucking universe for how amazing his ass looks in just black boxer briefs.

"I was trying to get out from underneath you."

"You'd love being underneath me." His voice is tired and slurring, like his default setting is being flirty. And, not gonna lie, but I don't think he's wrong.

"In your dreams, perv."

"Literally," he mumbles, eyes still closed.

Well, that caused my stomach to dip. "I don't think friends are supposed to get off to friends," I inform him, just in case he didn't get the memo.

His eyes pop wide open. "Have you gotten off to me, Zo?"

Ah. Fuck me. Why does his voice sound so sexy when it's all growly like that? "No," I lie.

He smirks at me like he knows I'm lying and I scrunch up my face at him. He turns on his side, props his head in his hand so he can stare at me. I desperately try to keep my eyes from dipping down his body.

And fail.

My greedy gaze eats up every inch, all the way down to where his package is straining the front of his underwear. Holy mother of—

Alex reaches out, a finger under my chin, tilting my gaze back up from where it got stuck, back to his face where he's full-on grinning now.

"Oh shut up, Mr. Big-Ass Ego," I grumble.

"That's not all that's big."

I can't help myself from laughing. He's not wrong. But this is getting ridiculous. We both know we can't act on this. "Is that what you say to all the girls?" I tease.

"Yeah. My go-to pick-up line is *my dick is huge, come home with me.*"

"Oooh, look who has game," I say sarcastically.

"I've been telling you I had game since the very beginning. You just didn't believe me."

"You seemed like one of those guys who talks the talk but couldn't walk the walk."

"Really?" He frowns. We've been teasing this whole time, but his face looks so serious now I almost bust out laughing, because, no, I didn't really think that. He carries himself with such a cocky confidence, I know he's earned it. But it's fun to egg him on. "Yeah, I mean you talk so much about all the girls you used to get, it seems a *little* unbelievable." I grimace at him. "I'm honestly starting to doubt your sexperience."

"My what?"

"Sexperience. Experience with sex."

He shakes his head. "Why the hell would you doubt my sexperience?"

I shrug. "The elaborate lengths you're going to cover it up." I bring my fingers up to do air quotes. "Celibate." I waggle my eyebrows at him. "Or virgin?"

Alex bursts out laughing, his head falling back with full-bodied laughter. It causes the tattoos on his abs to dance. "Not a virgin, babe." He finally chokes out. "Besides, I've never had any complaints."

"Mmhm. Sure."

"Zoey," he warns.

"It's just *awfully* convenient that there's no way to prove you exceeded expectations in bed."

Alex's thumb moves against my ribs, rubbing my bare skin. I feel it everywhere. He shifts forward, so our fronts are pressed up against each other. When he talks, he's so close I can feel his breath on my cheek.

"What do you want to hear, Zo?" His voice is low and quiet and makes me squirm. His smirk is cocky, his eyes watching my reaction carefully as he continues to speak. "How I can eat a girl out for hours? Until she *begs* for my cock? Lick her until she doesn't even know her own name?" I can't stop the shiver that barrels through me and his cocky smirk gets bigger. "You're just as sex deprived as me, sweetheart, two can play at this game."

I cross my arms in the very little space that exists between our bodies, and it just smushes up my tits between us. Even though my breasts are covered by the T-shirt I borrowed from Alex, his gaze dips down to check them out. It's my turn to smirk. "I might be sex deprived, but I can hold my shit together better than that."

"Meaning?"

"You. Don't. Affect. Me." I poke his chest with each word. "'Cause you're not even good at it."

He rises up on one elbow so he's hovering over me. His eyes trail down my face, over my tits, down the expanse of my stomach to where my panties are clearly on display, over my bare legs. When he meets my eyes again, they're blazing with determination, like he's about to absolutely destroy me. "There's an easy way to test both theories."

"Aren't you forgetting something?" I bite my lip, toying with him, and his desperate eyes go right there.

"What am I forgetting?" I love hearing the rasp in his voice.

"That Responsible Alex doesn't fuck."

TWENTY-TWO

ALEX

I've never been a word guy. I've always stuck to math and dealt with the few letters math decided to use. I thought people who called words beautiful were crazy.

But when Zoey says the word "fuck"?

I get it. I've never heard anything better than the way she elongates the word, making her mouth a perfect oval while says it. It's a sound that goes straight to my dick.

Oh Christ, this is a bad idea. But Zoey has the power to find the button for my self-control and flick it off with a smile.

"I don't need to," I respond. "I just need to prove that I can satisfy a woman." Zoey's hips shift on the bed when I say that. She wants this as bad as I do. But she still has this haughty expression across her face like she thinks she'll win this, and—goddammit. I want to prove her wrong.

"Fine." She smirks at me. "I'll call your bluff."

"What bluff is there to call?"

"I don't think you'll actually do it."

In one swift movement, I roll over on top of her, pulling her arms from between us and pinning them to the bed above her head. She lets out a tiny gasp, and then her cheeks instantly turn pink, as if embarrassed she made that noise.

Or maybe she's already flushing.

Hell, I've been imagining this moment for so long—Zoey's warm body underneath me, Zoey at my mercy—and nothing's compared to the real deal of feeling her here. The way her big blue eyes gaze up at me, twinkling like she's always a second away from laughing. The defiant tilt of her chin, challenging me with her expression.

There's a sick feeling in my stomach, the shame of giving in to something I never meant to give into. But I shove it away. Zoey doesn't believe I can get her off and I desperately want her to know just how damn good it would be if I did.

I bend down, pressing a soft kiss to her neck, right in the crease where it turns into her titled chin. I drop feather-light kisses along the side of her neck, nipping every so often. I press my lips to her pulse point and smirk at the way I can feel her racing heart rate.

"Sure you're not into this, babe?"

"Positive," she chirps, her voice all breathy.

I drag one hand to the hem of her shirt and then glide it up against her perfect skin. Over her obliques, her ribs, stopping right under the swell of her breast. Dammit. I drop my head, feeling dizzy. Even if I ran all the sprint and conditioning drills I've ever done in my life, I don't think my heart rate would ever get any faster than this. I've maxed out.

"How are you holding up?" I ask, knowing full well she can hear how affected I am in my voice. Her back is arched, and her lips are parted. She shakes her head at me. "What was that?" I tease.

She narrows her eyes at me. "I'm good if you're good."

"I'm great."

She spreads her legs underneath me, and I fall right against her center. Fuck—fudge—Goddammit. I almost curse out loud. There's only two very thin pieces of clothing separating us and I can feel *everything*. She's soaked through her underwear. I barely stop myself from rolling my hips into her. "How are *you* holding up?" she asks. I freaking love her defiance.

"Just waiting for you to give in and beg," I mutter, annoyed she's gotten the upper hand when she's freaking pinned underneath me.

"In your dreams, Mr. Big-Ass Ego." We glare at each other, in a standoff, but my head keeps lowering and hers keeps tilting up. We stop, just a millimeter away from each other's lips, electricity zapping between us.

I'm honestly not sure who moves first. One minute, neither of us is going to give in, and the next my lips are on hers. My hands are in her hair, and her newly released hands are scraping across my back, gripping my biceps.

Christ, she tastes good. It's just kissing. But it still feels like I'm one second away from exploding in my pants as she grinds against me, her tongue fighting for control. Always fighting, always stubborn, always so freaking *good*. I was kind of hoping a second kiss with her wouldn't be as good as the first. That I could be done with this and go on with being Responsible Alex.

How the hell was I supposed to stop this though? How was I supposed to—

There's a knock on the door.

I freeze. Panic washes over my body.

Oh fuck—fudge. Oh freaking fucking fudge. Did I lock the door last night? I normally don't in case Lucy ever needs me. Oh god, what if she comes in here right now? What the hell am I going to say?

"Alex?" Lucy's voice calls from the other side of the door. "We have to go in five minutes."

I squeeze my eyes shut. I can't believe I forgot about taking Lucy to school. Did she hear anything? My dirty talk? Zo's gasp?

How could I be this ridiculously irresponsible?

"Okay," I call. "I'll be right out."

My parents were right not to trust me. I was the biggest idiot on the planet.

I wait until I hear Lucy's footsteps retreat from the door, and then I scramble off Zoey and jump out of bed. Zoey has a hand pressed to her lips, her face just as panicked as mine.

"Oh fudge, Zo, you have to leave." What if Lucy catches her here? I mean she's in middle school now. It's not like she's going to think Zoey just spent the night here and we did nothing. She'll tell my parents about it, and then I'll be burned alive and chopped into a bunch of tiny pieces and thrown out in the ocean for the sharks to feast on.

All I had to do was keep it in my pants for a few goddamn months.

"I know, I know," Zoey whispers, finding her pants and pulling them on. "Shit, I'm sorry, Alex."

"You shouldn't have spent the night," I say, even though I'm the one who invited her in the first place. I tear through my clothes drawers, wrenching on the first thing I can find.

"I'm so sorry," Zoey repeats.

"We're just fake dating. You know that, right?" I can't stop the venom that's coming from my voice. I know I shouldn't take this out on her. But knowing and doing are two different things apparently.

"That's crystal clear."

"Then it should be crystal clear that this," I say, gesturing to the bed, "shouldn't be happening."

"We were just fucking around Alex. It's not a big deal. I mean, I'm into Z. You know that, right?" she snaps. Well, that's like a soccer ball to the nuts.

"Oh yeah, and you're really committed to that, aren't you?"

"What's that supposed to mean?"

"You're over here feeling up other guys in the middle of the night. I'm starting to get why he chose someone else." God, what was wrong with me? Zoey's face darkens to a purple shade, and she opens her mouth to yell at me, but I cut her off. "You need to leave. Lucy can't see you."

"I'll just wait until you guys leave and then sneak out," Zoey says quietly. I yank on my hair, turning in a circle, trying to think.

"She'll see your car out front. She'll recognize it." I stop turning, finally settling on the window.

"No," she says, seeing where I've settled my gaze. "Absolutely not." She's angry and scared and I get I'm being terrible right now.

But I really don't have any other options.

ZOEY

Alex is being a grade-A dickface right now. I get that he doesn't want Lucy to catch us and that he isn't supposed to have women spend the night, but I'm not about to crawl out the fucking window like his wife just came home and caught him fucking his sidepiece.

He runs his hands through his hair again, looking so

panicked that he seems on the edge of tears. Serves him right. He should be crying after the shit he said to me.

But a little piece of my heart breaks for him too.

"Zoey, please?" He's never begged me for anything before. "I'm trying so hard not to mess this all up." The pain in his voice is the worst. I stamp my foot, not wanting to give in.

But what exactly is my other option? To leave through the door right now and try to explain to Lucy what me and her brother were doing in here? She's warming up to Alex, but I know she'll still go straight to her parents with this information.

As pissed as I am right now, I don't want to mess up his relationship with his family.

"Yeah," I breathe, suddenly near tears myself.

He lets out a breath of relief and then pops out the screen to his window. I crawl out, drop onto the soft ground, and then dash around the side of his house. I have the urge to puke in his bushes, but I make it to my car and drive away, the sick feeling setting into my body.

I'm someone's dirty little secret. Again.

TWENTY-THREE

ZOEY

"And where have you been, little missus?" Tessa asks when I step through the door. I bend down to take off my shoe and lose my balance. It gets caught on my foot, and I end up hopping on one leg, trying to keep myself up. I yank the fucking thing off and throw it at the wall in front of me, cursing. Tessa pauses dancing around the kitchen to raise her eyebrows at me.

She's cooking eggs and hash browns for breakfast, because not only does she get up early enough to take eight a.m.'s (which, really, no self-respecting college student should do), but she wakes up with enough time and energy to cook a full-blown meal. I move to start scooping eggs onto my plate.

"Uh uh," she says, taking the plate away from me. "You have your stash of granola bars over there. This is my breakfast."

"So you're just going to sit there and make me watch you eat and not share *any*?"

"Oh good, you understand." I don't even crack a smile. I flop down into the chair at the table and groan, hiding my head in my hands. "So, I thought if you were coming back this morning it would be from happy happy fun times," Tessa says, slipping into the chair across from me. "But apparently it's not."

I snort. "It started out as happy happy fun times. Ended more like sad sad stupid times."

"What happened?"

"I was at Alex's—" I start, but Tessa lets out this huge sigh of relief. I narrow my eyes. "What?"

She looks sheepish. "I was worried it was going to be Z's."

I bang my head against the table and groan again. "Was Z really that bad?" I recall everything Eileen, Naomi, and Derek ever said about him. It wasn't all that positive. In fact, he came across as kind of a shit. Was I just an idiot when it came to guys?

"No, no," Tessa rushes to say. She twirls a curl of hair around her finger and takes a careful sip of her tea before continuing. "He was a good guy, Zo. Really, I believe it. You wouldn't have chosen him if he didn't have a good heart. It's just... he seemed to have a good heart with a lot of girls, too, and you went head over heels obsessively fast."

I grimace. Of course I did. And now I'm doing it all over again with Alex.

Tessa continues. "And that wasn't why I was hoping you weren't with Z. I—you haven't seen the post, have you?"

"What post?"

Tessa sighs. "Last night."

I yank my phone out of my pocket. Sure enough, there's a picture of Z and his girlfriend. *Several* pictures of Z and his girlfriend. They're celebrating their three-month anniversary. Who even does that?

The worst part though is the caption: **Happy three months to my favorite girl! I love you**!

I love you.

They're at the *I love you* stage. And it's posted for everyone to see.

"Well, shit."

Tessa is gauging my reaction. I'm pissed. But not about them being at the *I love you* stage.

"He kept me a secret for over a year," I say, awareness washing over me in seismic waves of rage. "He didn't even tell his friends we were hooking up, and yet he doesn't have a problem telling the whole world he loves his new girlfriend." I ball my hands up, death squeezing my phone.

"Keep going, babe. Let it all out," Tessa says around her bite of food.

"What the actual fuck," I demand. "It's not like dating me is anything to be embarrassed of. For goodness sake, he was just fucking me. He should have been bragging about it. I shouldn't be sneaking out of windows."

"Wait what?" Tessa asks. "He made you sneak out of a window?"

"I don't want to be anyone's secret anymore. I need someone who's going to be shouting about me from the rooftops, or I don't need anyone at all."

"Damn right," Tessa agrees. "But let's go back to the window thing."

"And did this whole fake dating thing just not work at all? Am I really that undesirable?" I question, throwing my hands in the air. Tessa's about to interrupt, to tell me how desirable I am, I just know it. But isn't my golden rule to be your own pump-up squad? "You know what? Fuck that. I'm desirable as hell. He's the one with the problem."

"Absolutely, babe. You're above and beyond what any guy could ever want."

"I'm done with Z," I announce. And I realize, it's true. Somewhere along the way, my heart stopped twinging every time I heard his name. I stopped caring about what he was up to in life or wondering if he was thinking about me. I stopped replaying memories of him in my head.

It wasn't even because of my crush on Alex. It just *happened.*

Heartache is like a hole. Sometimes, it's like a huge cavern that's been gouged out of your chest, and sometimes it's just a small dip. Either way, the only way you can get over it is to just keep filling it in, day by day, living your life until it's so full it's like it was never even empty in the first place.

"No more of this fake dating crap. He can suck a dick."

"I mean, he can if he wants," Tessa says with a shrug and a slight smile. "It's not the worst punishment." I give her a face. She's well aware of my hatred toward blow jobs. "But I'm with you. We hate Z."

Hate. No, that isn't quite right. I don't hate Z.

I just don't care.

My smile spreads. It feels damn good to be done with that phase of my life. "And I'm done with Alex too."

"I do have questions about possible happy happy fun times that you may or may not have had with Alex Adams."

I shake my head, the high of my anger dissipating thinking about the fight we got in this morning. Tessa awkwardly pats my hair.

"Another time, then. Another time." She jumps up from

the table and walks toward the stove. "How do you want your eggs?"

ALEX

I haven't seen Zoey in four days.

I know, I know, it's just four days. I didn't know her for years and I was fine. But four days of radio silence from Zoey?

Yeah. I'm feeling like crap.

Lucy hasn't mentioned anything about the other morning. My parents have called twice this week and haven't mentioned anything about Zoey, so I'm hoping that forcing Zoey out the window worked and Lucy had no idea she was here.

I still can't believe I was so stupid.

Looking at Zeus's stupid face in my class makes me want to punch him. I can't believe what I said to Zoey. Of course I think Zeus is an absolute idiot for choosing anyone over her. I'd never choose anyone over Zoey.

I just can't choose anyone at all right now.

I half expect Zoey to meet me after class for a fake date. Even if she hates me, she's still trying to win *him* back, right? And why the hell am I so hopeful that she's trying to win another guy back?

I step out of the classroom and glance around the crowded hallway, hoping to catch a glimpse of blonde.

Nothing.

Kinda makes me want to punch Zeus again.

. . .

"This is stupid." Lucy crosses her arms over her chest and leans back in her chair, propping her legs on the table. I think there's some small part of her that likes me being in charge, because Mom would never allow that to happen in her eyesight.

"It's not stupid. It's actually really important," I try to explain patiently.

"Why does it have triangles? Math shouldn't have triangles." She frowns at the paper like it slapped her in the face.

I chuckle. "You're in for a hell of a time when you get to trig."

Lucy harrumphs again but grabs the pencil in her hand and turns back to her homework. Her class is just starting to learn algebra, and her teacher decided to introduce the concept of isolating variables and canceling out like terms through giving them equations with shapes. No numbers or X's. Just circles, squares, and triangles. I get the concept, but I also get Lucy's frustration. She's never done math with shapes before like this.

I walk her through the next two problems. Lucy doesn't normally ask me for help with her homework, but I think she's just trying to get it done before Zoey gets here. *If* Zoey gets here. I'm actually pretty sure she's not coming, and I don't have a clue what I'm going to do. Would Lucy be pissed if I bring her to practice with me and make her sit on the sideline?

I glance over at her screwed-up face where she's writing on the paper with harsh, stabby strokes.

Yeah, I'll probably end up taking a pencil to the eye socket if I suggest that. Might be worth it though.

The doorbell rings when I'm helping Lucy with her next problem. I shoot off from the table, explanation forgotten, and race to the door.

Zoey's scowl greets me. I can't help the wide smile that spreads across my face. I want to hug her. But the death glare she sends me when I reach my arms out has me placing them right back down at my sides.

"I'm here for Lucy, not you," she says, marching by me into the house. Her hair swings as she weaves around me, and I'm struck stupid by the smell of her shampoo, rocking back on my heels. Her boots clack against the tile floor, my racing heart matching the heavy rhythm.

"Can I talk to—"

"Nope. Get dressed for practice and get the hell out of here."

"You just want me out of my clothes," I tease, because I'm an idiot apparently.

Zoey spins, narrowing her eyes at me and stopping me cold. I can feel the blood rush from my face with that glare.

I definitely said the wrong thing.

"Please, Zo—"

She holds up her hand to stop me, then mimes pointing at me, then zipping her lips shut, locking them tight, and giving me the middle finger.

Lucy comes around the bend and runs up to Zoey, giving her a hug. Zoey hugs her back, and dammit, now I'm jealous of my own sister. "Did you finish your homework?" Zoey asks.

Lucy nods.

"Did you actually?" I question, because she and I had about three problems left.

She shakes her head. "But Zoey knows math better than you. You can go."

And just like that, the attitude is back. Zoey smirks at me. "We'll finish that up first, and then I brought over all my nail supplies."

I'm still standing here, trying to figure out how the hell I'm going to apologize and get Zoey to talk to me in front of my little sister, who absolutely can't know that Zoey spent the night in the first place. I move to run my hand through my hair and freeze guiltily as Zoey turns to me again, my arm halfway to my head.

"Go get dressed for practice, Alex." Her tone is condescending. Final. She's done. My chest drops like I just got the wind knocked out of me. I don't know what else to do. If I stay here any longer trying to convince her to talk to me, I'm going to be late.

I'm halfway down the hallway. It's Lucy's voice that guts me in the chest this time.

"He'll never choose anything over soccer, you know."

It's official. I'm the worst person in the world.

ZOEY

I twirl my nail file in my hand and watch Lucy sing along with my favorite Nothing But Thieves song. I know she'd never admit it to Alex, but I think I just might be able to make a rock girl out of her yet. Her nails are a bright yellow with little white flowers. It seemed a little summery for November, but that's what she wanted.

Mine are black. Like my cold brew. And my mood.

Not my soul, though. Alex can't take that from me.

Lucy's so cute though as she sings while dancing around the kitchen, dark hair flying with a spin. She's gotten more confident these last few months and I love that. And while she's certainly not innocent, and goodness knows I've dropped more f-bombs than Alex would like around her, I wouldn't want to be the one to explain to her in the morning what I was doing in Alex's bed half-dressed. Their relationship is slowly getting better, she isn't as angry anymore. But...

I glance to the wall. The list of rules Alex's parents set out for him are still taped right there, the paper a little worn from hanging out there for the past few months.

But there it is. Number two. *No random girls.* If Lucy had seen us in the morning, I know she would have automatically assumed what we had been up to. She'd be disappointed in Alex for not following the rules, and then she'd stop talking to him again.

Alex was a dick.

But I kind of get why he did it.

When he gets home, he pushes open the door hesitantly, like he's bracing for attack. Part of me wants to hold my ground, but the guilt that washes over Alex's face and the sheepish smile he gives me when he sees me leaning against the counter makes the other part of me want to forgive him.

"Hey," he says, nodding at me. I roll my eyes to cover up my stupid heart flutter. My hormones haven't caught up to the fact that we hate him right now. And how does he make a nod look sexy?

"I cleaned your kitchen, Asshole Alex."

He winces. "I can see that."

"Like my new nails?" I raise my middle finger at him.

The corners of his lips tug up in a smile. "Love them."

Lucy comes from around the bend of the hallway, the book she wants me to borrow in hand. I pull my hand down before she can catch me flipping her brother off.

"Alex," she says surprised, *and* if I'm not mistaken —excited.

Alex can sense it too. His smile is huge as he turns to her. She tells him about our night, and they make plans to watch a movie together. Lucy asks if I want to join them, but I shake my head.

"I've got to get going, babe," I say. Lucy pouts, and Alex looks like he's considering tackling me if I don't agree to listen to his apology. I take a deep breath. "You want to talk?" I ask.

Alex nods, but then glances to Lucy, looking pained. "Not here."

"No," I agree. "Not here. Tomorrow."

TWENTY-FOUR

ZOEY

We settle into the big swinging chairs in Nerd Corner at my favorite boba place. It's the first time I've been here since the start of the semester and operation Make New Friends went down.

Which is sad, because I love this place.

"I used to love this place as a kid," Alex says, grabbing a plush Captain America shield from beside him and moving it out of his way. I reach forward and grab it from him, holding it to my chest. I could use the support. Alex frowns at me, glancing down at the pillow like he knows exactly what I'm doing.

"I forget you grew up around here."

"Yeah, once I graduated from high school I was ready to leave this place and never return."

"And now you're back." I push my feet into the ground, rocking the swing chair back and forth.

"And now I'm back," he agrees. The chain squeaks as I rock, and you can barely hear the hum of the air conditioning over the chatter of other students. Alex runs a hand through his hair. "I'm so sorry, Zo," he says, looking me dead in the eyes. They're shining with regret and determination, and I don't doubt for a second that he really means it. "I shouldn't have said any of what I said. I was mad at myself for instigating and asking you to spend the night and I took it out on you."

"No shit?" I ask sarcastically.

Alex frowns deeper. "I really do feel bad. I shouldn't have handled it like that." His knee bounces. His jaw is tense. "You know I didn't mean it, right? Any of that stuff I said about Z. Or you. I—" He trails off, shaking his head, like he's absolutely sick to his stomach with his actions. "Hell, I'm sorry."

"I'm glad you feel bad," I say, my voice full of attitude. I'm being childish and I know it, but my stubborn side just wants to come out right now.

Alex raises an eyebrow at my attitude, then takes a deep, calming breath. "Zoey, this whole talking about my feelings crap isn't something I would attempt with anybody but you. I really want to fix this. How can I fix this?"

"Why me?" I ask. Because I'm a button pusher like that.

Or maybe I'm just a little too invested in the answer.

"I *sometimes*" —he makes sure to stress the word some-times, but his slight smile is teasing as he says it— "like having you around as a friend."

Friend is both the best and worst word in the dictionary.

"So talk," Alex demands, settling into the chair. I release the pent-up breath I've been holding. All this drama isn't me. If Alex wants to have an adult conversation, I can rise to the occasion.

"I don't like feeling like a secret," I mutter. So I've decided to talk. It doesn't mean I need to be excited about it.

"A secret?"

I shake my head, glancing away from him to look at the rest of the store. The students around us are all smiles and bright and cheery, while I feel sick to my stomach saying this out loud. "The whole time I was with Z, he didn't want his friends to know we were hooking up. He wouldn't even stand close to me on campus. Made me feel like shit."

Alex growls. "I hate him. Honestly hate him. Next time I catch him cheating, I'm kicking him out of the room and reporting him." He cracks his knuckles, looking excited about the idea. "I'm going to make my tests really hard from here on out."

I laugh. "I appreciate that."

"You think I'm joking, but I'm not."

"Oh, Alex. It's fine. Don't worry about it."

"That's why you were so mad about leaving out the window though, isn't it?"

I kick at the floor, taking a deep inhale of the sweet air. "And I get it. I totally understand. Lucy makes it different. I don't want to sabotage your relationship with her or anything. And I didn't mean to make you break your rules. That wasn't my plan." I return the intensity of his gaze. I want him to know that I mean that. And, as much as I hate to admit it... "You were right. Sneaking out the window really was the only option. I just overreacted."

"You didn't overreact. I didn't know." He runs his hands through his hair again. The frown lines in his forehead, and the grooves where his fingers crawl through his hair, might be permanent by the end of this conversation. "I have no problem letting my class see that I'm all over you every week. I'm not exactly keeping you a secret."

"That's different. You're required by contract to do that."

Alex is up and out of his chair in a heartbeat. His hands come to cup my face as he stands, bent over in front of me. His eyes search my face, landing on my eyes with such unwavering intensity I gasp. "Zo. If we were ever in a relationship, or—hell, just hooking up—I would have no problem making sure the whole world knew how awesome you are." That might be the most romantic thing anyone has ever said to me. And then he ruins it by smirking. "Need me to make out with you to prove my point?"

"No." I shove him away, even though there's a small voice in me desperately screaming yes.

"Suit yourself." He shrugs, settling back into his chair. Then—yup. He runs his hand through his hair again. "Actually, I should probably stop with crap like that."

"The flirting?"

"Yeah." He nods, looking pretty damn sullen about it. "It confuses my celibate brain."

"I'm not sure that's the head it's confusing," I joke. Alex snorts, smiling for a quick second before going back to that sad expression again. I tap his toe with mine. "Lighten up. I think it's just our personalities. We're both flirty people."

"I don't think the fake dating helped. I think the fake relationship chemistry bled into our friendship."

"Well that's okay, we don't have to fake date anymore."

"What?" Alex asks, panicked. "Why not?"

"I've given up on Z," I say.

"You've given up on Z?" he repeats, looking absolutely appalled by that idea. I don't know why he's taking this so hard. Wasn't he the one that told me this was unhealthy in the first place?

Maybe he's realizing he won't get to touch me anymore. Kiss me. "If anything was going to happen, it would have happened already," I say, not giving him the real reason I'm quitting the fake relationship. He'll think I'm too flighty, instantly jumping from one guy to the next.

"Will you still babysit?"

I almost laugh out loud. *That's* why he sounded panicked. "Of course."

Alex nods. But his mouth is pressed into a hard line, like he's still dissatisfied and wants to say something more. But he doesn't.

"So back to being just friends?" he asks, leaning forward to stick out his hand.

"Just friends," I agree, sliding my hand into his. It's calloused from all the weights he lifts in the gym, and a spark of electricity shoots up my spine from just this.

We seal the deal on a handshake.

TWENTY-FIVE

ALEX

Apparently, the friendship gods were against me.

That's the only reason I can think of for the sudden November heat wave that had Zoey prancing around in shorts and tank tops again. Or the way I constantly imagined how she would feel underneath me.

Strike that. I didn't have to imagine anymore. I *knew* what her body felt like, warm and soft under mine. And every time I was around her I was half hard imagining it again.

She didn't pick me up after class anymore. Instead we get coffee and study for approaching midterms. Grad school is a fudge ton harder than I thought it would be. And now that we weren't putting on a show for Z, there was no reason to have my hands all over her, so my joints were buzzing with the need for release.

Hell, I passed her on campus once while she was giving a tour. She spotted me and winked and *that* was enough to turn me on.

Two weeks. Two whole never-ending mind-assaulting weeks. That's how long we've been just friends.

I hated it.

Zoey was good about it. She stopped flirting with me, just like I stopped flirting with her. I knew *why* it had to be this way. But it didn't stop me from hating it.

I'm rushing across campus, with just enough time to make it to my midterm, when my phone rings.

I groan, pulling it out of my pocket.

It's Lucy's middle school. I swipe to answer faster than I would swipe right on Zoey's Tinder profile.

"Mr. Adams?"

"Yes?"

"We just wanted to let you know that Lucy went to the school nurse with a fever and will need to be picked up."

I come to a stop in the middle of campus. Hell. She can't be serious. I have a midterm. I can't just miss that. But I can't leave Lucy either. She needs me. "Of course," I say. "I'll be right there."

I hang up and run my hand through my hair, rocking on my heels while I debate what to do. Students swarm around me. This couldn't have happened earlier? It had to happen the ten minutes before my midterm?

I feel like absolute crap doing this, but I call Zoey.

"Hello, Mr. Big-Ass Ego, my class is about to start. What do you want?" I know her class is about to start. I know her schedule as well as mine at this point. And I know she shouldn't skip this class. It's the week of her interview.

"I feel terrible asking this of you," I start.

"Shoot," she says.

"The school just called, and Lucy needs to go home sick." God, I wish I didn't have to ask this of her.

She gasps. "But your midterm."

"Is there any way..."

"You want me to go pick up Lucy?" She doesn't even sound that upset.

"Can you?" I breathe out.

"Yeah. Shit, yeah, I'll go right now. Eileen can take notes for me."

It's like a huge weight is released from my chest. I can hear her rustling around on the other end, packing up her stuff. She has a muffled conversation with Eileen, asking her to take notes for her, and I start jogging to my classroom.

"Okay, on my way," Zoey says.

"Thank you so much."

"Honestly, I've taken years' worth of notes for Eileen. She owes me this. It's not a big deal."

But it is a big deal. I wouldn't have asked her if I could have come up with literally anything else. I don't deserve Zoey.

"Thank you." That's all I can manage to tell her. "I'll call the school to let them know you're coming."

"Go ace your midterm," Zoey says, and then hangs up the phone.

I quickly dial the school's number and explain the situation before hanging up and ducking into the classroom. The professors just started passing out exams, but I manage to slip into the back of the room just in time.

I grab the stack of stapled papers, but when it's time to start, the problems swim in front of me. My mind keeps spinning in circles, worrying about Lucy's fever and Zoey's class and how my parents would react if I fail this midterm.

I take a deep breath, put my pencil on the page, and pray that I get enough questions right to pass this class.

. . .

I unlock the door in a rush once I get home. Zoey waves at me from the chair facing the door. Lucy lies on the couch, wrapped in a ton of blankets, her head propped up on about seven different pillows taken from different spots in the house. She looks miserable.

"Hey, Luce," I say, making a beeline straight toward her before I even set down my backpack or take off my shoes. "How're you feeling?"

She glares at me. "You're blocking the TV."

Well. Okay. Wasn't exactly the welcome home I was expecting.

I shoot Zoey a look, asking with my eyes why the hell I got such a hostile welcome. Zoey shrugs. "This show is very entertaining?" she offers.

I turn my attention back to Lucy and press the back of my hand against her forehead. I can feel the heat before my skin even makes contact. "What's her temperature?" I ask.

"101.7," Zoey says. "So it's okay, we're just chilling. She took some Tylenol earlier and can have more in four hours."

"I'm right here," Lucy mutters, but it sounds like she can barely get the words out.

"I know you're right here," I say, taking my hand away from her forehead.

"Then stop talking like I'm not."

Okay. Apparently Lucy gets irritable when she's sick.

"Do you need anything?" I ask. "Water? Food?" I try to think back to what I do when I have a fever, but it's usually a lot of staying in bed and watching TV, drifting in and out of sleep.

Lucy shakes her head and then grimaces from pain. "Zoey's got it."

Ouch. My eyebrows shoot so far up my face they're like

a goalie trying to reach a shot at the crossbar. Christ. What the hell did I do?

I walk to my room to put my stuff away. I know I can't yell at a sick kid, but dammit, I've been trying so damn hard with her. Can't she see that?

"Alex?"

I spin around. Zoey's standing in the doorway.

"What the hell was that?" I ask.

She cocks one eyebrow at me, crossing her arms at my aggressive tone. "I was just coming to see if you're okay."

"Well, I'm not."

"I can see that." She smirks.

"Why is she upset?" I demand.

Zoey shrugs. That just pisses me off more. "People do weird things when they're sick. I can't stand clothes. It's actually a thing, like they feel all claustrophobic when I'm already struggling to breathe. Maybe Lucy gets mean?"

My brain takes a detour, imaging taking care of a sick Zoey who thinks clothes are claustrophobic. I don't think I'd mind at all taking care of her when she's sick. Hell—my pants are getting tight imagining it, and I have to glance at the ceiling to focus back on the problem at hand. "She wasn't angry at you, though."

"Maybe because I picked her up?"

I run a hand through my hair. Is that what the issue is? Does Lucy think I just couldn't be bothered with her?

"I'm sorry, Zo." I sink down at the edge of my bed, propping my elbows on my thighs. "You did all that for me, and here I am attacking you."

She comes to stand in front of me, practically in between my legs. I prop my head in my hands, glancing up at her. I have the urge to reach for her, wrap my hands around the back of her thighs and pull her against me. But I don't.

"You should be sorry, because that was unnecessary." She pokes at my chest. "But it's okay." She sits on the bed beside me, and I bump her shoulder with mine.

"You're the best, Zo. I wouldn't be able to do this without you." It's true. I'm absolutely failing at this Responsible Alex thing. In order to do well in school, I couldn't pick up Lucy. In order to be a good teacher's assistant, I have to push off my own studies. Everything is such a mess, and if I hadn't met Zoey this semester, Lucy and I probably would have died from a vegetable deficiency.

How the hell did I think I was going to be able to do this all by myself? I'm a mess and I'm failing and even *with* Zoey's help I still can't get Lucy to forgive me.

"Why don't you go talk to her?" Zoey asks softly. "I should probably get going anyway."

I nod. Zoey stands and then reaches a hand out to me. I slide my hand into hers, and she pulls me up off the bed. I don't want to take my hand away.

But Zoey pulls away and walks out of the room. I follow.

She's telling Lucy that she has to leave, but Lucy keeps shaking her head. "Don't go,"

"I'm leaving you in good hands, I promise." Damn right Lucy is being left in good hands. I'm her freaking brother.

Lucy glares at me. "Don't make her go."

Zoey glances back at me, uncertain.

"Zoey has stuff to do. But she's welcome to stay if she wants to." Because there's no way I'm pissing off Lucy any more.

Zoey blows air into her cheeks. I can tell she wants to

give Lucy and me space to talk, but she doesn't want to make things worse. "Can I borrow your laptop to study?"

"Of course," I say. "You can have anything you want. I'll make Lucy do pushups right now if you request it." Of course I wouldn't do that. I'm just trying to get Lucy to laugh.

It doesn't work. Lucy rolls her eyes and then groans in pain. Maybe being sick will condition her to roll her eyes less. "Calladito te ves más bonito."

I narrow my eyes at her.

"You speak Spanish?" Zoey says in surprise, glancing between Lucy and me.

"Lucy does. I don't," I say.

"How is that possible?"

"Well, I mean my mom tried to teach me. I just didn't speak it that much, and my dad never spoke it, and I've forgotten most of it at this point." I shrug, a little embarrassed honestly. "I can say some words still, but like if Lucy got kidnapped in Spain I would not be able to speak enough Spanish to rescue her."

"Why do I have to be kidnapped?" Lucy grumbles. "Why not say..." She trails off, looking even sicker than she did before, her eyes unfocused. "Why not say." She finally continues. "That you can't order food in Spanish."

Zoey giggles. "The sick girl has a point." She bites her lip, glancing between us. "Why don't I go pick us up something to eat?"

She's still trying to give Lucy and me alone time, which I appreciate but— "No. I can cook something." Lucy would want that. "What do you want?" I ask.

She thinks it over, then smirks. "Chicken noodle soup."

I have no clue where to start for that, and Lucy knows it. She's challenging me. But it was just last year I was one of the best college athletes in the US. I'm not about to back down from a challenge.

"You got it."

Lucy eyes me, obviously not believing I can do it. Her attention drifts back to the TV though, so I square my shoulder and get to work.

"Can I see your phone?" I ask Zoey.

"Sure?" She's confused but unlocks her phone and hands it to me anyway. I open up her recent calls, and just like I thought she would be, Tessa is at the very top. I dial her number.

"Hey babe," she answers.

"It's Alex actually."

"Eh, you can be babe too."

I laugh. "Zoey is going to love that."

"What? What am I going to love?" Zoey asks, tugging on my shirt like a child. I wink at her.

"Do you happen to know a good recipe for chicken noodle soup?"

"Of course I do," Tessa says. "Here, I'm actually at home, let me pull out my recipe cards."

"You have recipe cards?"

"Oh, you called Tessa?" Zoey laughs. "Yeah she has a whole stack of them, they're great."

"Someone has to keep Zoey and me from starving," Tessa says. Wow. Even when they can't hear each other, it still sounds like they're having a conversation. "Here, I'll text it to you. Or Zoey I guess. How do I not have your number?"

"I don't know. I've never actually had to reach you before."

"We should rectify that. I want to brag about having the great Alex Adams on speed dial."

I laugh again. "We can make that happen." I hang up and then text her off my phone before handing Zoey back her phone.

Tessa texts me the recipe minutes later, and the ingredients list throws me for a loop. I double check our pantry but, yeah. I don't have large quantities of chicken broth or egg noodles just lying about. I groan, running my hands through my hair.

Okay, this is just a minor setback. I can figure this out. I—

"Need me to do a grocery run?" Zoey asks, leaning in the archway separating the kitchen from the living room, holding up her car keys in her hand. "I know Tessa makes some fancy-ass shit." She mouths the last two words so Lucy can't hear, and I grin.

I'm reminded of that very first day I showed up to practice and West freaked out, calling me his savior. That's how I feel about Zoey today. I could kiss her.

"Could you?"

"Of course," she says. Then she gives me a pointed look. I know what she wants me to do. Talk to Lucy. And I have every intention of doing it, once I figure out what I'm going to say.

Zoey texts herself the list, and then disappears out the door with a flounce of blonde hair, leaving Lucy and me alone.

When I was sick as a kid, my mom would always make me mint tea with honey and lemon in it. It turned me off tea for the rest of my life. I always associated the taste with being sick. I can't deny that it helped though. I microwave some water for Lucy now and track down the tea in the back of our pantry.

"Hey, Luce," I say, setting the boiling hot liquid on the

coffee table in front of her. She's lying against the pillows, her eyes closed, her face pale. "I brought you tea."

She doesn't respond. I sit down on the floor in front of the couch.

"Are you actually asleep? Or are you just pretending to be mad at me?"

She doesn't crack a muscle. But her breathing is still shallow and irregular. I had to share a room with plenty of guys when traveling for away games. I know what it sounds like when someone's sleeping, and Lucy's not sleeping.

"I'm sorry I didn't pick you up at school today. I sent Zoey because I had a midterm. If I had missed it, I would have failed the class."

"Zoey missed her class," Lucy rasps, her eyes fluttering open to a glare.

"I knew you were awake," I cry. Wait—that sounded too excited. No wonder my mom didn't want to leave me with Lucy. I'm bad at this. And that rasp in her voice didn't sound good. "Here, drink your tea." I shove it toward her.

"I don't like tea."

"Neither do I. Mom still made me drink it." And I know she would make Lucy drink it too. There's no way you could say no to that woman.

Lucy sticks her little T-rex arms out of the blanket, reaching for the cup. I pass it over to her carefully. Steam billows off the top, the lemon smell filling the room, and—oh Jesus. What if it burns her?

I should have let it cool off more. I almost snatch it out of her hand, but then she takes a sip. And then another. She makes a face of disgust, but she doesn't cry out in pain.

Thank the tea gods. I already burned Zoey with hot liquid once. I don't need to add Lucy to the list, too.

"I know Zoey missed her class, but it was different. She

didn't have a test." I push a hand through my hair, trying to find the words to explain. "If it was anything else I would have skipped to come get you."

Lucy snorts. Or tries to. It kind of gets caught somewhere in her throat and she ends up coughing. I grab the tea to stop it from splashing, simultaneously leaning back to stay out of the germ zone. "Liar," she finally chokes out.

"Am not."

"You wouldn't skip soccer," she counters.

Hell. That hurts. Yeah, a year or two ago, I wouldn't have skipped practice for Lucy.

"I used to be stupid, Luce," I say. "But now it's not even a contest. I'd skip soccer for you every time. Even if you called me 'cause you just desperately needed ice cream in the middle of practice, I'd make fun of you, but I'd come get you." Lucy closes her eyes in disbelief. "I promise you, I've changed." My voice cracks like a freaking middle schooler.

Lucy shakes her head, but she doesn't open her eyes. The conversation has worn her out. "The chicken noodle soup better be good," she mumbles.

"It will be. Get some rest," I say. I push myself up from the ground and head back to the kitchen.

Zoey comes back with groceries half an hour later. Lucy is passed out and I've spent the time googling the best ways to care for someone with a fever. Zoey sets the bags on the table, and I walk up behind her, wrapping my arms around her.

"You saved my butt today," I whisper into her hair. Why does it always smell so sweet? Like vanilla and home. She melts into my chest. In another world, one where we actually wanted to date each other, we'd be so compatible. "Thank you."

"Ass saving is what I do," she says grimly. "You owe me money by the way." She fishes the receipt out of the bag.

I shouldn't be crossing lines like this, not when I'm the one who drew them in the first place. But I see that line and I run straight out of bounds. "My wallet is in my back pocket."

"Do you plan on grabbing it?"

"No."

She flips around in my arms, glancing up at me. Her cheeks are flushed, and because it's Zoey I know it's desire, not embarrassment.

She probably doesn't want to kiss me again after everything I put her through last time. But damn. I want to kiss her. I remember after our first kiss I racked my brain, scrolling through my past hook-ups, trying to remember if any other kiss I had was ever that good. Some girls were extremely talented with their tongues, I'll give them that. But kissing Zoey was like scoring that winning goal—that perfect shot that would be replayed for decades to come.

I plaster on my best unfazed smirk, trying to pretend I'm unaffected by all this. "Are you gonna get it or what?" I ask.

"The things I do for money," she sighs with an eye roll. Her hands reach around me, dipping each one into a butt pocket. And then she gives me a flirty squeeze, smirking up at me. Ugh. What I wouldn't give to ditch our clothes right now.

She draws the wallet out of my pocket and collects a couple bills. I don't actually care how much she takes. I might be broke, but I trust Zoey not to rob me blind. She glides her hand down her body, running it over her breasts, her stomach, circling the button on her jeans, before slipping the money into her front pocket. My eyes follow her all the way down. Then she leans forward a little, and I can see right down the neckline of her shirt.

I groan. I can't help it. I know she's teasing me on purpose. I'm sure it's obvious to her that I'm a boob man. Always have been, always will be. And Zoey's are out-of-this-world amazing.

"Are you going to give me back my wallet now?" I rasp.

She twirls it in her hand. "Nah," she says. "Finders keepers." She tucks it into her own back pocket.

These games are messing with my head. I want to lift her up, place her on the edge of this table, step right between her thighs, bury my hands in her hair and kiss her until the semester ends. But, dammit, I'm Responsible Freaking Alex, and Lucy is in the next room over. So I don't. "Pretty sure that's not how it works." I place my hand on her lower back, my splayed fingers following the curve of her jeans. Her muscles spasm when I make contact.

I slide my hand down, drawing my wallet out of her pocket.

Don't think about where your hand is. Don't think about the shape of her ass. Don't think about how perfectly it fits in your hand.

"You are literally the worst influence," I grumble, giving her butt a light slap when I've finally finished taking my sweet-ass time removing my wallet.

"Never claimed to be a good one," she says with a grin. "Besides, you started this." She slips out from between me and the table.

TWENTY-SIX

ALEX

I survey the ingredients Zoey bought and then get to work, following Tessa's recipe to the best of my abilities. Zoey makes herself comfortable at the table with my laptop, tossing me the ingredients I need every so often.

I chop carrots and onions, boil chicken, measure out herbs, add the noodles. Soon the kitchen smells out-of-this-world amazing, and I'm actually pretty impressed with myself. And the detailed instructions of Tessa's recipe card. But damn. Look at me.

When the soup is finally done, Lucy is fast asleep and Zoey is hard at work. At some point during her study session, Zoey borrowed a sweatshirt of mine and has the hood pulled up over her head. I don't know if she's even aware that she does it, but once she gets a flow going, she always puts her hair up in a bun, and if she has something with a hood she'll pull it up, as if to block out the outside world around her. It's cute as hell.

I don't bother her and instead head back to the living

room, dropping into one of the chairs and messing around on my phone. I feel like I should be doing something, but I don't know what. Lately it's just constantly been something, so actually having a moment to just sit is new. Wrong.

Too wrong.

Oh hell. I'm forgetting practice.

I glance over at Lucy. She's still passed out, and Zoey is already here, food is ready. In theory, I could go and it would be fine.

But Lucy would hate me. And I can't do that to her right after I freaking told her she was more important than soccer.

It feels like blasphemy to skip. In my whole undergrad career, I'm not sure I even missed one practice. Class, sure, I skipped all the time. But practice? Never.

I know the club team is different. People have different priorities, and they come less regularly compared to my D1 team, but I still feel absolutely terrible when 8:30 rolls around and I'm still at home, pacing around my house.

My phones buzzes twice, within seconds of each other.

Eddie: Everything okay?

West: WTF WHY WOULD YOU ABANDON ME ARE YOU DYING I FEEL SO ATTACKED

I chuckle, typing out my responses. I actually explain to Eddie that Lucy is sick. For West I just ask him why he feels so attacked if I'm the one dying.

"You're not at soccer?" Lucy croaks from the couch. I startle, glancing up at her. She blinks at me from the coach, looking slightly more alert than she did earlier. It's dark outside now, so she probably slept for a few hours.

"Nope," I say brightly, bringing her water. "I needed to

make sure you got some soup in you." I help her into a seated position and then go grab her a mug full of soup.

"Mugs are for drinks. Bowls are for soup," Zoey says when I walk past. The hood is down now and she has her feet propped up on the table, my laptop in her lap. She must have finished her assignment.

"Mugs are easier to hold, especially for sick people," I argue. "Engineering logic. Come at me."

"You're ridiculous," she says while laughing.

"Want to join us for dinner?" She nods and then helps herself to a bowl out of the cabinets. I find a can of plain tomato soup in my pantry for her and toss it to her to microwave.

I hand Lucy the mug and spoon, and then wait for the moment of truth.

She eats one spoonful. Then another.

"Stop staring at me," she says.

"Do you like it?"

She shrugs. I grin. If she has nothing bad to say, that means she *does* like it.

"I have mad cooking skills," I say, doing a little dance while silently thanking the cooking gods.

"Said no one ever," Zoey says from behind me. "If it's good, I'm attributing that all to Tessa's recipe card."

The three of us talk about nothing for the next hour, until Lucy drifts off to sleep again. I collect her dishes and carry her to her bed. Skipping practice was less terrible than I thought, and Lucy seems to like me more.

And Zoey's so good with Lucy. Every time I glance over at her, my heart beats a little faster for no good reason. She's literally the only reason I survived today though.

When I get back to the living room, Zoey's tidying

things up. She glances up at me and smiles, and there goes my stupid heart.

"I guess I should head home then," she says. I shake my head.

"Crash here." It's a stupid move. We both know it. But I don't want her to leave. "You've already finished your work, you don't have an early class tomorrow, and I'm sure I can find you an extra toothbrush somewhere."

"We'd have to share a bed," Zoey says. She gestures to the couch. "I'm not about to sleep on germ city."

"We would," I agree. That's kind of the whole point of getting her to crash here. "I mean, what's the big deal? You're not affected by me, right?" I ask with a smirk.

"I like to think I've matured since then," she says loftily.

"Since two weeks ago?"

She flips me off.

"Come on, Zo. Spend the night. We can watch something. Lucy is asleep for the night, anyway. And there's no way she's getting up for school in the morning."

She thinks it over, biting her lip.

Maybe I was wrong. Maybe Zoey isn't the bad influence. Maybe *I'm* the bad influence. I know I shouldn't be pushing boundaries like this.

"I really shouldn't," she says, shaking her head.

Damn. That sucks. I rub dirt off the tile with my bare foot. I'm not gonna force her to stay if she doesn't want to. But it absolutely sucks that she doesn't trust me enough to stay.

"I mean, last time I spent the night you made it sound like it was an issue I was sleeping around. And I wasn't even sleeping around."

"I know. I'm sorry—"

"You said that you understood why Z chose someone

else." Her arms are crossed now, and she's glaring up at me, some of the anger from that fight coming back to her.

Hell. I did say that. I didn't mean that though. "I was talking out of anger at myself, Zo. I—" I break off, knowing I need to be real with her. My heart is doing flips in my stomach, and I open my mouth again, whispering softly. "The truth is, I can't fathom why any guy would choose not to be with you."

She's silent. She stares at me, arms still crossed, practically tapping her foot against the floor while she thinks. "You're not going to yell at me in the morning again, are you?" she asks. "Or make me crawl out of any windows?"

It breaks my heart that she has to ask that. I shake my head. "You're not a secret, Zo. It's just...Lucy. We'll set an early alarm." She's still debating. I think we both know if she agrees to stay, the whole friendship thing we've tried for the past two weeks is going to blow up in flames. My logic? As long as we don't go all the way, I'm still fulfilling the Responsible Alex commandments.

And Christ almighty, I'm done with this friendship bullcrap. I want to spend the whole night tangled up with Zoey.

Her eyes search my face. And I wait. "Let me just text Tessa that I'm not coming home tonight," she whispers.

I grin.

Hell. Yes.

TWENTY-SEVEN

ZOEY

We get ready for bed in silence. We brush our teeth side by side in the bathroom. He splashes some water on his face, which I guess is like the guy equivalent of washing his face.

The silence gives me space to think.

I know, after everything I said to Tessa about not wanting to be someone's dirty secret, I shouldn't be spending the night here. I don't want a repeat of what happened with Z to happen again. I want to be with someone who is proud of being with me.

But I also know, Alex is not Z. Alex wants me here. I want to be here. I don't have any proof that this time with Alex will be any different than last time, but...

I think he's worth the risk.

Alex shuts the door to his bedroom, then clicks the lock.

My heart rate spikes. Without words, the tension builds between us. Anticipation rises inside me, racing through the veins in my body.

Responsible Alex doesn't fuck. But I wish he did. I

haven't been able to keep my eyes off him all night. The sweet way he cares for Lucy, the way he eye-fucks me every time we're in the same room. I love it.

We start undressing. Alex doesn't bother turning away from me as he strips out of his shirt. I love his tattoos and his muscles and his unabashed confidence. I want my hands on his body so badly, *my* body is practically vibrating.

He unbuttons the top button on his jeans, and I have to turn away. I can't handle that right now. I select a shirt from his drawer and then pull my sweater over my head.

I can feel his eyes on me, tracing the curves of my back. I imagine his hands on me, wrapping his arms around me from behind, sliding his hands up my stomach until he's cupping the weight of my breasts. They feel swollen now, practically begging for his touch. My skin is hot and buzzy.

I slip his shirt over my head and then shimmy out of my jeans. When I turn around, he's already in bed, still shirtless, sitting up against the headboard. His eyes are on me, tracing the shape of my thighs with a gaze so intense it almost feels like he's touching me.

"Nice shirt," he finally says, breaking the silence. His voice sounds calm, and I wonder if I'm blowing his invitation to spend the night out of proportion.

"Thank you," I smile. It's an old Linkin Park concert T-shirt. It barely covers the tops of my thighs. He must have gotten it years ago. I climb into bed next to him, trying to figure out how close I should sit to him. I settle in a few inches away from his body, but close enough to feel the heat wafting off from him.

"Want to watch something?" He reaches for his laptop, and when he returns we're so close every part of our sides touch. We have this huge bed, and I'm practically in his lap. I can feel the hair of his thigh sliding against my smooth skin. My panties are damp, practically begging him to make a move.

Alex tries logging on to his computer. It doesn't work. He retypes his password. It takes everything in me to keep a straight face as his computer rejects him again. He turns to me, raising his eyebrows. "Do you have anything you want to tell me?"

"No," I say innocently.

"What's my new password?"

"I don't know what you're talking about." He sighs and types something in. Then gets rejected again. "What'd you try?" I ask.

"Zoey is awesome."

"Aw, I thought you knew me better than that."

He looks at me, his head tilted to the side, thinking. Then he chuckles and shakes his head and types in a significantly longer password. It lets him in.

"What'd you try?" I ask him again. I can't keep the grin off my face anymore.

"You are *such* a bad influence."

"Come on, you already typed it. You can say it."

"See? Bad. Influence."

"Say it. Say 'Zoey is fucking awesome.'"

"I will not, you demon."

"Pussy."

Alex bursts out laughing. "If I had to choose between you and Thanos, the better villain would definitely be you."

"Really? I'm worse that Thanos? Who wiped out half the universe's population? Because I want you to say the word 'fuck'?"

"We have a population crisis! He was just trying to help. You're just doing it to be evil."

"No, I'm doing it because it would be fucking sexy hearing it come from your mouth."

He groans. Then he shakes his head and pulls up an action movie. Something we've both already seen. Nothing we need to pay attention to. "Shut up and watch the movie, Zo."

I slouch down next to him, resting my head on his shoulder. If he's allowed to push boundaries tonight, then so am I. I expect him to tense. But he doesn't. He wraps an easy arm around me, tugging me against him. Like we're a couple or something. Which we aren't. We're nowhere near being a couple. But it still feels nice.

I can't ignore the fact that he's in just his boxer briefs, and his skin is taut and warm beneath me. Why the hell did athletes have to look this good, and why did it take me this long to jump on the athlete band wagon? Throughout the movie we sink further and further into the bed, tangling closer and closer together, until, when the credits finally roll, we're lying down in the bed, my leg tossed over his hips, his thigh pressed in between my legs, and our arms wrapped around each other.

He closes the laptop, engulfing us in darkness. I feel him more than I see him turning away from me to set the laptop on the bedside table. Then he turns back to me, pressing his thigh more firmly against my center. I gasp. It's so loud it echoes throughout the room. I'm positive he can feel how drenched my panties are.

His hand slides underneath my shirt, resting on my waist.

Fuck it.

I grind my hips tentatively against his leg. Alex tenses beside me, his muscles flexing against my center, and I can't help the way I shiver. Fuck me. Why does something so simple feel so good?

"God, don't shiver like that, Zo," he whispers, his hands tracing my body. "I'm trying so hard to be good."

"Really? Inviting me to spend the night was your idea of being good?"

I see a flash of his teeth as he grins at me. "Probably wasn't my best plan." He pulls me closer to him, his hand cupping my ass, dragging me against his thigh. My hips do this little involuntary roll.

"Not your worst though," I whisper, letting my hand drag across his lower stomach, feeling each hard ridge of his abs. I want to trace them with my tongue. That's a normal thing to want, right? I've never actually been with someone who has muscles like these before. I grind against him again. God, I'm close. How am I already so close? I can feel how tight all the muscles in my stomach really are.

"I've sworn off sex," he reminds me—but he says it in a voice like he's dying. Like it's literally killing him not to be inside me right now.

"We don't need to have sex." My hips are rolling in a constant motion now. I'm riding his leg. I'm desperate.

"Can you actually—like this?"

"Yes," I breathe.

Alex rolls me over, so he's on top of me, his thigh still nestled firmly between mine. Gravity helps. I prop one leg up, and he grinds against me like we're teenagers. I can feel his hard-on pressing against my hip. It's so good, I whimper. His body, all six foot four of pure muscle is hovering over me, propped up on his forearms. I grip his biceps, run my hands over his abs, his pecs, squeeze his tight ass. Everything I've wanted to do for weeks. It's even better than my imagination.

My sight has adjusted to the dark, and I glance up to see his eyes boring into mine with an intensity I've never seen before. His brows are scrunched together, and he's enjoying every slice of pleasure that crosses my face. It's really his expression that does it, that pushes me over the edge. It's how turned on he is, how all of his concentration is on me. I place a hand on his cheek, cupping his chin in my hand. I pull him to me, and this kiss is light and searing and perfect. When we break apart, I can feel his breath on my cheek, but I can't tear my gaze away from the way he's staring at me like I'm a treasure.

"Oh fuck," I whisper. "Oh fuck, Alex, I'm gonna—" I break off in a moan as the orgasm overtakes me.

ALEX

Zoey's breaking apart on my thigh. On my freaking goddamn *thigh*. I'm watching her shatter underneath me, her body shaking, fingers digging into my skin. And the *noises* she's making. If I could only listen to one thing for the rest of my life, it would be Zoey's breathy moans and whimpers. I'd give up Linkin Park forever.

She deserves better. I *know* I can give her a better orgasm than this. I literally spent four years refining my skills and none of those methods involved my *thigh*.

"Hell, sweetheart, take your shirt off."

"Huh?" Her face is still filled with the aftereffects of her pleasure. I tug at the bottom of her shirt, pulling it up and over her skin. When she finally realizes what I'm doing, she yanks that shit off in a nanosecond.

Holy. Hell.

This women was blessed with perfect breasts. Absolutely freaking perfect.

"You sure?" Zoey asks, her voice heavy with need.

"God, yes." I dip forward, pressing a kiss to one breast, then the other. I slide one hand up her body, until I'm cupping the left one in my hand, feeling the smooth swell, the weight of it. "Goddamn."

"Thank you, I know."

I'm gonna come in my pants it's been so long. She wraps a hand around my neck, pulling me to her, sliding her tongue between my lips. I tweak her nipple and she lets out a moan that vibrates through our kiss.

One thing is clear to me now.

Zoey is *loud.*

And I'm loving every second of it, thanking the gods that Lucy is passed the hell out in a fever sleep tonight. There is no way we will ever be able to do this again while Lucy is home.

I tweak Zoey's nipple again. Once again, I'm swallowing her moan.

I tear myself away from her lips and then kiss my way down her neck, biting sensitive spots along the way. She's so responsive. I love it. When I suck her nipple into my mouth, she lets out a loud groan that makes me chuckle.

I continue to kiss my way down her stomach, feeling her muscles contract against my lips. The closer I get to her panties, the faster she pants. I trace the edge of her panties with my tongue, sliding it across her stomach, in the creases of her inner thighs. She reaches down to grab my hair and pull me away from her so she can glare at me. What the hell?

"Alex, I swear to God." Her face is flushed, and her breasts rise with each heavy breath she takes. "It's been months. This is not the fucking time to be a tease."

I laugh. Hard. This is what she's so upset about? That's an easy problem to fix.

I briefly wonder if I'm messing up by letting this happen. If I'm a failure for giving in. But really, isn't giving my woman a proper orgasm the responsible thing to do? Look at me, Responsible Freaking Alex.

I slide her panties off.

She guides me down with greedy hands in my hair. I don't mind. I'm just as greedy as her. I'm desperate for a taste of her. Without any more teasing, for fear of losing my hair, I trace my tongue through her folds, circling her clit.

I moan against her skin. "You taste good, baby," I tell her. "So damn good."

"Damn right I do," she mumbles, gripping my hair harder, dragging me back down. I chuckle against her, and her hips buck against my face. I capture her clit in my mouth, sucking and nibbling gently, until she moans out. "Lick me," she gasps. And I do. With soft strokes, until she's shaking violently underneath me, her legs practically vibrating in my hands. I appreciate her telling me what to do, but it doesn't exactly surprise me. I doubt that the one place Zoey would develop a filter would be during sex.

I glance up at her. Her head is tossed back in pleasure, and her breasts are on display for me, pointing up toward the ceiling. I've died and gone to heaven. That's the only explanation for how Zoey sounds so perfect and tastes so perfect and looks so perfect. I never want to leave this moment. Ever.

I know there might be repercussions tomorrow, that none of this is a good idea. But we can deal with that then. For now, I need this. I slow my licks, lighten the pressure, until she's squirming beneath me, asking for more.

"Alex." It starts out as a warning, but when I plunge two fingers into her halfway through my name, it ends on a pleasure-filled gasp.

"Holy hell, you're tight," I say, pumping in and out of her slowly, curling my fingers against the spot where she needs it most.

Zoey lets out in unintelligible response. She tries again, but then loses her train of thought once more. I reach my free hand up to play with a nipple. Her body is squeezing my fingers. She's getting close.

"And remind me who was making fun of my sexperience the other day?" I lay my head on her thigh, glancing up toward her. I slow the movements of my fingers until they're barely dragging in and out.

"No no no," she moans, trying to ride my fingers. "Alex, I swear to God, go show off your big-ass ego somewhere else."

"Just admit I know what I'm doing." I grin, pressing a kiss to the crease of her inner thigh on one side and then the other. Then I press a light kiss against her clit. "Admit I know what I'm doing, and I'll get you there."

"Please," she gasps. Holy hell. That's a sound that goes straight to my dick. Involuntarily I grind against the bed. She yanks on my hair, hard, dragging my head back to where she needs it. "Alex, please."

I can't resist that. I give her what she wants. I pump my fingers in and out of her. I lick her clit. I worship her body until her thighs are sweaty and shaking around me, her stomach is as tight as it can be, and her breath stills as she approaches the edge. I flick my tongue over her once, twice, three more times, and then she's falling. Her body is unraveling, pulling up off the bed as she arches her back. She muffles her moans with my pillow, but it still sounds beautiful.

After I've helped her through wave after wave of her orgasm, I ease away, wiping at my mouth, feeling pretty damn good about that.

That's the type of orgasm Zoey deserves.

I lie down next to her, and Zoey plasters her sweaty body against me. Apparently, she's a cuddler after sex. I don't mind it so much when it's her. Having her naked body pressed against mine as she goes through aftershocks isn't exactly a hardship. I wrap my arms around her, holding her tight.

"Holy fuck," she finally breathes out. "I can die happy now."

I chuckle. "That good?"

"I mean, not actually, universe. Please don't drop an elephant out of the sky and kill me. There's a lot I still want to do with my life. I need to research all the rocks and have about twenty million more orgasms just like that."

"You done?"

"Just making sure I didn't jinx anything. I'm not ready for death by a post-orgasm elephant."

"Is that a common occurrence in your life?"

"Alex, shush, some dude just gave me the best orgasm of my life, my brain no work."

"Some dude, huh?"

"I mean it couldn't have been you, because he had loads of sexperience."

"Zoey, I mean this in the nicest way, but you're the worst."

She bursts out laughing. She looks up at me, her face still plastered against my chest and I can't help but feel a little proud at that happy, relaxed look across her face. "You really shouldn't insult the girl who's about to give you a hand job. I know you don't have much experience with this, but it's a pretty standard rule."

"The girl who's about to do what?" I ask. Did she just say—oh hell, she did. Zoey gives my dick a squeeze over my underwear, rubbing her thumb up and down my shaft. She pulls my boxer briefs down, easing me out.

"Fucking hell, man," Zoey whispers, her eyes huge. I smirk at her. "Are you sure I can't ride Responsible Alex?"

I shiver. God, I would like nothing more. "Positive."

"You know you don't actually have to stick your penis in my vagina for this to qualify as sex. There's lots of other way to fuck."

"Shh, don't ruin it with logic for me, baby. I can pretend."

Zoey wraps her fingers around me, gripping hard, and then starts jacking me. After months of my own hand, Zoey's feels incredible, the sensation tingling all the way up my spine. Zoey knows what she's doing, and she's not shy about it either. Lots of girls grip too lightly, but her grip is firm, and steady, and so freaking hot.

"Goddammit, baby. This is going to be over way too quick." Every time she moves her hand up and down, her tits jostle. I'm mesmerized

"That's hot," she whispers into my ear. I reach out to grab her breasts in my hands, and then groan when she starts jacking me with two hands at once.

"It isn't."

"No, it is. The fact that it's me, making you lose control." She nips my earlobe. "It's. Fucking. Hot." She presses a kiss against my neck, her tongue flicking out, and damn if I don't feel it all over.

I growl, thrusting up into her hand. And I was right—I

don't last long at all. Within minutes I'm spurting all over my abs and her hand.

I'm still panting, my body heavy and tired and unresponsive while she finds the tissues and cleans us up. Then she snuggles in bed beside me. I wrap my arms around her and chuckle, kissing the top of her hair.

"If I had known what I was missing out on, I would have stopped being Responsible Alex at the start of the semester."

She tilts her head up to look at me. Her eyes are serious as she drags a soft hand over my chin. "You're still Responsible Alex," she says. I snort. "No, you are. You're doing everything right, you're careful not to do anything in front of Lucy. The alarm is already set. Let's both get dressed right now. That way if Lucy needs anything in the middle of the night, you're already prepared. See? Responsible." I'm about to cut her off, but she presses a soft kiss to my lips.

She has no clue how much those words mean to me. And the fact that she's waking up early for me to satisfy my stupid rules? I know how much Zoey hates mornings. Suddenly, there's too many feelings. I gently untangle myself from her and then pull on a clean pair of boxers. I toss her back her discarded shirt and panties. She makes a face as she catches them.

"What?" I ask.

"Can I borrow underwear? Mine are all wet for some reason."

"Of course. Best friends privileges, right?"

"Which part, the underwear or the orgasms?" I don't respond, just wink at her and toss her the underwear. Honestly, this was good. This was really good. I'm just not sure I can let it happen again.

We crawl into bed together again, and she snuggles up

against me, and I hold her tight. If this one night is all I have, I'm going to make the most out of it. I let my hand drift up and down her back, and it isn't long until she melts into me and falls asleep, using my chest as a pillow.

I can't sleep though. I don't even feel remotely tired. I stare up at the ceiling, wondering how the hell I got here, to this point.

At the beginning of this situation I promised my parents and myself that I wouldn't bring random girls home to hook up with them and expose Lucy to that type of behavior. She's too young. It's the main philosophy of Responsible Alex. No sex.

In my defense, though, when I first started bringing Zoey over, I never thought I was going to hook up with her. And if I only hook up with her and no one else, does that make her a random girl? What are the rules on that?

And does Zoey even want to continue this? We started this whole thing because she was madly in love with another guy. That's the cold hard truth that I don't want to think about. Isn't that the whole reason that we've gotten this close? The whole reason we even kissed in the first place? She's pining after a different guy.

Is it inappropriate to be competing with my student for a girl? And fudge—competing? It's not a competition and Zoey's not a prize. She will make the decision that's best for her.

But I don't miss the jealous looks Z shoots her way. It's happened since the beginning, and when I kissed her? That prick couldn't stop the yearning look he gave her. Plus, he's giving me attitude in class. I'm tempted to be spiteful and mark him down a whole letter grade for the shit he put Zoey through. I know she can't see it, because otherwise she wouldn't have fake dated me in the first place, but she deserves way more than his sorry ass. No guy with Zoey should ever even *think* about another girl.

Hell, my mind is constantly centered on Zoey. I don't know what that means, or what the hell I'm going to do about it. I'm not even sure *I* can be the guy she deserves.

TWENTY-EIGHT

ZOEY

Alex didn't even fuck me and I still feel like I can't walk two days later. That's how good that orgasm was.

Tour Guide Fun Fact #5: It's exactly three miles around this whole campus. We cover two of those miles on tour.

I do the whole thing on autopilot, on shaky legs and with Alex's name inked into my brain. It's not only his name—it's his body, the feel of his tongue against me, the way he felt in my hand. It's all I can think about.

If there was any residual part of me that still had feelings for Z, it's effectively dead. Alex destroyed it.

I want to get back in his bed again. It's not fair to only get to feel heaven once and then never again. And what's really not fair is the fact that the semester I met him is the one, *one* time in his life he's supposed to be celibate.

I feel a little guilty that I let things get as far as they did. He didn't exactly try to stop me though. In fact, I think he loved every second of it as much as I did.

I just hope he doesn't regret it.

ALEX

"Why are we doing this?" I groan.

"Wow, never would have guessed Alex Adams was a whiny baby," Eddie says.

"Blasphemy," West says. "Wipe that shit from your mouth. Alex Adams is, and always will be, a god."

"You only say that 'cause you couldn't score on him," Eddie says with a shrug. "But you wanna know who stopped his shots?"

Both West and I flip him off. "I'm pretty sure I remember scoring a couple on you."

"Pretty sure you shot way more than a couple."

"Who knew hikes made Eddie get so cocky?" West laughs.

"And made Alex get so whiny." Eddie gives me the side-eye, a smirk on his face. I know he's totally joking with me, but I am being kind of whiny. I take a deep breath and try to state my concern, without the whine.

"We should be practicing right now."

"We are. We're hiking. Hiking is fitness," West explains.

"Not this hike. This is paved." I gesture to the asphalt, slightly uphill road we're taking up the mountain.

"Look, man." Eddie gestures back to the rest of the team behind us. They're jostling around, knocking into each other. A group of them are in a loud and passionate argument about a kids' TV show. "The club team is a different vibe. Sometimes we have team bonding days instead of practice. It's not the end of the world."

I grumble. After skipping practice earlier this week and having a stupid hike instead of practice today, I'm going through withdrawals. There were times, back at Heyward, when we'd have three-a-days, every day of the week. A gym session, a field session, and a reviewing tapes session. I lived for those weeks. Cutting down to only twice a week, and a fat total of none this week, has made me antsy. My touches are starting to get sloppier than I'd like and I was hoping to buckle down on that during today's practice.

"Last year Eddie and I *might* have pushed them too far."

"Might have?" Eddie asks sarcastically.

"It was bad," West admits. "Fitness was great but team morale was low."

"We learned," Eddie says.

"How'd y'all wind up with the coaching gig anyway?"

"It's a volunteer position." Holy hell, they're volunteers? I should probably tone down my whining. "They had a long string of shitty coaches before us is what I heard. So they asked if anyone on the D1 team wanted to coach."

"And all of the sane guys said no." West grins. "But my bitty baby second year over here was willing to volunteer with me."

Eddie smacks him in the arm. "It was more of an 'if I'm not playing soccer, I want to be coaching it' thing, you know? It's good experience to have for the future."

"Obviously we can't be there all the time," West says. "A lot of times we're away for our own games. We figured having someone decent that was there most of the time was better than having someone coach who had never played soccer before. But we just email Matty a lesson plan, and we *hear* that he runs practice."

Matty, our team captain, hears his name and jogs up next to us, wrapping his arms around Eddie's and my necks and hanging off us. "'Sup, coaches." I wouldn't have pegged him as one of the best players on our team, but he *is* one of the most dedicated and he tries to boost everyone up around him. He's a good choice for captain.

"Adams isn't a coach," West says. Then he waggles his eyebrows at me. "Although, if you want to be one, I am graduating this year. Eddie's gonna need an assistant coach next year."

"I'm not so sure how great of a coach I would be."

"You'd be awesome," Matty says. "You already give us great advice from the field. You'd just do that from the sideline instead."

See what I mean? Always boosting people up. But my issue is with that tiny stupid word *sideline*. I hate it. Even when I was little I couldn't stand being pulled out of a game to sit on the bench. I wanted to be on the field. I wanted the ball. I *still* want it.

But the sad truth is, coaching might be my only option anymore. Hell. I hadn't thought of that before. I run my hands through my hair, trying not to let my disappointment show all over my face.

"Aren't you a TA already, man?" Eddie asks. "If you can do that, you can coach."

I snort. "Not quite sure my TA skills are up to standard."

"What drills do you think we should be doing based on how we're playing?" West tries a different tack and the four of us fall into soccer speak, naming drills and analyzing plays and discussing how we've been doing in our games recently. Soccer speak is easy. It's good. I don't have to think about my future or anything going on with Zoey.

Because lately? The only thing my mind has been on is Zoey. I can't stop thinking of her face when she comes or her voice when she's whimpering my name or the way her hand felt wrapped around my cock.

And I'm pissed at myself for letting it happen. We haven't hooked up since, but seriously, what was wrong with me if I couldn't even complete a *one-semester vow of celibacy*? That's not even that long.

We make it to the top of the mountain in no time because, like I said, it's a freaking walk, not a hike. But the view from the top is gorgeous. Zoey would love it. I take a seat on a rock at the edge of the mountain, looking over at the lights of the city.

"So why do you look extra stressed?" Eddie asks, coming to sit next to me on the boulder.

"Yeah, I've been wanting to ask you that all night but I didn't want to be rude," West says, giving Eddie a pointed look. Eddie shrugs.

"It's nothing."

"Class trouble?" West guesses.

"TA trouble?"

"Sister trouble?"

"Parent trouble?"

"Girl trouble?"

"Holy hell, I've told you guys way too much about my life," I groan.

West nods. "I know that groan. It's girl trouble."

I raise an eyebrow at him. "That's creepy."

He shrugs. "Daniel said you're always making out with some blonde after class."

"Christ, why does that even come up in your conversations?"

"Apparently she has great tits."

I screw up my face. They are freaking spectacular. And, honestly, I don't think Zoey would be all that upset that the guys are talking about how great her breasts are. She owns her body. But still. I don't want the whole team talking about them.

I end up dumping the whole story on West and Eddie, complete with my vow of celibacy, fake dating, and then practically breaking that vow early. We're walking back down the mountain and it's fully dark by the time I'm done explaining my situation.

"I say screw your vow, take the sex and run. Just don't do it around Lucy." West offers in advice.

Eddie's more thoughtful. The only sound is our footsteps against the path. "Do you like her?" he asks.

I nod. I'm not lying when I call Zoey my best friend. We can talk for hours about nothing and still not be bored around each other.

"What if she was your girlfriend? Like West says, just don't fool around when Lucy's home. But would you feel as bad about breaking your vow if you were in a serious relationship?"

I almost trip over a piece of gravel. Girlfriend? I wouldn't know the first thing about having a girlfriend. I don't think I'm ready for that step, at all.

What would it even be like having Zoey as my girlfriend? It'd be time-consuming, right?

But then again, maybe not. Zoey and I spend all of our free time together anyway. And when we were in a fake relationship, that wasn't a huge suck of time.

And even though we're not in a relationship they have a

point that Zoey is the only one I'm bringing home. Showing Lucy a committed relationship is healthy. I mean, that's what my parents do, isn't it?

I don't know anything anymore. Life was easier as Athlete Alex.

I wave away Eddie's logic. "She doesn't even like me. She likes the other guy."

"'Cause girls spend the night with guys they don't like all the time," West says with an eye roll.

"We're friends."

"Who have sex."

"I mean *technically* we haven't. Yet."

West hoots. "Just don't do it when Lucy is home and I think you'll be fine. Honestly, Adams, a vow of celibacy was stupid."

"It's not stupid," Eddie argues. "He's just trying to do the right thing."

"If he doesn't get laid soon, though, he might become permanently this grumpy."

I let them bicker. I still don't know what to tell Zoey. If we should pump the brakes or not. I don't even know what she wants to do.

I guess that should have been my first step. Talking to Zoey instead of these idiots.

Behind us, the team grows louder, yelling into the night. West sighs beside me. "I haven't yelled at those fuckers in a bit, huh? They're getting too used to their freedom." He flips around to walk backward and shouts to the team. "Eddie and I have some away games next week. If I even hear a snippet of a rumor that you lot aren't practicing or listening to Matty I will triple your suicide sprints. Understand?" The team grumbles. West turns back to us.

"A snippet of a rumor?" I smirk.

"Shut up. I'm a great spokesperson. I inspire fear."

"Sure you do."

"We've all seen your victory dance, West," Eddie says. "You inspire fear in no one."

"I haven't seen your victory dance." I grin. "Must be because you never scored on me."

"Oh fuck off."

TWENTY-NINE

ZOEY

I stretch my arms above my body, gripping my hands together as I shift in my seat. I'm in the one lonely chair in the geology hallway, staring at the gray door in front of me. I've been here for twenty minutes, and usually with downtime in the geology building I'll check out the rock and fossil collections that line the walls. But not today.

What are your strengths and weaknesses? What is your experience and how does it prepare you for this position? Why do you want this position?

I run through every possible question I can think of in my head, rehearsing my answers till the last minute. I think I've studied harder for this than I've ever studied for a final in my life—and that's saying something. Tessa mock interviewed me last night, Alex the day before.

I take a deep breath, letting the air fill my nostrils, running down the back of my throat. The hallway even smells like rocks. It's calming.

I thought I'd feel more jittery, more nervous. But I don't.

I feel ready to destroy this thing.

The door to Professor Heath's office opens and I stand, brushing off my dress pants. Eileen walks out into the hallway, closing the door behind her.

"He'll just need a few more minutes," she says.

"How'd it go?" I ask, even though I can tell by her smile.

"Fantastic. I think I really have a shot." She winks at me. "All thanks to you, of course."

I nod. I swear to God, universe, if you give Eileen this job instead of me, I will sic Tessa on you for the rest of existence.

Eileen looks down the hallway and then bites her lip, looking likes she wants to tell me something she shouldn't.

"What is it?" Does she know something about the position I don't? Will she tell me what questions he asked in there? She wouldn't be that selfless, would she?

"I just—never mind, I don't know if I should tell you."

"Tell me what?"

"It's nothing. I just—I overheard Z talking about you the other day."

Oh. Well, that was anticlimactic. I lean backward in disappointment, not really caring, but Eileen's face is telling me this is important, so I ask anyway. "What did he say?"

"Well, I was with Derek and Naomi, and Naomi wanted to say hi." Eileen offers a sympathetic shrug. "He was our friend too, you know?"

"Of course." That's bullshit, but who am I to deny them the power of his magical friendship?

"And he and his friends were talking about their shittiest sex experiences, and you know Naomi just had to jump in on that." I laugh, despite myself. I'm honestly not sure how Naomi manages to get herself into these situations.

I feel a little pang for my friends. I spent the last three years listening to stories of Naomi's wild adventures and gossip, Derek's shitty home life, Eileen's laid-back drawl.

But I also got torn down by them for three years straight. I don't regret for a second what Tessa and I did. Besides, Tessa's found her new group. Alex brought us to meet up with some of the soccer guys at the library. Most of them were freshmen, and Tessa spent half the time freaking out because Jonah West was actually talking to her, but she found her group. She, Brandon and Kacen have been practically inseparable lately.

And I've got Alex.

Then Eileen says something that causes my thoughts to stop in their tracks.

"Z said *what*?"

"That you were his shittiest sex experience." Eileen pouts like she feels bad for me, but I also notice she didn't have a problem repeating this information to me.

What the actual fuck. "Are you sure?" I ask. I'm taking a leaf out of Alex's book and trying to be Responsible Zoey right now. I can't drop the F-bomb right outside of Professor Heath's door. But honestly, that's such *bullshit*.

Eileen shakes her head. "I don't know, he was talking about how you just didn't really do it for him. That it was overall mediocre."

"Didn't *do* it for him?" I ask. "*Mediocre*? I—"

"Trust me, none of us believe him," Eileen cuts me off. "I wasn't really sure if I should tell you or not, but he's spreading this shit to all his friends. Just so you know."

Not that great, my ass. I'm fantastic. Honestly, he was coming in minutes every time. I know he didn't fake that he was into me—so why the hell was he saying this stuff?

And *now* he's okay with telling his friends about us?

The door to Professor Heath's office opens. "Ah, Zoey," he says smiling brightly, like we're two old friends instead of a professor and student. "Come on in."

I take a deep breath, trying to calm my rage and get refocused.

"Good luck on your interview, Zoey," Eileen says, her voice full of sugary sweetness. She disappears down the hall of the geology building.

I follow Professor Heath into his office, sitting in the chair opposite of his desk.

Did Z really think I was bad at sex? Is that why he kept choosing other girls? Our whole relationship was *just* sex. Why the hell would he keep coming back to me if he didn't like it?

Oh god. Was I just his fluffer? And worse, was I *bad* at being his fluffer?

"Zoey?" Professor Heath asks gently. Oh fuck me, now I'm zoning out during the most important interview of my life.

"Sorry, could you repeat that? I'm just a little nervous." I plaster on a smile.

"No worries. I wanted to let you know I'm thrilled you're interested in this position. You've always been one of my top students in my classes."

My heart swells with pride. "And your classes have always been my favorites," I say, honestly. "Last year's class on volcanism is the whole reason I went to Italy this past summer."

"Yes, I saw that on your resume. Do you want to start there and tell me about your research project on that trip?"

Once I start talking about my research experience, everything else floats away. I know these topics. I'm excited about these topics. The whole Z drama pales in comparison.

Professor Heath seems genuinely interested and impressed with the work I've done, and he doesn't ask me cheesy questions like "what are your top three strengths," which I appreciate.

There's only one question that throws me. "What did you think about my lecture on magma chambers? I'm applying for a grant to start another research project in that area. I know granitic plutons in this area has been fairly well researched, but I think there's an opportunity to explore further with applications to eruption predictions. You remember how and why granite forms beneath volcanos, right?"

My heart beats in my chest, so hard and fast I can hear my pulse racing through my body, drowning out the air conditioning and Professor's Heath's papers shuffling around.

That's the lecture I missed. The one Eileen gave me notes for. I can practically see her notes in my head, highlighted in pink pen, arrows drawn to the answer to this question. I open my mouth to respond...but something about what she wrote seems off. I think she's wrong.

My internship in Italy this summer briefly touched on this. There's a couple volcanoes there—but they don't have the granite formations like we have in Northern California, so it was only mentioned once for comparison purposes.

I debate. Eileen's notes were clear. My memories are fuzzy, but I think... "Granite forms beneath the volcano due to silica rich magma that gets trapped underneath the Earth's surface because of loss in buoyancy. The slow rate of cooling gives granite it's coarse grain texture. If the magma were to travel to the surface of the volcano, it would then become an extrusive rock known as rhyolite."

"Exactly, Zoey," Professor Heath says, tapping a finger

to his nose, a gesture that makes him seem older than he actually is. He quickly falls into a lecture about his theory, and I nod along, willing the adrenaline in my system to calm down. "Sorry, I've been rambling." He chuckles to himself. "Do you have any last questions for me?"

Of course I do. I prepared them beforehand.

At the end of the interview, he shakes my hand, and I'm all smiles. He tells me he will follow up to let me know either way.

I step out of the room and the door closes behind me. I sigh in relief. I think that went well. Really well. Except for my mess up in the beginning, and my brief hesitation over that last question, I feel good.

But then I realize what just happened.

The two times I messed up were because of Eileen.

Eileen tried to sabotage me.

Straight-up fucking sabotage me.

She tried to throw me off with all that bullshit about Z before the start of the interview and she gave me fake notes. When I've been giving her notes—goddamn good notes—for *years*.

I'm sick of letting people walk all over me. I should have confronted Z the *first* time he chose another girl over me and then came crawling back, and I definitely should have confronted him the third time. I should have ditched my ex-friends years ago, like Tessa said, but I just kept putting up with every shitty thing they said to me.

I thought I was blowing things out of proportion, being too emotional, that it wasn't my place to confront them with how I was feeling. But now? My strides are long, powerful, and merciless as I stalk out of the building.

Eileen and I are going to have a fucking conversation.

THIRTY

ZOEY

I find Eileen at work.

She exits the tour office, where I'm waiting for her, arms crossed, practically steaming. Her face registers her surprise at seeing me—I'm not working today—and then quickly she rearranges her features to an aloofness that I want to slap off her face.

"Wanted to get some extra hours?" she asks, moving to walk by me.

My muscles tense. I can't believe she's just going to blow this off, act like nothing happened. "Why'd you try to sabotage me?" I demand.

Eileen shakes her head as if confused and then walks around me. I turn around, spreading my arms wide. She glances back at me. "Get off your high horse, Zoey. I have to go scout for a group, I don't have time for a conversation."

I seethe. She walks away from me again, and I curl my hands into fists. I know as well as she does that scouting for a group does mean she has time. School groups are never here on time, so all she's going to do for the next thirty minutes is wait on a bench.

I walk to catch up to her. "Fuck this," I whisper vehemently. "You've missed so many lectures in the past four years you probably have more notes from me than your own notes. I recommended you to my boss to get you this job. I've—"

"Dropped our entire friendship like it doesn't matter?" Eileen spins to me, placing her hands on her hips. "I've seen you for three seconds this quarter. Today is the most we've talked in weeks. Normally we'd be six pans deep in slutty brownies right now."

"You sabotaged me because I was being a bad friend?" There's *so* many times I could have done the same thing to her if that's the requirement for sabotaging someone. "This is my career."

"And your career matters more than my life?" Eileen questions, walking toward the bench again. Then she gives me a haughty little noise and an eye roll. "You know, I thought because you and Z had finally split, you'd finally have time to focus on something besides yourself. But no, it's always 'Zoey this and Zoey that.' You turn your life into a soap opera, and suck us all into your drama, and there's never a moment for anyone besides you."

"What the hell are you talking about?" Do I really do that? I try to think back to our past conversations, and I have to admit... most of them are about me and what's going on in my life. But, if I were a terrible friend, wouldn't Tessa have said something?

Eileen takes on a mocking voice "'I love this boy, but he only wants to sleep with me,' let's all take the next two months of our lives figuring out what Zoey should do. 'This boy broke up with me,' now let's all take the next month of our lives to feel bad for Zoey. 'Work was horrendous today, let me tell you the terrible story of what happened.'" Eileen levels me with a look. "We have the same job, Zoey. It's not that bad."

"I never said it was that bad—" I start, but Eileen barely lets me get those words in.

"I'm just tired of everyone being a terrible friend. I just wanted something for myself for once. It's like you have Tessa, and Naomi and Derek have each other, and then there's poor Eileen, always being forgotten and having no one." She shakes her head as we arrive at the bench, and then she plops down into it. Then she smirks up at me. "I just wanted to see your face when I got the position instead of you. Finally someone will take the great Zoey down."

I hate that she was lonely. I do. If I had known, I would have tried to fix things. But why didn't she come to talk to me sooner? Why didn't she have this conversation three months ago?

Instead of being an adult, she gave me fake notes. She tried to distract me before my interview. She went after a job just because she knew I wanted it.

"So you sabotaged me?" I yell, standing in front of her. "Do you know how messed up that is to straight-up sabotage someone?"

"I didn't *plan* on sabotaging you."

"Bullshit."

"I was just going to tell you about going for the job, and maybe you'd notice me again. But nope. You couldn't bring your head out of your ass for one second—"

"I told you I supported you!"

"And you kept on ignoring me after that. Then you missed class that one day. I could have done worse than give you fake notes," Eileen says. "Did Professor Heath ask you about granite? I told him you were really into the subject."

I can't believe this. One part of me wants to let her know that I suspected her notes were fake and she didn't get away with her stupid plan. But I don't want her to escalate to anything worse. "Why couldn't you just talk to me, like a normal fucking human?"

"Word is you're playing games just as much as I am." Eileen shrugs. "Naomi says you're dating Z's TA. Does the poor man know you're using him to get back at Z?"

"I'm not using him," I growl, because, first off, Alex and I had an agreement, it was mutually beneficial. And second, we effectively killed our decision to be just friends last time I was in his bed. And honestly? I'm kind of okay with that.

I just need to figure out if he is.

"And how does me dating someone become the equivalent of ruining my job interview?" I ask Eileen.

"There's other jobs," she says with a flippant wave of her hand.

"Not. Like. This." Besides all the backstabbing, this is the real reason Eileen doesn't deserve this job. She doesn't understand how big of an opportunity it is. She doesn't even *want* to do the work.

The school buses pull up to the curb in front of us. Eileen stands up from the bench and adjusts her microphone over her head, dusting off her jeans like literally nothing just happened. I was supposed to tear her apart for this and she's acting like she was the victim.

"What you did is absolutely unacceptable. And so fucked up. Trying to mess with my head before the interview, giving me fake notes. I gave you—"

"Real notes for years, blah blah." Eileen cuts in, looking bored. "Get to the part where you de-friend me for life."

I silently glare at her. I'm not going to give her the satisfaction of—

"'Cause here's the thing, Zoey. You're a shitty friend. I don't want to be your friend for life anymore."

The students are piling off the school bus, and we only have a few more seconds before she'll have to go over there to talk to them. I open my mouth to try to get the last word in, but once again Eileen beats me to it. "By the way? It wasn't all lies. I really heard Z complain about your sex life. I guess you haven't earned all the confidence you have." She flounces away from me, literally flounces, and turns her microphone headset on. "Welcome everyone to Olympia University!" she announces, approaching the group of students.

I stand there, watching her, before shaking my head and walking away.

Am I really that bad of a friend? Do I always make everything about myself?

It's true I don't know anything going on in Eileen's life right now. But I know about Tessa's life. I know she wants to add on a last-minute double major in mythology. I know she has to stay an extra year to do so, and when she told her parents they exploded about the money. It's the biggest fight they've ever been in. I held her while she vented.

And she's never once told me stop talking about myself. She always wants to hear my stories. I'm sure she'd be her usual dramatic self and tell me to shut up if she really needed to.

But maybe I should have been a better friend to Eileen.

And did Z really say those things? Was I terrible at sex?

Alex didn't complain last time I spent the night, but all

he really got was a hand job. And now that I'm thinking about it, Alex hasn't had sex in months. Even if I was absolutely terrible, he would have finished.

Dammit. Maybe I'm terrible at sex. Which would really suck because Alex was really good, *like really good*. Like still made my toes want to curl three days later good.

I'm stalking across campus, the rage still racing through my veins. My body is on autopilot. I'm not even sure where I'm going until I reach my car. And then it's clear what I need.

Alex.

"How'd the interview go?" Alex grins as soon as he answers the door. His hair is wet, like he just got out of the shower, and it's dripping down, leaving fat dark drops on his blue shirt. The fact that he looks so good that I want to jump into his arms pisses me off. I don't like feeling out of control.

"Like fucking motherfucking shit," I growl angrily.

Alex's eyebrows shoot up. "You know what?" Alex says, inching out the door to come meet me on the porch. "I'm just going to close this." He pulls the front door closed, sealing us both outside and away from Lucy's prying ears. "Now rant away."

"It wasn't even the interview," I groan, pulling on my hair as I pace in a circle, trying to figure out how to even start explaining the day. "It was Eileen, it was Z, it was my inability to just—fuck." I let out a few more curse words, yelling them toward the sky.

"Zoey?" Alex sounds concerned. "You okay?"

"Do I seem okay?"

"Not really. No. You're kind of acting like the creepy person you don't want to sit next to on the bus."

I glare at him. "I'm going through something."

"Obviously," he says with his stupid fucking smirk. I shove him lightly, and he laughs, and then wraps his arms around me, dragging me against his body.

"Today sucked," I moan, my head falls forward, banging into his chest. I fold my arms tight around his middle and let his warmth take over. Being surrounded in his strong arms, his scent—it rights me.

"What happened?" he asks. He says it into my hair, and that's kind of nice.

"It turns out that Eileen was trying to sabotage my internship position." I pause. "Oh, and that Z is a total ass."

"I believe it."

"Are you allowed to say that about your students?"

"When they're jerkholes, yeah."

I snort. I've barely even talked with Alex but I already feel so much better. "Apparently he's told people that sex with me was awful." I pull myself out of Alex's arms and throw my hands in the air. "Who goes around telling people that?"

"A jerkhole."

"But what if this whole time I was the one without sexperience?" I groan, my voice laced with horror. Alex's serious eyes are suddenly alive with humor, and one side of his lips quirks up.

"I'm sure you're not awful at sex, Zo."

"Easy for you to say, you haven't fucked me." It comes out more bitter than I intended it to. Like biting into a piece of chocolate that you expected to be milk but is actually like eighty percent cacao. Alex laughs, but it sounds pained.

"It's not because I don't want to. Trust me."

"Then fuck me," I say.

Alex raises an eyebrow at me. I tilt my chin up at him,

challenging him. We're less than a foot away from each other, meaning I have to tilt my head up just to meet his eyes anyway. His jaw is tight, clenched, but I don't miss the heat in his gaze.

I just admitted, straight to his face, that I want him. I know I shouldn't be pushing him into this, and if he says no I'll walk away. But I'm desperate.

Finally, after what feels like years of this silent standoff, Alex speaks. "If Z was available right now, would you still choose me?"

"What?" I ask, thrown off by the question. I expected him to be worried about his celibacy rules or Responsible Alex responsibilities, not Z.

"The only reason any of this started is because you were head over heels for him. Hell, even now you're here because of him."

"That's not true," I say. But it is *kind* of true. I did rush over here partly because of the things Z said. But not because I'm attracted to Z anymore. Between Z and Alex, there's no contest.

"You still care about what he thinks," Alex says. "That's why you want to have sex with me, just to prove Z wrong. What're you going to do afterward? Rub it in his face that you're not a starfish and then beg him to take you back?"

"Don't put words in my mouth, Alex. It's not about proving Z wrong." I cross my arms over my chest. "I just need to know I didn't imagine that I was good at it."

"Christ, you already know you didn't imagine it." Alex says. He reaches out and grabs my upper arms, pulling me flush against his body. My stomach drops likes it's on a roller coaster. He growls in my ear, "I came harder than I ever have in my life, just from your hand job. Hell—"

He spins both of us around until his body is pressing me into the door. I uncross my arms, relenting to the feeling of having Alex against me, and instead glide my hands up his chest. He slides his hands up my legs, until they come right under my butt, and then he picks me up. I eagerly wrap my legs around his waist, my arms circling his neck. His hard-on presses against me, demanding and insisting and fucking huge. His nose drags against my cheek until he can whisper in my ear.

"Do you feel how hard I am just remembering last time we were in a bed together? Trust me, you know what you're doing. And I *know* you know that you know what you're doing. So what do you really want?"

"You."

Alex groans. "What am I supposed to do with you, Zo?"

"Fuc—"

"Don't say it." He sighs. One of his hands slides up my body to grip my hair. "Christ, do you know I don't go a day anymore without jacking myself to the thought of how it would feel to be inside you?"

Holy. Shit.

Does he really? That's an image that'll be burned into my brain forever. Alex, shirtless, tattooed, one hand gripping himself, my name on his lips. He wants this and I want this, so why is it so goddamn difficult to make it happen?

"I want you." My voice is quiet and raspy when I speak, so I take a shaky breath and try again. "If Z was available right now, I'd choose you. It's not even a contest."

I can't see Alex's expression, but I can hear his shaky breath in my ears. That statement affects him more than I thought it would. But when he speaks, it still sounds like he doesn't believe me. "Really? After months of this you're just suddenly through with him?" He also sounds like he doesn't want to get his hopes up.

"Fuck Z," I say. "Honestly, fuck him. Here." I tap his arms. "Set me down." He does, and I untangle myself from him before going to sit on the edge of the porch. Alex comes to sit beside me.

The sky around us has started to turn golden as the afternoon slides into evening. There's a soft breeze, but not enough to cause me to shiver. I dangle my legs off the edge of the porch, observing the empty street, breathing in the crisp fall air, trying to figure out how to tell Alex how much he means to me.

He's right. Things between us started because of Z. But it wasn't months of just thinking about Z though. Somewhere along the way I stopped thinking about him entirely, and his name popping through my head stopped mattering.

And then, Alex's did.

His name started to mean something, make my heart pound a little faster. I'm not as obsessed with Alex as I was over Z. I'm not as hormone-crazy, heart-poundingly nervous around Alex, and I don't feel the need to constantly be trying to make him happy just so he'll choose me.

I'm completely myself with him. It's like hanging out with Tessa—casual, comfortable, fun—except for the fact that most of the time I'm with Alex I'm turned on. He's just so fucking hot. Honestly, ask me on any given day what I want to be doing, and the answer would probably be hanging out with Alex. He just gets me.

And when you compare them like that, there really is no contest.

It's kind of a scary thought, though, going straight from one guy to the next. It's not exactly the woman I imagined being.

"Look," I start, glancing over at him. His lips are pressed into a thin, straight line instead of the normal smirk he has, and he's glancing at the ground in front of him. "I'm over him. Truly. I liked him and he didn't like me back, and he handled it poorly. Then I handled his rejection poorly. And *maybe* might have taken it too far."

Alex snorts. There's that smirk I was missing. I bite my lip, not really sure if I should say this last part or not, but when his eyes land on me, I gain confidence.

"Being with you is like when you get to the top of the mountain, looking down at the view below. That moment when you're totally at peace with the world? I never felt that way with him." I can feel myself blushing as I say this, but Alex doesn't look uncomfortable. "There's no one else I'd rather prove my sexperience to."

Alex's eyes crinkle. "Immediately ruined the whole mature thing. Sexperience isn't a real word." He can't keep the smile off his face though.

I roll my eyes.

He runs his hand through his hair. He's thinking.

And I just put myself out on a freaking limb here. The least he can do is hurry up and make a decision about whether he wants inside me or not.

Finally, he gives me a side-eye. "You know, reviews would mean more coming from me."

"Why's that?"

"I'm a much better lay."

My heart pounds. "That wasn't a no?"

Alex shrugs. "This is a problem that needs to be solved. The responsible thing to do is to help my friend in need."

I laugh. Then scoot closer to him, so all along our thighs are touching. "I'm very much in need."

He dips his head to whisper in my ear. "Well then, I would very much like to help you."

Fuck. Yes.

Me. Alex. And a bed. Or a wall. Or a couch or a chair or a car or any space, really. Shit, even here would work.

"So... now?" I ask. Alex bursts out laughing.

"No, you crazy. Lucy is home. Get out of here."

"Why can't I hang out?"

"'Cause if you stay, I'll end up dragging you back to my bedroom."

"So... now?" I repeat. He presses a soft kiss to the side of my neck, and I tilt my head so he can have all the access he fucking wants.

"I'm still Responsible Alex, Zo."

"There's a perfectly good door right here."

He chuckles, his lips dragging against the skin on my neck. "You're perfect. But no." He doesn't make a move to push me away though. His lips continue across my neck, pressing soft kisses against my skin. When he bites, I squirm. He soothes the spot with his tongue and I moan. And then I hear another noise. A grumble.

Both Alex and I look toward the sidewalk.

"Hi Mrs. Parkons," Alex says with a wave, completely unperturbed that he just got caught performing some intense PDA. The older lady is walking a dog that looks way too big for her to control, but the dog just stares up at us, wagging its tail. She grumbles something again, and I think I hear the word "youths." I try my best to smother my laugh. She walks away.

"Are you sure you're okay with this?" I ask Alex. "I don't want to make you break your rule."

"I've thought about this a lot since the last time you were here," he says seriously. I get that it's a big deal for him. His brown eyes smolder into mine and I practically melt just from his gaze. "But yeah. I'm okay with this." He grins at me, and it seems dirty as hell the way he does it. "As long as we don't do it when Lucy is home." He gives me a pointed look.

I hop off the porch, my hands in the air. "Okay, I'm leaving, I'm leaving." I walk backward toward my car, so I'm still facing him. "But when should I come back?"

"Lucy is going to a sleepover this Friday," Alex says.

"Friday is far away," I whine.

"And I promised West I'd go to his party that night."

"Is it a soccer party?" I ask. Alex nods. "Can you get Tessa in?"

He nods. "I was going to ask you two anyway."

"So then after the party we..." I waggle my eyebrows at him, because Mrs. Parkons looks like she might still be in hearing range. Alex chuckles.

"Oh yeah. Expect a whole night of hot, sweaty, eyebrow waggling."

I've reached my car now, but I make no move to unlock the door. Alex and I are still grinning at each other, the sexual tension between us still intense even several feet away from each other.

"So, want me to be Unresponsible Zoey for a second?" I call out to him, glancing at Mrs. Parkons' retreating back.

"Aren't you always?"

"Dick."

"See, this is what I mean. All the swear words, all the—"

I reach for the hem of my sweater and yank up, flashing him my tits. I don't know why I do it. I'm happy and excited and want to tease him.

Alex stops talking completely.

He kind of looks like he just got punched in the face he's so stunned.

"Holy fuck," he whispers.

I throw my head back and laugh, letting my shirt drop.

"Atta boy, Adams."

THIRTY-ONE

ALEX

Zoey and Tessa are standing in the parking lot. Zoey clutches Tessa, who is almost toppling over laughing. They're both in jeans and skimpy crop tops and Zoey has her hair in two braids and it's honestly super hot.

She could be dressed up in a dinosaur costume right now and I'd still find her ridiculously attractive.

"Get in the car, it's freezing," I call out the window. Zoey slides into the front seat and Tessa crawls into the back, buckling herself into the middle.

"Ah, it's okay," Tessa says with a hand wave. "We're going to drink our way to warmth."

Zoey laughs. "Damn right we are."

I shake my head but make eye contact with Zoey. Her eyes are filled with mirth and heat and—is it terrible that I want to ditch this party and take her home right now? Our gazes burn with the knowledge of what we're going to do after, and then I let my gaze rake over her.

Her light skin has started to turn red from standing in

the cold, and her breasts are practically bursting out of that top, and they rise and fall with each breath she takes. Her nipples are standing at attention and I don't know if that's because she's cold or because my gaze is on her but I desperately want to get my mouth on them.

"Y'all are making me feel lonely back here. Stop eye-fucking each other," Tessa whines from the back.

I drag my gaze away from Zoey and focus on the road, pulling out of the parking lot. "Have you two already been drinking?" I ask.

"I don't know what you're talking about," Zoey says innocently. I see right through that. "Although I do appreciate having a designated driver." She pats my jean-covered thigh as she says it, and even though her hand feels like an ice cube, heat spreads through my leg.

"I can't believe you got us an invite to the soccer team parties," Tessa babbles from the back. "I've literally been trying to break into one for years, haven't I, Zoey?"

"I have climbed a fence with her, yes."

Insane. Together they're insane.

"And all the guys are so beautiful. If you and Zoey weren't going to bang tonight there'd be no shortage of guys she could rebound with."

I cut Zoey an amused look.

She shrugs with a smirk. "I told you. Tessa and I are a package deal. I tell her everything."

When we get to the party the windows are open, blasting out music, and even though it's a residential neighborhood, almost all of the houses belong to college students. I'd like to see someone try to shut down an Olympia soccer party with a noise complaint.

This house is home to several upperclassmen on the team, including West and Eddie. It's been a soccer house since forever. I used to crash some of these parties when I was in high school and it feels almost nostalgic approaching it.

We walk over a half-alive, half-dead lawn and toward the five concrete steps that lead up to the house.

"Wait wait wait." Zoey spins around on the stairs, pressing a hand to my chest to stop me. She's a couple steps above me, so she's slightly taller than me. It's so cold I can see the breath leave her mouth when she speaks. "Before we go in there, I want to say something."

"Yes?" I ask, amused.

Her eyes twinkle down at me. Her lips quirk up on one side, and she twirls the end of a braid in one hand, looking innocent and cocky all at once. "Well, I plan to get super drunk tonight..."

"Super drunk," Tessa agrees from where she's standing by the door. "Out of solidarity."

I raise my eyebrows at Zoey in question.

"Tessa's parents are pissed Tessa's staying an extra year. We're drinking our problems away."

Tessa has apparently fallen in love with the Greek mythology course she and Zoey are in and has decided to add on a second major. She has to stay one more year. I know Zoey is bummed they're not graduating together, but I like that she's willing to support her friend despite that. Zoey really is the best person I know.

I nod in agreement. Not gonna lie, I'm a little disappointed that she's planning on getting wasted when we're supposed to be having sex for the first time tonight. I've been counting down the days, and I know she has too, based on the texts she's been sending me.

"And while I'm still sober," she says. I screw up my lips in a flat line, letting her know I'm fact-checking her statement. "While I'm still mostly sober and just a little bit tipsy," she amends with a giggle.

"Just a little bit?" I chuckle.

"It is just a little bit. I swear. I'm mostly getting second-hand drunk off Tessa. Here, look—" Zoey then proceeds to recite the alphabet backward, walk back and forth on the step she's on in a straight line, and when she starts hopping on one foot, I reach out to stop her. My hands settle on her waist.

The perfect curve of her waist.

"Okay, okay, you're mostly sober and just a little bit tipsy."

She grins at me. Then she places one hand over her chest and raises the other in the air. "Well, I want you to know that I, Zoey Hawthorne, consent to having sex with you, Alex Adams." Wow. Okay. Didn't know we were going there with this, but dammit if my dick isn't already perking up at the prospect. "Even if I'm super drunk, as long as I want it then, I am a willing and more than happy partici-pant and am very much hoping that's where the night leads." She lowers her hands and bites her lips. They're covered in a light pink and I want to capture them in my teeth so badly. "As long as I'm not peer pressuring you and you still want to fuck me." She gazes up at me through her eyelashes, a question in her eyes.

I groan. Like there's any way I'm saying no to that. I lean in closer and whisper in her ear. "I want to have sex with you, Zo." I've already made up my mind. I'm not changing it now.

"No, no, you're doing it all wrong," Zoey says, straight-ening back up. A group of guys walks by us, jogging up the stairs and jostling each other on their way into the house.

"Get a room," one guy calls, and the rest of them wolf

whistle behind him. Zoey rolls her eyes, unbothered by their comments.

"Put your hand in the air," she says. She reaches over and grabs my hand, pulling it into the air. Then she pulls my other hand over my chest. "Now repeat after me. I, Responsible Alex Adams."

I smirk at her but repeat the words. "I, Responsible Alex Adams."

"Consent to sex with Zoey Hawthorne."

"Consent to sex with Zoey Hawthorne."

"And only Zoey Hawthorne, because Zoey Hawthorne is pure awesomeness."

I repeat after her, fighting and failing to keep the smile off my face.

"Even in the event that she's drunk tonight, because I should have been balls deep weeks ago, but I was being a fucking idiot."

"Really, Zo?" I ask dryly.

She nods solemnly at me.

"Even in the event that she's drunk tonight, because I should have been balls deep weeks ago, but I was being a freaking idiot." I repeat after her, even though I know if she's not feeling it later there's no way in hell I'd ever suggest we do anything.

"Close enough, I guess," she grumbles. But she's smiling and looking adorable, so I place my hands back on her waist where they belong. I want to pick her up and carry her right back to the car.

"What are we even doing here?" I ask, dropping my voice.

She looks about ready to jump into my arms, and I know she's questioning it too.

"No way, you're not ditching me," Tessa says from

where she's still standing by the door. She grips Zoey's hand and pulls her up the stairs. Zoey bursts out laughing and follows Tessa inside the house. Light spills out of the door, illuminating their figures as they disappear inside.

Okay. Just a couple hours of this, and then I get to take Zoey home. I can do this. Hell maybe we just say hi to everyone once, make sure Tessa has friends, and then get the hell out of here. I could do that in fifteen minutes, tops.

"Adams, get your ass in here," West calls, sticking his head out the open door. "We don't just leave doors open like this, dude, we might get a noise complaint." I laugh and jog up the stairs. I don't bother pointing out that every freaking window in this house is open. "Come on, honestly, who raised you?"

I can't keep my eyes, or hands, off Zoey. The whole night I watch her light up the room. She and Tessa laugh twice as much and twice as loud as everyone else here. I'm convinced that most of party culture is just pretending to enjoy parties, but the two of them seem so comfortable in their own skin, and with each other, that they're actually enjoying themselves.

When Zoey and I dance together, I can't stop from grabbing her hips, her waist, her hands. When we stand around talking to our friends, I pull her so her back lines up against my front. I'm following her around like she's the soccer player I've been set to mark, and I don't let her out of my sight.

She annihilates at beer pong. I'm thanking the party gods for that because it's Eddie and Maia against Zoey and me, and let's just say I play soccer for a reason.

Eddie on the other hand is one of the best college

goalies in the country right now, and it's a very close battle between him and Zoey.

"Damn girl, you have skills." Kacen pops up by the table. "Where's Tessa?"

"Fangirling over West." Zoey nods toward the corner of the room. Kacen frowns. If I hadn't seen him go home with a different girl every time we hung out, I might have thought he was actually into Tessa. "Where's Brandon? I thought you two were a package deal."

"Didn't feel like coming out. Home shit. It's okay though 'cause I have my boy Carlos." Kacen stands on his tiptoes, looking around the room as if suddenly noticing Carlos isn't standing right next to him. Zoey laughs and returns to the game.

We have two cups left, and they only have one left. Zoey shoots, and her ping pong ball lands perfectly in the cup. Eddie curses. One to one.

"Let's see this, Athlete Alex." Zoey grins. I shoot. It goes wide. Embarrassingly wide. She throws her head back and laughs. "Is this really the guy you recruited for your team?" she asks Eddie, jerking her thumb in my direction.

"Hey," I protest. I reach for her, dragging her against my body, burying my nose in her hair. I can't keep the grin off my face, even as Eddie sinks his shot.

"Well, fuck." Zoey pouts at the table. But her hand lands on my abs and slides up to my chest. I don't give a crap about this game as long as she keeps touching me like that.

"I'll make it up to you tonight," I whisper in her ear.

She doesn't even blush, just grips me tighter. "Damn right you will." Christ, do we really have to stay at this party any longer?

"Bet I can beat Maia at beer pong." Carlos appears out of nowhere, swooping Zoey's and my spot.

We leave them to fight it out and weave through the overcrowded party.

The way I'm all over Zoey, I'm treating her like she's my girlfriend. And even though I never wanted a girlfriend, holding her like this doesn't freak me out as much as I thought it would. Zoey just gets under my skin, and I like her there.

"What the hell are you doing?" I ask when we find West, Kacen, and Tessa folding a blanket over the back of the couch and taping it to the wall, making a covered space between the couch and the wall.

"Wait can I guess?" Zoey asks. "Is it a sex cave? Wait—can Alex and I use it?"

I almost spit out the sip of soda I'm drinking. "How drunk are you?" I ask, spinning her to face me. Her cheeks are rosy, eyes a little glassy, and she's a little wobbly on her feet. But she still seems with it—not wasted. She grins at me, toying with her bottom lip with her teeth, like she's just trying to mess with me.

"No, it's a secret hideout. Don't turn this into something nasty," West says. He crawls into the space. "The party was getting too crowded." I shake my head. This has got to be one of the weirdest things I've seen happen at a party. "Come in," West gestures animatedly.

"I'm not going in a sex cave with you," Tessa says.

"It's not a fucking sex cave," West argues.

"Still," I say, also hesitant to be the first to go in. West sighs, and then he peeks his head out from under the blanket.

"Eddie," he yells through the house. A couple of people give him curious glances, but then continue dancing and drinking and getting half naked. Most people are already familiar with West's antics. "Eddie!"

"Calm your tits, West, I'm coming." Eddie lazily walks toward the blanket fort.

"Come in the sex cave with me," West yells, even though Eddie is only two steps away from him.

Eddie laughs. "You've got to know how that sounds, man," he says, but he crawls under the blankets anyway. Once Eddie breaks the seal the rest of us follow. We sit on the ground, and there isn't a lot of room in here, so I pull Zoey into my lap. She gets comfortable there, with all her smooth skin against me, and I can't stop my brain from going through every single thing we're going to do later tonight.

Every thought is foggy with lust, and I run my hands up and down her jean-clad thighs. I drag my finger along that little slice of skin between her shirt and her jeans. She feels so soft and warm and I can't wait to get her out of these clothes. Zoey shifts in my lap. I suppress a groan. I'm starting to harden underneath her. Around all of our friends.

I close my eyes and try to run through game plans in my head. Zoey squirms more though, arching her back against me, and my eyes fly open. Her breasts are arched up in the air, giving me the perfect view of her cleavage over her shoulder. Her top is so low cut, I'd barely have to tug it down to see everything. Her body is flushed red and I'm hard as stone beneath her looking at the view.

I know she notices because she lets her head fall back against my shoulder and nips at my ear. "I can't wait to be dicked by you." I burst out laughing before pressing a soft kiss to her shoulder. Sober Zoey isn't one to mince her words, and apparently drunk Zoey isn't either. "Honestly, Alex, how is it fair to have a dick the size of your ego?"

"That," I tell her, dropping kisses along the side of her neck, "is the best compliment anyone has ever given me."

"I stressed several times that this wasn't a sex cave. They do know this is *not* a sex cave, right?"

"Better question: They do know we are in here with them, right?"

I flip them off, my other hand circling around Zoey's waist, stilling the tiny movements she's making. If she keeps that up I'm never going to be able to make it back to my house.

"We really don't need to know everything about your sex lives," West whines.

Zoey shakes her head. "I'm not a secret."

"No, you're not," I murmur, pressing a kiss to her hair. I wrap my arms around her waist tighter, and I feel my heart trying to pound its way out of my chest. I hate that I ever made her feel like she was someone I had to hide. I hate that Z ever put that idea in her head. If Zoey wants me showing her off and touching her all night, I'm never going to object to that.

She tilts her head back and whispers, "Let's go."

I nod so eagerly I almost give myself a concussion.

"Ditching the sex cave," she announces, crawling off my lap.

West groans. But they wave to us and promise to get Tessa home safely, and Zoey and I race out of there.

THIRTY-TWO

ZOEY

We're barely in the door to his bedroom before I have his shirt off and my hands all over his abs. We're making out against the wall, and *damn,* my man has skills. His tongue drives deep into my mouth, fighting eagerly against mine. He lifts me up against the wall, pressing against my center, and I moan out, wrapping my legs around him.

This is the make-out session every girl dreams of since they're old enough to be dreaming of this. There's not a single girl I know who *doesn't* like getting pinned against a wall. It's just about the hottest experience ever, being trapped between the wall and the uber-gorgeous, uber-muscled, uber-tattooed guy of your dreams.

Alex separates us for a moment, his free hand coming to rub the side of my face. "Just checking, are you sure—"

"God, yes."

"I mean I know you gave that whole speech earlier, but you can still change your mind."

"I'm not changing my mind."

He grins at me and then attacks my mouth with his again. I melt into his kiss, gripping onto his hair, pulling myself closer, needing more, and more, and more.

"Shirt off," Alex grunts, yanking at the bottom of my shirt. We separate long enough for him to yank the scrap of fabric over my head and set my breasts free. "I love that you don't wear a bra," Alex says, "Honestly freaking love it." Between each word, he drops a kiss to my breasts, before taking a nipple in his mouth and sucking on it. I groan. He mumbles about how perfect I am and thanks Jesus and *did he just say boob gods?*

I can't think though because his lips are covering every square inch of my breasts, sucking and biting until I'm jelly in his arms.

I want to give him a blow job.

My thoughts are a hot mess right now, all over the place, but I can make that one out.

I almost never want to do this. There are very few guys I've actually blown. But Alex—

Yeah. I want to get on my knees for Alex.

I wrestle myself out of his arms, spin us around, and drop to my knees in front of him.

"Uh, Zoey?" he asks, sounding a little panicked. I unbutton the top button on his jeans. "Oh shi—Zo." I lower the zipper, and the sound slices through the air, making my stomach spin. I make a big show of licking my lips. He groans, letting his head hit the wall. When I start to pull his pants down his legs though, he hooks his hands under my arms and yanks me back up.

"Nope. No no no," he says.

"What's wrong?" I'm so confused. I've never had someone turn down a blow job before. I'm usually the one trying to finagle my way out of giving them.

"Sober Zoey did not give me permission to let you give me a blow job."

I laugh, pushing away from him and sinking back down to my knees. I push his pants down out of the way and suddenly he's just in his boxer briefs.

"Oh Christ, Zo. I can't let you do this."

"Don't you want me to?" I pout up at him, playing with the waistband of his underwear. His jaw is tight, and all the muscles in his neck look tense, like it's taking all the strength in his body to turn me down. "I want to," I whisper.

"Hell, of course I want you to." His voice is raspy. "But you can't perform the blow job test while you're drunk."

"I'm not drunk." I ease him out of his boxer briefs and he hisses. I slide my hand from base to tip and whimper, getting really turned on at the thought of having my mouth on him. "You're so huge. Like honestly, Alex, it's not fair to the rest of mankind. You're like that top score they're always throwing out of the test for fucking up the curve."

He chuckles above me, running his hands through his hair, biceps on display. "You're not drunk?" he whispers, clearly disbelieving me.

"Please," I whisper. I want him in my mouth, desperately.

But I also want to give him the blow job test now, while I can still blame it on the alcohol. Because if I end up liking it as much as I think I will, that means...well, it means I love him. Or close to it. And I'm not ready to admit that to him yet.

It's sweet though, that he remembers how much I hate blow jobs. That he's trying to protect me from anything I might regret in the morning. Alex is the best of guys.

"Zoey," he groans. "This is literally the hottest thing I've seen in my life. You on your knees for me, topless, begging for my dick. But I can't let this happen."

I lean forward, and without any warning, I wrap my lips around his cock and suck him deep.

"Oh fudge," he curses, involuntarily pumping into me.

I release him with a pop. "No, no way," I say and point a finger up at him.

"See, I knew this was—"

"Swear like a normal fucking human adult."

"What?"

"None of this Responsible Alex, no cussing bullshit while we're fucking," I say, glaring at him. "You're not saying 'fudge' or 'fudge nuggets' or 'fudge balls' at any point during this. It's a serious mood killer."

Alex smirks, not breaking eye contact with me. "You do know you're the one who just said all of those words, right?"

"I'm not sucking you off until you say 'fuck,'" I say, crossing my arms and rocking back on my knees. His eyes go straight to my tits. When he finally manages to drag his eyes away from my nipples, which are practically begging for his touch, he's looking at me like he wants to fight me on this. Just because he's stubborn like that.

So I wrap my hands carefully around his shaft and give him a good tug. "C'mon, Alex," I whisper, slowly sliding my hand up and down, "Say fuck."

He grips my wrist, stilling my movements. I can see all the veins in his forearm as he pries my fingers from him with a strength that shouldn't be possible. Everything stills around us, and I hold my breath, my heart pounding out of control.

"Get on the bed." He growls. "Get up and take off those jeans and get on the bed."

I shake my head. "I want to—"

"You're not going to suck me off tonight." He shakes his head, sounding so final about it, so in charge and demanding. My legs shake. "But I am going to fuck you until you can't walk straight tomorrow. Now get on the fucking bed."

I obey without thinking. I end up lying on the bed, waiting for him in just a red lace thong. He stands by the side of the bed, and *holy motherfucking hell*. Alex Adams fully naked might be the most beautiful thing I've ever seen in my life. I have a bucket list full of geology landmarks to see, and none of them will ever top this.

"You're better than the Grand Canyon," I murmur.

"What?" He laughs.

"I think I'm still a little bit tipsy."

"No shit, Sherlock."

"Wow, throwing swear words all over the place now. Seems a little irresponsible."

He laughs again, climbing onto the bed over me and capturing my lips in a searing kiss. Before long, I forget what we were laughing about. I forget everything except for the feel of Alex's lips against mine, and his tongue in my mouth and the feeling of his bare chest sliding against my breasts. His cock is hard and heavy between us, and within minutes we're both desperate and panting and rubbing against each other.

"These are gorgeous," he whispers against my mouth, fingering the waistband of my panties. "They are so fucking sexy, and if I had known this is what you were wearing under your jeans I wouldn't have lasted a second at that party." He presses another long, hard kiss against my mouth. "Just thought you should know before I rip them off."

I lift my hips, and he yanks my underwear down my legs and then off. His hand trails over my hip bone, dragging across my skin until he reaches my center. His thumb applies the perfect amount of pressure to my clit. Barely any at this point, the touch soft and wonderful and—

"Inside me," I demand. He slips two fingers inside of me. I gasp, the walls of my vagina squeezing around him. "No, Alex, I want your cock."

"But..." He looks torn between wanting to be inside me and feeling the need to warm me up first. But I'm plenty warmed up. In fact, I'm fucking dripping for him, and I've been waiting way too long. I turn away from him and open the second drawer on his bedside table, finding what I'm looking for in the back corner. I toss a condom at him.

"How do you know where those are?" he asks, glancing between me and the condom in his hand. He leans back on his knees and rips the package open.

"Best friend privileges," I say softly, thoroughly distracted watching him roll the condom over his length.

"Uh-huh," he murmurs. But then he positions himself at my center and neither of us care anymore. I line him up, and he pushes in, slowly, sinking in inch by inch.

Holy shit.

I will forever be grateful Alex dumped his coffee on me that first day. Because he feels so good, stretching me, filling me. I've never been this full before and I think Alex might have just ruined me for other men forever. My walls clamp down around him and we both moan out.

"Oh fucking hell, Zoey, why do you have to be so goddamn tight?" He's groaning into my shoulder. I shift my legs so they're wrapped around his waist, and he sinks deeper into me. We both groan.

And when he starts to move? Well, let's just say I'll never doubt his sexperience again. His strokes are steady and deep and my hips rise up to meet each thrust. It lights up places inside of me that have been neglected for a long time. Pleasure courses through my body, my stomach tightens. I run my hands over his body, clawing his back, fisting his hair, gripping his backside. Alex is in possession of one of the finest asses in the universe, and I don't know what the hell kind of workout he's doing at the gym to make it this tight, this powerful, but it's working. It's really fucking working. I slap his ass and he lets out a sharp breath.

"Why did we wait so long to do this?" he asks, picking up the pace, slamming into me. I gasp underneath him. He reaches a hand in between us and uses his talented fingers on my clit. I moan, tossing my head back. "Zoey, babe, holy fuck."

It's almost hotter, though, when he starts to lose control. His breathing is ragged, his touches get sloppy, his thrusts fast and choppy. His face is drawn up, lips parted like he's in pain. I'm the one making him lose control like this. All of those orchestrated touches are flying out the window, because of me. I lose track of what I'm saying, shouting out random curses and praises and prayers. I repeat his name, over and over. Because that's all that exists in the world now.

"Fuck me forever," I tell him. "This is all I want for the rest of my life. Never stop fucking me."

"Okay, Zo," he whispers, pressing a soft kiss to my lips. "Forever."

And this is the point when I break.

My orgasm hits me hard. Hard enough that I see stars when I come, my body arching, shaking, and gripping onto his with everything I have. I feel him get harder inside me as he comes. The fact that he's coming inside of me just sets me off again.

When our breath finally calms, we're gripping onto

each other, arms and legs and bodies intertwined. I'm hugging him hard against my chest. We stay like that until I can no longer feel my pulse throughout my whole body.

"I don't really want to get up." He sounds muffled. His lips are against my shoulder. "But I do need to get rid of this condom." I release him, and he eases out of me.

I pout. "I thought you said forever." He laughs, and the bed dips with his weight when he returns after disposing of the condom. He pulls the blankets up and over us, scooting closer to wrap his arms around me and press a kiss to my cheek.

"Give me five minutes," he says. "Trust me, Zo, I have lots more fucking planned for us."

THIRTY-THREE

ALEX

"I come bearing donuts," Zoey says as she walks through the door. I don't know at what point she stopped using the doorbell and just started letting herself in, but I'm okay with it.

"Thank goodness," I say, reaching for one covered in chocolate, but she whisks the box away from me.

"These aren't for you. You have a game." She's looking at me like I'm stupid.

"But you came bearing donuts," I say.

"For Lucy and me," Zoey says as if she's explaining what two plus two is to a high schooler. Lucy comes running up and grabs the exact donut I had been eyeing before sticking her tongue out at me. I scrunch up my nose at her. Not cool. "Honestly, Alex, weren't you a division one athlete?"

"You got half a dozen donuts for just you and Lucy?"

"We can finish them, can't we, Luce?" she asks. Lucy sits on top of the dining room table, chocolate frosting on her lips, already mostly done with the first donut.

"Heck yeah we can," she says. Zoey high-fives her.

"You're a bad influence," I say, shaking my head. "Lucy shouldn't be having so much sugar."

Lucy pouts at me. Zoey turns toward me and pouts at me too. It's cute, and I have to glare at them harder to suppress the urge of reaching for Zoey. I *constantly* want to reach for Zoey.

It's been a week since we first had sex, and we've done it every single day since then. Any moment we can find during the day when Lucy is at school, we'll sneak off to Zoey's dorm. I kind of thought finally sleeping with her would stop the constant parade of sex images when I'm around her, but no. They've gotten worse. Being inside her again is all I can think about. I want Zoey bent over this counter right here, I want her in my bed again, I want her up against the wall.

I turn my back on Zoey and Lucy. I don't want either of them to guess my train of thoughts. "Do you two want to come to my game today?" I ask over my shoulder, walking back to my room to get ready.

"I'm not dressed to go outside," Zoey says. I glance back toward her and then wish I didn't. I'm not in the correct mindset to be checking her out right now. She's in gray sweatpants and this black long-sleeve shirt that is so tight on her I feel a little dizzy. Is that the outline of her nipple?

Lucy is right there, you idiot, pull yourself together.

"You look fine," I tell her.

"Oh I know I look hot," Zoey says. I laugh at that. "I mean it's as cold as ball—" I glare at her and flick my eyes toward Lucy. "—lloons. Balloons."

"Balloons aren't cold," Lucy points out.

"Neither are balls," I mutter under my breath.

"Balloons can be cold if they're ice balloons," Zoey fumbles.

"We're in Southern California," Lucy points out. "There's no ice."

"Thank you, Lucy," I say.

"Okay, point is, it's cold. And I can't stand out there for a whole hour—"

"Ninety minutes."

"—in just this." She gestures to her outfit, and again my eyes get caught on her chest. I avert them quickly, but damn. I really want a peek.

"You can borrow a sweatshirt," I say.

She glances over at Lucy. "What do you say?"

"Can we get ice cream afterward?"

Zoey throws her hands in the air. "What is wrong with you people?"

"Nothing?" I say.

"Hot coffee is for cold weather. Ice cream is for warm weather. It's not that hard."

"Well, that's just not true," I say.

"Ice cream is for every weather," Lucy says.

"I've trained you well." I jog over to her for a fist bump.

"You two need life help," Zoey says. "We can go get soup after the game. Maybe hot chocolate. Something *warm*." She motions for me to continue down the hallway. She knows I'm running out of time to get ready.

"What if it's ice cream with something warm?" Lucy asks. "Like ice cream and a warm cookie?" I don't hear Zoey's response as I duck into my room and rush to get dressed in my uniform. I reach for my phone and get my pregame playlist started.

"Turn it up," I hear Zoey call from the kitchen, and I

think, just maybe, I might know what it feels like to fall just a little bit in love.

I miss hearing the stands fill when I warm up. Normally the sound of chatter and feet against metal would all combine together into this buzzing background noise that would fuel me, get my heart pumping as I ran drill after drill, pushing myself to go faster each time.

The club game warm-ups are almost eerily silent. My team is here, together, yelling at each other through the fog. Zoey, Lucy, and Tessa are sitting on the grass by the side-line, surrounded by blankets. It looks like Kacen, Brandon, Maia, and Carlos have come to watch too. A couple of other parents sit in camping chairs along the side of the field.

I take a deep inhale. At least the morning fog and dew against the grass still smells the same. My socks are already wet and muddy. My jersey sticks to me.

And the snap of the ball against my feet. That will always be the same. A sound that leads to pure adrenaline skyrocketing through my system.

A coach once told me that soccer is the most mentally challenging sport there is. It's one of the only sports where there are no time outs—just forty-five minutes of straight play, usually with no subs. There are no chances to stop and chat with your team, reevaluate your strategy. You have to do that on the fly, being constantly aware of your surroundings, so when you get the ball and have a half second to make a decision, you already know what you're going to do.

It's why I wanted to play center mid. If the most mentally challenging part of soccer is making decisions then hell yeah, sign me up for the position where you have to make the most decisions. I always wanted to challenge myself, always wanted to be the best.

When the whistle blows at kickoff, the level of team I'm playing for no longer matters. I'm off like a rocket, pressing the other team hard and fast, shutting down their options, forcing a mistake.

Matty's the one to get a handle on the ball first, and he immediately passes it to me. My touch on the ball is quick, and I tap around my defender. I only hang on to the ball for a second though before I feed it to my winger who's tearing up the line. He has to pick up his pace to reach the ball in time, and the strikers and I are already rushing the box, running in the patterns West and Eddie drilled into us.

The cross comes, arcing across the goal box. I jump a full head higher than the defender marking me, and the ball connects with my head. I drive it toward the ground, and the goalie makes a diving save, but it's too late.

Goal.

In the first three minutes, I have a goal.

There's really nothing in the world better than this.

ZOEY

I'm trying not to drool in front of Lucy. But I don't think I've ever seen anything as sexy as Alex on a soccer field. God, I didn't even need his sweatshirt. My body is heating up plenty just watching him.

Four years ago, I wouldn't have been able to tell you what a goal box was. Tessa grew up in a household that ate, slept, and breathed soccer. She dragged me to every home game at Olympia, made me watch her Premier League team, and got me obsessed with the US Women's National Team. Now, I'm practically an expert on the rules and watching soccer has become a staple of my life.

I agree with Tessa. It's the best sport there is. The sheer fitness it takes to sprint the whole field, which is larger than a football field, only to have a couple seconds of recovery and then do it all over again, is insane.

Alex is faster than anyone else out there. He's so light on his feet, executing turns and changes so quickly it's almost blurry. For someone who's six-four and packed with muscle you wouldn't believe his speed and agility.

And don't even get me started on his technical abilities on the ball. Alex is a god on this field.

And I am here for it.

Tessa's here for it too. "Holy fuck," she whispers in awe as we watch him dribble down the field again, juking out two people and megging a third before passing the ball off and making an overlapping run, constantly in motion. I elbow her in the ribs and glance toward Lucy, shaking my head. "Shit. Sorry."

"Oh my god, Lucy, don't tell Alex about that." He'd never let us hang out with Tessa again.

Lucy snorts and gives me an eye roll. "Don't worry."

"I never thought I'd be this close to Alex Adams playing live," Tessa says, shaking her head. "One day people will be paying hundreds for seats like these."

I think we could start charging people now. I'd pay thousands.

Lucy looks at Tessa curiously though. "They will?" she asks.

"I know he says he's done, but he can still go pro in a heartbeat. US men's soccer sucks. This man will be dominating in a few years' time, just watch." Tessa nudges Lucy, and I think she's trying to cheer her up or give her encouragement, but Lucy's face pales with dread.

I try to make eye contact with Tessa to get her to shut up, because something about what she's saying is freaking Lucy out, but Tessa's eyes are glued to the field again.

I poke Lucy. "You good, babe?"

She nods and gives me a quick smile. She drops her hands to the grass, wraps a blade around her finger, and then pulls it out of the dirt. I'm not sure why she's upset, but she is. She obviously doesn't want to talk about it though, and keeps her gaze glued to the sideline.

The wind blows harder, and I snuggle further into Alex's sweatshirt. It smells like him, and I tuck my nose into the collar when Lucy's not paying attention to take a deeper inhale. We've done a good job of hiding our activities from Lucy so far. And it needs to stay that way.

I take another inhale of his sweatshirt. I like being surrounded in his clothes. It feels like I'm *his*.

I didn't think I would want to do another friends with benefits situation so soon after the first one blew up in my face, but it's different with Alex. Our friendship is deeper and more stable than my friendship with Z ever was.

And the sex is good. Real good. I'm not about to give that up, even if this is a bad idea.

Suddenly Tessa is standing beside me, shouting at the field. I glance up and Alex has a breakaway. It's just him and the goalie. He fakes a shot and the goalie jumps, but Alex does a roll-over instead and taps it neatly into the corner of the goal.

It's beautiful.

"You've got to stop breaking out the victory dance, man. It scares people." I think it's Carlos who yells this at West. West's dance is a mess of flailing arms and legs, and it makes me wonder if this is actually how he dances, or if he just does it because it's his signature move. Kacen, Brandon, Maia, and Carlos have all come to watch the game, but mostly to heckle the coaches.

"Wait until you play with him for years. You get used to it," Eddie says.

"Correction," West says, finally letting his limbs calm down. "You grow to love it."

Lucy giggles beside me, watching them.

But I can't keep my eyes off Alex.

After the goal, he doesn't do any sort of crazy celebration. He barely even acknowledges he scored. He pats his teammates on the back when they run up to hug him, but otherwise, his face is serious, ready to start playing again. The sheer intensity radiating off his body puts my mind right in the gutter. I want that look on his face when he's slamming into me. God, I just want his hands on me again. Period.

I glance at Lucy, grateful she can't read minds.

Because lately? Every single thought I have is a dirty thought about her brother.

THIRTY-FOUR

ZOEY

We've made zoodles—zucchini noodles—from one of Tessa's recipe cards for dinner. I've had it before, and it's delicious, but Alex isn't convinced that any form of vegetables should be pasta. Lucy grabbed a bowl of pasta and headed back to her room to call her parents. Alex and I are seated on the couch in the living room to eat our food.

The theory is that if we hang out in public household spaces like this we'll be less likely to maul each other.

I poke his toe with my sock-covered foot. He raises his eyebrows at me while shoving a huge forkful into his mouth. Doesn't like zoodles, my ass.

"You were great in your game today."

He shoots me a cheeky grin once he's done chewing. "Thanks, I know."

I narrow my eyes at him.

"You can't have a monopoly on a phrase, babe."

"Have you played Monopoly against me? I can get a monopoly of anything."

"I'd like to see you try against Lucy."

"No, she's scary when she plays games." I pause, biting my lip. "Actually, you have the same sort of intensity on the field that she has playing board games."

Alex laughs. "Only I'm hotter while doing it, right?"

"So much hotter," I whisper, remembering exactly how he looked at the end of the game. Sweat was dripping off his forehead, his shirt was sticking to his skin, and that cocky smirk on his face. I was ready to run into his arms right there.

His eyes darken. He licks his lips. I lean forward.

And the door to Lucy's room opens. We listen to her footsteps and then the bathroom door close. Water for her shower starts.

My heart is pounding in my ears and I inch away from him again. Alex shakes his head ruefully. "Farther."

I sit as far away as possible from him while still being on the same couch. It still doesn't seem to be enough space to stop the raging need flowing through me.

We eat in silence until I finally ask a question that's been bothering me. "What do you want to do after you graduate?"

Alex frowns at me, and I do feel a little bad about asking him the dreaded question. "Do we have to do this?"

"We do." I nod. Because there are times that he gets this sad, faraway look on his face when talking about soccer.

He sighs, sinking backward into the couch and crossing his arms. I refuse to be distracted by his biceps bulging out from his T-shirt. "I don't know, Zo. I figure I still have a year and a half before I finish my master's. I'll figure it out then."

"Do you want to go into engineering?" I press.

"I guess."

"What did you want to do before?"

"Before?" he asks, pretending like doesn't have a clue what I'm talking about. He sets his bowl on the coffee table, refusing to make eye contact.

I spell it out for him. "What did Athlete Alex want to do?"

His sigh is resigned. "Play professional soccer. That's all I ever wanted."

"So why don't you?" I ask, excited that he's opening up on this. "Tessa follows it obsessively and she thinks you're still good enough."

He runs a hand through his hair. "It's just... I feel like I had my shot. Most people don't even get a single shot, and I had one, and I fucking blew it. How the hell am I supposed to get two shots at something most people think is impossible?" He makes eye contact at the end of his speech, as if daring me to say something different. I know this is emotional for him though. Responsible Alex wouldn't accidentally drop the F-bomb if it wasn't a big deal.

"I mean, I watched you score a hat-trick today. I think you can take more than one shot."

The left side of Alex's lips quirks up. But then it falls as he shakes his head again. "What if I get back there again and I just fall into the same trap? All the girls, the partying, the drugs. It's all more intense at the professional level." He doesn't trust himself, and it breaks my heart.

I ignore the stupid twinge in my chest at the thought of him with other girls. I know what this is. "You're not that guy anymore," I tell him. He doesn't look convinced. "Alex, I promise you. You wouldn't make the same mistake."

"How can you be sure?" His whisper sounds so pained that I scoot closer to him and slip my hand into his.

"I would never be your best friend if you were still that guy."

He thinks it over, his jaw ticcing back and forth. "What if being a millionaire changes me?" he asks, and I love that the joking tone is back in his voice.

"Wow, Mr. Big-Ass Ego. Millionaire, huh?"

"Hey, you're the one who said I was good. Don't you *want* me to be a millionaire? Think about all the best friend privileges."

I snort. "And in return you'll get the best friend privilege of me whipping you into shape if you're being stupid."

Alex nods. "Actually, that is a little terrifying." Then he looks at me with heat in his eyes. "Would you actually whip me?"

I burst out laughing, shoving him away. "We're keeping this PG-13 tonight."

Alex grumbles, but he smiles at me. I know he's grateful I roll with his boundaries so easily. I'm about to ask him another question when he groans. "Oh god, do you know how out of shape I am though? Imagine the effort to get back to my peak."

"You're out of shape?" I've had my hands all over his body this past week, and there isn't one inch of him that feels out of shape. I poke at his abs, just to make sure. Yup. Hard as a fucking rock.

"Babe, I went from three-a-days to twice-a-weeks. I try to make it to the gym as much as I can, but I've lost a lot."

"What does that make me then?" I demand, gesturing to my body. I don't work out nearly as much as Alex, but I go hiking and running and sometimes swimming. I've always liked my body.

Alex leans in close to me so he can whisper in my hair. "Fucking gorgeous."

I snort, suppressing the shiver trying to run through me. "Smooth."

"Kacen has been giving me unsolicited pick-up tips."

"Well, at least you finally have game."

Alex shoves me and I laugh. The conversation stays light after that. Alex walks me out to my car when I leave and gives me a quick hug goodbye. I want to pull him against me and kiss him senseless under the stars, then drag his ass back to his bedroom, but I settle for the hug.

I know he thinks he just gets one chance to have the life of his dreams, but I don't believe it. He still wants it, and as long as you still want something, it's possible to get it. There's always another way.

Even with Professor Heath's lab position, I realize. Even if Eileen gets the job over me, it would suck. But it's not the only path to my future. I know what I want from my future, and I'm not going to let anything stop me from achieving my dreams.

And the same applies for Alex. He needs someone to believe in him and a little shove in the right direction.

And if I'm the one who has to shove him, so be it.

THIRTY-FIVE

ALEX

"Are you sure it's okay that we're here?"

"Of course, why wouldn't it be?" Zoey rolls her eyes at me from the passenger's seat. We're sitting in the driveway at her house, but we haven't gotten out of the car yet. Mostly because I'm panicking just a little bit. I've never had to meet a girl's parents before.

"Because it's Thanksgiving," I fumble. "I feel like I'm intruding on your family time."

"My freshman year, my mom walked around the dorms looking for lost souls who weren't going home on Thanksgiving to invite them to our dinner. Trust me, she'll be thrilled that you're here."

"But what if she thinks we're like..." I trail off and gesture between us. I love the way things are between Zoey and I right now. Friends, like always, and sex every freaking moment Lucy isn't around. It's the best situation ever. But showing up at her house for a family holiday? That seems like a big deal and I know exactly what my mom would assume.

"Dating?" Zoey laughs at my reluctance to even say the word. I nod, uncomfortable. But honestly, why else do you bring someone home for the holidays? "I told her we were friends. You'll be fine."

"Can we just go in already?" Lucy grumbles from the back seat. "My legs are tired of sitting."

I've been trying to get a gauge on how Lucy feels about Thanksgiving. I asked her if she wanted to stay home, just the two of us, or go home with Zoey. She said she didn't care, so I decided for us. And I decided homemade food not cooked by me. But something still seems off about Lucy.

I'm also pretty sure I made the wrong decision now. Zoey's mom is opening up the front door, or at least I assume it's Zoey's mom. She's tall and blonde too, but looks much older, her hair cropped short around her face. My heart is panicking in my chest and I haven't even gotten out of the car yet.

I'm not sure if Zoey has noticed, but I'm not exactly the bring-home-to-meet-the-parents type. I wore a button-down long-sleeve shirt, but you can still see the edge of one of my tattoos peeking out of my collar.

What if they don't like me? And, Christ, why does it matter so much if her parents like me? It's not like I'm dating her.

Although, it is kind of close to dating. We're banging, exclusively. That's something I'd never thought I'd do. But it's kind of the best deal ever. Zoey's *always* down. Hell, last week we did it in my office.

And now the image of her bent over my desk is in my brain as I'm about to go meet her mom. What is wrong with me?

Zoey and Lucy have both gotten out of the car, and Mrs. Hawthorne already has arms wrapped around both of them.

I take a deep breath. It's game time. I've got this.

I push open the car door and step out. I've barely taken a few steps toward the house when Mrs. Hawthorne has wrapped her arms around me too.

"You must be Alex," she says warmly, rubbing my back a few times in a motherly way before releasing me. My joints feel stiff as I hug her back. "I'd like to say I've heard so much about you, but Zoey doesn't call me nearly enough."

"I call you twice a week, Mom," Zoey grumbles.

"See? Not nearly enough. Both your brothers called me daily."

"And where do they live now?" I hear her say under her breath.

Her mom nods decisively. "Where they should be. And where you'll be soon." Her mom says it with so much enthusiasm that I feel a twinge of guilt. I know how hard Zoey's working to not move back home, but apparently she hasn't given that message to her mom yet. Mrs. Hawthorne grabs Lucy's overnight bag and ushers us inside. "Come on, come on, I know it's California but it's cold out here."

Zoey already warned me before we came that we wouldn't be staying in some fancy guest room—her words, not mine—but instead the couch and air mattress had been reserved for us. I told her it wasn't a big deal, but she still seemed a little embarrassed as she confided in me.

We walk into her house now, and her dad meanders into the entryway to meet us too. My heart kicks into gear again as I give him a handshake. He nods at me. "I hope the drive wasn't too bad."

"No, I drove, so it was fine," I joke.

Hell.

Horror rushes over me as I realize what I said. I just made fun of Zoey's driving, *to her parents*. And worse, it was the first freaking thing out of my mouth to her father.

Jesus, I'm bad at this.

Zoey just rolls her eyes though, and her mom smiles. "Thank goodness," she says, gripping Zoey's shoulder. "I worry about this child on the road sometimes."

"We don't know where she gets it from," Mr. Hawthorne says. "Both my other two are great drivers."

A timer goes off in another room, and Mr. Hawthorne runs to take care of it.

"We do know where she gets it from." Mrs. Hawthorne drops her voice to a stage-whisper. "Her dad is just as bad."

Thanksgiving dinner at Zoey's house is huge. We got there early enough to help with some of the food and get settled, but for the last hour aunts and uncles and grandmas and cousins have arrived one after the other until it's just a sea of blonde.

It's overwhelming. Usually I'm a guy who's pretty comfortable in his own skin, but I can't help feeling like all eyes are on Lucy and me. My shirt feels itchy, and I keep readjusting it. I wish I had worn my lucky shirt underneath.

I glance down at Lucy who is practically glued to my side. She's staring around the room with wide eyes too.

"Hey, anytime you want to get out of here, we can," I tell her. "I'm the one with the car, remember?"

She smirks up at me though. I think me being nervous just made her less nervous. "Why? Are you scared?"

"I'm not scared," I grumble.

"You sound scared." She raises her eyebrows at me, daring me to ask to leave again. I scrunch up my face at her, not about to give in, but I kinda wish she wanted to get the hell out of here. "Is it 'cause you're meeting Zoey's parents?" she taunts.

"Shut up," I groan. "Fine, if we're staying, you have to be my shield then." I grab her shoulders and push her in front of me to weave through the crowd. Lucy giggles.

And then I make eye contact with Zoey, who is bringing a stack full of plates to the table to lay out, and she smiles at me so huge it makes my insides go fuzzy.

Yeah. That's why I'm here. Suffering through her family party. For that damn smile.

Zoey's mom has introduced me to everyone saying, "This is Alex, Zoey's *friend*." I don't miss the way she stresses the word friend. Every. Single. Time.

The first couple times make me stiffen up when she says it. I told Zoey they'd think we were dating. After a while though, I loosen up and chuckle every time her mom says it. It's not that big of a deal, I guess, and honestly, most people seem more interested in Lucy than me. She's the perfect shield.

No one is giving me judging glances. No one seems to disapprove of my "relationship" with Zoey. No one has even taken a second look at my tattoo except for Zoey's cousin Karen. In fact, her parents have been nothing but accepting, and the more I tell them about my life, the more they seem to like me.

Granted, I've left out some pretty important parts. But I figure that information is on a need-to-know basis.

Zoey comes up behind me, bumping me with her hip. "Has my cousin Karen tried to hit on you yet?"

"I've got the best human shield in the world." Karen has definitely tried to hit on me. Multiple times. But I brushed her off each time, because it really didn't matter. I swing

Lucy around by the shoulders and she giggles, but then she just stands there between Zoey and I. "Luce," I fake groan. "You were supposed to karate chop her."

"Wow, this is how you treat your friends?" Zoey asks. "I invite you here and you hire your little sister to attack me? I see how it is."

"Once we take you down, we can steal our rightful place in your family. They'll never know the difference."

Zoey laughs, but Lucy tenses in my hands. I glance down at her, but as quickly as that tension came she replaces her sullen expression with a smile.

Zoey directs us to a table where everyone is starting to sit down. The table is really like five tables pushed together, expanding from the dining room into the kitchen. They're mismatched, all at different heights and covered with different table clothes, but it feels homey. I'm sitting on a piano bench that they stole from somewhere in the house, with Lucy squished between Zoey and me. Which is probably a good thing. Even though it's the worst idea in the world, I am still tempted to run my hand up and down Zoey's thigh through the whole meal.

Luckily, Karen and her two sisters are on the far end of the table, away from us, sitting in rolling desk chairs.

"Just wait till later," Zoey whispers to us. "When we're supposed to be cleaning up, my brothers and I always race those chairs up and down the hallways. Drives my dad crazy."

"I bet I can beat you," I nudge Lucy.

"Never," Lucy says, some of her old spirit there. Besides when she was challenging me earlier, she's seemed off this whole night. Quieter than normal. More forced giggles. I don't know what's up though.

"I'd like to see you try to beat her." Zoey laughs. "I'm convinced soccer is the only sport you're good at."

"Is chair racing a sport?" I question.

"I mean, I was counting beer pong as a sport." I shoot her glare for mentioning beer pong in front of Lucy. But Lucy doesn't seem to care. "But fine, we can change it to soccer being the only *physical* activity you're good at." She smirks at me, knowing damn well that's not true. And also knowing I can't say a freaking thing to argue my point.

"Really? That's how you want to play this?"

Zoey nods, an impish look on her face.

"Then I'll prove you wrong. Tonight." I let that hang there for a moment. She raises her eyebrows at me, a half grin on her face. "At chair racing."

She laughs.

And bless the Thanksgiving gods for bringing me here. Despite my worries when I first got here, this is one of the best Thanksgivings I've had in years.

Don't get me wrong, I love my family. But ever since I started college—hell, maybe even before that—all my parents have done is pick apart things I'm doing wrong. And I am well aware of the fact that I was doing a lot wrong. Sometimes it's nice to hang out with people who think I can do no wrong. Like Zoey.

Once everyone is sitting and the food is served, Zoey's mom asks us all to go around and say what they're grateful for.

Most say family and friends. Karen says "family, friends, and cute boys" while looking right at me. Zoey snorts at that. Zoey's grandma rambles forever on how wonderful her family is, coming all together for an event like tonight's. Zoey's uncle gives a five-minute speech with pictures about his Belgian Malinois.

We're about ten people thankful for their families in, and three people away from it being my turn, when Lucy pushes away from the table and runs from the room.

I stare at the spot she just occupied in shock. Zoey does too. Then she looks up at me, her face panicked. It propels me into motion.

"Sorry about that," I say, scooting away from the table. "I'll be right back."

I hear the conversation start up again behind me as I move through the empty house, looking for Lucy.

I find her sitting on the ground in the hallway, her back against the wall, her arms wrapped around her knees. She's crying.

Lucy is tough as nails and full of attitude, so to find her actually crying is a shock to my system. What do I do? I have almost no experience with crying girls. The last time I tried to comfort Lucy when she cried, I think she was two years old and all it had taken to solve the problem was finding the toy that she wanted.

"Hey, Lucy," I say, gingerly sitting down beside her. I lean my back against the floor in the hallway. It feels a little weird, making myself at home in a house I've only been in for a couple of hours. But Lucy is in need, so I'm sitting on the floor and gathering her up into my arms. "What's up?"

She shakes her head and tries to wrestle her way out of my arms. "I don't need you."

"I know you don't need me," I say, still holding her despite her struggle. "But I'm here if you do."

"Not always," she counters. I suck in a breath. She's right. I still feel terrible for not reaching out when I was in college. "Why does everyone leave?"

My heart breaks when she finally lets me hold her and she collapses, crying into my shoulder.

Sometimes, I forget how young she is, how this all must look to her. It makes a short span of time a huge deal. For the past four years of her life, I was essentially gone. And right after I got back, our parents left.

"Oh, Luce. It's not you. You know that, right?"

"They haven't even called."

I glance down at my phone.

"'Cause of the time change. They're not up yet."

Lucy continues to cry into my shoulder.

"I'm sorry," I say, and I hope she can hear how sincere I am. "I'm the one who messed up. I should have called home more when I left for college. I should have spent more time with you. That's my bad though. It has nothing to do with you." She rubs snot off on my shirt and I smirk at her. "For the past few months, spending this time with you, it showed me just how stupid I was. I'll spend every minute of every day trying to make it up to you."

"I overheard you and Zoey," Lucy accuses. I freeze, my arms stiffening around her. Hell. We've tried to be good and not flirt in front of Lucy, but we've been far from perfect. What did she hear? Was it the night she was sick? "You want to play professional soccer. You're going to leave me again."

I breathe out a sigh of relief. "I don't know if that will ever happen. But yeah, eventually I'm going to have to leave." I poke her in the side. "And you know what will happen then? I'll video chat you every day. You can come stay with me whenever you want *and* the parents can't object because we already know I'm fantastic at taking care of you. All it takes is ice cream."

Lucy snorts at that. We both know it takes a lot more than ice cream. She's stopped crying now, but still seems sad. "We'll call the parents tonight. The minute dinner is over," I offer. She just nods. "You want to know what I'm grateful for?" I ask. This whole conversation is starting to get outrageously cheesy. A year ago, I wouldn't have even considered saying these things, but I know she needs to hear them. "I'm grateful for you, Lucy. You're my favorite sister ever."

"I'm your only sister."

"You're forgetting our ghost sister."

"Mabel doesn't count."

"Dad *named* her?" I demand. Last time I talked to Dad about the ghost family that lived in our house, he hadn't given them names yet. Granted, I missed a lot of time.

"Dad named all of them," she responds.

"Do you believe they exist?"

"No." She shakes her head. "I think Dad just does something stupid and then is scatterbrained enough to forget about it."

"See, I'm on the fence about it. There's some weird shi —stuff that's happened. Remember when all the books off that one shelf went missing?" As I say it, though, I realize her explanation works in that situation too. It's very possible Dad was just looking for a book and then forgot the next day that he had moved all the books. Shit. Had my childhood been a lie?

Lucy giggles and I'm happy she's not crying anymore. "You know I hear swear words at school, right? Mom and Dad made that rule a bigger deal than it needed to be."

"Yeah, but I've committed to it now."

"You've followed most of their rules, haven't you?" Lucy muses. "Except for the 'no random girls' clause."

"Zoey isn't a random girl."

"She *started* as a random girl."

"We've been through this." I groan. "Should we *not* be at Zoey's for Thanksgiving?"

"I mean, ideally, we would have been home with Mom and Dad and the ghost family like always." Lucy pauses and then bites her lip. I swear she picked up that thinking trait from Zoey. "I guess this as a second option isn't so bad though."

"Those mashed potatoes smelled bomb," I agree.

We both sit against the wall. My arm is still thrown around Lucy's shoulder, but she's supporting herself. Her eyes are all red and puffy from crying, but she's smiling now. She wipes at her face, clearing it of any dried tear marks.

"Alex?" Her voice is soft.

"Yeah?"

"I'm glad I stayed home with you."

It's like a whole stadium is chanting my name, that's how good it feels to hear those words. It's exactly what I've wanted to hear all semester. I hug her to me, tucking her under my chin.

"Me too, Luce." My smile is huge. "Me too."

THIRTY-SIX

ALEX

No one makes a big deal about our disappearance from the dinner table. Only Zoey raises her eyebrows at me, the question apparent in her eyes. But Zoey and I excel in the art of having a conversation without actually saying anything. Well, she at least understands enough to know that I'll explain later.

I was right. The mashed potatoes were bomb.

After dinner, I bested everyone at chair racing. And Lucy won a couple board games. We helped clean and said our goodbyes to Zoey's extended family, and finally, hours later, Lucy and I are alone in the living room and have a moment to call our parents.

We sit on the couch together. I pull out my laptop, placing it on the coffee table. Lucy's in better spirits now, but when I hit the button to call, her brows furrow. Some of that anger is coming back.

"Have you seen my chair racing bruise yet?" I ask, twisting my arm to show her the bruise on my bicep.

"Yes. Several times." She looks at me like I'm crazy. "You know that's not something to brag about, right?"

I shrug. The ringing on the laptop stops and my mom's face appears on the screen. I breathe out a sigh of relief. I don't know what I would have done if she hadn't picked up.

"Happy Thanksgiving." Her eyes crinkle at the camera. "Well, at least for you guys."

"Happy Thanksgiving," we chorus back.

"How are my babies? Lucy? How's your week off school been?" Honestly, for me, it's been stressful. What do parents do with their kids when they're off school but they still have to work?

"It's been good. I've mostly just been hanging out at Jenna's a lot," Lucy says. "I got to see Alex teach his class."

"Was he any good?" my mom asks.

"Wow," I comment.

Lucy giggles. "He's terrible," she says. I poke her in the side, and she giggles again.

"Wow," I repeat. "She's joking, Mom." At least I think she's joking.

"And Alex? Are you studying for finals yet?" Of course my mom's first question is about school.

"Yeah, Mom. I've got it."

"I'm glad." She glances around her room. "I don't know where your dad ran off to. He should be back in a few minutes." She turns back to us and narrows her eyes at the screen. "Where are you two anyway?"

Shit. I was hoping we could avoid that question. "We're at Zoey's," I say. I don't talk to my parents about Zoey because I know they wouldn't approve of how often I leave her with Lucy. Or how often she comes over. All I've told them is that Zoey is a friend I made at the start of the semester and I've left it at that. No need to get yelled at more than I already do.

"You went to Zoey's. For Thanksgiving?" I can hear the judgment in my mom's voice, and her eyebrows shoot up. But what did she expect us to do? Sit at home just the two of us?

"It's been great," Lucy starts. Then she proceeds to tell the story of winning at board games. I guess bragging about ourselves runs in the family.

Zoey walks into the room, a stack of blankets in her arms. When she sees we're on the phone she sets them quietly by the door. I wink at her over the top of the computer screen.

"I'm sure it was fun," my mom says. "It just surprises me that you're at Zoey's. I would have thought you'd go over to West's or Eddie's. You talk about them more."

Zoey smirks at me and then leans in the doorway, eavesdropping on our conversation.

"What was I supposed to do? Invite myself over to their houses?"

"Did Zoey invite you to hers?"

"It's not a big deal, Mom."

"Are you spending the night there?" my mom asks.

I close my eyes. I can hear it in her voice. She thinks I'm hooking up with Zoey, even after they told me not to. Hell. I knew they wouldn't trust me to have a girl who is a friend. And, yeah, okay, I *am* hooking up with Zoey. But it's not like we're doing it in front of Lucy. In front of Lucy I'm PG-13 as hell. In fact, this is the most PG-13 I've been since before I was thirteen. And it's not like I planned this whole Thanksgiving thing just to get into Zoey's bed.

I wish my mom would just trust me not to be an idiot.

"It's not like that, Mom," I say.

"I didn't say anything. I'm just trying to understand." She obviously doesn't believe me. I glance up to Zoey. She looks uncomfortable, standing in the doorway, hesitating on whether she should stay in the room or not now.

I know my mom is just trying to make sure I keep my shit together, but she's making this situation so much worse than it has to be.

She's frowning at me now. The disappointment is clear in her face. She is never going to believe I'm capable of keeping my dick in my pants. That's the only reason I add, "She's my girlfriend."

Because dating Zoey instead of just fucking her has got to seem more responsible, right?

The whole room freezes. There are three pairs of eyes staring at me. Oh hell.

I check in with Zoey first. I glance over the laptop screen, wondering if she is about to freak out.

Her face looks calm as ever. She's smirking at me, eyebrows raised, clearly amused by this turn of events. Oh thank the relationship gods. She knows it isn't real. Zoey is so chill. She never blows anything out of proportion, and right now I appreciate her levelheadedness more than ever.

And then I hear it as she does—fast footsteps racing down the hallway. Her mom pops behind Zoey in the doorway.

"Zoey," she whispers excitedly. "I thought you said you were just friends."

I watch all the color drain from Zoey's face.

I can't even help her because my mom is calling my name. I glance back down at the screen, just as Zoey is pulling her mom out of the room by her elbow, talking to her in hushed voices.

My dad is on screen now too. "Did you just say 'girl-friend'?" he asks. There's that disbelief again.

"When did this happen?" my mom asks.

"Why didn't you tell us you had a girlfriend?"

"Is it serious?"

"Are you two being responsible?"

"Alex, we told you not to."

Instead of answering, I look over at Lucy, begging her to bail me out of these questions that are still coming at rapid-fire speed. Lucy rolls her eyes. The look she gives me is clear: You dug your own hole. Climb your own way out.

I just messed up. Big time.

It's hours before I close the laptop screen. I drop my head into my hands and curse under my breath. Lucy snorts.

She's made herself a bed on the couch with the blankets Zoey brought. There's a stack on the floor still that I assume are for me.

"I'm sorry," I breathe. Lucy needed to talk to our parents tonight and I hijacked the whole conversation.

"It's okay."

"You know I'm not actually dating Zoey, right?" I ask, a little panicked. "I wouldn't hide that from you."

"That's dumb."

"I should hide it from you?"

"No. You should be dating Zoey." I stare at her, open-mouthed. I'm not even sure how to respond to something so ludicrous. Lucy shrugs. "Just saying."

I shake my head and pick myself off the floor, where I had been sitting with my back leaning against the couch. "I need to go clear things up with Zoey. Are you okay if I leave you here?"

Lucy nods, gaze already glued to her phone. I make my way out of the room to go find my not-girlfriend.

THIRTY-SEVEN

ZOEY

I just survived the inquisition of a lifetime. I groan, closing the door to my room and leaning my back against it. Finally breathing in peace and quiet. Fuck. Tell my mom about job opportunities and she changes the subject. Tell her about a boy and she can talk for hours. Hours.

There's a knock on the door.

"Who is it?" I'm wary. I can't handle any more questions about my "new, budding relationship with Alex. How exciting!!!"

"It's me." I'd recognize Alex's voice anywhere. I open the door and he barely acknowledges me before stumbling into my room and face planting on the twin bed.

This room was mine when I was growing up, and there are still bits and pieces of me all over it. Linkin Park posters on the walls, my rock collection lining the window shelf. My brother has taken over it while I've been at college though. There's a whole gaming set-up on my childhood desk, video games and energy drinks stuffed under the bed.

My brothers are in the same room again tonight so I could sleep here, but it's weird. It's like it's still partly mine, but not. And seeing Alex hanging off my childhood bed makes the whole situation seem even more out of place.

He lets out a groan. It sounds the exact same as mine.

I close the door and then walk over to the bed, sitting beside him, sinking into the mattress.

"You suck," I tell him.

He groans into my blankets again. Even looking as exhausted as he is, the man is still gorgeous. There are deep grooves in his hair from all the finger dragging he's been doing for the past few hours. His dress shirt has been pushed up to his forearms, revealing a couple tattoos. His ass is right freaking there, filling his jeans perfectly. It would be so easy to just grab a handful.

God, I want to kiss every inch of him.

"I just went through an hour of questioning because of you."

He flips his head to the side, resting it flat against my quilt. "Yeah," he says slowly, in agreement. "I fucked up."

I snort. It's still weird hearing him cuss. He only ever does it if Lucy isn't around. Or if we're in bed together. Which we kind of are now.

I fall backward onto the bed, lying beside him. I turn my head toward him. The quilt feels cool against my cheek. Our faces are only a couple of inches away from each other now. "That you did."

"I thought it would make it better."

"How?" I laugh. It's obvious he just went through an atrocious amount of questioning too.

"My mom thought I brought Lucy over to your house just so I could get in your pants."

"Ah. That's fucky."

"And I didn't want her to think that. And I *knew* she wasn't going to believe we were just friends."

"Why not?" I demand. "Even if we weren't fucking on the regular, you would have still come here for Thanksgiving."

"I know. Look, *I* know that. You're my best friend, Zo. But my mom would never believe me if I told her a girl was my best friend."

"You've never been friends with a girl before?"

"I'm still not convinced you can be just friends with a girl."

"That's stupid. I'm friends with Brandon and Kacen and West and Eddie—"

"Okay. I'm still not convinced *I* can be just friends with a girl."

"You were. For a whole two months."

"But I wanted to bang you the whole time." Yup. Alex still doesn't say "fuck" if he can avoid it.

"You were sex deprived."

He just shakes his head. He looks so disappointed in himself. He closes his eyes and winces. "What did you tell your mom?"

"I just went with it."

His eyes pop open, crinkling at the corners as he cracks a half smile. "You did?"

"Yeah, as far as our families are concerned, we're now in a relationship." He thinks that over, a smile still tugging on the corner of his lips. He's happy, I realize. Happy I'm okay with telling my mom we're in a relationship. That I didn't try to change the story. Is he really so down on himself that he needs this kind of approval?

"What did she say?" he asks.

"She's extremely excited. I haven't actually told her

about a guy in years, so she's one drink away from throwing a party."

"You mean you *didn't* tell her about your friends with bennies relationship with Z?"

"Nope. She doesn't need to know about my sex life."

"But you loooooooved him," he sings.

I laugh, glad he's joking again. "I didn't. Or I don't anymore. Fuck. I don't know. Feelings are hard."

Alex snorts. "Tell me about it. At least your mom isn't upset you're dating a fuck-up."

I reach over and run my fingers through the grooves in his hair, exactly where he's been running his hand through it. The curls are soft beneath my fingers. It's longer now than when I first met him and I wonder if he's gotten a haircut at all this semester. He's been so busy.

His eyes close at my touch. "You're not a fuck-up." I hate that he gets in this mood every time he talks to his parents. I wish they could see him the way I do. "You made some mistakes in the past. But it made you the Alex you are today. You're loyal and honest and disciplined and so fucking *responsible*."

He smirks slightly.

"Honestly, Alex?" When he opens his eyes, the eye contact between us is intense. I feel like I can barely catch a breath, I'm drowning in his eyes. My throat feels tight when I speak. "You're the best man I know. I just spent an hour explaining this to my mom." I laugh, trying to keep this lighthearted.

Alex isn't laughing though. He's watching me. Intensely. Then he reaches for me. He wraps a hand around the back of my neck, pulling me toward him. He presses his lips firmly against mine. The kiss is sweet. There's no tongue or devouring of each other. It's just a firm press of the lips. And it feels like he really, really needs this.

He breaks apart, staying close enough that his eyes have to flick back and forth between mine.

When he speaks, his voice is hoarse. "Why *aren't* we in a relationship?"

THIRTY-EIGHT

ZOEY

What the...

Did he really just ask me that?

Did Alex Adams—avoider of all things relationship—just ask me why were *aren't* in one?

And my heart needs to calm it's fucking fluttering right now. This can't be a thing.

"Because," I scramble. "It wouldn't work."

Alex sits up on the bed, a new light in his eyes. I can see the idea gaining steam in his head and I need to stop it before we go flying off the tracks. "Why not?" he asks. "You're already my best friend. Sex with you is the best I've ever had in my life. It'd be the perfect relationship."

"No, it wouldn't. You need other things in a relationship." I'm sitting now too.

"Like what?" he demands.

"Like—like... the cute stuff. Like dates."

"We get lunch together all the time."

"That doesn't count."

"Sure it does."

"You don't know anything about being in a relationship."

"Like you do? You were trying to date Z."

"Wow. That's judgy."

"I'm obviously a way better option."

He is. But I'm not about to admit that. "Mr. Big-Ass Ego," I mutter.

Alex's face is bright and excited right in front of me. He reaches forward with two hands to cup my cheeks. Goddammit, why does he have to be so gorgeous?

"C'mon, Zo." He flashes me a panty-dropping grin—and yup. Heat buzzes in my center from that stupid smile. "Be my girlfriend."

ALEX

I don't understand why Zoey is resisting this so much. It's like the relationship gods and goddesses uploaded an epiphany straight to my brain. I understand now.

Zoey and I would be perfect together.

Literally. The definition of perfect.

Look up the word "perfect" in the dictionary and you'd see a picture of Zoey and me. In a goddamn motherfucking relationship.

I mean, we're practically in a relationship now. It isn't time-consuming or annoying. It's just Zoey and me. The only difference between what we're doing now and a relationship is the word "official."

Zoey shakes her head, pulling my hands from her face. I don't get that upset though. I don't know why she's resisting, but I can find out. Because this thing between us? I'm going to make it happen.

"Why not?" I demand.

"You don't actually want this," she says, standing up, as if the idea of it is just too much for her to handle. "You just want your parents to think you're responsible."

Well that's just not true. Sure, it would be an added bonus, but I want Zoey and me together because I honestly can't imagine wanting any other girl ever again. "No. I want this because I want you."

"Really? Why'd you never bring this up before the conversation with your parents then?" she asks sarcastically.

"Because I didn't realize before then."

"Uh-huh."

"No. I'm serious. My parents aren't part of the equation."

"I find that hard to believe when the whole freaking semester you've been like 'I can't have sex with random girls. No, Zoey, stop making me come, my parents wouldn't approve.'" She's pulling at her hair and pacing around the room.

"Pretty sure that's not how it happened," I chuckle.

"That's exactly how it happened. And if I was your girlfriend, your parents suddenly wouldn't think I'm a random girl."

"My mom obviously isn't convinced of that," I counter. "But that's not the point." I stand up, moving across the room toward her. She crosses her arms. She lets me approach without backing up, just tilting her chin up the closer I get. She has murder in her eyes the whole time and I fucking love it. "The point," I say, dropping my voice, "is that I would be happy fucking you, and only you, six ways from Sunday for the rest of my life." I don't miss the shiver that goes through her body. She glances away from me. "Trust me when I say my parents aren't part of *that* equation."

I reach an arm out, placing my hand on her hip. Her curves feel perfect under my touch. She doesn't push me away, but she keeps her arms crossed firmly between us. Her eyes slide back to mine. They have significantly fewer murder vibes this time. That defiance is still there though. She refuses to be affected by my touch.

"I already told you fucking isn't the only part of a relationship," she says dryly.

"But it's the most important part," I wink.

"Remember that thing I said about you being responsible? Strike that from the list."

"Aw, come on." I step one half-step closer to her, and her head tilts even farther to maintain eye contact. "It'd be so good," I whisper. "You know it would."

"I know," she yells. It bursts out of her, echoing off the walls. Then she blushes, glancing around the room. Christ, I hope her walls aren't thin. Oh hell. What if her parents overheard us? And now they knew exactly how much I like to have sex with their daughter?

Hell. I really am bad at this.

"That's the thing." She moans, turning out of my grip. My hand falls from her hip. She faces the wall, biting her lip. "I know it would be good. It's just you... and..." She glances back to me again. She looks vulnerable as hell. "Last time hurt so bad, and I wasn't even in a relationship."

Sometimes I forget Zoey went through a huge heartbroken phase less than three months ago. Z seems like such a non-issue now, and Zoey always seems so put-together. There's always a smile on her face.

I try to reassure her. "I'm not going to break your heart, Zo."

"You can't promise that."

I run my hand through my hair. She's right. I can't. "Well, if it's any consolation, if things go south I will be just as messed up as you."

She smiles at that. It's a reluctant smile, but a smile all the same.

"I feel like I should have gotten down on one knee or given you a Ring Pop or something. You know, properly asked you."

"You need a Ring Pop to properly ask me to be your girl-friend?" she asks, half laughing. "I mean, I have nothing against Ring Pops, but honestly—what the fuck?"

"Isn't that what people in relationships do?"

"No."

"Ah. Wouldn't know."

She jerks her chin in my direction, quizzing me. "What do you think happens on Valentine's Day?"

"Sex in giant chocolate fountains," I respond instantly.

She bursts out laughing. "That would be great. But no."

"I don't see why not." I shrug. "I'm sure we could find a way to make that happen."

She shakes her head at me, grinning and biting her lip at the same time. It's hot as hell. I want to go to her, gather her up in my arms, kiss the hell out of her. But I'm not going to pressure her when she hasn't said yes yet. I know it's a big step for her.

There's a knock on the door.

Zoey's dad pops his head in. "Hey, how about we keep this open when you're in here with your boyfriend?"

"Dad," Zoey complains. "I'm twenty-two."

"And this is my house," her dad responds. He walks off, leaving the door wide open.

We're both silent for a second.

"I can't move home," she whispers to me.

"Hell no, you can't." I shake my head. Not if it means we'll never have a moment alone ever again. I'll do whatever it takes to keep her in my bed.

She sits back down on her bed, chewing the side of her cheek. I sit beside her. I want to sit right beside her, thigh pressed to thigh, just so she's reminded of how awesome it would be. But I give her two inches of space. Because I'm a good guy like that.

Finally, *finally* she says, "'Boyfriend' does have a nice ring to it."

I glance up at her. She has a teasing smile on her face, but I think she's being serious. Shit. My chest feels a little warm. Is that a yes?

I know what I'm going to say next is cheesy but I need to put the nail in the coffin. So I step out of my comfort zone and speak. "I vow to continue being your best friend, making sure you and Tessa don't get arrested, to always put you first, after Lucy, and to—" I drop my voice to a whisper, almost just mouthing the words, kind of terrified now that the door is wide open. "Continue giving you mind-shattering orgasms." When I'm done, I hold my breath. The bait is out there now. She just has to take it.

"And I vow," she says, tucking her hair behind her ears, a little half grin on her face, "to continue abusing my best friend privileges, keeping your big-ass ego in check, helping you see the best in yourself, and..." She waggles her eyebrows at me, then whispers, "To continue receiving those orgasms."

Hell. Yes.

"I get none in return?" I joke, but I'm sure I look like an idiot, the smile on my face is so big.

"It's up for discussion."

"That's fine. I'll take it. By the power vested in me by the caffeine gods who threw me in your path—"

Zoey rolls her eyes.

"I now pronounce us *real* boyfriend and girlfriend."

"You may now fist bump your girlfriend," Zoey says, holding her hand out.

I do. And then I kiss the hell out of her.

Well, as much as I can with her door wide open.

THIRTY-NINE

ZOEY

Tour Guide Fun Fact #6: Olympia University's entomology department is nationally ranked, and our undergraduates can take a course in beekeeping.

When Tessa was in that class, she accidentally killed her queen bee three times. Three. She still got an A in the class. I always ask my tour groups if they think she should have gotten a B for that.

But each time she did, her hive was able to recover. Move on and move forward.

Eileen and I don't sit next to each other in class anymore. I'm the one who had to relocate though. First day after she tried to sabotage me, she was sitting in class right where we normally sit, her head held high, looking haughty as fuck. I decided it wasn't worth it to argue.

I've gotten over it. Kind of. I mean, I've stopped being

filled with rage every time I see her, so that's a plus. I guess this is the semester of learning how to get over people.

I sit in the front row now, which kind of sucks, because Professor Heath is like right freaking there. My phone lights up in my backpack with a nonstop stream of texts from Alex and I desperately want to check them, even though I know they're just nonsense. Probably *Firefly* memes.

Instead, like the good student I am, I take diligent notes. At the end of the lecture, I'm still wrapping up my last couple sentences when Professor Heath calls to me.

"Zoey? Do you have a minute?"

"Of course," I chirp. On the inside, though? I'm panicking. Is this good news or bad news? This could be *the* news.

I weave my way out of the aisle and toward the front of the room. My pulse buzzes around my head. My heart is pounding harder than when Alex and I are fucking. Which I *really* shouldn't be thinking about right now.

Professor Heath is stuffing his laptop and papers into his bag when I reach him. "Zoey!" he exclaims excitedly. He has a swirling orange and red tie on that I'm pretty sure is supposed to represent Red Rock Canyon. "I just wanted to let you know while you're here that you got the position. You should be getting the email later today. I was really impressed with all your experience and I'm excited to see what you bring to the lab. The email will tell you your starting dates, and I know finals are coming up, but we want to get you introduced to the lab as soon as possible so you'll be ready to hit the ground running next semester."

My brain stalls out.

It takes a whole flabbergasted second for me to process what he's saying.

I can't believe it. It doesn't seem real. I've been

dreaming of hearing those words since I was a freshman here.

I got the position.

I got the fucking position.

"Thank you," I sputter. "Thank you so much. I've been wanting this for years. I—thank you."

"Good, good. I'm happy you're happy. You've been a good student these past few years." He's nodding casually as if he didn't just drop life-changing news on my head. Literally. Life. Changing. "Bring your hiking boots the first day and don't be late. We're going to be collecting samples. I look forward to working with you, Zoey." He sticks out his hand, and I shake it. My hand is probably sweaty I'm so overwhelmed.

"Uh, thank you again," I remember to say as he's already walking away. He lifts a hand in acknowledgment and makes his way out of the lecture hall.

Holy fuck.

Thank you, universe.

I exit into the sunlight, a huge grin on my face, and throw my hands in the air. I don't pay attention to the weird looks I get from the next incoming class. This is my moment.

And all I want to do is find Alex and jump into his arms. Tell him the good news. Celebrate the day away. Ride him until neither of us knows our own names. I dig in my backpack for my phone.

"Congratulations. I guess you really do get everything you want." The bitter voice pulls me out of my self-celebration. I turn. Eileen is standing against the building, waiting for me. She's dressed in her standard flannel pajama bottoms and Olympia sweatshirt. She looks... sad.

And I feel bad for her. I really do.

"Hey, listen, why don't we get everyone back together again? Go have boba this weekend?" I'll convince Tessa to come. She won't like it, but she will for me. Maybe one last hang out for old time's sake.

Eileen shakes her head. "Naomi and Derek are out of town this weekend. They're having their first weekend away as a couple."

"Oh shit. They finally got together."

"Yeah," Eileen says. The conversation falls flat. This is why I hate small talk. I never know what to say. "What about you?" Eileen asks. "What's your new man's name again?"

"Alex."

"Are you and Alex the real deal?" she asks. I remember her accusing I was only dating him to get Z's attention. I wonder if that's what everyone thought all along. I can't be bothered to be embarrassed though, because that whole process gave me Alex.

"Hell yeah we are," Alex says, walking up behind me. My stomach spins at the sound of his voice and my already huge smile gets bigger. I can't help it. He passes me one of the hot coffees in his hand before he wraps his arm around me and presses a kiss to my neck. As long as we're not around Lucy, Alex has no problem with PDA. I love that. "I got out of class early. Decided I'd meet you here."

"Good decision. You shouldn't be sitting on Hades's Fountain any more than you already have." I finally drag my eyes away from the six feet and four inches of god-like hotness that is my boyfriend. "This is Eileen," I say, putting on that overly sweet tour guide voice again, but she's already backing away from the conversation. She lifts her hand in a wave.

"I'll see you at work, Zoey. Congrats again."

"Why is she congratulating you?" Alex whispers, watching Eileen go. He flips her off behind her back and I laugh.

I spin into his arms, wrapping one arm around his neck. "Guess."

"Congrats on getting dicked by me?" he guesses, pulling me to him as tight as he can without spilling our coffees.

"Oh my god, Mr. Big-Ass Ego. No, that wasn't it." I lean in and drag my lips across his cheek before whispering evilly in his ear. "Even better."

"Not possible," he says matter-of-factly. I pull away a couple inches so he can see how big my smile is. He's confused, glancing between my eyes and smile. Then his eyes go wide. "Holy shit. You got the position?"

"Damn right I did."

"I knew you would." He grins. He squeezes me even tighter. And I know if he didn't want to spill coffee all over me again, he'd be picking me up in his arms right now, just like I imagined. We're on the same wavelength like that. "I'm so proud of you, Zo."

"Want to go back to my place to celebrate?" My voice is drowning with innuendo.

Alex presses a hard kiss against my lips. Then, without breaking contact, he murmurs, "Fuck. Yeah."

The celebration is perfect. In fact, everything between Alex and me is perfect.

I spend the next two weeks with Alex in relationship bliss. Granted, most of that time is spent blissed out in bed, but when we're not in bed, it's *still* perfect. Life goes by in these moments I want to keep forever. I take Alex and Lucy to my favorite hike in the area, showing them one of the best views in the world. Alex takes me out to an actual fancy restaurant for a lunch date, since we can't leave Lucy home alone for dinner. The two of us study together for finals on the couch, my legs in his lap, his hands on my shins.

Being with Alex is so out-of-this-world perfect, it's hard to believe I ever wanted anything else.

"Tessa, my love, where are thou?" I call into her room, wading through the crazy amount of junk covering her floor. I pretend to look around and under various objects. I'm baffled how someone can have this much stuff in one room. I pause, tilting my head in half laughter when I spot a giant stuffed penis in the corner of her room. Where did she even get that?

"You brat." She looks up from where she's sitting at her desk studying and throws a pen at me.

I clear off a space for myself on her bed and take a seat. "So this is where all of our plates have gone."

"I can't both cook and clean." She spins around in her desk chair to face me. "So I assume you kicked Alex out then?"

"His alarm kicked him out. I'm proud. As long as he doesn't hit traffic, he should be on time to pick up Lucy." He was late once when we first started hooking up. We lost track of time all tangled in each other. Ever since then, he's set an alarm.

"Wow. Shit has changed."

"It really has." I can't help grinning. I've been so happy lately. Everything in my life is coming together. The world after college doesn't seem so scary anymore. I can finally just relax and enjoy my last year here.

"Did you register for classes today?" Tessa asks.

"Yeah. Can't believe we're about to start our last semester already," I say. "Well, some of us." Tessa officially declared a second major and registered for her class in Greece over the summer. So she now has a year and a half left. "I got into the dance class."

"Oh thank goodness." Tessa, Kacen, Brandon, and I have all decided to take a dance class together next semester. Tessa shimmies at me, I assume preparing for our dance class. I already know she's going to be great. She's musically talented like that.

"I still can't believe the freshmen got to register before us," I complain.

"To be a student athlete is to be a god," Tessa says with a shrug. "Speaking of gods, any progress with the Get Alex Adams Back On The Field Operation?"

I play with the ends of my hair. I feel terrible not telling Alex about what I've been up to. But he doesn't think he deserves to play again and I know he does. "Yeah, I've been talking to West trying to figure out what I need to do," I say quietly. "I've contacted a couple agents and scouts and stuff for him. There's definitely still interest."

"I told you there would be." Tessa clasps her hands together. "Have you seen that boy play? It's like getting a glimpse of heaven."

I snort. I know exactly what she means. Watching Alex play is definitely a religious experience for me. I could worship his body all day. "He has a tournament in Arizona this weekend."

"And?"

"And there may or may not be a couple of scouts coming to watch," I confess. Tessa bounces in her chair with excitement. I think she's more excited than I am about this plan to get Alex back in the professional soccer sphere.

"Are you going to tell him?"

"Should I?" I ask, flopping backward on her bed. It's something I've been trying to figure out for a couple of days now. "What if he gets stressed or something and doesn't play up to standard?"

"You mean what if he gets mad at you for going behind his back?" Tessa asks dryly, using her psychology witchcraft powers to single out what I'm actually worried about. "That man couldn't play bad if he was blindfolded and his hands were tied."

"Well, I mean, you don't need your hands for soccer."

"What's your plan?" she asks, brushing away my jokes.

"Maybe an agent will just call him up out of the blue, you know? My name will never have to be mentioned." I don't sound confident in my answer at all, and Tessa can hear it. She makes a disbelieving sound. I pop up on my elbows, trying to defend my actions to her. "I know he wants this. And he's going to come up with all these stupid reasons of why he doesn't deserve it. But he *does* deserve it. And—what?"

I break off when I notice how hard she's smiling at me. "You looooove him," she teases.

I grab a pillow off her bed and throw it at her. She bats it away and it lands on her floor in the sea of discarded clothes and notebooks. "I do not."

"You do. You love him."

"We barely just got together, Tessa. I can't love him yet."

"You've *basically* been together for a whole semester. Besides…" She waves her hand through the air and her bracelets jingle. "Time doesn't matter when it comes to love."

I shake my head. But I think about it. I do constantly

want to be with Alex. I want to be in his arms, surrounded by his scent. I crave his laugh and his jokes and his stupid cocky attitude. Practically every moment I'm with him, I feel like I'm on top of the world. "How can I love him? I don't even know what love is."

"Eh. You love him. I can tell." I think she can tell this conversation is freaking me out though, so she changes the subject. "So what's he doing with Lucy this weekend?"

"Oh. I'm taking care of her."

Tessa's eyes go wide. "No shit? Zoey in charge of a little human's life." She fake shivers. "That's a scary thought."

"She's practically an adult."

"She's what, thirteen?"

"See, an adult."

"You and I aren't even adults yet."

"She's like the same as us then."

"Are you sure you can handle it? Caring for a kid can be a lot."

"It's one weekend. What could go wrong?"

FORTY

ALEX

My shin guards always stay in my soccer bag. Or, almost always, I should say. Of course, this is the one day that one of them isn't there. I'm sprinting through the house, trying to find it, and instead keep noticing other things I haven't packed yet. Like my phone charger. I throw it into the mound of stuff in my duffel bag.

Zoey lets herself in and I rush right by her. "Hey babe," I call over my shoulder.

"You're late?" she guesses.

"I can't find anything." I spin in a circle. Then I rush back to my bedroom to look in there one last time. I check my phone again and curse. I really am running out of time. "Lucy!" I yell through the house.

"What?" she calls back. I don't think she even bothers coming out of her room even though she knows damn well I need to talk to her. I drop to my hands and knees and exhale in relief when I spot my shin guard under my dresser. I fall flat to my stomach so I can wiggle my arm in there and retrieve it.

"Do you have everything you need?" I yell as I make my way back to my soccer bag. I drop my shin guard in there.

"Yes." I can sense the eye roll from here. I've been over-planning and over-worrying all week. I grab my laptop and slide it into my bag on the off chance I get a moment to get some grading done. I glance around my room again. I don't spot anything else I need to pack. So I jog to Lucy's room.

I knock on the door and then push it open without waiting for an answer. She's lying in her bed watching TV on her phone.

"You're going to be okay with Zoey, right?" I ask.

"Yes." There's that eye roll.

"And you'll behave for her?"

"What do you think I'm going to do? Throw a temper tantrum over broccoli? Sneak out?"

"I don't know. What does Mom normally do before she leaves you home for the weekend?"

"Hugs me and makes sure I have food."

"Oh fudge," I curse, straightening up and running a hand through my hair. Do I have time to make it to the store? I glance at my phone again and almost panic laugh. I don't even have time to make it to the meet-up location before we're supposed to leave.

Lucy smirks at me. "Did you forget to go grocery shopping?"

"I didn't forget," I grumble. "I just ran out of time."

"It's fine," Zoey says in a soothing voice, coming up behind me and placing a hand on my shoulder. My body practically melts into her touch. "Lucy and I will make do. We can order out."

"You can't just eat donuts all weekend." They both pout

at me. "No way, that won't work on me," I say, shaking my head and leaving the room so I don't have to look at their puppy dog eyes. Because, yeah, these are my two favorite people in the world. If they pout enough, they could probably get anything they wanted from me.

I pile my two bags by the door. I glance around the house again. I've left a mess for Zoey, but I don't think she'll mind. Everything else should be ready to go.

I feel a little guilty about leaving. Even though my mom knows who Zoey is now, I still don't talk to her about my relationship much. Every time she calls me, she asks about Zoey in that disapproving tone of hers. So I avoid the subject as much as possible.

Which means I haven't told my parents that I'm leaving their daughter in the care of someone they've never met before for the weekend.

I know if I did tell my mom, she'd be pissed. She wouldn't approve of the situation and she would forbid me from going to the soccer tournament. And then I'd either have to go behind her back or not go at all.

And Zoey's right. I need to start trusting myself more, not just doing everything that my parents want me to do. I trust Zoey. I trust her to take care of Lucy for the weekend.

If everything goes according to plan, I get to play soccer for the weekend and my parents never have to know I was away.

Lucy drags herself out of her room to say goodbye.

"You can call me if you need anything, you know that, right?" I ask.

"It's just a weekend," Lucy says. I swear, one of these days, her eyes are going to get stuck in the back of her head.

I look over her shoulder. "Zoey. Call me if anything

happens." I say it with all the seriousness I can manage, because, dammit, I'm worried.

"I will." She smiles reassuringly at me. "But we're going to be fine. We're just going to watch TV and eat *healthy* food and play board games. Maybe paint."

Lucy high-fives her.

"You need to get your homework done too, though," I say. I keep thinking of more things. "And don't forget—"

"Alex," Lucy cuts me off. "It's one weekend. I'm going to be fine." She pushes forward and wraps her arms around me. It feels damn good that she's finally the one initiating a hug. I hug her tightly back, patting the top of her head. "Go kick butt in your game, okay?"

She only sounds a little bitter when she says that. I grin. I release Lucy and reach for Zoey next. I press a quick kiss to her lips, careful to keep it PG-13. Even though one touch is all it takes for me to want to shove her against a wall.

"We're going to be fine," Zoey promises against my lips.

And I believe her.

They push me out of the door, and I wait until I hear it lock behind me.

Now I just have to focus on soccer. That's something I can do any day of the week.

ZOEY

The rest of that Friday was uneventful. It felt weird sleeping in Alex's bed without him. It smelled like him, which made me miss him all night long.

Alex didn't help the situation by sending me dirty texts throughout the night.

Saturday has been drizzling all day. It's the perfect day for Lucy and me to stay inside and drink hot chocolate and watch movies. So that's exactly what we do. We fuck around with watercolors a little bit midday, but we mostly just stay couch potatoes.

Alex's first game of the tournament is late this afternoon. They play two games today and one tomorrow. I managed to get a couple scouts to agree to come this weekend, but I'm not sure if they're coming to today's games or tomorrow's. It's abnormal for them to even consider coming to a club soccer game at all. Even if a player is good, it's impossible to tell how good if the competition isn't up to standard.

But they're going to be there this weekend. I mean, it's freaking Alex Adams.

"Ugh," I say, refreshing the website for the bajillionth time. "Why don't they do live updates for club soccer games?" I sit cross-legged on the couch. Lucy sits on the floor, her legs spreading under the coffee table. We have attempted starting a puzzle, but after about an hour of half-assed work, we don't even have the edge pieces yet. Lucy connects another piece.

"Because no one cares," she says, not bothering to look up from the puzzle.

"I care," I grumble. I texted Alex good luck before his game, but I didn't confess what I had been up to. I didn't want to jinx anything and tell him more, but there was a thirty-three percent chance a scout was at this game.

I'm fucking praying he has another one of those hat trick days.

Lucy glances up at me suspiciously. "Why are you so nervous?"

I am nervous. I'm practically shaking. My palms are

sweaty. I shouldn't tell Lucy, especially if I haven't told Alex yet, but I want this off my chest. I rub my palms off on their couch. "Can you keep a secret?"

She nods.

"From Alex?" I clarify.

She narrows her eyes, obviously not liking that idea. "What did you do?"

"Nothing bad," I rush to say. I don't know where her brain is going, but the way her glare is building makes me want to shut down that thought process fast. "I mean, I don't think it's bad."

"Zoey?" she prompts.

"So you know how Alex still kind of wants to keep playing soccer?" I lead. Lucy nods, but she doesn't look particularly happy about it. "I might have sent an annoyingly large number of emails around, trying to see if there was still any interest in him. And there is. So scouts are coming to his games this weekend."

Lucy thinks this over. She twists a puzzle piece in her hand, staring at it. The silence is deafening. The rain picks up outside. It beats a steady thrum against the window. That, and the creepy whistle the heater makes are the only sounds in the room. "Does Alex know?"

Way to cut right to the heart of the problem, Lucy. "Well, I haven't told him yet," I hedge.

"I think..." Lucy bites her lower lip. "I think he'll be okay with it. Especially if it works out. You're just trying to help."

She sounds so sad. And she still hasn't torn her gaze from the puzzle piece. It dawns on me that there's a bigger issue here. "Are *you* okay with it?"

She shrugs, her hair falling forward and obscuring her face from view. "I mean, he's going to leave eventually, right?" She turns back and tries to connect the pieces in her hand together, but they won't fit. "I just don't want him to forget me again."

"He won't, Lucy," I say. "He's different." Not that I knew him before. But I know who he is now, and there's nothing he wouldn't do for Lucy.

She nods. I think most of her believes me. She isn't thrilled about the prospect of him leaving so soon, but she knows he's different now.

I lean toward my computer and refresh the page one more time. Nothing. They might not even post the final score until tomorrow. I consider texting West, but I'm sure he's busy.

I groan, shutting the laptop. "Wasn't there that movie you wanted to go see?" I ask.

"It's already after nine," Lucy says.

"So? Responsible Alex isn't here. You have no bedtime."

"You're the worst babysitter ever. I love it."

"So, to the movies?" I ask. I desperately need the distraction.

"To the movies."

It's just past midnight when we leave the theater and make our way back to my car. The rain has stopped, but the sky is filled with fog, and the pavement is shiny, reflecting the lights of the parking lot. Our breath leaves streaks of white steam in the air as we run back to the car giggling, trying not to slip in the puddles.

We yank the car door open and throw ourselves inside. I slam it shut behind me. "It's so cold," I moan, instantly turning up the heater to full blast. This is the first day of good rain this year and I'm not prepared. It's fucking freezing. I'm a summer child through and through.

We pull out of the parking lot after I've double-checked that Lucy is seat belted in properly. She puts her hands over the vent blowing hot air at us and sighs happily as they start to defrost. We come to a stop at a red light. When the light turns green, I'm careful to look both ways first, instead of just trusting it. Then I accelerate slowly. Alex freaks out about my driving for no good reason, and I know I said I'd never change for a guy, but if driving a little more carefully with Lucy in the car makes Alex happy, then I'm going to do it.

It's a short drive back to the residential streets near their house. We've been talking and laughing the whole way back. Lucy yawns now, then asks, "Will you still babysit me when my parents come home?"

I bite my lip, unsure of how to respond. We pause at a stop sign and, again, I look both ways before proceeding forward. "I don't know if I'll be babysitting you, but I'm sure I'll see lots of you—"

I see it happening out of the corner of my eye, like slow motion. A dark car blazing through the intersection, not even slowing at the stop sign. It's headed straight toward Lucy's side of the car. I accelerate, trying to escape its path, but it catches the tail end of the car, sending us spinning into the street. We skid across the wet asphalt. I hear more than see the sickening thunk as Lucy's head hits the window. I slam on the brakes, but the car continues to glide until we hit a small tree on the side of the road.

The whole thing doesn't take more than a second. But it feels like so much longer.

My heartbeat is erratic and everywhere. I can't think. The smell of smoke fills the car, and I can't figure out where it's coming from. The airbags? I banged against the side of the car, but I think I'm okay. I think—

"Lucy?" I spin toward her. My neck spasms with the sharp movement but I ignore it. "Are you okay?" She's whimpering beside me. "Lucy?" I'm full-out panicking now. Her head is bleeding. Oh fuck, there's a lot of blood.

I'm babbling. I keep telling her she's going to be okay as I search my car, slapping random parts and throwing things around. Where the fuck is my phone?

Finally I find where it was flung under my seat. I dial 911.

The air around us smells metallic and sharp. It's heavy. Suffocating.

Lucy continues to whimper.

"We were in a car accident," I tell the operator when they pick up. I don't notice until I'm speaking that I'm on the verge of tears. "I have a minor in the car."

"Where are you?"

I rattle off the street signs and the calm voice of the operator talks me through the situation. I glance in my side mirror and notice the man who hit us has gotten out of his car. He's standing at the hood, inspecting it. I'm glad to see he's okay, at least.

EMTs will arrive in minutes. I reach over to hold Lucy's hand and she squeezes mine. I'm still on the phone with the operator.

Out of the corner of my eye, I see movement again. The man who hit us is getting back in his car.

He's driving away. The motherfucker is driving away. He peels out of the intersection, and I've been so worked up about Lucy that I never managed to write down his license plate number.

Waves of blue and red flashing lights wash over the

street. A firetruck gets here first. Then an ambulance seconds after. They exit the truck and—

Walk. They're walking. Do they not understand that someone is in pain over here? Why the fuck aren't they sprinting to the car?

When they finally, finally reach us, they inspect Lucy first.

They reach to pull her from the car. Lucy glances over to me, her face wide and panicked and so trusting. I nod, trying to tell her everything will be okay.

They keep trying to take a look at me and make sure I haven't broken anything, but I keep waving them off, and then I climb into the ambulance with Lucy.

I put my head in between my knees and take deep breaths.

Holy fuck holy fuck holy fuck.

Alex is going to kill me.

FORTY-ONE

ALEX

There's a party spread across five different hotel rooms right now. An intense game of king's cup is going down in one room, rage cage in another. In the next, some of my team members are sprawled across the bed, eating edibles. It's kind of a choose-your-own-adventure hotel room party scene.

Guests have complained, but every time there's a noise complaint, we just file out of the room and walk down the hallway to a different room.

This is way less disciplined than it was for Heyward's D1 team. Coach had us on a strict curfew and an even stricter "no party policy" the night before a game. Not that we didn't find ways to make it happen, but for the most part, we respected the system because we respected the game.

These motherfuckers are drunk off their asses with no care whatsoever that we have a game tomorrow.

It's funny. When I first got home, I would have killed for a chance to party like this. It's one of the first nights that

I'm not somewhat responsible for a thirteen-year-old. I could let loose if I wanted to. I don't have to drive anywhere, and how I perform in my match tomorrow doesn't matter anymore.

But I don't want to.

It's like some part of me actually did become Responsible Alex. For months, I've been faking it, pretending that I have my shit together.

And now I do. Kind of.

I weave out of one hotel room, down the hallway, and into another. I haven't seen Eddie or West all night. I need something to do besides sit on my ass and watch my teammates get drunk, and I'm pretty sure Eddie will be sober too. He almost always is.

But I can't find either of them. I've been through every room now. The jerks probably have a coach's room to themselves and are fast asleep by now.

My phone rings. I can barely hear it over the music they have blasting in this room, but I do hear it.

It's Zoey. My heart stumbles. Why the hell is she calling me at one a.m.?

"Zo?" I yell into the phone, trying to be heard over the music.

"Alex, I'm so sorry—"

"Are you crying?" Now I'm panicked. I've never seen her cry before. Hell, even when she was heartbroken she wasn't crying. "Are you okay?"

"I'm okay," Zoey says. She hiccups on the other end. "We got into a car accident—"

"Is Lucy okay?"

It feels like my heart has stopped. Waiting for Zoey to respond to this question takes an eternity. I'm in Arizona. I'm in Arizona and Lucy is in danger and I don't know how the hell I'm supposed to get back in time to help. My mind just keeps offering up all these worst-case scenarios and my heart—it's stopped fucking working. I rub my chest.

"She's okay," Zoey says. "We're in the ambulance—"

"You're in an ambulance?" I screech into the phone. I immediately cough afterward. I don't think I've ever screeched before.

I'm not there to help Lucy. Because I left her for soccer. Again. I'm six hours away. Five, if I drive like... Zoey.

If I drive like Zoey.

Fucking hell. I told Zoey to be more careful. I told her to—

"Is she in pain?" I don't recognize my own voice.

"I-I think so. I don't know what's wrong," Zoey says. "I'll call you when I know more." She pauses. "I'm so sorry, Alex."

"I'm coming home." It's all I can manage. I hang up the phone.

The party is raging around me, but instead of the amused disinterest I had moments ago, I'm pissed. People keep stumbling in my way, refusing to move. I'm literally shoving teammates aside, trying to reach the door.

"Hey man, what the fuck?" Caleb mumbles as he bounces against the wall.

"Where's Eddie and West?" I demand. Caleb shakes his head. Fuck. They're the ones who have all the keys to the vans. I can't get home if I can't find them.

I call West. Then Eddie. It goes to voice mail both times.

I tear through hotel rooms, yelling for them.

They're not there.

Why the hell did I think coming here was a good idea? Why did I think any of this was a good idea in the first place? I'm terrible at being Responsible Alex. I should have sent Lucy abroad with my parents.

Fuck. My parents. They're going to kill me.

Matty finally hears me yelling and leads me to Eddie and West's room. I bang on the door.

"Calm your tits, calm your tits," West mutters from the other side of the door. "I'm coming." He opens it, shirtless. "Adams!" He grins. "What—"

"I need to get home." I barge into the room. Eddie is lying on one of the beds but sits straight up as I come into the room, looking around for the van keys. "Lucy is in the hospital. I need the keys."

To their credit, neither of them fights me on this, despite the fact that going from three vans to two vans is going to mess everyone else up on the drive home. Eddie even offers to drive me back, claiming I'm not in a fit state to drive. West frowns at this, but he lets us go.

We've barely crossed the California border when Zoey calls me again. I drop the phone I'm so panicked and then have to root around for it on the floor of the passenger's seat side.

"Is she okay?" I ask the minute I have the phone to my ear.

"She's okay." I can hear the relief in Zoey's voice, and I know she's telling me the truth. "I'm about to take her home."

"What happened?" I ask.

"She just got a couple of pretty good gashes. She needed stitches, but it was nothing serious. Didn't even have a concussion." Zoey drops her voice to a shaky whisper. "It looked like a lot of blood. Alex. I thought..."

I don't even want to know what she thought. "Are they

sure that's all that was wrong with her?" I ask. "Did they run tests?"

"Yeah, I think so. I don't know. I couldn't be in the room."

"Why not?" I demand. I'm still freaking out.

"I'm not family."

I groan. What if they missed something important and she has internal bleeding?

"Alex," Zoey says softly. "She just needed stitches. She's fine."

"Is she with you?" I ask.

"Not yet."

"Let me know when she is. I want to talk to her."

"Good. I think she's pretty rattled."

I can't believe I did this to her.

When I hang up the phone, Eddie glances over at me. "Is she okay?"

"Yeah. Just needed stitches," I mumble.

And really, it isn't a big deal. There're loads of times when I needed stitches in my life. The time I was ten and tried to build a treehouse by myself and fell out of the tree, hammer in hand. I sliced open my arm. Or, just last year, I went up for a header in a game at the same time as my opponent. His head slammed into my chin and it burst open, blood everywhere. They taped me up, and I finished the game. They stitched me up after.

But Lucy was my responsibility. This never would have happened if I had just stayed home.

And why was Zoey even driving her around at one in the morning? Hadn't she said they were just going to stay home and watch movies and order in?

If I had just kept it in my pants for one full semester, Lucy wouldn't have been in a car crash.

. . .

The third call of the night is from my parents. My mom is video chatting me. I don't know why she's calling me, because I've neglected to tell her the news until I'm home with Lucy, but I pick up anyway.

"Alex," she starts in with rapid-fire speed. "Oh god, are you okay, is everything okay? Wait—where are you?"

"In the car."

"Where's Lucy?" she asks. My dad is sitting in the background, a worried scowl across his face.

"Back home," I say. "She just needed stitches."

"The hospital, they called me..." My mom trails off as we both start putting things together. They thought I was with Lucy.

"I was in Arizona. For a soccer tournament. Zoey was taking care of Lucy." My voice is sick with guilt. They both stare at me for a second. "I'm on my way back home now." As if that makes it any better.

"You left for the weekend? And left Lucy home alone with a stranger?"

"She's not a stranger. She's my girlfriend."

"Alex. We said no girls." My dad is glaring at me. "Not only did you break that rule, but you put Lucy in danger."

I hang my head in shame.

"This is why we were going to take her with us," my mom says. "You can't handle this."

"I *can* handle this," I argue. "I was handling it just fine."

"You went to parties, you had random girls over, you left Lucy with people we don't even know—"

"I went to one party. One. When Lucy spent the night at her friend's!"

"Which means if anything had gone wrong you would

have been too drunk or high or whatever it is you do to handle it."

"That's not true!"

"Did you forget we're friends with you on social media?"

I shake my head. This is so frustrating. "I don't know what the fuck you saw, but it wasn't like that. I've been here for Lucy the whole time."

"Don't curse at us, Alex," my mom yells. Disappointment is etched on her face, probably more permanent than my tattoos.

I don't know who I was kidding with this Responsible Alex bullshit, but my parents sure didn't fall for it.

"If you were here for Lucy the whole time, why were you in Arizona? And why didn't you tell us you were going?"

"I left her with Zoey. I trust—"

"We've never met Zoey. You had no right to leave our daughter with her. You've trusted a lot of things in your life, Alex, and most of them just proved you were an idiot."

"Tom," my mom admonishes.

"What?" he groans, his hands flying in the air. This is the exact opposite of my dad's personality. He's normally the kooky, gentle one. So distracted by a book that he doesn't even have time to talk to you. Now his face is so screwed up it's an angry red and purple color. "I don't know what to do for him anymore. We've tried everything. If he wants to live the rest of his life as a fuck-up, that's on him."

My dad thinks I'm a fuck-up.

I don't know why I'm surprised.

"I have a flight booked—" my mom starts.

"You don't need to come home. I've got this."

"You don't," my dad says. "And don't interrupt your mother."

"It's just two weeks early, Alex. Your dad is going to stay here the remainder of the semester. Then we will all be home."

"Mom, you really don't have to."

"She's my baby. And she's probably scared." Lucy probably *is* scared, but also, she's a beast. If what Zoey says is true and it really is just stitches, she'll have no problem getting through this. "You need to pick me up at the airport tomorrow."

I nod in agreement.

God. Motherfucking. Dammit.

I couldn't take care of Lucy for one semester.

One goddamn semester.

The call ends shortly after that. We continue at record speeds down the freeway. I stare out the passenger's side window, but it's so dark I can't see anything out there.

I'm willing Eddie not to say anything. I know he just overheard that whole conversation.

And because Eddie is Eddie, he can pick up on the mental signs I'm putting down.

He grips my shoulder before returning both hands to the wheel. He doesn't offer any condolences, any false "everything will be okays." I appreciate that.

Because, honestly, I don't know if everything *will* be okay.

FORTY-TWO

ZOEY

I've been up all night. Lucy and I are both sleeping in Alex's bed. She didn't want to be alone. She's fast asleep now, snoring lightly beside me, but I'm still staring at the ceiling.

The sun is barely starting to rise, a mist of sunlight sneaking in through the window, when I hear the front door open.

I ease myself out of bed. My whole body hurts. I can barely twist my neck, it's so stiff. I tiptoe into the living room. The cold of the tile floor seeps into my skin, chilling my soul.

Alex is setting his stuff by the side of the door.

"Hey," I say. My voice is soft, timid, uncertain. I want to reach my arms around him and hug him tight, soak up all the comfort and warmth from his body. His face is pressed into hard lines, though. He looks like he's had less sleep than me, if that's possible.

I don't hug him.

"Where's Lucy?" he asks.

"Your bed," I say. "She's asleep."

He nods. Then weaves around me. I follow him back to his bedroom. He stands over Lucy in the bed. She has a small cut on her temple and cheek that's been stitched up and a couple more along her arm. Alex's face is impassive, unexpressive. I rarely see him like this. It's jarring. Scary, almost. He's a tall wall of tattooed muscle that could do some serious damage on the guy who injured Lucy.

He's just looking down at her, and I don't know what to say to make anything better. "The doctor said she wouldn't scar," I whisper, trying not to wake Lucy. "Or shouldn't," I amend. These words affect Alex. He rears back like he's been hit. The prospect of scarring hadn't occurred to him.

He runs a hand through his hair. The movement is comforting and familiar, but the expression on his face is anything but that. He reaches out toward Lucy, like he wants to touch her and make sure she's okay, but instead, he draws away, thinking better about waking her up.

He walks out of the room and gestures for me to follow. When we're back in the living room, he starts to speak.

"Zoey—" He breaks off when his voice ends in a squeak. I can't help it anymore. I reach for him, wrapping my hands tight around his midsection. He holds me just as tight, biceps coming around my shoulders. He smells like sweat, honestly, but I don't mind. I bury my face in his shirt, feeling the hardness of his muscles, the softness of his skin, the rhythmic pounding of his heart behind his ribs.

We stand like this for several minutes, each seeking comfort in each other. Then Alex breaks away. "Zoey," he starts again, louder this time, more resolute. "This isn't going to work."

"What isn't going to work?" I ask, refusing to hear what he's saying.

"Us." He says it so simply, like it isn't rocking my whole worldview right now.

"Alex?" My voice cracks. It fucking cracks. I suddenly appreciate the way Z did this over text.

"It's my fault, Zo. I didn't think any of this through." His eyes are on the floor.

I poke at his chest. He doesn't even flinch. Just lets his head hang more. I jab at him again. "Two weeks, Alex. Two weeks ago you asked me to be in a relationship."

"I was stupid, okay? I thought I could do this and I can't." He glances to me, and then away at the wall.

"Why not? You were doing fine—"

"I wasn't doing fine. I should have known this was how it was going to turn out."

"How?" I throw my hands in the air. "How could you have known this was how it was going to turn out?"

"My parents gave me a set of rules for a reason. And I broke them." Alex groans, running a palm over his face, his fingers stretching out his cheek. "It was bound to be bad for Lucy."

"One person making a stupid decision on the road does not suddenly make you a failure."

"One person?" Alex snorts.

"What does that mean?" I ask, crossing my arms over my chest. It's cold all around me, but my body feels on fire.

"Okay, here's the thing, Zo. When I left, I should have left *you* with the rule not to drive Lucy anywhere."

"Alex," I say, reaching a hand to his shoulder, hoping he will listen to me. His muscles are tense and spasming beneath my hand. "I swear, I was being careful."

"If it's one in the morning and no one else is around, do you really need to stop?" Alex quotes our conversation from the amusement park.

My hand falls. "I stopped."

"I find that hard to believe."

"I knew you would be worried. I—"

"Damn right I would be worried. My parents entrusted a child to me, and then I go and let her get in a car with you."

That hangs between us for a moment.

"So that's why this is your fault," I breathe out, a weird calm taking over my body. I inhale anger, exhale shock and sadness. The energy courses through me and I turn it all on Alex. "It's not that you think you're stupid for attempting a relationship. You think you're stupid for attempting a relationship with *me*."

I don't phrase it as a question, because it's not a question. I see it on Alex's face. He winces, as if knowing this will be hard for me to hear, but the validity of the statement is in his eyes. At least he's always been honest with me, I'll give him that.

"You know what?" I ask. "Fine. Fuck it. You're right. I don't need to be in a relationship with someone who isn't going to listen to my side of the story."

I glance around me, wondering where I left all my belongings and what I need to grab before I storm out. I groan when I realize I'm wearing Alex's pajama bottoms and T-shirt. I have the choice to either strip down in front of my now-ex boyfriend or leave wearing his clothes. I almost laugh at how similar this is to when we first met. Me, in his clothes.

"Zoey," Alex says. "It's more than that too." He sits

down on the couch, his normally perfect cocky posture a mess as he folds in on himself. "You have this big, bright future ahead of you. And I'm the fuck-up who's not going anywhere else in his life."

"Only 'cause you choose that," I counter.

"I know I'm the one who messed up."

"*Messed*. Alex. Messed up. As in past tense. You literally can change that all now, do whatever you want to, but you're stuck in your head as if what you did was this big bad thing."

"It was."

"It's not insurmountable."

Alex glares at the coffee table. "You deserve someone better." His voice is soft and tired. And honest. He really believes what he's saying.

"Only I get to decide who I deserve," I tell him, my voice hard. "But yeah, I deserve better." He glances up quickly, and I see the flash of hurt across his face. "Just so you know, it's not because of your past. It's because you're being a dick right now."

I spin away from him, walking back to his room so I can grab my backpack and start throwing things in.

Lucy is sitting up in the bed when I get there, her eyes wide. I don't know how much of that conversation she heard. I give her a halfhearted wave.

"Are you leaving?" she whisper asks.

I nod.

"Oh."

I finish gathering up my things. I walk over to Lucy and hug her, careful to avoid her cuts and bruises. Just because her brother is a dick doesn't mean she is.

"Call me if you ever need anything," I say, releasing her. She hangs onto me tightly before finally letting me go.

When I turn to leave, Alex is standing in the doorway, watching us. I don't know what the hard expression on his face is, but I do know he's blocking the exit he's demanding I walk out. That's it. I'm taking his damn pajamas with me. I flip him off, not caring that we're in front of Lucy. He moves to the side, letting me scrape past him, and out of his life.

FORTY-THREE

ZOEY

"Oh god," Tessa says. "It smells like someone died in here."

I peek my head up from where I'm curled up under a mound of blankets and pillows. Tessa wades through the mess of dirty clothes in my room, covering her mouth with her arm.

"I'm okay." My voice is thick from lack of use. "You don't have to come in."

"How did you make this much of a mess already? I don't understand how you even got the supplies for this."

"It's an art form."

"That's something I would say. Don't turn into me, Zoey."

"But you're so great. I love you."

"And I love you," she says. She climbs into bed behind me and wraps her arms around me. "That's why I want you to stay you."

"You don't have to spoon me."

Tessa shushes me. "You need comfort."

"Tessa, it's fine. I'm alright."

"Your room says otherwise."

"Okay, but spooning? That's your first solution?"

"I'm pretty sure this is what I would want if I was going through a breakup."

"I'll keep that in mind."

"You do that." Her hands are on the outside of all my blankets, squeezing me in, and it's starting to get a little sweaty in here, but I make no move to escape. "Remember the previous three years, when you were never heartbroken and your room was always clean?"

"Good times, good times," I agree. And then I moan, "How did this happen twice in a semester?"

Tessa laughs a little. "Maybe you were finally brave enough to date someone you actually liked?"

"I've had boyfriends before."

"Exactly."

"What?" I wiggle up a little farther out of my blankets, trying to get a bit more air.

"I mean, sure, you dated them, Zoey. I'm just not sure you were their biggest fans."

"They grew on me. Like mold."

Tessa snorts. Her hand finds my head, and she starts petting my hair. Literally petting it. It feels kind of nice though, so I let her continue. "I think with Z you were ready to fall in love, so you pushed yourself over that edge. Z could have been anyone. And then Alex was Alex and you really did love him."

"The stupid fucker," I mutter. She laughs and pats my head. "Why are you giving up this psych thing again?" I ask.

"I'm not giving it up. I'm just adding another major. I never realized how cool mythology was until I was in this class and it feels like such a waste to be at the best university for it and *not* study it."

"I can't believe you're doing a whole second major in a year."

"It's only 'cause I'm taking that class in Greece this summer."

"I'll be all alone," I whine. I don't really want Tessa to leave me. I don't feel at all emotionally prepared to handle life without her right now. Although, hopefully by summer, I won't be as heartbroken.

I shift in the sheets, rolling out my shoulders, trying to get that haunting feeling in my chest to go away. Fuck. Why does everything hurt?

"Don't worry. I can still psychoanalyze you from abroad."

"Good. 'Cause you're good at this."

"I know. Now let's get you out of this god-awful place and get you to class."

"I'm not going." Once again, I don't want to be seen on campus. There's a chance I'll run into Alex, and I'm not looking forward to that. At all.

"Yes, you are."

"No, I'm not."

"Next week is finals."

I groan.

"Come on, you can't skip any more classes," Tessa says.

"Why not?"

"I don't want to be alone in myth."

"So for selfish reasons, then."

"And you need to graduate."

"I guess. I mean, what am I even going to do after this research lab—" I break off, panic reaching for my phone to check the time. "Oh fuck."

I'm officially late for my first day on the job.

Professor Heath is frowning when I get there. I still haven't showered. My greasy hair is thrown up into a tight bun. At least I remembered hiking boots. All in all though, not my best foot forward.

"I'm so sorry." I don't have a reasonable excuse, so I don't give one. "This will never happen again."

Professor Heath's frown grows bigger. He shakes his head. "Let me show you around then, Zoey." His voice is short and snippy. I've never heard him talk like this before. He's normally so warm to me.

He shows me around the lab. We don't have time anymore to go collect samples, and I can feel the annoyance wafting off him.

The whole point of getting this position was to use Professor Heath's connections to get a better job after graduation. If he hates me, how am I supposed to do that?

I can't believe how colossally I just messed up.

Losing Alex feels like someone is hacking at my chest with an ice pick. But that's no excuse to throw my future away. My whole semester so far has been about boys. But I'm done with that.

I'll prove to Professor Heath that he made the right choice. I'll be here early, put in extra hours, work harder than anyone else he's got. I'll have all of next semester to become the best assistant he's ever had.

And all of next semester to forget Alex Adams ever existed.

FORTY-FOUR

ALEX

Grad school sucks. I never thought I'd be up before six for anything in my life besides soccer. But here I am, sitting at the kitchen table with all my papers spread out in front of me, studying for my last final. After that, all I have to do is conduct a couple review sessions for my students and then proctor their final. I'm almost done with my first semester.

And I don't care. At all.

My mom's cooking oatmeal. She's adding apricots, apples, and blueberries. These are all things I never would have thought to add to oatmeal for Lucy. It's just another reminder of how I fell short.

I feel like I'm back in high school. Only worse. My parents trust me even less now. Didn't think that was possible.

"Eat," my mom says, setting the bowl in front of me. I sigh. She's been like this the whole time she's been back. Normally she has a hard outer personality, but you can see the softness in her eyes or hear it in her voice.

Nope. My mom's been all hard, all business around me for the past couple days. Like we're not even family.

"No, I was planning on starving," I respond, full of sarcasm. She turns around to glare at me, arms crossed over her chest. Honestly, the full power of her glare is kind of scary. She's an intimidating woman. The hardball to my dad's softball.

Today though, I don't have time to fight her. I really need to cram this last bit of information. "Thank you." I scoop a spoonful of oatmeal into my mouth. I turn back to studying.

I wonder if our relationship will always be this icy silence, or if she's just waiting for my dad to get home before she explodes and lets it all out.

Lucy comes in an hour later.

"How's my baby doing today?" my mom calls, suddenly all smiles and sweetness. Freaking hell, I'm going to have to start using Lucy as a human shield. She sits Lucy down at the table and places a soft kiss to the top of her head, placing a bowl of oatmeal in front of her. "How do you feel?" she asks.

"I'm fine," Lucy says, shaking her off. "I already told you, everything is fine." My mom nods and ruffles her hair, and then shoots a glare in my direction.

My mom leaves the room to get ready to drive Lucy to school. That's no longer my responsibility.

I take a sip of my coffee.

Which reminds me of Zoey.

Freaking caffeine gods. Will coffee always remind me of Zoey? Am I going to have to think of her every morning for the rest of my life?

Will I always feel this shitty about the things I said to her? Or miss her so goddamn much? I rub my chest.

"You're a moron," Lucy says dryly.

"Good morning to you too." I glance in her direction. The cut on her cheek is healing well, but it's still obvious. Her bruises have faded to an ugly yellow, but she doesn't look any worse than I look after a hard game. Her glare, though, is practically the same one my mom was giving me. "Why am I a moron?"

"Because you're all sad over here."

I bark out a laugh. "Am I not allowed to be sad?"

"Not when it's your own damn fault."

"Oh god, don't let Mom hear you say that."

"I got it from Zoey, not you."

"Don't let Mom hear you say that either."

"It wasn't Zoey's fault."

"Lucy—"

"No, listen. The other car didn't stop at the stop sign. It would have happened if you were driving, or Mom was driving. It wasn't Zoey's fault," she repeats.

I sit back in my chair. I push my hands against the table and push until the front two legs are tilted off the ground.

I never did listen to what Zoey had to say. But it doesn't matter. I would never be able to forgive myself if something I did put Lucy in danger.

As much as I tease Zoey about her driving, it isn't terrible. She's a fine driver. I've trusted her with my life all the time. She just has a tendency to break some rules on the road.

"It doesn't matter," I say.

"It does matter," Lucy persists. "If you broke up with her because she crashed the car—"

"I didn't break up with her because she crashed," I say, letting the chair fall back to the ground, front legs slamming into place.

"Then why?" Lucy demands. "I liked Zoey."

I did too, I think. "Because," I say. "She deserves someone who's not a fudge-up."

Lucy rolls her eyes. "Zoey doesn't think you're a failure."

"Failure. That's the word I was looking for," I say, reaching over to ruffle her hair. She slaps my hand away. Hard. "And see? That's the problem. I'll just end up letting her down too once she realizes she's wrong."

"I don't think you're a failure," Lucy says. This conversation is getting too deep for this early in the morning.

If there's anyone in the world who deserves to feel the most betrayed and hurt by my actions, it's Lucy. I start to speak, and she cuts me off.

"Honest. You were a great substitute parent." Lucy tucks a strand of hair behind her ear, an uncharacteristically shy trait for her. "And I don't think you'll abandon me when you play soccer again."

"Play soccer again?" I ask, confused. I have a year and a half left playing for the club team. And then... that's it. Hell. I'm not ready.

"Yeah, Zoey said..." She trails off, her face going pale.

I narrow my eyes at her. She shakes her head in response. "Zoey said what?"

"Nothing."

"Zoey said what?" I repeat.

"It doesn't matter," Lucy says, shaking her head.

"It does matter," I argue.

"You came home early anyway."

"Lucy," I warn.

Lucy hesitates for half a second more and then blurts it all out. "Zoey lined up scouts to come watch you in your Arizona tournament."

It feels like the whole world stills around me, while my heart starts beating faster. I glance at my homework spread out on the table. Numbers and drawings and proofs and equations.

God, I know a final isn't exactly supposed to fill you with happiness and make your blood buzz, but even the mere idea that I could actually be playing again brings me more joy than this ever could.

Zoey did this. For me. Because she believes in me.

It might be the nicest thing anyone has ever done for me.

And then it all comes crashing down. "And I didn't play."

"You played two games, right?" Lucy asks, hopefully.

I glance at my phone. The lack of calls and notifications tells me everything. "Fuck," I whisper, running my hand through my hair.

"Alex," my mother snaps, choosing that moment to walk back into the room.

"Sorry," I mutter. But I can't be bothered to care that much. Cussing in front of Lucy seems like a minor issue now.

There's a little flicker of hope in my belly.

And Zoey put it there.

I realize now how numb I've been, committing to a lifetime of things I don't love. Only Zoey recognized it and did something about it.

I run my hands through my hair again, whispering "fuck" under my breath.

Zoey's the best thing that ever happened to me and I just about banished her from my life.

"Alex," my mom repeats again, angrier this time. "Did

you follow any of the rules we gave you? How are you this irresponsible?"

I start to mumble another apology, because she's right. I shouldn't be dropping swear words around Lucy. Lucy pushes back her chair though and stands up on it. She crosses her arms, glaring at my mom.

"Alex followed all of your rules. All of them."

I barely hold in my laugh. It warms my freaking heart that she's doing this for me, but this is ridiculous.

"Lucia Adams, bajate."

I raise my eyebrows at Lucy. I'd get the hell off the chair if I was her, but she stands her ground.

"He did a great job," she says, shooting rays of fire out of her eyes. "The crash would have happened to you too. You need to stop blaming everything on Alex."

"He left you with—"

"With Zoey, a responsible adult that he trusts," Lucy finishes. "And I trust Alex. If you wanted to be this angry at him, you shouldn't have left me in the first place."

"We wanted to take you with us."

"And I didn't want to go to some—"

"Alright, Luce, it's good," I say, placing my hand on her back. "Thank you." She glares at me too, as if she wants to argue with me for stopping her roll. But she steps down from the chair. "We got to get you to school."

"I'm taking her," my mom cuts in, frowning.

"It's okay, I'll just take her on my way to campus."

"You need to study. You don't have time."

"I'll study on campus."

"Alex—"

I feel like shit cutting my mom off, but I do it anyway. Lucy's right. They need to stop blaming me for everything. "I'll take her."

"I want to go with Alex," Lucy says, her arms crossed again.

My mom isn't a crier. But I don't really want to tempt fate by Lucy choosing me as a surrogate parent over my mom's actual parenting. I tap Lucy on the shoulder to go get her backpack. She stomps out of the room.

I walk over to my mom. She's standing there, stiff, holding the oatmeal spoon. She looks a mixture of pissed and shocked. I wrap my arms around her. I dwarf her. Her personality is so bold and larger than life, I forget sometimes how tiny she is. I can tuck her under my chin. She smells like citrus and spice, a smell I've associated with home and movie nights and long drives to away games for so many years. The good things.

"I love you," I say truthfully. I want to repair our relationship, and I know it'll take time for them to trust me again, but I'm willing to put in the work. "Can we talk later?"

I squeeze her tight, not waiting for a response, and not expecting one. My mom isn't sappy like that.

The drive to Lucy's school is comfortable. I drop her off on time, and she actually gives me a full-blown smile before she gets out of the car.

When I'm alone again, I try to focus on my final.

But I can't. All I can think about is Zoey. She did so much for me and, repeatedly, I took my own insecurities out on her. She deserves so much more.

I'm an idiot for not keeping her when I had the chance.

ZOEY

I feel like a zombie, dragging myself across campus. My body aches as I drag it from a final to a study group, to my research lab, to work.

I can't stop my brain from wandering to its happy place: Alex's arms. His inked biceps surround me, his body warm, comforting. The imagery is so vivid I can feel the stress release from my body as I imagine him supporting me. Just because I've officially sworn off men doesn't mean I can't use and abuse them in my imagination.

I'm so lost in the fantasy, Z has to call my name twice.

I've walked right by him without even noticing.

"Hey," I say, hugging myself. This is just one more thing I don't want to handle right now.

"Hey yourself." He shoots me a grin. When I don't return it, it slides off his face.

I would have killed for him to be shooting that grin at me in the beginning of the semester, and now, frankly, I don't have time. There're no heart flutters anymore. It's just Z, my ex of sorts. His girlfriend ducks into the bathroom, and it leaves the two of us, just standing here like a couple of idiots.

"I heard you and Alex broke up," Z says.

"How? We're not in middle school," I grumble. It's a stupid comment, but I'm in a mood and don't want to deal with Z right now.

"It was pretty easy to put together when he showed up for class looking miserable. And you weren't there to cheer him up with a cold brew." Really? Did Alex look miserable? And Z noticed that I used to bring Alex a coffee every time I greeted him. Maybe Z was paying more attention than I thought.

He wasn't paying enough attention though. "It's December," I say. Because cold brew in December is not okay.

He just nods. "It is December." He wrings his hands together, looking as uncomfortable as this situation is.

"Listen, I'm gonna go—" I start, but Z cuts me off.

"Is there any world where we still have a chance?" he blurts out.

I'm sorry. What?

Those are words I was desperate for him to say at the start of this semester. And now it's the last thing I want him to say. "It's just, you left. And I was lonely. And then you came back and I had forgotten about your laugh and your voice and your little hair tosses. It's so different hanging out with you in person" —because we had been doing so much of that lately— "and it made me realize how much I missed you. So I guess I'm just wondering, how badly did I mess this all up?" He stares up at me, hope growing in his eyes. Apparently there *aren't* laser beams shooting out of my eyes if he still looks so damn hopeful.

I sigh. "Z, I wasted so much time on you because I thought you were a good guy."

"I am a good guy."

"No, I mean, I thought you were a genuinely good guy. That you had a good soul, a good heart. A hero type. Those were the vibes you were putting out into the universe." He opens his mouth to protest again, but I hold up a hand to cut him off. "How long were you fucking around behind my back?"

His mouth stumbles open and closed like a fish searching for oxygen in the desert. He looks pained and glances away before glancing back to me. "We weren't in a relationship, Zo."

"Don't call me Zo. We had an agreement."

"You were on the other side of the world."

"And you're here, right now, asking me if we still have a shot, while your girlfriend is in the bathroom right over there." As if on cue, his girlfriend walks out of the bathroom, a bright and cheery smile on her face. As much as I wanted to hate her in the beginning, I just can't. She had nothing to do with his behavior.

Z drops his voice to a whisper as his girlfriend approaches us. "We're still friends though, right?" I snort. "No, no, really. I'm still your forever friend. I promised you that." I stare at him, flabbergasted. Z's girlfriend arrives and links her arm through his, but his eyebrows are raised in my direction, waiting for an answer from me.

"Bullshit."

"Zoey?"

"Bull. Fucking. Shit. You're not my forever friend. You're not even my friend. I mean, that was the worst part of this whole thing," I say, gesturing in between us. "Losing you as a friend."

"We're still friends. I mean, we're Zeus and Zoey, right?" he says with a shrug. I notice his girl glaring at him a little bit.

"No, we're not still Zeus and Zoey." I snort. "And what is up with your name always coming first?" I look up at the sky as I say this. "Honestly, it's a little fucked up. It's always Zeus and Zoey, never Zoey and Zeus. I'm obviously the one carrying the goddamn relationship."

Zeus moves his mouth a little to respond, but I've waited way too long for this and I have way too much to say.

"I waited for your weekly text. I waited a whole month before I finally gave up."

"I'm sorry I never texted," he mutters, glancing around as if he feels awkward being put on the spot.

"You leading me on sucked. Treating me like shit when we were together sucked. Not choosing me multiple times sucked. You dropping my ass as a friend altogether?" I shake my head at him. "It almost broke me."

But then I smile at him and spread my arms wide, as if to say but I'm still here, not even caring that we've gathered an audience "But then I realized how much of a little shit you are, how much shit you put me through. And for you —*you*—to do that to *me*" —I gesture at myself— "is not okay. You don't get to be my friend."

"Hey," his girlfriend speaks up. "He's a great guy. Don't say that stuff."

I roll my eyes at her. I can't help it.

"I'd tell you to go choke on a dick," I tell her with a smirk. "But I know he's way too tiny for that shit."

I feel a chorus of oohs around us from our impromptu audience. I think I see a couple people with phones filming this.

"I didn't mean to hurt you," Zeus says. He says it with such sincerity that I want to believe him. I'm just not sure I do. I mean, even after we were over he spread all those lies about me being terrible in bed. Why?

But I don't want to yell at him anymore. I just want to leave. This whole situation is just so goddamn insignificant.

"I'll see you around, Zeus," I tell him, circling my middle finger around in the air in lieu of a wave goodbye.

FORTY-FIVE

ALEX

"Adams! Get your stupid, fucking, demented ass over here."

I turn around immediately, honestly a little terrified.

Students around me chuckle and weave by me. It's easy to spot who yelled at me. Tessa is glaring at me, hands on her hips, and Zeus's Fountain is exploding behind her. It's like a scene from a movie.

I speedwalk to Tessa. There's no way I'm about to risk death and refuse her.

Zoey isn't with her. My chest aches with disappointment. When I saw Tessa, I thought for a second Zo would be there too. It's like being down a goal, taking a shot, praying it'll go in, and watching it go wide.

I don't even know what to say to Zoey yet. I just want to see her.

"Hi Tessa," I say when I reach her. "Demented ass, really?"

"Don't 'hi Tessa' me." She glares, pointing a finger at

me, bracelets jangling as she does. "What is wrong with you?"

"A lot." Or maybe a little? Wasn't that Zoey's whole point? That I wasn't as much of a mess as I thought?

"Damn right there is." She shakes her head, looking thoroughly disappointed in me. "Why would you even—" She breaks off on a groan and throws her hands in the air. Several students glance toward us. "Sit," she orders, pointing at the fountain. Almost no one sits on the edge of the water's spray during December, but I'm not about to argue with Tessa. Once I'm seated and shivering, Tessa narrows her eyes at me. "Why the hell is Zoey so heart-broken right now?"

Heartbroken? She's heartbroken? My chest fucking cracks. I never wanted to hurt Zoey. That's the last thing I wanted.

"I thought it was a mistake." Still can't believe I shot myself in the foot like that.

"You're an idiot."

"Trust me. I know."

"Why the fuck did you think it was a mistake?"

"Because I was messing everything up at home. I thought she deserved better."

I still think she deserves better. Zoey deserves the world. But I want to become the type of man who is good enough for her. She sacrificed so much for me, skipping a class that mattered for her interview, just so I could make my midterm, continuing to babysit Lucy, even when she was getting nothing in return, constantly supporting me, encouraging me and seeing the best in me, even when I didn't believe in myself.

She showed me how good it is to be loved.

Loved. Not a word I ever thought I'd say, but I think it's

pretty obvious at this point that I'm in love with Zoey. I mean, I want to spend the rest of my existence showing her how good it is to be loved too.

Tessa is still frowning, but I can see the flash of sympathy in her eyes. She looks like she's going to say something else. I cut her off. "I want her back."

She snorts. "Men. Just because you want her doesn't mean you can get her. You broke her heart."

"I know."

She stares at me, hands on her hips. "The only reason I'm just mildly pissed—"

"Mildly?" I smirk. If this is mild, I'd hate to be the person who really pissed Tessa off. Tessa narrows her eyes at me and I instantly regret interrupting her.

"—is because I think you're a good guy. You did a stupid thing, but you didn't know any better."

"Thank you, I think?"

"But it still doesn't mean you can have Zoey back just by asking. She's way too strong for that."

I sigh, leaning back and welcoming the cold from the fountain. Tessa is right. Zoey doesn't even want to speak to me anymore, much less take me back. Not after I completely ended things with her and refused to listen to her side of the story. I close my eyes and run my hand through my hair. Losing Zoey might hurt more than failing that drug test ever did.

"Do you think I have a shot?" I ask Tessa. I'm hoping she blames the shakiness of my voice on the fact that I'm full-on shivering now from the cold of the fountain, and not the fact that I'm way closer to crying than I've been in years.

Tessa regards me with disappointed anger. I could have played a whole soccer game in the time it takes her to respond. "If you grand gesture this shit and talk it out with her, you might," she offers.

There's that little beacon of hope I need. "I'll do anything."

"But it can't *actually* be anything. You need something good."

"So let's think of something good." An idea I think of with Zoey's best friend is going to be so much better than anything I could come up with on my own. For a second, I think Tessa's going to turn me down. But then she relents, shaking her head at me.

"Here, let's go get tea. We'll talk it over." She spins toward The Bolt, and I don't hesitate to scramble after her.

Tessa and I have officially spent an hour drinking coffee and tea and bouncing ideas off one another. This grand gesture shit is way harder than they make it seem in romcoms. We sit at a table inside The Bolt, inhaling the smell of espresso. I chose a table directly beneath the heater vent, but it still took me most of this time to dry off.

"What if I get her name tattooed?"

Tessa throws her hands in the air. "Dumbass."

"That's a no?"

"Why are you like this? Zoey will laugh at you for getting her name tattooed. Laugh."

"Okay. Fine. No tattoos," I grumble. I sit there in silence for another thirty seconds. "What if I find a boom box? I'm sure they still sell them somewhere. And then I play Linkin Park outside her window."

"We live on the fifth floor."

"So?"

"What would you even play? That song about a tampon?"

I look at her in horror. "Did you just say *song about a tampon*?"

"'Bleed it Out.'" She gestures her hand, as if expecting me to fill in the blanks on the lyrics.

I blink. I blink again. "No."

"You've got to admit—"

"No."

"But—"

I hold up a hand to stop her. "Stop trying to ruin the greatest band in the world."

"It's not ruining them." She shakes her head. "It's bringing them a new audience. That's the only song I listen to because I think it's funny."

"I used to like you, Tessa."

"I used to like you too. And then you were a dick and broke my best friend's heart."

Ouch. Yeah. I deserve that. "I would play 'In Between,'" I say softly.

"No idea what that is." Tessa shrugs. "And anyway. No. That's a terrible idea."

"Okay. Maybe I'm just not an ideas person."

"Aren't you an engineer?" she questions, raising an eyebrow at me.

"Fuck off."

"Wow, you can cuss now. You're not a child in a man's body anymore."

I shake my head, looking away from her. "Wait," I say. I stand up out of my chair. It's like a freaking light bulb hits me. "I've got it."

She looks at me and starts shaking her head vehemently. "No. I'm going to veto it. Any idea that came from the sentence 'child in a man's body' is a bad idea. Trust me. Anything to do with children at all is a bad idea."

"No. Not that. Forget that," I say, waving away that horror-ridden minefield. Then I tell her my plan.

Tessa drums her fingers against the table. Her eyes are thoughtful, flicking around the coffee shop while she thinks. Finally, she looks up at me. "That just might work," she admits. "But be prepared to do some groveling. Lots of it."

"I was already planning on it." I would do all the groveling in the world if it meant I could have Zoey back.

"Do you think you can pull it off?" she asks. "The semester ends in three days."

Three days. That's hardly any time at all.

"Yeah, I can do it," I say. Tessa's lips press into a line, her eyebrows raise. She doesn't believe me. "Number one rule of an athlete," I say with a shrug. "Never give up."

FORTY-SIX

ZOEY

There's a coffee cup with my name on it sitting on the kitchen table when I get home from another miserably long, cold day on campus. My joints are achy and my back wants to curl in on itself to conserve warmth.

I reach for the coffee cup and yell out a grateful thank you to Tessa.

The coffee cup feels light. I lift it toward my mouth with a frown. When I drink, nothing comes out. Something clunks against the lid. I pop it open.

There's a note inside. A folded-up sheet of college ruled paper. A little wrinkled and soft, like someone held it too long before dropping it in the cup.

I unfold it.

I'm still kind of thinking this is Tessa. She always did have a flair for the dramatic.

But no. I'd recognize Alex's handwriting anywhere. Fuck, I'd recognize anything Alex-related anywhere.

I should just throw it away. Not even read it. That would show him.

But I can't convince myself to do that.

Dear Zoey,

Hell, Zoey. From the moment I met you, I haven't been able to get you out of my head. I was too busy checking you out to stop before crashing into you. It's just one of the many things I need to apologize for. I'm sorry I burned you with the coffee. I do wish I had done the "proper" thing and gotten iced coffee that day. That way, I could still crash into you, dump it on you (on accident ofc), and meet you in the exact same way.

Because meeting you was the best fucking thing that has ever happened to me.

I'm sorry for everything I put you through. I never meant to hurt you. It seems like that's all I've been able to do since this has started, though. I'm sorry for dumping hot coffee on you. I'm sorry for ever making you feel like I wasn't desperate for you. I'm sorry for when I kept you a secret. I'm sorry for all my stupid rules getting in the way of us. I'm sorry for breaking up with you. I'm sorry for ever thinking you couldn't decide for yourself what you wanted or what you deserved. I definitely had the big-ass ego you always claim I have. You were right. You're always right.

Love,

Mr. Big-Ass Ego

P.S. There's an actual coffee in the microwave for you. I figured you could nuke it to proper Zoey winter temperatures.

. . .

I reread the note. Then I reread it again.

Honestly, I don't know what he wanted to accomplish with this note. All he did was apologize. I'm glad he recognizes what he did was wrong, but... he doesn't want me back. And even though I don't want *him* back either, it stings.

I move to the microwave. Sure enough, there's a coffee sitting in there, waiting for me. I heat it up, then grab it and curl up on the couch, letting the coffee warm my frozen fingers.

I reread the note. Again and again and again.

The next day, Alex is waiting outside my door when I get back from the lab. His back leans against the wall across from my door, legs straight out against the cold concrete. His posture looks determined, like he'll stay out here all night if he has to, even as the wind continues to pick up.

I have half a mind to turn around and walk my ass right back to the elevator. My hands shake and sweat at the same time. I wipe them on my jeans.

His eyes track my every movement as I approach. They roam over my body, and the hungry, desperate way they soak me up makes me feel like I'm wearing something way cuter than jeans and a ratty sweatshirt. My already speeding heart picks up the pace when he bends his knees.

He sits up from the ground, using only his legs. He has a coffee cup in each hand. It's an impressive feat, actually, that reminds me just how strong he is, how powerful his thighs are. Jeans cover those thighs, and he's in a gray, long-sleeved shirt. I don't like the way it grips his arms. At all.

Fuck. Why does he have to look so good?

I'm a hot mess right now.

"Zoey—"

"Nope," I say, darting around him. I unlock my door with record speed and let it slam shut behind me.

I fall back against the door, hard enough that my hair flings around my face before settling over my shoulders. My chest rises and falls quickly. I don't understand how a single interaction can have me feeling like I just backpacked up Mt. Whitney.

But shit—when he said my name?

My body couldn't handle the heart flutters. My knees wanted to collapse right there.

I can't talk to Alex. I'll either end up slapping him, crying, or hate fucking him against my door. None of those are things I want to do, so thank the universe there's two inches of wood separating us now.

Alex knocks on the door. I think he uses his forehead to do it. "Do you at least want your coffee? I promise not to talk to you." His voice sounds resigned.

"You're talking right now."

He's silent on the other end. I glance through the peephole. He's still standing there, shoulders thrown back. Waiting.

I'm not sure he'll leave, honestly.

I whip open the door. Alex takes a startled step back. He recovers quickly and holds a coffee cup out to me. I narrow my eyes. They both have my name on it. One is probably another letter, and the other is actual coffee.

I reach for the one he isn't offering and let the door slam shut.

The coffee cup is way too light. I pop the lid. Yup. There's that letter.

"Fuck," I yell. I throw the cup to the ground.

I can hear Alex chuckle outside. I yank the door open again, and this time he's prepared.

He leans in the doorway, his free hand resting on the top seal.

His biceps look massive.

That's my weakness. I never knew it before Alex, but boys with muscles might forever be my weakness.

God, why couldn't he be wearing a sweatshirt with spaghetti stains or something? And how did he always smell so good? It brings me right back to everything we've done together—movie nights, amusement parks, fake dates, and real dates.

Fucking. Lots and lots of fucking.

I want to bury my nose against his neck.

Instead, I snatch the coffee out of his hand and let the door swing shut again. Alex doesn't try to force his way in. He just lets me have the coffee, and stays outside, where he belongs.

"You can go now," I tell him.

I hear him rest a fist against the door. I inch over to the peephole. There's a distorted, way-too-close Alex head right there.

A miserable expression flits across his face, and I find I don't like it there as much as I thought I would. Even though I'm angry right now, I still don't like the idea of him being in pain.

"I miss you, Zo," he says softly. He taps the door again.

Then walks away.

It takes all of my willpower to keep my legs rooted to their spot and not chase after him. What would that say about me? Forgiving him so easily?

I bend down to grab his letter from the floor. It's a

folded piece of lined paper again. I run my thumb over it, knowing he must have touched this too.

I make my way to my room, taking a sip of coffee as I go. It's warm on my tongue. Not burning hot, like it just came from the store. But warm, like he was sitting out there for a while.

I have one last final tomorrow, but I'm ready for it. All studied out. I *was* going to run through my flash cards one last time.

But instead, I find the shirt I stole from Alex the day he broke up with me. I shimmy out of my jeans and T-shirt, slipping into it.

It hardly smells like him anymore.

Dear Zoey,

Remember the conversation we had when we became official? I said, "If things go south, I will be just as messed up as you." Well, things went south, and it was definitely my fault. But I'm just as messed up as you. Unless you're not messed up at all. In that case, I'm all sorts of messed up over losing you all on my own.

The point is, you mean the world to me, Zo. I will regret for the rest of my life breaking up with you.

Lucy filled me in on the full story (while calling me an idiot, btw). I should have listened to you in the first place. She also told me what you did for me in Arizona.

I think that was the kick in the ass I needed to believe in myself too. I was being an idiot before. One mistake didn't ruin my life. My attitude did. And that I can change. I'm so grateful for you. I'm glad I might have a soccer-filled future now. I just hope it will be soccer and Zoey-filled.

Love,

Alex Adams (also, here's my autograph for when I get famous. You got it first).

P.S. The actual coffee is in my hand this time. So, like, you probably already have it. If you didn't dump it on me.

I should have dumped it on him. Because this letter makes me want to cry.

I was finally done with my last day of the semester.

And I felt like shit. Alex and his stupid letters were on my brain. I had almost talked myself into forgiving him. I knew the amount of stress and pressure he was under, trying to be responsible for Lucy. I knew the amount of trouble he got into because of my car accident.

It was a hard situation. Anyone would be making rash decisions.

I wasn't mad that he broke up with me though. I was mad because he refused to listen to me and trust me. And that wasn't something I was sure I could get over so easily. My heart and head battled it out, and I felt the stabs of pain as they sliced at each other, in a war to forgive, or not to forgive.

There was a third coffee cup with a letter on my desk when I got home that day.

Just because I hadn't yet forgiven Alex doesn't mean I didn't greedily reach for that letter.

Dear Zo,

I considered not writing this because it was inappropriate, and then I realized who I was talking to. I miss being inside of you. I miss all those way-too-loud moans, gasps, and faces you make. I miss the feel of your legs around me, the weight of your breasts in my hands.

I miss your laugh and your jokes and how much you tease me. I miss your intelligence and your fierceness and your positivity. I miss your totally bangable body. I miss your weird opinions on the time of the year and the temperature of food and drinks. I miss your awesome music and movie preferences.

I want you back. You make me a better person. You're just fucking awesome.

I love you.

I do. It might have taken me longer than I needed to to figure that out, but I love you.

I want to tell you in person. And hopefully have a conversation about the possibility of us in the future.

I'll be waiting at The Bolt tonight. I really hope you show.

If you don't want to talk to me, you can at least slap me in person this way.

Love,

Alex.

P.S. There's an actual coffee in the fridge for you. And I'll buy you all the coffee you want forever if you come tonight.

"You're a traitor." I walk into Tessa's room and sit cross-legged on her bed, my freshly microwaved coffee cupped in my hands. She has an open suitcase on the ground, but nothing is in it. She leaves tomorrow, like me, and, like me again, it looks like she hasn't packed yet. Tessa comes to join me on the bed. She wraps her arms around me.

"Is it really treachery if I mean well?" The fact that she doesn't question what I'm referring to just further proves she's a traitor. I finally realized that the only way Alex could be getting these secret notes into our apartment was from help on the inside.

"Uh, yes?"

"Oh. Well then, yup. Sorry. I'm a traitor." She releases me and sits back against the wall, hugging a leg to her body.

"He wants me to meet him at The Bolt tonight."

"Are you going to go?"

I tuck my hair behind my ear, glancing at the letter still gripped in my hand. I loosen my grasp. I don't want to ruin it. It's the type of letter I might want to keep forever. "He says he loves me."

"He said *what?!*" Tessa exclaims, eyes wide, leaning forward. "Oh my god."

"I'm guessing the fact that you snuck all these notes in for him means you approve? Even after everything?" I ask.

Tessa shakes her head. "I'm always on your side, babe. If you still hate him, I'll hate him too." She pauses and bites her lip. "Let's just say, though, that I never would have done that for Z."

I snort. "God, remember when I thought I liked Z?"

"Three months ago?" Tessa asks, giving me the side-eye.

"I mean he passed the blow job test and everything." I smile. She's right. Three months feels like a lifetime. Everything happened in these past three months. A whole world inside this tiny space in time. I guess that's what falling in love feels like. "I never gave Alex a blow job." I moan.

Tessa smirks at me. "By choice, I presume?"

"Yeah, but I wanted to give him one. Now I'll never know if he'll pass the test and I really like him."

"Show up tonight and be like 'Alex, I want to talk to

you, but I can't until I give you a blow job.' And then get on your knees in the coffee shop. He'll love it."

I groan, throwing my arm over my eyes.

"Okay, this drama isn't you, babe. You don't need to suck his dick to know you like him."

"It's just an added bonus," I joke. Because yes, even picturing giving Alex a blow job is a turn-on. Everything about Alex is a turn-on.

"See? He's already passed the test. You like him."

Yeah. I really do like him. Maybe even love him. Is that enough to forgive him though?

Tessa and I have this theory about the universe. Meeting Alex isn't fate. I'm the one in charge. Each time I make a choice, I change, and my path changes. But maybe... maybe the universe was shoving Alex and me together all along. I mean, I never would have met Alex if I hadn't met Z. It was little choices I made, and a little help from the universe that pushed us together.

And I am grateful. At least I know how great it could be now. Fuck.

"I'm gonna go," I say finally. At least hear what he has to say. See if he's worth forgiving. It would be a betrayal to the universe to *not* at least talk to him.

"Good luck," Tessa says, hugging me. "Also, piece of advice? Shower first."

I smack her with her pillow.

FORTY-SEVEN

ALEX

I've had my eyes glued to the door all night. It's the type of intensity I only reserve for soccer—and Zoey apparently. I'm practically glaring at the door and anyone who gets in the way of my vision.

It's already dark, and the hanging lights inside the building reflecting off the windows mean I can't see outside. I just keep praying the door will open and I'll see a flash of blonde.

The rest of the room is fairly empty. It's the last Friday of the semester. Most students have already gone home or have parties to go to.

The door opens. I suck in a breath.

And then release it in a disappointed exhale. It's just some guy. He pauses, though, on his way inside, and holds open the door. Honestly? I can feel it all through my body that it's going to be Zoey. My body buzzes, like the adrenaline rush I get before a game. It's the way the guy is checking her out. I can't even see her yet, but from the look on this guy's face, whoever is about to walk through that door is hot as hell.

And sure enough, Zoey walks through the door.

I can't fight the reaction my body has to seeing her. My heart slams in my chest. My hands shake. My smile is stupid huge. I'm giddy. Actually giddy.

She's dressed in a sweatshirt, tight shirt, and jeans. I want to slide my hands past her unzipped sweatshirt and settle them on her waist. I want to kiss her right here, under the glow of the orange lights. I want to push boundaries with her until they kick us out.

Zoey, though, doesn't look quite as giddy as me. She stops at the edge of the table, crossing her arms over her chest, her lips pressed in a line, and makes no move to sit down.

I wince. "Are you here to slap me?"

"It's up for debate."

Well, that's not what I was hoping for. But I did give her that option. I nod at the line of coffees in front of me on the table. I ordered a new one every fifteen minutes, just to make sure it was hot when she got here. "If you take one from the end there, it'll be cold enough to throw at me. Get me back for the beginning of the semester."

Zoey's mouth falls open at the line of coffees. She hesitantly reaches toward one—

"That's a hot one," I warn. Because I'm going to try to avoid death by coffee if I can. She smirks at me and then lifts it to her lips. And I watch, mesmerized by her perfect pink lips pressed to the rim of the cup. When she lowers the cup, her lips are still slightly open, and she licks a stray drop from the side of her mouth. I nearly groan. My letter did not do my desire to get back inside of her justice. It just said—

"Oh shit. I love you," I blurt out. That was supposed to

be the first thing I said to her. But *hell*. That's not how I wanted to deliver it. She shakes her head at me, and I know that's probably not how she imagined getting the news, either. "I don't mean—well, I *do* mean I love you, Zo. I didn't mean to say it like that. And—hell. I'm messing this up."

Zoey pulls out a chair and sits down.

Thank the relationship gods she's staying.

"Talk, Adams."

Is it bad that her death glare is turning me on a little bit?

She waits silently, taking another sip of her coffee, eyebrows raised. I clear my throat. No more stalling. Time to burst out the big guns. I take a deep breath.

"Zoey. First off, thank you for coming here tonight—"

She bursts out laughing. "You have a speech prepared?"

"No," I lie.

"Do you have notecards or something?"

"No." That one's not a lie. There's a paper outline crumpled in my back pocket. "Now shush and let me profess my love for you."

"You honestly love me?" she asks, looking up at me again with her eyes shining. I don't know whether that's a good thing or a bad thing. Are they shining from laughter? Is she crying?

I haven't ever said these words to a girl before. It's nerve-wracking.

But I know with Zoey, I without a doubt mean it. "Yeah. I do," I say. Neither of us are laughing anymore. My body finally stills, the nerves washing away as I'm filled with certainty. "I love you, Zo."

ZOEY

He means it. The full force of Alex Adams staring at me with that much sincerity and determination and *love*? It's too much. My body is melting. It's responding like it loves him back.

My body is stupid.

"It definitely was not my shining moment when, you know, I came home and freaked out, pushed the blame card around and broke up with you." He runs a hand through his hair, and I have to stifle my smile at seeing that action. "I was really scared. And worried. About Lucy. And you. I never asked you how you were after the accident, but I was freaking out about you too. And I handled all that poorly. And for that, I'm sorry."

I nod. I get it. I would have been scared too.

But tons of people are put in scary situations all the time. Do I really want to be with someone who is going to take his fears out on me?

"I've changed," he says, glancing at the coffees. There are six that line the table. It's sweet that he kept buying coffee so it would be warm when I got here, but that's just money and time. There's no proof that he's changed. "I know you probably don't believe me, since that was only two weeks ago. But I realized..." He looks up at me, making direct eye contact as he says these next words. "You were right all along, Zo. My past doesn't define me. It's what I do now that does."

I drag my finger back and forth across the table. We both watch the movement. "And what are you doing now, then?"

"Trying to get my favorite girl in the world back." He gives me a cocky grin. My stomach spins when he calls me his favorite girl, and I have to look back down at the table, away from his grin. "But if she doesn't agree to come back to me, then maybe she'll consider being my friend? I'm okay being friend-zoned for life, as long as you're in it. And if even that is too much, maybe you'll consider being Lucy's friend? That way I can see you from time to time?" He leans forward so he can tap at my hand with a finger. When I glance up, he winks at me. "Not ashamed to admit I'm desperate, Zo."

He's putting on a show of being cocky, but I see through him. His eyes are shining with worry and hope, his knee won't quit bouncing and the coffees on the table jiggle ever so slightly.

"I'd never abandon Lucy," I say. Like I said before, her brother may be a dick, but she's the best.

Alex lets out a breath, like he really is grateful that I'll still be in his life in some capacity. "That's why I love you, Zo. You're so selfless and sweet. You're hardworking and funny and confident. You *get* me. I can't imagine my life without you."

I can't imagine my life without Alex either. Somehow, in the span of one semester, he's wormed his way into my life.

And I don't think I want him out of it.

But I'm scared. Worried. Nervous.

"How do I know you won't do this again?" I ask, looking down at my coffee. Looking directly at him is kind of like staring at the sun—so beautiful it might kill you.

His fingers reach forward, brushing against my chin. He applies light pressure until my eyes are on his.

The skin-to-skin contact makes everything else drift

away. Like we're not in an almost empty coffee shop, underneath fluorescent lights, surrounded by the faint sound of shitty music and a buzzing heater, like there isn't a table full of burning coffee separating us. It's just him and me and the endless expanse of his eyes. "Do you trust me?" he asks. His eyes flick back and forth between mine, his body impossibly still as he waits for an answer.

I shouldn't. That's what my brain is telling me. He's betrayed me before, and he'll do it again. I've already made this mistake with Z, forgiving him time and time again.

But my gut says yes. That Alex is telling the truth. That he loves me. That I can trust him with anything.

My heart is pumping out a heavy tune, trying to break free from my chest. "Yes," I whisper.

Alex closes his eyes for a moment. The relief washing through his body is palpable. His fingers tighten on my chin before returning to his loose hold. He opens his eyes, and his thumb brushes over my lips.

I shiver.

Alex doesn't even smirk at my reaction to his touch. His voice is growly and intense and I melt. "Then I will work to prove to you every single goddamn day that I love you. That I can be the person you deserve. I'll always put you first, no matter what. I'll—"

His phone rings, loud and jarring. He growls, reaching into his pocket to silence it without even looking.

I've heard enough anyway. I feel almost nauseous my pulse is racing so fast through my veins. I know what I need to do.

But I've never been one for trusting my emotions over my brain. There's no safety net if I fall.

But every time he tells me he loves me, I feel like I'm floating.

"If you'll have me, Zoey—" His voice cracks, and he shakes his head, a smile crossing his face. He tries again. "If you'll—"

"Okay," I say. I've never been one to take the leap before. But I want to be that person.

Alex freezes. His fingers are tight on my chin. "Okay, what?"

"Okay." I smirk, waving my hand through the air. "I want a relationship with you."

Alex releases my chin. He stands—slow. Purposeful. Like he has all the time in the world.

He stalks around to my side of the table, like a predator who's spotted his meal.

I expect him to say something more.

He doesn't.

He takes my face in his hands, tilting my gaze up to his, bends down, and then slams his lips to mine.

I let out a surprised sound, and he captures it with his mouth. Rough and insistent and desperate. I wrap my arms around his neck, keeping him here.

Don't leave. That's what my arms are saying.

As if I would. His lips say.

The kiss is electric. I feel it all the way down to my toes. I've been missing this for weeks. His tongue tangles with mine, his lips and fingers pressing harder and harder and harder. Like he can't get enough of me. Like there will never be enough of me. Like I'm all he needs forever.

What feels like hours later, we break apart. Our faces still pressed together. We're still under the fluorescent lights of the coffee shop, and it's still playing shitty music, and we probably have an audience. I don't bother looking away from Alex to check.

"Come home with me?" I ask against his lips.

His fingers, which have traveled to my waist, squeeze tight. "Always."

FORTY-EIGHT

ZOEY

"Oi. Love birds. Stop canoodling. Let's go out."

"His dick can't be that great. He wasn't dropped from heaven. His face isn't nearly messed up enough to have taken that fall."

"What if only his dick was dropped from heaven though?"

"How the fuck does that work?"

"It would explain the moans."

"It means he would have a misshapen dick."

"No—he'd have a giant one."

I look over at Alex. We're wrapped around each other in my tiny twin bed, sweaty and tired and honestly well on our way to starting up round three.

"Is that West?" I ask in horror.

"And Kacen and Brandon," he confirms. The three of them have gathered outside the door of my bedroom and are currently discussing the size of angel cocks. "What are they doing here?" he asks.

"They're friends with Tessa now," I whisper. I can't help but giggle at their conversation outside. I'm in a good mood right now. A really good mood.

Alex looks over at me and smiles softly. Like he can't believe he's here. A strand of hair is stuck to my face from sweat, and Alex reaches over and pushes it away. He then presses a soft kiss to my cheek. Then another on my jaw. And then square on the lips.

"Maybe if we ignore them long enough, they'll go away," he whispers.

"I will continue to bang on this door until your banging ceases," West yells, whacking the door with his fist again.

"Come on. It's the last night of the semester," Brandon complains. "Let's go do something fun."

"We are doing something fun," I shout at the door.

Alex chuckles. "Damn right we are." He presses a kiss to my neck. Sucks a little. My brain goes hazy enough that it takes a lot more yelling from outside the door to pull me out of my Alex-induced trance.

"Fine, fine, we're coming," I yell. They cheer on the other side of the door. Literally cheer.

"We are?" Alex mopes, pouting at me. "'Cause honestly, I think there's a lot more fun we can have right here."

He kisses down my body. His hands come to cup my breasts. When he sucks a nipple into his mouth, I can't help but cry out.

The peanut gallery behind the door groans in protest.

"I thought you were coming."

"She is coming, you dipshit."

"Oh. *That* coming."

I laugh, pressing a hand to my forehead. I'm equal parts turned on and amused. "Alex."

He releases my nipple with a sigh. "I know, I know. They've ruined the mood."

"It's my sole purpose in life," Kacen calls from behind the door.

Alex chuckles, letting his head rest on my shoulder. We both lie there, letting our bodies deflate. "Shall we go?" he finally asks.

"I guess," I groan. Alex pushes himself up out of the bed first. I sit up and watch him search for clothes around my room. Honestly, I think his shirt might be in the kitchen still. I'm not entirely sure.

Watching Alex's powerful backside, though, makes me wonder why I ever agreed to leave this room in the first place. He has muscles in places I never even knew *could* develop muscles. I probably should have paid more attention in that anatomy class I took freshman year. He's found his boxers and moves to step into them, but I move first. I stand up, pressing my front to his back. I wrap my hands around his torso, let my hands grip his abs. I let them run freely, my fingers finding the dips in his muscles, sinking into his skin. I kiss his shoulder. I can't help it.

"Sweetheart." It's a warning. "I don't have a problem with an audience. If you keep touching me like that, I'll fuck you against the door."

"Is that a promise?" I whisper in his ear, nibbling his earlobe. Alex groans. "'Cause I might be able to think of another option."

I press my hands into his skin, using the pressure to move him around until he faces me. He moves easily, willingly. His expression is hungry and eager. It's like this every time we're together. I've been missing this.

He's so. Fucking. Gorgeous.

I drop down onto my knees in front of him. Grip his rock-solid member in my hands.

"Oh sweet mother of fuck," Alex whispers. "Zoey, are you su—"

I stop his words by sucking him deep into my mouth. He lets out a strangled groan as his abs contract.

Someone knocks on the door. We ignore them. Someone bangs on the door. We ignore them too.

"Zoey," Alex whispers my name like it's a prayer. He slides a hand into my hair, guiding my movements. "Baby, that's so good. That's *so so* good."

"Maia and Carlos are already at the bar. I repeat, Maia and Carlos are already there and alone. I do not want the bar to blow up or catch fire or for either of them to die, so we really need to get over there and be a buffer," Kacen yells at the door.

Alex shakes his head and presses his fingers to the bridge of his nose. Then he reaches his hands to my face. Lets his fingers glide softly across my cheek. Removes himself from my mouth. "Give me a second?" He asks it so gently, staring down at me so sweetly, that I'm honestly surprised when he stalks over the door and whips it open with so much aggression. He only has it open a crack but that's enough for him to yell at our audience.

"I swear to God. Text me the address and we'll meet you there in half an hour. Leave. Now."

"Dude, maybe you were right. I think his dick really came from heaven."

"Look at the size of that thing. Angel cock."

"Maybe he's part god, part human."

"Get the fuck out."

"Jesus, Adams, you get scary when—"

"If the three of you aren't out of this apartment in the

next minute, none of you will be playing soccer again." Alex slams the door in their faces and turns back to me. He waits until he hears the front door slam, then grins. We are surrounded by absolute silence.

"So, how's the test going so far?" Alex asks. Still standing right where he is, still grinning.

I roll my eyes at him. "You're passing with flying colors."

"That's what I like to hear."

I want to knock that cocky smirk off his face. I want to make him feel good, come apart on my lips. I stand up and pull him toward the bed. Alex is still smirking at me, so I shove him down on the mattress.

When I swirl my tongue around the head of his cock, he's not smirking anymore. He's back to worshipping me, praising me. I'm eager and I take him as deep as I can take him. And before long, Alex is shuddering, his abs tight, near release.

When he becomes impossibly harder between my lips, I know he's close. I can't help moaning in response. I'm *that* turned on. There's so many times that giving a blow job feels like a chore. But with Alex, it's anything but that. I love knowing that I'm making him feel good. That it's me he's choosing to spend his time with. That I'm the woman in control of when he comes. It's hot as hell.

"That means you love me, right?" Alex growls, referring to my moan.

I flick my eyes up toward him. He's propped up on his elbows, panting and sweaty, waiting for my answer. I nod yes, and he groans as the orgasm hurtles through him. His muscles contract beneath my fingers. My hands are running all over his body, desperate for this response. I swallow every last drop.

"Jesus, Zoey," he finally pants out, pulling me up toward

him, tugging my body against his. His arm is around my neck, and he tucks my head into his side, pressing a kiss to my forehead. "Jesus."

"I love you," I whisper against his neck.

"Best fucking thing I've heard all day."

ALEX

"Do you think we get extra credit if we've heard our TA have sex?" Kacen asks eagerly, bouncing up and down in his seat.

"What are you on about?" I raise an eyebrow.

"Next semester." Brandon grins brightly. "We had our choice of beginning engineering courses, but don't worry, we chose yours. Of course."

"Motherfucker," I curse, mostly joking though. I think they would make my class way more entertaining to teach. The table laughs. Zoey, Tessa, and I are on one side of the booth, West, Eddie, and Maia facing us, and Kacen, Brandon, and Carlos have managed to squeeze chairs together on the end of the booth. I can't keep the smile off my face. This group has become my Olympia University family.

That and the woman I love loves me back. And gave me the blow job to end all blow jobs. For someone who hates it, she sure as hell knows what she's doing.

"What about extra credit if we've seen our TA drunk?" Brandon muses.

"You haven't seen me drunk," I argue.

"But we're about to." Brandon grins.

"Yeah, what can I get you to drink?" Kacen says, looking

me right in the eye and propping his chin in his hand. I shake my head, chuckling at his antics.

"Absolutely nothing from you two. I won't take bribes." And honestly? Even though my mom is back to watch Lucy now, and I'm back to swearing and fucking again, I'm still planning on living the sober life. I'm an all or nothing kind of guy, and in this case, I think the nothing is better than the all.

"Are you sure?" Kacen asks. "I'd love to show you a good time tonight."

Then he winks at me. It's a motion that only requires a single eyelid, but Kacen does it in a way that uses his whole body. The table groans.

"This is your fault," I tell West.

"I know, I know, I made a monster," West agrees. "At least you'll have something to remember me by when I graduate."

We stay out late, and for the first time ever, I'm not in a rush to get home. My mom is with Lucy and I'm crashing at Zoey's tonight. At least I assume I'm crashing at Zoey's tonight. That had been the plan before this lot dragged our asses out.

At some point, Tessa and Zoey disappear to the bathroom and Maia and Carlos leave to get more drinks. Kacen is trying to convince Brandon to come with him on the "staircase run of hell" tomorrow.

"I can't, I'm moving this weekend," Brandon says.

"Moving?" Kacen's head swivels around. "Don't leave me."

Brandon chuckles. "Nah, dude, I'm not moving from the dorms. My mom and I are moving. I have to help pack and drive the moving truck."

"Why are y'all moving?" Eddie asks.

Brandon shrugs. "The weather is nicer in Oceans Edge."

"Oceans Edge?" Kacen practically screams. "That's where I live. And I can finally introduce you to my siblings. There are six of us."

"We know," the whole table says in unison. Because Kacen talks. A lot.

"Well, did you know that we're all named K names?" he counters, sticking his tongue out.

"All of you?" I echo.

"All of us," Kacen confirms solemnly. He ticks off his fingers with each name. "There's Kenneth, Kendrick, Me, Kylieann, KJ—Kayden James—and Krista."

"Are they all as crazy as you?" West asks. "'Cause I'm torn between wanting to meet them and running for the hills."

Kacen waves us off. "Bummer I'm not going to be there this summer, we could have hung out."

"Where are you going to be?" I ask. Kacen never blushes, but at this, he starts to turn a little pink.

"I'm taking some classes over summer," he says.

"Same," Brandon says. "It's not that far of a drive."

"I might be taking them abroad," Kacen mumbles.

"Would any of these classes happen to be in Greece?" I ask, starting to laugh.

Kacen's eyes widen. "Don't tell Zoey. You know if you tell Zoey she's going to tell Tessa."

"Bro," Carlos says, walking up to the table, drinks in hand. "Give it up. Tessa's way out of your league."

"Look who's talking," Maia says right behind him, depositing the other handful of drinks on the table.

"What's that supposed to mean?" Carlos asks through narrowed eyes.

"Just that you have experience with the situation. Literally everyone is out of your league."

"Only 'cause I'm on a whole other playing field, baby," he says. "I just like dip down, throw a bone to the mere mortals every once in a while if you know what I mean."

Eddie coughs out a word that sounded suspiciously like "bullshit," before turning to Kacen. "Isn't she graduating this year anyway?"

"She's staying an extra year," Kacen and I both say in unison. I give him a smirk. Kacen turns back to Brandon, changing the subject. "But I can introduce you to my sister. She can show you around. Honestly, she's as dedicated a soccer player as you are, you'd like her." Kacen turns pensive again for a second. "Actually, I was supposed to coach her this summer. I didn't think this through."

"Do you ever think anything through?"

"Valid question." Kacen nods. "The answer is rarely."

We laugh. I glance at my phone. The little notification light is blinking at me. I have a voice mail. I don't recognize the number, but I listen to it anyway.

And my heart stops.

Zoey slips into the booth beside me. "Are you okay?" she asks immediately.

I nod. I feel like I'm in a daze. "You know that call I kept getting when I was trying to convince you to take me back?" I tell her softly, not wanting the rest of the table to overhear. She nods. "It's an agent. They caught my first game in Arizona and want to represent me. They say there's a couple teams already interested in signing me."

Zoey breaks into the most beautiful grin. "No fucking way."

"Don't sound so surprised."

"Holy fuck. I'm dating a professional athlete."

"Well, not yet."

"All this money is going to go straight to my head, just so you know."

"You're getting money from this now?"

"I'm going to buy the Captain America shield. The actual movie prop. First time you get a million-dollar contract, that's my first purchase."

"At least that way you'll stop stealing my Captain America shirt."

"Nah bitch, that's best friend privileges." She laughs, showing me she's just joking about all of this. "But honestly, Alex, that's so great. I'm so proud of you."

"I'm proud of me too." I smirk.

"Of course you are, Mr. Big-Ass Ego."

I tuck a piece of her hair behind her ear. It's all wild from what we were doing in her bed earlier. I like it like that. Strike that—I love it like that. I lean down to whisper in her ear. "But honestly, Zo? This never would have happened without you. Thank you."

"Most of the good things in your life are because of me," she says, a serious expression on her face.

"Brat." I poke her in the side and she laughs. Then I whisper in her ear exactly what I want to do to thank her. She raises her eyebrows at me in an obvious question: *Really, dude? Again?* At the exact same time, Tessa claps her hands over her ears.

"No!" she roars. "Indoor voices. I don't need to hear that."

"Do you have superhuman hearing?" I shoot at her.

"I got bit by a radioactive elephant as a child. Giant ears." She gestures at her perfectly normal-size ears.

"I was bit by a radioactive elephant too," Kacen says. "He gave me a different body part though."

Tessa throws her napkin at him.

I chuckle, but I put my hand on Zoey's thigh and slowly drag it up her leg until I'm cupping her center.

"Yup," Zoey says, jumping up. "We're going to blow this popsicle stand. I'll see you next semester everyone." She grabs my hand, dragging me after her. The table boos us.

"Do you need a ride, Tessa?" Zoey asks.

Tessa shakes her head. "Knowing you two, you won't even make it home. I don't want to be there for the car sex."

"That was one time!" Zoey shouts.

"You told her about that?" I ask, sounding madder than I am.

"Oh shush, you don't care. You have no shame," she says. I laugh at that. She's not wrong. "You do know you're basically dating both of us, right?" Zoey says with a grin. "Anything you say or do can then be repeated to Tessa. It's all fair game."

"Are you reading me my Zoey rights?"

"Damn straight," she says with a grin.

Zoey gives Tessa a look though, because suddenly Tessa is waving us off and saying, "Go, I'll get a ride."

"I'll drive you home," Eddie offers.

"I can drive her," Kacen immediately butts in, turning from his conversation with Brandon and Carlos.

"You," I say, pointing at him, "better not be driving anywhere. That goes for all three of you," I say, pointing at the freshmen. How come the ones who aren't even allowed to drink yet are the ones that drink the most? And how are they even getting their drinks? Brandon's fake ID is the shittiest piece of trash I've ever seen.

Carlos flips me off, Brandon just looks kinda sad, and Kacen lets out this long whiny noise.

"I'll get them home," Eddie says, looking at me. "You two go."

I don't need to be told twice. Zoey was already dragging me out the door, our fingers interlaced, and I already knew I would follow her anywhere.

EPILOGUE

ZOEY

Tour Guide Fun Fact #7: Because of the heat in Southern California, Olympia University always holds its graduations during the evenings. Not only is it cooler, but the sunset makes for perfect pictures.

If you had told me when I started college how quickly four years passes by, I never would have believed you. High school dragged on. But college? That passed in the length of a Kacen wink.

I've officially walked across the stage. Moved my tassel from one side to the other. Threw my *Firefly* decorated grad cap in the air.

I motherfucking graduated.

I'm searching for my parents the minute the ceremony is over, but like the universe keeps wanting to shove us together, Alex, Tessa, and Lucy are the first people I run into.

I launch myself into Alex's arms and he catches me easily. He spins me around in a circle, my feet flying off the ground like I weigh nothing to him. If I thought he was ripped before, it's nothing compared to the pure strength he has now that he's been actually training again for a professional team.

"Let her go. You're getting enough of her in the future," Tessa complains.

Alex ignores her. "Congratulations." He grins, his head dips and he plants a searing celebratory kiss on me. People swarm all around us, finding family members, cheering and celebrating. It reminds me of our first kiss, how the swarms of students just faded away until it was just him and me.

When the kiss ends, I break away from him to hug Tessa just as tightly.

"I can't believe you're not walking across that stage with me."

"I can't believe you're leaving me," she cries. She's literally wiping tears from her eyes.

"I'd never leave you," I say, shaking my head vehemently. "I'm still going to video chat you for hours every day. And I'll visit all the time." Tessa and I, for the first time in three years, won't be living together. Alex officially was signed with a professional team in Northern California, and I was able to score an entry-level job as a structural geologist near him. Through a semester of hard work, I was able to repair my relationship with Professor Heath, and he was happy to recommend me for the position. Alex and I will be moving in together officially in a month. Which is crazy, but I'm honestly excited. "Alex will have to leave for away games all the time, so I'll just come visit you. I expect you to welcome me into your bed with open arms."

"Of course." She laughs. "I'll even consider cleaning for

you." Then she points at Alex. "You better score me tickets to every game. You owe me for stealing my best friend."

Alex chuckles but agrees.

We take pictures together. I hug Lucy loads. She and Alex are super crazy close now, so I expect she'll be visiting us all the time too. Eventually I manage to find my parents and my brothers. My mom's crying even harder than Tessa. But they're happy tears.

I even see Jonah West stride by, weaving through the crowd, the image of pure confidence, his graduation gown billowing behind him. I hug him too. I'm hugging everyone I run into. This might be the last time I see some of these people.

The sun is setting around us, and once we've gotten our fill of pictures, Alex tugs me to him again. His arms circle around me from behind, and he presses a kiss to my neck, right below my ear.

"I'm proud of you, baby," he murmurs as we watch our friends and family laugh and mingle.

I reach a hand behind me, wrapping it around his neck and weaving it into his hair. I turn to give him a quick kiss. "I'm proud of you, too." His parents are pissed he dropped out of grad school, but I think he knew from the very beginning it wasn't for him. And sometimes you just need someone to acknowledge that the path you're on is acceptable too.

"I can't wait until we can celebrate, just you and me," he whispers.

"It might have to wait until tomorrow. I think my parents want to take everyone out to dinner."

"At least we're going to be living together soon. We can celebrate as much as we want."

"What if we fuck too often though? Forget about our

other responsibilities?" Alex laughs, and I poke him in the side. "I'm honestly concerned."

"That's not my top concern about us living together," he says. "That's not a concern at all actually. It will never be *too often*."

"What is your concern then?" I ask.

"Probably Tessa breaking in at one a.m. 'cause she misses you too much."

"Tessa can't drive."

"She can talk Kacen into driving her anywhere. And where Kacen goes, Brandon will follow. That's too many people breaking in at one a.m."

I laugh, because that's something that will probably happen. And I'm glad he's not worried about us. "What if we just sleep in until noon every day and never cook for ourselves?"

"That sounds perfect." I can hear the smirk in his voice. "Besides, I've become a way better chef now. I took pictures of all of Tessa's recipe cards. You should strive to be me."

"No—I mean it as a bad thing. We both hate mornings. What if we end up missing work and practices?"

"Zo." He flips me around so he can laugh at me face to face. "Stop worrying. It's going to be perfect."

"Yeah?" I ask. It's golden hour right now all around us, and Alex looks impossibly more handsome in the light.

"Yeah. Anything that comes up, we'll work through it."

"'Cause you love me?" I tease.

"'Cause I love you," he agrees. "And coffee fixes every-thing anyway."

"Do you ever wonder if we drink unhealthy amounts of caffeine?"

"Nope." He grins. "Never." His eyes tell me to trust

him, and finally, I relent. I lean into him, resting my head against his chest, and he holds me tight. "It'll all be perfect," he whispers into my hair, inhaling deep. "I promise."

ACKNOWLEDGMENTS

Writing a book, especially a first book, is an adventure. It's been a crazy two years working on this project, and I'm grateful that so many people were willing to help me on this journey.

First and foremost, I want to thank you, the reader. None of this would be possible without you and I'm so grateful you decided to take a chance on a new author like me!

Next, a huge thank you to my early readers and beta readers, Robert, Kristina, Steph, and Shayna. You dealt with the hot mess that were my early drafts of this book and helped create the beautiful story it is today. Thank you for your time and excellent notes!

To Mikaela, Evelyn, and Kristen. My best friend, my soulmate, my love. I'm grateful to have not one but three Tessas in my life. Your constant support and read throughs have been so unbelievably helpful, and I never would have made it to the finish line without you.

To Evelyn Chavez, an out-of-this-world diversity reader. Thank you for multiple read throughs, invaluable advice, and lending me your Spanish! You are amazing, and your insight was fantastic. Any mistakes made in this book are entirely my own.

To Hot Tree Editing, for an awesome critique that helped me whip this story into shape!

To My Brother's Editor, for everything you did to push

through and continue working on my book. Thank you so much for correcting so many of my mistakes!

To Aquila Editing, for an outstanding proof job. Thank you so much!

Thank you Y(a)sabella for being one of my very first fans and illustrating the beautiful cover! I'm grateful you've stayed with me from the very start of this journey and are willing to share your unbelievable talent with me. The cover is everything I ever wanted it to be!

To all my new Edinburgh friends who gave me advice and helped me along the way.

To the roommates of L-106, I love you all! Thank you for your unwavering support and for always being there to pick me back up when I need it!

Most of all, I need to thank my family. They're the ones who listened to my rants, my struggles, my moments of panic. They're the ones who said hilarious things that I was then able to steal (with permission) and put in my books. They're the one who enthusiastically celebrate all of my wins and help me when I encounter my lows.

To my parents, thank you for everything. This book is for you, even if you're not allowed to read half of it. You didn't even bat an eye when I told you I wanted to be a romance author. You just continued to love and support me, and that's more than I could have ever asked for. I love you!

And, finally, to my siblings. I love you both more than anything. Thank you so much for putting up with all my crazy. You mean the world to me, and there is no way any of this would have been possible without you.

Made in the USA
Middletown, DE
25 March 2022